For my dad, Ron.
I could get all flowery and wordy. Thank you for teaching me to work hard and never give up on my dreams. Thank you for teaching me the value of family, of right and wrong. I could go on and on about how much you mean to me, and that without you in this world life would never be the same. But because you and I are so much alike, I know you'd prefer if I kept it simple. So…

I love you, Dad. This book is for you.

ACKNOWLEDGMENTS

Special thanks to Jamie Denton, Christy Esau and Mary Ann Chulick for their help with this book. Another big thanks to my cover artist Kim Van Meter, KD Designs.

I also want to thank Nikki Erickson, Jenny Gyurky, Renee Seefeldt and Sunny Thompson. You ladies were an enormous help to me while writing this book. Knowing how important this book was to me and how limited I am with time, you took care of my kids and gave me the chance to write. Your friendship and encouragement means the world to me.

PROLOGUE

"WHO DID YOU piss off?"

Detroit homicide detective Nick Merretti looked at the dead man lying on the bed in a pool of blood. After twenty-eight years on the force, with only two left until retirement, he'd thought he'd seen it all. Until today.

"We got any ID?" he asked no one in particular, but after years of experience knew one of the half dozen cops or CSI techs would give him an answer.

"Nothing," a tech called from across the shitty, no-tell motel room. "No wallet, jewelry, clothes. No prints either. Whoever did this, cleaned up after themselves."

"Yeah, well, they still made one hell of a mess." From the opposite side of the bed, Medical Examiner, Joyce Wilson, leaned over the victim, wrinkling her nose in disgust. "I've never seen anything like it."

Nick hadn't either, and he'd seen some fucked up shit. "Time of death?" he asked.

"I'll have a more concrete time once I do the autopsy, but best guess?" Joyce looked at the dainty watch on her thick wrist as if it had the answer. "Twenty-four to thirty-six hours ago."

"According to the owner, the cleaning lady found him," his

1

partner, Leon Smith, said as he entered the motel room. Leon looked at the body and winced. "That's fucked up." He looked to Joyce. "Sorry, Ma'am."

"No worries, Detective." She tossed Leon a pair of gloves. "You're right. It's totally fucked up. And I'm the one who gets to spend all kinds of time with him. Lucky me."

Leon held up the gloves. "What do you want me to do with these?"

His partner had only been with Homicide for six months and had some growing to do. "Put them on and do whatever Joyce asks."

"Okay," the ME began, and gently touched the dead man's head. "Looks as if he was bludgeoned with…" She glanced at the lamp lying haphazardly on the filthy carpet. "Likely the lamp."

Nick nodded to the nearest CSI tech, and asked him to check the lamp for any evidence. "What do you think was used on his face?"

She shrugged. "I'm assuming some sort of acid. Look at the way the skin melted."

Swallowing down the bile that had been burning his throat from the moment he walked into the room, he stared at the dead man's face—or what was left of it. The acid, or whatever had been used, had practically liquefied the man's skin, leaving behind only bits of reddish brown flesh and tufts of brown hair over the partially exposed skull. "I'm assuming the acid took care of the eyes."

After righting the dead man's head, Joyce checked the eye sockets. "Acid would do that, and probably did. But look." She pointed a Latex-gloved finger to the cavity. "See these grooves here?" she asked. "Again, I'll know more during the autopsy, but those grooves are consistent with knife marks." She pointed to the other eye socket. "They're here, too."

"You're saying he was *stabbed* in the eyes?" Leon's caramel face grew ashen to the point where Nick wondered if his partner would lose his lunch. "What about his teeth? Do you think he wore dentures?"

Joyce examined the man's mouth, dipping a finger inside and along the area where gums and teeth *should* have been. "Most of his gums were destroyed by the acid, but based on some of the holes I can feel where his back molars were, I'm thinking they were ripped from his head."

Nick rubbed the back of his hand along his chin, and glanced at the man's torso, where it looked as if he'd been stabbed dozens of times. "Total overkill," he said. "In every sense of the word."

"No doubt he suffered." Joyce also looked to the deep, jagged slices tattooing the man's chest and stomach. "Someone thought he deserved it."

"I don't know," Leon said, his voice filled with dread and anguish. "Slicing off a man's dick, sorry, I mean penis is...is..."

"Personal," Nick finished.

Joyce met his gaze. "Based on the amount of blood, I'd say it was done while he was still alive." She moved to the end of the bed. "I have a gut feeling my findings will prove he was alive during most, if not all of this." She picked up the man's gnarled, partially skeletonized foot. "Looks like acid was dumped on his feet, too."

"Let's roll him," Nick suggested. "I want to see his hands and back." They were screwed. No ID, no recognizable facial features, and no teeth meant no dental records. They wouldn't have been able to run a footprint through AFIS like they could with a fingerprint. But just like fingerprints, a footprint was unique to each individual.

"Put those gloves to work, Leon," Joyce said. "Help me roll him on his side. Good, now hold him steady."

Leon stood across the bed, his head turned to the side and his face contorted in a deep grimace as he held the victim's bloodied shoulder and hip. "Don't take too long." His partner's shoulders lurched and his Adam's apple bobbed as if he fought to keep from vomiting. "I...I don't know how long I can do this."

Ignoring Leon, Nick viewed the dead man's backside. His

hands had been tied behind him, the flesh around the fingers melted away, leaving behind nothing but bone. Small puncture wounds, likely from the force of a knife as it had been gouged into the victim's torso over and over, lined his lower back. He glanced to the man's shoulder blade, where a large chunk of skin had been removed. Swearing, he stepped away and ran a hand over his bald spot.

Two more years. That's all he had left. Two more years of dead bodies.

When he glanced back toward the bed, Leon had just stepped away from the victim. "Get some air," Nick told his partner. Once Leon left the room, he turned to Joyce. "They took his tattoo."

"That was my first thought." She sent him a wry smile that didn't reach her eyes. "Glad you waited until Leon set the vic back down before you brought it up. I really didn't want a mutilated corpse on my head."

"Right." He propped a hand on his hip, and stared at the dead man. "She made sure nothing was left to ID this guy."

"*She?*" Joyce removed her gloves. "How can you be so sure? You're obviously the detective here, but based on this motel, based on some of the prostitutes I saw when I was coming in, I figured this was a pimp putting a john in his place."

"I've had my share of run ins with plenty of pimps." He shook his head. "They might beat the hell out of a john who did one of their girls wrong." He shrugged. "They might even stab him. But acid? Ripping teeth from his head? This wasn't a pimp." He glanced at the mutilated genitalia and the gouged eyes. "This was a woman. This was personal. It was also premeditated."

"Maybe. But, and I'm guessing here, the vic is about six foot two and probably one ninety to two hundred pounds. Unless he was drugged or highly intoxicated, I can't see a woman capable of subduing him, then mutilating him while he was still alive."

"She didn't drug him." With a tired sigh, he moved toward

the door, then glanced over his shoulder at the disfigured corpse. "She wanted him coherent...for every single slice."

CHAPTER 1

MONDAY

Eighteen months later...

RACHEL DAVIS STARED at the ringing cell phone, at the Michigan area code. Panic clamped her heart and tightened her chest. Her brother, Sean, lived in Michigan, but only called her from his cell phone, which used a Chicago area code. She glanced at the alarm clock beside her bed. He also never called her at six in the morning. Hoping something had happened to Sean's phone and he was calling from the dormitory landline, she quickly answered.

"Rachel Davis?"

Not Sean.

Panic morphed into utter dread. "Yes, who is this?"

"Sheriff Jake Tyler. Dixon County, Michigan."

Mouth dry, mind racing, she reached into the nightstand drawer and grabbed a pencil. "Why are you calling, Sheriff?"

Please let Sean be okay.

"It's about your brother."

She closed her eyes. Not caring that she'd just finished her hair and make-up, or that she was dressed for work in a freshly laundered suit, she slumped onto the bed and curled into the fetal position. Sean was her only family. Whatever news the sheriff was about to give her, she'd take it lying down. Fainting onto the hardwood floor would hurt like a bitch.

"Ma'am?"

"Is Sean…?" She couldn't say the words. Hurt. Missing. Dead.

"Your brother is at Dixon Medical Center. He's been beaten, but the doc working on him says he'll recover without issue."

Anger suddenly surged through her veins. She shot off the bed. "Beaten? When did this happen? Where? At the university?"

Although she'd tried to encourage Sean to remain in Chicago and attend Northwestern, he'd chosen Wexman University, in northwest Michigan, instead. He'd liked the idea of going to a small school, loved the campus, the engineering program and the fat scholarship the school had awarded him for his academics. While she'd respected his wishes, and the scholarship had definitely been a Godsend considering she was paying for his education, she still wished he'd stayed closer to home. She loved his company and missed seeing his face on a daily basis.

Now he was lying in a hospital bed.

"Actually, we're not sure where the beating took place. The doc thinks, based on the way Sean's wounds have healed, that your brother was hurt sometime Saturday."

"Saturday?" Pinching the pencil between her fingers, she paced the bedroom. "In case you're not aware, Sheriff, it's Monday."

"I'm fully aware of the day," he replied, his tone holding a hint of irritation. "But your brother wasn't found until last night around midnight. He had no ID and was considered a John Doe until a couple of hours ago."

Rachel stopped pacing and snatched the picture frame off the dresser. Staring at the photograph of her and Sean at a Chicago Cubs game last summer, memories of the cheering crowd, the mouthwatering aroma of hot dogs and popcorn, filled her mind and made her want to cry. They'd had a great time at the game, then later pigged out on pizza and wings. He wasn't just her brother, he was her best friend. And she could have lost him.

Tears filled her eyes as she set the photograph back on the dresser. Swiping a stray tear from her cheek, she drew in a deep breath.

She needed to maintain control. Think. Obtain the facts. Analyze the situation. Leave emotion out of the picture—for now—and use every resource she had available to find out who had hurt Sean. She worked for CORE (Criminal Observance Resolution Evidence), and had helped the agency investigate and solve hundreds of cases. She'd solve this one, too. And when Sean was well enough to travel, she'd haul his ass home. Maybe even force him to be the next bubble boy. Anything to ensure he remained safe.

"Miss Davis? You still there?" the sheriff asked.

She tucked the pencil behind her ear, then rubbed her temple where a deep throb began to build. "Sorry, Sheriff, I'm still here and didn't mean to snap at you. My brother..." He was the only family she had left. After their mother had run off with a musician six years ago, she'd become Sean's legal guardian. Had she been old enough, the courts should have given her that right when he was born. Even at twelve she'd been a better parent than their mom. The woman had spent more time trying to land her next husband than paying attention to her children. Rachel loved Sean. Without him in her life...

Clearing her throat, she said, "I work for a private criminal investigation agency and we specialize in—"

"I'm aware you work for CORE. One of your agents recently helped the Detroit PD with a case. A few months back, another of your people helped bring down a serial killer in Wisconsin."

"That's right," she said, and headed into the kitchen to where she'd left her laptop. "So, I understand that you might not be able to give me all the details while you're still running this investigation." She paused. "You *are* considering what happened to my brother as something worth investigating, correct?"

"Of course. Actually, I was hoping CORE might lend us a hand."

While she'd planned to use CORE's resources to find out who had hurt Sean, the sheriff's hopes bordered on extreme. CORE didn't usually handle cases like this unless they were high profile or the client had deep pockets. "What about the Michigan State Police?"

"They...have no interest in what goes on around these parts."

"That doesn't make any sense." She closed the case file she'd been working on before her shower and the sheriff's call. CORE had worked with the FBI, law enforcement in different cities around the country, as well as numerous state agencies. During the four years she'd been with CORE, she'd had the opportunity to work with the Michigan State Police a few times. In her experience, their personnel were both capable and professional.

"It will once I explain. Now, the county can't afford to pay your agency—"

"We do plenty of cases pro bono." More concerned over her brother than the sheriff's issues with the State Police, she shifted focus. "Forget about that and give me details. It's the end of January. Last night the temperature dipped to fifteen degrees in Chicago, and I'm betting it was even colder where you're located. Did my brother suffer from exposure? Who found him and where? What are his exact injuries? Do you have any suspects or—?"

"Hang on, and slow down," the sheriff said. "Let me start at the beginning. Your brother was found by a local guy. He was heading home from work and spotted his body on the side of the road. Sean couldn't have been outside for too long because his body temperature was normal. The guy who found him even said he was surprised your brother's skin was warm when he touched his neck to find a pulse."

Somewhat relieved that Sean hadn't been lying in the freezing cold for over twenty-four hours, Rachel began to type notes onto her laptop. "Who was the man who found my brother?" She'd like to thank the Good Samaritan. If he hadn't seen Sean, he could have frozen to death.

"Hal Baker. After he brought Sean to the hospital, Hal took me to where he found your brother. Based on the way Hal described the state of Sean's body, the doc and I both think that he was thrown out of a vehicle. Something high off the ground—maybe an SUV or a truck—and that's how he suffered the concussion and broken arm. The broken ribs, and bruising to his face and body...I think that happened somewhere else."

She paused her fingers over the keyboard and fought back the worry, anger and grief. Whoever had done this to her brother would pay dearly. "Did you find tire tracks on the road, or any fibers or DNA evidence on Sean's clothes?"

"While there's snow on the ground, there's none on the road. There weren't any fresh tire tracks, and I didn't find any shoe imprints in the snow near where Sean was found. As for DNA evidence, we're small time here, Miss Davis. I did bag Sean's clothes and could probably send them to the Michigan State Police, but like I said, they really—"

"Don't have any interest in what's going on in those parts," she repeated what the sheriff had said earlier, and shook her head. "I'm still having a hard time wrapping my brain around that nonsense, Sheriff."

"Right. We...ah...have had some past events that have made the Michigan State Police look bad and my department look like a joke."

"Unless these past events are in any relation to what happened to my brother, I see no reason—"

"Miss Davis," the sheriff interrupted. "I'm afraid they do. Over the past twenty years we've had well over a dozen missing person reports in our county. Nineteen to be exact. Out of all of the cases, only five of those missing persons have been found. The couple of times the State Police came in to help investigate, the reports ended up being nothing but a hoax."

Shrugging, she said, "I don't see why that would keep the State from helping with future investigations."

"Look, I've got a meeting with our town council and honestly don't have time to go into the details right now."

"Fine, then you can explain when I get there," she said. "It's about a six hour drive from Chicago, and I'll need to stop by CORE on my way out of town." She glanced at the clock and did the math. "Will you be able to meet with me around three? I want to see my brother first."

"Sure. I'll meet you at my office in Bola. If you've been to the university, you would have had to pass through the town."

If Wexman University wasn't located near the town, and she hadn't had the best breakfast of her life there, she probably wouldn't have remembered the forgettable Bola, Michigan. Located near the Menominee River, the small town thrived on tourism during the summer, and the students and faculty from the university throughout the remainder of the year. Except for the small manufacturing company at the edge of town, and the place she'd eaten breakfast, she couldn't recall anything else about Bola, other than it being boring.

"I'm familiar with Bola," she said.

"Good, then I'll see you at three."

While the sheriff gave her his contact information, the missing persons he'd mentioned nagged at her. Bola's population—she remembered from the town's billboard—was around twelve hundred. Last fall, the university's enrollment had been almost equal to the number of residents living in Bola. Granted, those missing person cases had occurred over the course of twenty years, but with approximately twenty five hundred people living in the area nine months out of the year, the number of missing persons seemed...staggering.

"Before you go," Rachel said, and headed for the bedroom to pack a bag. "You'd mentioned that what happened to my brother relates to the missing persons you've had over the years. How so?"

"I'd planned on telling you when we met. It's also the reason why I was hoping CORE could help us." He paused, exhaled deeply, then said, "With almost every one of those missing persons, a note was left behind. Same writing, same message. Only this time, the note wasn't left behind. It was left *on* your brother, stuffed in the pocket of his jeans."

She stopped packing, and sat on the edge of the bed. "What did the note say?"

"'Welcome to Hell Week. You have seven days to find him.'"

A chill swept over her and prickled the hair on her scalp. During fall semester, Sean had participated in the university's rush week, and had decided to pledge the Eta Tau Zeta fraternity. Over winter break, he'd told her he was excited to join the Zetas, that they were a great group of guys, but had worried about the expense. She hadn't worried about the money. The cost to join the fraternity and live at the frat house wasn't much different than that of the dorms.

What had worried her, though, were the hazing rituals that occur during Hell Week. Sean had assured her that the university didn't allow any form of hazing, that the school's policy was strict and if any member of a fraternity was caught or even suspected of hazing, they would be expelled. Although the universities no-tolerance rules had eased her mind, and she'd met most of the boys from the fraternity, she'd still worried about her baby brother. She'd practically raised him and couldn't help being overprotective.

Now he was six hours away, lying in some rinky-dink hospital.

"That note might make sense if you'd found it in Sean's dorm room," she said, more as a way to alleviate her unease. The missing persons, the note, Sean's beating, the way he'd been left along the road…something wasn't right in Bola.

"I don't think the message was meant for Sean. Have you met your brother's roommate?"

In an instant, the image of a handsome, athletic, blonde hair, blue-eyed kid jumped into her mind. Although Josh

Conway was the polar opposite to her redheaded, brown-eyed, lanky, bookworm of a brother, the two boys had become close friends, and both were pledging the Eta Tau Zeta fraternity. "Yeah, I know Josh. What about him?"

"According to the dormitory residential assistant, both Sean and Josh were last seen leaving their dorm room Saturday evening. They were supposed to meet a few others at the library for a study session. Neither showed."

"Is Josh…?"

"We have no idea of his whereabouts."

And her brother had been beaten and left for dead.

Welcome to Hell Week.

Dread settled in the pit of her stomach as a grisly thought came to mind. "Sheriff, these missing persons your town has seen over the years…were any of them students at Wexman University?"

"Not all, but most of them. Nine to be exact. With Josh Conway's disappearance, we're now up to ten."

Ten? "The students, were any of them pledging a fraternity or sorority?"

"Fraternities. They were all male."

Rachel tightened her grip on the cell phone. "When? Was there a specific time of year when these boys went missing?"

"January."

"And their bodies?"

"They've never been found."

While she wasn't a criminalist like some members of CORE's team, her years spent with Army Intelligence, along with her hacking skills, had prepared her for the job and had made her valuable to Ian Scott, the owner of the agency. During her tenure, she'd been involved in some seriously twisted cases. Her mind worked quickly and zeroed in on one thing.

"You have a serial killer in Bola."

"That's right, Miss Davis. Welcome to Hell Week. We have only seven days to find Josh Conway."

****

With a yawn and a stretch, he climbed out of bed and toed on his slippers. After shrugging into his robe, he raced down the staircase and into the kitchen like a kid at Christmas. Eagerness and excitement hummed through his veins. Better than Christmas or a birthday or any other holiday, today marked a special day, a special beginning. The time of year he anticipated the most.

Hell Week.

As the coffee brewed, the strong, rich aroma of hazelnut and cinnamon wafted throughout the kitchen. While he waited for that first delicious cup, he did a mental checklist of today's schedule. Monday was always a full workday, filled with meetings and preparations for the upcoming week. Pity. He'd love to play hooky today. He'd love to play with the pledge in his basement.

The pledge would have to wait until this evening. Work came first. Deviating from his daily routine was not an option. Besides, he knew in his heart, now, this moment wasn't the right time. In the past, he'd made mistakes with his pledges. In his overzealousness, he'd rushed things, which had made for some...deadly results. He couldn't rush anything with the new pledge. Twenty years ago, what began as therapy had now become legend. *He* had become legendary. No. There would be no rushing, no overzealousness. No more mistakes.

After what Junior had done on Saturday, there had better not be any more mistakes. He poured coffee into the mug, then blew on the liquid before taking a sip. Although still angry over Junior's screw-up, he couldn't stay mad at his only child. Hell Week would become Junior's legacy. The gifts of dominance, control, power...definitely the kind of inheritance that keeps on giving.   And he wanted his child to feel, to truly understand, what it is to have power over another human being. Over their pledge.

Although Junior had been born a disappointment, he never wanted his own flesh and blood to experience what he had twenty-five years ago. The powerlessness, the helplessness, the utter degradation at the hands of a monster. While it had taken him years to battle the nightmares that still haunted him, he'd made his mark on the world. Well, at least in Bola, Michigan.

Chuckling, he shrugged and looked out the kitchen window. He glanced at the trees in his backyard, now naked save for the clumps of icy snow resting on their branches, then to the path which led to the Menominee River. When he'd been a child, that path had terrified him. His parents had warned him never to walk through the forest alone, to never go near the river, or bad things would happen. Too true, he chuckled again, then took another sip of his coffee.

He no longer knew what it was like to be afraid. The Townies knew. They knew and they feared him.

Just like his parents had done, the town folk of Bola had spun terrifying stories to their children in order to keep them from venturing too far into the dense forests surrounding Bola. The university students, most of them spoiled, coddled, little shitheads, didn't buy into the Townies' fears and beliefs. They'd considered him a myth, akin to the celebrated Bigfoot many of the ignorant Townies had claimed to have seen roaming the area.

Fools.

He was no myth. But he should be feared. Every male student at the university should agonize and wonder.

Will he come for me this year?

While he'd bet there were a few young men who worried, they wouldn't have to concern themselves any longer. He'd taken his pledge. By noon today, word of the boy's disappearance would reach every corner of the campus and county. And so it would begin.

Seven days of torture.

Seven days of hell.

The front door opened, sending in a loud gust of wind, then quickly shut.

"Junior?" he called as he left the kitchen and moved down the hallway into the foyer. He stopped, leaned against the stair rails and eyed his favorite mistake. "What have you learned?"

"They found Sean Davis late last night. He's recovering at Dixon Medical Center. Depending on the severity of the concussion, he'll likely be released in a few days."

"And the note?"

"Sheriff Tyler didn't mention it, but it's obvious he found it. Around four this morning, he questioned the boys at the Eta Tau Zeta house, as well as the RA and some of the kids living at the dorm."

He sipped his coffee, then said, "I wonder if our dedicated sheriff has tried to contact his family."

"Davis's?"

Waving his hand, he shook his head. "I don't care about that whiney, little skid mark. Idiot, I'm referring to our pledge."

"Yes, sir." Junior looked to the floor. "Sorry. I don't know. As you're aware, the university administration offices open at eight. I wouldn't be surprised if they receive a call from the sheriff then. Does he need Josh's parents to file a missing person report?"

The mug, filled with his delicious coffee, smashed and splattered on the tile. In an instant he had Junior by the throat and up against the door. "*Pledge*," he said, and tightened his grip. "*That* is his new name. *That* is what you will call him. Do you understand?"

Junior nodded, and whispered, "Yes, sir."

He reined in his anger and loosened his hold. "Josh Conway is dead, figuratively speaking of course," he said, calmer now, and stepped over the mess on the floor.

"Yes, of course."

Turning his back, he walked down the hallway toward the kitchen for a new cup of coffee, but stopped at the threshold. "Clean up the mess you caused and meet me in the basement."

"I thought we wouldn't begin with the pledge until this evening."

"You're right, we won't. But he must be given a taste of what's to come."

****

Owen Malcolm stifled a yawn and waited for Ian Scott, his boss and founder of CORE, to end his phone conversation. He glanced around Ian's luxurious, yet comfortable office, particularly at the large, leather sofa near the fireplace, and ached for a nap. Not about to curl up on his boss's sofa, he leaned into the plush office chair instead.

The past couple months of travelling might have finally caught up with him. November, there had been California and Las Vegas. December had him in San Antonio for a few weeks, then from there, he'd flown to Virginia to spend the holidays with his family.

While he'd loved visiting his parents, sisters and nieces and nephews, he couldn't count the trip as a vacation. If he hadn't been working odd jobs around the house for his mom and dad, his sisters had been ushering him, and his nieces and nephews, to the obnoxiously loud, germ- and kid-infested Play World. How many times can a kid go on the same humungous, inflatable slide without growing sick of it? Infinity, he assumed, because his sisters' kids never stopped until they'd left, then had begged to go back the next day.

He'd take the raucous Play World over this last assignment, though. While Miami in January had its perks, beautiful, warm beaches, wild nightlife, and even wilder women, he didn't have the chance to enjoy any of it. Instead, he'd spent three weeks helping the Miami-Dade police track down the man who'd been robbing, raping, then murdering elderly women. He'd found the guy. But the prick had put a bullet into his head before the police could arrest him. The suicide might not give the victims' families total closure, but it had made his part in the investigation easier. Now he wouldn't have to travel back to Florida for a long, drawn-out trial.

He looked out Ian's office window. Nothing but gray sky. Maybe a long, drawn-out trial in Miami wouldn't have been such a bad thing. Chicago plus January equaled snow and freezing temperatures.

Ian hung up the phone. "How was Florida?" he asked.

Owen straightened. "I didn't get much of a chance to work on my tan," he said, then leaned forward and handed him the case file.

Ian glanced through the paperwork. "When did you get back?"

He looked at the clock. "My flight got in about an hour ago. I haven't even been to my condo yet."

Arching his black brows, Ian leaned into his chair and shrugged. "Go home then."

"I didn't mean to imply—"

Ian shook his head and offered him a slight smile. "I know you didn't."

"Then why are you sending me home without giving me my next assignment?" In the six years he'd worked for Ian, other than his annual holiday trip to see the family and the occasional vacation, he'd never ended a case without being handed another.

And he needed another.

When he visited his folks, they kept him too busy to think. When he took a vacation, he always made sure they were well-scheduled trips, packed with a full itinerary. Downtime, lounging on the beach or poolside, didn't work for him. If he stopped moving, his mind would go into overdrive. Bringing up the past. His mistakes. His regrets.

Ian moved, as if to run his hand through his salt and pepper hair, then instead, scratched the back of his head. "I don't have anything for you."

During his time with CORE, he'd only seen one member of the team let go. And it had started with, "I don't have anything for you."

Flashbacks from his days with the U.S. Secret Service suddenly shifted through his head. The cover-ups. The bullshit. The lies and dismissal.

He'd been loyal to Ian because the man had helped him salvage his career. His boss could be manipulative, but it was done with purpose. Ian, although not as blunt as he'd like, was still an excellent employer. He didn't want to lose his job with CORE. Sure, with his background, he could find a position with another private agency, but he had no interest in working elsewhere. CORE had become his life. He liked his fellow agents, his hefty salary, the bonuses and the benefits.

"Is this the start of your firing process?"

Ian's bark of laughter filled the office. "God, no. Why in the hell would I fire you? I can work you like a dog, and you never complain. *I* have no complaints." He grew serious, then said, "You've been working cases back-to-back, and I don't want you to burn out. I thought you could use a week to regroup. Paid, of course."

Most people would have jumped at the opportunity of paid time off. And while he appreciated Ian's intentions, he didn't want a break. He'd rather work. The assignments kept his mind busy, his thoughts focused.

"I appreciate the offer, but I'm good."

Ian eyed him, then nodded. "If you change your mind, just let me know. Meanwhile, I have an interesting cold case that needs solving." He pulled a file from the drawer and set it on the desk.

Owen liked cold cases, especially the older ones where modern day technology hadn't quite been invented. They were like puzzles. He enjoyed sifting through old paperwork, crime scene photos, and evidence. Seeing what fit and what didn't, then solving what no one else could.

A rap at the door caught his attention. As he turned, Rachel burst into the room. She came to an abrupt halt when she saw him, then looked to Ian.

"Sorry, Ian. I don't mean to interrupt, but I..." She looked away, stared out the window, then reached for the pencil tucked behind her ear.

Something had Beaver upset. Not once, during the four years Rachel had worked for CORE, had Owen ever seen her at a loss for words. The woman always had something to say, and had an annoying habit of doing so over a mouthful of pencil.

"I can come back," Owen said, sensing Rachel might want a moment alone with Ian.

"No, actually, I wouldn't mind if you stayed. I might be able to use your help."

Interesting. Rachel never liked having him around, and rarely asked him for help with anything. Why, he didn't know. All he knew was that whenever he walked into the room, she threw verbal jabs, snarky uppercuts, and sarcastic hooks. He didn't care, and actually liked Rachel. Although a bit…mouthy, he couldn't deny her capabilities as CORE's computer forensics analyst, plus he admired her intelligence and her quick-working mind.

"I'd be glad to help," he said, still dumbfounded that she'd willingly have him part of the conversation.

She moved to the leather office chair next to him, then sat. "Yeah, well, no one else is here yet, so I have no choice."

So much for thinking she'd been interested in *his* expertise.

"What's going on?" Ian asked her.

"It's my brother," she began. "Late last night, he was found on the side of the road just outside of Bola, Michigan, beaten and unconscious."

"My God, Rachel," Ian said, and leaned forward. "How's his condition?"

"He's okay. I'll know more when I see him."

Ian nodded. "Absolutely. Take all the time you need. It's a long drive to Bola. If you want to use the jet, feel free."

She smiled and shook her head. "Thank you, but I'm going to drive. I'm not sure how long I'll be gone, and I don't want to deal with a rental."

"Understood," Ian said.

"I'm sorry about your brother," Owen said, and meant it. He had three older sisters, and if anything bad had happened to them, he'd be devastated. And out for blood. While he doubted he'd ever have a family of his own, his parents, his sisters and their kids, meant everything to him. They accepted and loved him, faults and all. He knew Rachel had basically raised her brother, and couldn't imagine how she must be feeling. "Do you have any idea who did this to him?"

"The sheriff I spoke with doesn't have any leads. That's why I wanted you to stick around. I...ah." She paused and glanced to the ceiling. Seconds later she looked at him. "I'd like your advice."

Seriously interesting. Most times when he offered his opinion, she'd somehow find a way to either dismiss him or cut him down.

"When I get to Bola I plan to investigate my brother's beating," she continued. "I know where to start, and have already begun a list of the people I want to interview."

"Are you planning on running this investigation on behalf of CORE?" Ian asked.

She tapped the pencil to her lips. "Are you okay with that? If not, I can—"

Ian waved a hand. "Our resources are yours."

She tucked the pencil behind her ear. "Thank you. I have a feeling I'm going to need it. Sean's beating...based on what the sheriff told me, I don't think it was random."

"Why's that?" Owen asked.

"The sheriff said they found a note stuffed in Sean's pocket. It said, 'Welcome to Hell Week. You have seven days to find him.'"

"But they obviously found your brother," Owen countered.

"Right. They found Sean. His roommate, Josh Conway, is missing."

"Could this roommate have gone home for the weekend?" he asked.

"No. Sean told me his parents are overseas."

"Didn't you tell me that Sean planned to join a fraternity?" Ian asked.

"Yes. The Eta Tau Zetas"

"Based on the Hell Week reference," Ian began. "Is it possible that this could have been a hazing gone bad?"

She nodded, and hugged herself. "I thought about that, only..."

"What?" Owen asked.

"The sheriff said that over the last twenty years, nine male students from Wexman University have gone missing. Josh makes ten. These students always disappear in January. And with every one of these missing boys, the same note was left behind."

Owen rubbed his jaw, both confused and disturbed. "You're telling us that nine guys go missing, the same time of year, with the same message left behind...have any of the bodies been discovered?"

"No."

"Does this sheriff realize he has a possible serial killer in his county?" he asked, surprised that Bola, Michigan's local law enforcement, hell, even the university, hadn't pieced the obvious together and asked for outside help.

"He's well aware."

Irritated at the sheriff's ineptness, he leaned forward and asked, "Then why not bring in the Michigan State Police?"

"The sheriff tried that route. I'm still confused as to what happened when they participated in the investigation." She faced Ian. "I have vacation time, and you said I can use CORE's resources. The sheriff can't afford to pay us, but if it's okay with you, I want to investigate what's happening in Bola and find Sean's roommate."

"Of course," Ian said. "But there's no need to worry about vacation time and fees. Not when family is involved. Besides, this is an interesting case."

"Very interesting," Owen said. "A possible serial killer who targets victims at a certain time of year...strange, too."

Ian nodded, and removed the cold case file from the desk. "Agreed. This case can wait a few more weeks. Rachel has just handed you your next assignment."

Excitement pumped through Owen's veins. He'd gladly take the case. What had and was happening in Bola sounded like a huge puzzle with a lot of missing pieces.

"I didn't *hand* him anything," Rachel said. "And I told you *I'd* like to conduct this investigation."

"You can." Ian smiled. "Only you'll do it with Owen."

CHAPTER 2

RACHEL FINISHED SECURING the El Camino's truck bed cover as Owen approached.

"We'll take my car," he said.

"If Ian wants you tagging along with me, we go in my car." Because she had zero field experience, she'd suspected Ian might want her to have assistance on this case. But did that assistance have to come from Owen? She didn't have a problem dealing with his arrogance. Except for her, the entire CORE team was filled with cocky, alpha males and she'd grown accustomed to their ridiculous Neanderthal ways. Owen's phony, syrupy charm? Now that drove her crazy. Dozens of guys like him, charming womanizers who liked to take advantage of a woman's emotions, vulnerabilities and insecurities, had walked in and out of her mom's life. They were the bottom feeders of the dating pool, and Owen swam with them.

He shook his head. "There is no way in hell I'm driving six hours in that thing."

She eyed the El Camino she'd bought off of Hudson Patterson, a member of the CORE team, less than a year ago. From the moment she'd seen the car, all shiny black, with fire decals running along both sides, she wanted it. Having only two seats, the car had screamed impractical. But she hadn't cared. Hudson had restored the car himself, and had not only given it a modern twist—CD player, optional satellite radio—he'd added those fire decals. Super cheesy, yet super cool. The same way Sean had always liked to describe her.

She opened the passenger door. "We go in *this* car, or *you* don't go at all."

"Ian said—"

"Oh, but Ian said," she mocked him, and held a hand over her heart. "I'm in no mood to deal with your insecurities. So either climb in, or go home."

He snorted. "Insecurities? How about impossibilities? For example, it would be *impossible* to transport you, me, *and* your brother from Bola to Chicago in a two-seater."

Crap, she hadn't thought about that. "Well, then I guess you'll have to find some other way home."

"Really? For a bright woman, you make no sense."

"Are you calling me stupid?"

"Do I think taking this thing," he started, and pointed at her car, "is a bright idea? No. I don't. Do I think you're stupid? No. Hostile and antagonistic...absolutely."

He really thought that about her? Good. She'd worried she had been too soft on him lately. Still, he had a point. The El Camino wouldn't fit three people, and they were wasting time.

"Fine," she said. "We'll take your car. Actually, it's better this way. You can drive, while I do some research on my laptop." She couldn't let him think he'd won this battle or, even if true, that he was right. From the moment she'd met him, she had made it her mission to put him in his place and come out on top.

Not true, her conscience reminded her as she switched her gear to the back of his white Lexus LX. At one time, she'd wanted him on top of her. Naked, pressing his thick arousal between her legs.

Heat rushed to her face as she slammed the SUV's gate. She would not, could not, allow herself to relive the humiliation and hope he'd caused last year. Not only did they have to work together, she had her brother to worry about and an investigation to run.

She climbed into the passenger seat, then secured the seatbelt. When he didn't start the ignition, she turned to him. "What?"

"Unlike your tricked-out El Camino, this vehicle wasn't built in 1969. It has all kinds of modern features. Here's one I'd like you to take note of." He pressed a button and the back gate began to rise. "Now watch this." He pressed the same button and the gate closed. "Isn't technology amazing?"

"Was the show necessary? All you had to do was ask me not to slam the gate shut." She faced the front window. "FYI, the only people I know who refer to their car as a *vehicle* are pompous douche bags. Oh wait, I guess you should call this thing a vehicle, after all."

He turned the ignition, then adjusted the temperature and seat warmers. Within seconds her butt was toasty warm, and the Lexus's temperature a comfortable seventy degrees.

As he shifted the gear, then wove the SUV through the parking garage, he said, "I thought you agreed not to call me a douche bag anymore."

"I didn't actually call you a douche bag. If you recall, you asked me not to call you a DB."

"DB and douche bag are the same thing."

"No. DB could stand for dumb butt, dirt bag—"

"Dream boat," he interrupted with a smile that probably caught him more ass than a public toilet seat.

"Hardly." She glanced at his hair. "But ditzy blonde would work, or even *Daily Bugle*, the Berkeley DB, that's a cross-platform embedded database library, defensive back—"

"Defensive back?"

"It's a football term."

"I'm fully aware, but doubt you know what it means."

She folded her arms across her chest. Not into football, she had no idea what defensive back meant. "It's the guy who defends the back," she guessed anyway, hoping she could squeak by with the vague answer. Why didn't she end this childish "DB" discussion with the Berkeley DB? Computer stuff she knew.

"The back of what?"

"Look, sorry I'm not Chicago Bears head coach, Mike Dicky, and can't exactly explain every move a defensive back could possibly make...wait, why are you turning left? The freeway's that way," she said, and pointed out her window.

"I need to stop at my condo."

"For?"

"The clothes in my suitcase are intended for Florida weather. Don't worry, it won't take me long to grab a few things. We'll be on the freeway in less than twenty." He paused, then said, "And it's Ditka."

What was he talking about? "Come again?"

"It's not Mike *Dicky*, but Mike *Ditka*, and he hasn't been head coach for the Bears in more than twenty years."

Yep. Should have stuck with the Berkeley DB. "Dicky...Ditka, whatever. You still knew what I meant."

Minutes later, Owen parked the Lexus, and left the engine running while he went inside his condo to repack his suitcase. As she waited in the car, she had to admit his *vehicle* was a definite badass ride. Definite badass, there was another DB phrase. Based on the stories she'd heard about him, definite badass would fit Owen. Not that she'd know from personal experience. Until today, she'd never been given the chance to work side-by-side in the field with Owen or any of CORE's agents. For years Ian had told her he needed her in the office, that her computer skills were invaluable to the agents on assignment.

While she knew Ian was right, that she didn't have any experience with physically tracking down criminals or interviewing suspects, she'd wanted the chance to try. She wanted to prove she was more than a computer geek. After spending her childhood stuck in a crappy apartment while her mom searched for her next husband, then her teen years raising her brother, she had wanted action and adventure.

With a full academic ride, she'd enrolled in the University

of Chicago's Computer Science Program. An overachiever, she had graduated in three years, then had enlisted in the United States Army's Military Intelligence Corps where she'd thought for sure she'd find the adventure and travel she had craved. She'd learned all too quickly, while training at Fort Huachuca, Arizona, that the chances of her seeing the world were slim to none. This realization came to fruition after her training had ended and her career had begun at Fort Belvoir, Virginia, the Army Major Intelligence Command Center, where she'd spent her days tied to a desk.

Six years later, her mom ran off with an aging, hippy musician, leaving Rachel responsible for Sean. Because she'd served six of her eight-year commitment to the Army, she'd been placed in the inactive Reserves. While she'd been able to move back to Chicago and take care of her teenage brother, she had still longed for action and adventure. She'd thought applying to the Chicago Police Department might give her what she had wanted, but unfortunately, she—who'd graduated Summa Cum Laude from Chicago University and had been a U.S. Military Intelligence Officer—couldn't pass, of all things, their stupid psychological test.

Now might be her one chance to prove to Ian that she was more than a desk jockey. She hated that the opportunity had been spawned from her brother's beating, and his roommate's disappearance. But loved the chance to be able to make the person who had hurt Sean pay for his crimes, find Josh, and discover the reasons behind the missing persons Bola and Wexman University had experienced for the past twenty years.

"Twenty years," she said out loud, just as the Lexus's back gate opened.

After Owen dropped his suitcase inside and closed the gate, he opened the driver's door, then climbed inside. "Do you always talk to yourself?"

"It's a sign of intelligence." Rather than engage in another round of juvenile banter, she added, "I was reminding myself that this year marks twenty years of abductions from Wexman University."

He pulled the Lexus out of the parking garage and onto the street. "Yeah, the sheriff told you nine boys in twenty years."

"Sean's roommate makes ten."

"You're repeating yourself."

Ignoring Owen, she opened up her laptop, searched the Lexus's control panel until she found a power source, then plugged in the cord. "Each one of these missing fraternity kids are taken during January, and are never seen again."

"Still repeating yourself."

She reigned in her irritation. "This year marks twenty."

"Repeat. And unless the kidnapper left some china behind in the kid's dorm room, I don't see your point."

He actually knew china was the standard twentieth anniversary gift? In her experience—make that her mom's—most men could hardly remember their anniversary, let alone what to buy. "Maybe I don't have a point." She reached in her computer bag for a pencil. "Maybe I think…forget it."

"No. As much as I know you probably don't want to hear this—"

"Then please keep it to yourself. In case you haven't noticed, I'm not having the best morning."

"What I was going to say…" He paused, and blew out a deep breath. "Okay, so the Miami case I just finished."

A shiver ran through her. "That guy was a total sicko."

"Yeah, a sicko you helped me catch."

She glanced at him. "*You* did the catching, all I did was—"

"Lead me in the right direction after I told you about his second to last victim."

"Well, he was stupid. He'd left a credit card trail."

"A trail neither the Miami-Dade PD nor the FBI could find. Let's not forget my other assignments, or how about what you did for John when he was working in Wisconsin, or Hudson back in November?"

This was going to be the longest six hours of her life. She didn't want compliments from Owen, and would rather deal with his insults. Compliments led to hope, which led to dreams, which, in her experience, led to disappointment.

Although, now that she thought about it, other than the jabs about her pencil dependency, he didn't sling the insults, she did. Maybe ditzy blonde would have been the perfect nickname for him. He either had no clue as to why she couldn't stand being around him, or didn't realize how much he'd hurt her. Not that she'd bring that embarrassing situation up to him. How would she even broach the subject? 'Hey, Owen, remember the night you kissed me under the mistletoe, then turned around and left with the leggy Barbie doll?' Yeah. Not going to happen. He probably didn't even remember the kiss.

But I do.

Rubbing the knot at the base of her neck, she said, "What's your point?"

"I rely on you. Not only for the information you provide, but because you always have a way of coming up with new angles. So, if you're having a 'maybe' moment, let's hear it."

He relied on her? She glanced at the passing mile marker. This was *really* going to be the longest six hours of her life. His praise bothered the hell out of her. Sure, everything he'd said had been work related, and had nothing to do with her as a woman. A vital, somewhat attractive, yet somewhat geeky, under-sexed woman.

Still, it was a compliment.

A rather bland, boring compliment.

Not that she wanted him to confess to being hypnotized by her smile, or tell her that looking into her eyes was like staring into deep pools of emeralds. She'd heard her mother's past conquests spew that sort of flowery drivel enough to know empty compliments were worse than none at all. Hence the reason she preferred to date nerdy, nice guys who admired her intelligence and computer skills, and had no idea how to fake a relationship. Unfortunately, with those men foreplay would be pizza, wings, and maybe a discussion about the latest Mobile Ad Hoc Network they'd created. As for sex...discussing the Scalable Link Interface was usually more exciting. Regardless, she'd rather date bland and boring, than mix herself up with men like Owen.

Too hot. Too confident. Too good of a kisser.

Why was she even thinking about any of this? He'd admitted to relying on her skills and she'd turned that one, itty-bitty flattering remark into so much more.

Remember he's a bottom feeder. Stick to business. Think about Sean. Quit wandering into the past.

"Okay," she began, refocusing. "Maybe I think it's odd that whoever is behind taking these frat boys hasn't stopped. Not in twenty years. Or maybe…"

"What? We'll find the roommate on a china platter?" He glanced at her. "Sorry, bad joke."

"Very bad joke," she said, and shook her head as another thought occurred to her. "Maybe Hell Week is the anniversary of…something."

He shrugged. "Yeah, like how about Hell Week? Did the sheriff mention how many years in between disappearances? Because the more I think about it, if the Hell Week note wasn't left behind, one could consider these disappearances random rather than deliberate."

"The sheriff said he'd fill me in on everything when we meet. But you're right, if it wasn't for the note…"

"And that the kids go missing in January. But doesn't that seem too obvious? Twenty years of abductions, at the start of a weeklong fraternity ritual, and the local authorities haven't come to the conclusion that whoever is behind this might harbor a grudge about Hell Week itself?"

"Or it could be that the person behind this had been a victim of a Hell Week hazing," she said, then began typing. "I'm going to find everything I can about Bola, Wexman University and the long list of missing persons."

"Might as well go in armed with info. That sheriff sounds clueless."

She thought about Sheriff Jake Tyler. While they'd spoken, her focus had been on Sean's condition. She'd still caught the frustration in the sheriff's voice when he talked about the missing persons and the Michigan State Police. "I don't know about that. He couldn't be that clueless if he was smart enough to ask CORE for help."

"Oh, come on, Rachel," he said. "This Hell Week thing has been going on for twenty years. Your sheriff is probably old and counting down the days until retirement. The only reason he wants us involved now is probably because the university and the people living in or near Bola have had enough and want answers."

"He didn't sound old. Actually, he had a nice voice," she said, then popped the pencil in her mouth and began researching Bola.

"A nice voice? Whatever." He snorted, then a few minutes later asked, "Hey, Beaver, do you plan on chewing that pencil the whole time we're in the car?"

Without looking at him, or removing the pencil, she mumbled, "Yep."

He turned on the radio, then released a deep, exasperated sigh. "This is going to be the longest six hours of my life."

"Remove all of your clothes."

The chains cuffed to the pledge's wrists shook. "Why are you doing this?" he asked on a sob.

"Junior, hand me the baseball bat. No, not the wooden one, our pledge deserves metal."

After Junior gave him the metal bat, he wrapped his hands around the base, and moved into a batting stance. "You have two seconds to comply. If you don't, or you ask another ridiculous question, I'll use your genitals for batting practice."

Sniveling, the pledge quickly shucked his jeans, kicked them off, then removed his boots and socks. When he reached for the waistband of his underwear, Junior gasped.

"You're right," he said, and leaned against the bat as if it were a crutch. "Keep the underwear in place. The male genitalia are too vulgar for a delicate woman's eyes." He smiled to Junior.

"Thank you, sir," she said. "Should I go upstairs to the

31

laundry room and check the hose?"

"The hose is fine. But I do need you to turn on the faucet. Cold, please." With no running water in the basement, he'd learned to improvise. Connecting the garden hose to the sink in the laundry room had worked well. The old farmhouse he'd inherited from his parents had been built in the early 1880s. While the house itself had been modernized over the years, the basement had been left in its original state. Researching the home that had belonged to his family for more than one hundred and thirty years, he'd learned that the builder, his great-great-great grandfather, had used dynamite to blow a hole in the rocky ground near the Menominee River. He'd then covered the eight hundred square foot, dank, rocky cavity with the farmhouse. He'd learned the basement had been initially used to keep food items cold. Even in the summer, the basement maintained a comfortable sixty degrees. But in the dead of winter, the room could dip into the fifties and even the forties. Not a pleasant place for the pledge. But this wasn't Holiday Inn, and his pledge wasn't here for rest and relaxation.

He glanced up the ladder. His parents had sealed the basement access door after he'd been born. They'd worried over him constantly, and had feared he'd fall into the gaping hole and perish should he play with the old trapdoor. After he'd taken possession of the house, he'd found where the old access had been, and had reopened the basement. Thinking about the moment he'd climbed down the ladder and stepped onto the worn limestone still aroused him. Not in a sexual way, of course. A lewd, crude exchange of bodily fluids, sex was for animals. Only one time had he given into his body's disgusting needs. While he'd achieved physical gratification, emitting semen into his lover had stupidly resulted in an unwanted child.

"And here she comes now," he said, then offered his hand when Junior had reached the last few rungs of the ladder.

"The water is on," Junior said. "I also made sure the extension cord was plugged in, too."

"Good. Now hold this for me. I'm tired of watching this pathetic puke try to undress." He stopped short of the struggling pledge. "If he tries to harm me, break his knee cap."

She raised the metal bat. "Yes, sir."

When Junior had brought the pledge to him, the puke had been wearing boots, jeans, and a black-hooded sweatshirt with Wexman University emblazoned across the front in the university's trademark colors of green and gold. In his haste to rid himself of the sweatshirt and the long-sleeved thermal shirt he'd worn beneath, the fool had managed to tangle the material in the chains secured around his wrists.

With a schedule to keep, he drew a hunting knife from the belt at his waist and moved closer to the pledge.

The puke's eyes widened. His breath came in harsh bursts. "I did what you told me," he wailed, his voice echoing off the rock walls.

"Shut up," he ordered, then stabbed the material bunched between the pledge's wrists.

In seconds, the sharp blade tore through the fabric. Taking a step back, he glared at the devil's spawn. Naked save for a pair of underwear, and the torn clothing around his wrists, the pledge—if his memory served him well—was the spitting image of the demon who had tormented him for more than two decades.

With this year's Hell Week, his life would come full circle, and then he would pass the torch to Junior. She'd showed up on his doorstep eighteen months ago, as welcomed as a burning paper bag filled with dog excrement. He'd been immediately angered by her presence. But then he'd learned that her mother, Vivian, the vessel he'd once used to slake his lust, had died. Apparently Vivian hadn't told Junior about him. Instead, after cleaning out her deceased mother's files, his child had discovered not only who he was, but that he'd given up his rights to her when she'd been born.

That balmy, summer night eighteen months ago, he'd sat on the back porch with Junior, drinking iced tea and listening to her talk. He'd learned that Vivian had all but ignored her.

33

That, as a child, Junior had taken to torturing small animals. Later, she'd been fired from babysitting jobs due to the physical abuse she'd doled out to the children. And later still, she'd slit the throat of the man who had tried to rape her of her virginity. In that moment, he'd realized he might have found a kindred spirit in his daughter, that she could be the son he'd always longed for. The person who could share his vision and continue his legacy.

After their initial meeting, he'd spent months testing her. Spent nights ensuring that she not only respect, but fear him. Junior might be his protégé, but as her father, it was his God given right to mete out punishment. And while Junior had already made the mistake of bringing him two pledges when he'd distinctly said one—this one in particular—he couldn't stay mad at her. Like he had been in the past, she'd been overzealous with power the night she took the two pledges. He had learned, from her stories of neglect and physical abuse, she'd hungered for power all of her life.

He glanced at her. Her eyes, so much like his own, were fixated on the nearly naked pledge. They shimmered with what he assumed was excitement, and a small, triumphant smile played across her lips. Yes. She would definitely continue his legacy.

"Keep alert," he said to Junior, then using his fists, shoved the pledge against the rock wall. The pitiable crybaby sobbed and groaned. He ignored the blubbering and secured the pledge's wrists to the metal hooks he'd drilled into the rock years ago. After he replaced the shackles around the pledge's ankles, he did the same with those chains, then took several steps back. With the way he'd been chained to the wall, the pledge reminded him of Da Vinci's *Vitruvian Man* diagram, minus the extra set of arms and legs of course.

"Are we ready?" Junior asked, and handed him the metal bat.

"Yes. Care to do the honors?"

"Definitely."

"I thought as much," he said, retrieved the hose, then

handed it to her. "Begin."

Without delay she squeezed the nozzle, and at full throttle, sprayed the pledge in the face. He coughed and spat, shook he head as if doing so might thwart her efforts.

"Make sure you get the rest of him," he reminded her.

She did as he'd directed, and doused ice-cold water across the pledge's young body.

Minutes later he instructed her to turn off the nozzle. After coiling the hose, then placing it on the far wall, he turned to the pledge. The puke shivered, and his teeth chattered hard enough he wondered if the pledge might actually chip a tooth.

"What's next?" Junior asked, and pulled her heavy coat tight against her chest.

"We leave, then resume this evening after dinner. I thought we'd have roast beef."

She furrowed her forehead as she stared at the pledge. "It's freezing down here, will he survive the cold?"

"According to the thermometer, it's forty-nine degrees. Through my research, I've learned that hypothermia, for someone as unclad as our pledge, usually develops between the temperature ranges of thirty to fifty degrees. That, of course, is if he remained dry, had the opportunity to move and stay active, and the floor was well-insulated."

She half-laughed and shook her head. "Then I guess we'll be disposing of a body after dinner."

"Never fear, I will not leave you disappointed." He moved back to the wall, picked up the space heater, then set it on the rock floor approximately five feet from the pledge.

"Now I know what the electrical cord was for," she said. "No offense, sir, but giving him the heater…forcing him to strip, then hosing him down seems more like a show to me."

He shrugged. "Not a show, what I'm offering is false hope. I have the heater set on a timer. Every half hour the heat will turn on for ten minutes. As I explained to you, I've been doing this for a while, and know that the small amount of warmth will be enough to eventually dry the pledge and keep him from succumbing to hypothermia. We won't be removing a body…today."

"F…f…fuck you," the pledge stuttered, while his body shook.

In four strides he stood in front of the pledge, then gave him a swift, hard backhand to his wet face. "A lady is present. If you continue to use foul language I will remove the space heater and allow you to freeze to death. It's only Monday, I guarantee I can find a replacement pledge. Do you understand?"

The boy nodded.

"Good. Now apologize."

Tears streamed down the puke's wet cheeks. "I…I…I'm s…s…sorry."

"Good." He pulled a piece of cold, burnt toast from his coat pocket. "Open wide," he instructed the pledge, then shoved the toast into his mouth.

While the pledge chewed, he turned to Junior and ushered her toward the ladder. As she climbed the rungs, he doused the battery-powered lantern, and flooded the basement with utter darkness.

"We'll see you after dinner. I promise to bring you something more substantial than toast." He smiled. "I hear maggots are quite high in protein."

CHAPTER 3

OWEN STOOD IN the hallway of Dixon Medical Center, holding a Styrofoam cup filled with the worst coffee he'd ever tasted, and stared at Sean's closed hospital room door. Knowing Rachel the way he did, he'd declined visiting with her brother until she'd had the chance to see him first. He hadn't missed the relief in her eyes, or the way her body had relaxed when he'd lied about needing to find some caffeine.

Despite her strong aversion to him, he'd come to know and understand her. Mensa smart, she could crack computer codes, create her own programs, and hack into just about anything. Unlike most of the ultra brainy people he'd known, she actually had a high amount of common sense, too. When it came to the social skills department, though, she tended to be… unusual.

The youngest child of four, and the only boy, he'd learned the mysterious inner workings of the female psyche at an early age. His sisters had taken it upon themselves to make him the model male. They had taught him when to shut up and when to listen. That, when a woman asks how she looks, you never say, "fine." Even if the woman simply looks "fine," he should always find one thing to compliment. While they hadn't schooled him on how to deal with the rollercoaster of emotions females might experience, growing up with a gaggle of girls, he'd learned on his own that what makes one woman tick, will make another tock.

Computers made Rachel tick. Her brother and their coworkers made her tick, along with pencils, popcorn, Diet Coke, her El Camino and, strangely enough, hip hop and classical music. For whatever reason, he made her tock. Maybe, like a lot of women he'd met over the years then immediately steered away from, she preferred the brooding badass—a term that, with the exception of himself, would sum up all the men who worked for CORE. While he could be a badass when necessary, brooding wasn't his style. Dwelling on the shit life throws at you, then acting all dark and menacing over it, didn't work for him.

Living in the past only hinders the future.

Still, after spending six hours in the car with Rachel, he'd thought that *maybe* they'd actually have a decent, civil conversation. Instead, she'd kept her nose buried in her laptop while chomping away at a pencil. And that was fine. Just because they worked together didn't mean they had to be friends. Only…

Shoving off the wall, he went in search of a garbage can. Now wasn't the time to evaluate or even begin to try and process why in the hell he couldn't stop thinking about her lately. She didn't even like him.

But you like her.

He did, but couldn't figure out why. She chewed pencils, drove a tricked out car, probably couldn't go to a party or a bar without having a panic attack, and had to be the most abrasive creature he'd ever met. And yet he looked forward to hearing her voice when he was stuck on assignment, loved the way she challenged and mocked him. Unlike most women, she didn't care about his looks, and was immune to his charm.

Dumping the nasty coffee into the trash, he shook his head. He needed to have sex. That's all. Except for his mom and sisters, over the last six months, Rachel had been the only other constant woman in his life. After this case, when they were back in Chicago, he'd have to look up and hook up with one of the women he would date now and then. Angelica came to mind. A beautiful model with long blonde hair, longer legs, and bedroom eyes, she'd take his mind off Rachel.

"Owen?"

He turned, and guilt sucker-punched him in the gut. How could he consider using Angelica to help him overcome his urge to explore something with Rachel?

Bloodshot and red-rimmed from crying, her green eyes appeared greener. Her short, spiky red hair was even spikier, as if she'd been yanking it from the roots. While already vertically challenged, with the way she stood, shoulders slumped and hugging herself, she looked even smaller, almost fragile.

"Hey, how's your brother?" he asked, and shoved his hands into his pockets to keep from hauling her into his arms and taking the heavy weight off of her shoulders.

"Way better than I expected. He's hoping you'll stop in and see him before we leave to meet the sheriff."

"Of course," he said, and followed her into Sean's hospital room.

When he saw the kid lying on the bed, his nose broken, eyes and cheeks bruised, lips swollen and split, he tried to mask the anger pounding his skull. He didn't want to amplify Rachel's concerns and grief, or upset Sean during his recovery. But as he glanced at the kid's broken arm, then again at his bruises, the anger he'd been reining in morphed to both dread and relief. While his heart went out to the family of the missing roommate, he thanked God that Sean hadn't been the one to suffer the kidnapper's version—whatever that might be—of Hell Week. Based on Sean's injuries, he could only imagine what fate the other boy would suffer over the course of the next seven days.

After he cleared his throat, he said, "How you doing, kiddo?"

"I've had better days," Sean answered with a smile, then winced and touched the stitches binding his split lip.

Rachel moved to her brother's side and smoothed his red hair off his forehead. "Try not to talk, laugh or smile. Actually, I'd prefer if you didn't move at all."

"So you want me to just lie here."

"Yes, exactly."

"What about when I have to go to the bathroom?"

"Oh, do you have to go now?" she asked and reached for a bedpan. "Here, let me help you."

A blush stained Sean's face making him look like a bruised tomato. "I don't have to go now. I'm just saying..." He glanced at Owen. "A little help, please?"

"You don't need his help," Rachel said. "I not only used to change your diapers, but I also potty trained you."

"Oh my God, Ray," Sean said. "I mean, seriously?"

The poor kid had suffered enough, and although he might catch backlash from Rachel, Owen decided to put Sean out of his misery. His sisters had changed his diapers, too. And they still loved to remind him of that disgusting and embarrassing fact. "I'm on Sean's side," he said, then looked to the kid. "But your sister is right. You do need to take it easy. I wouldn't be getting out of this bed unless a nurse is here to help you."

"I know. I guess I won't be doing much of anything for a while."

"That's right," Rachel said, reached for the cup of water on the bed tray, then pressed the straw to Sean's lips. "Here, drink."

He turned his head away. "I'm not thirsty."

"Are you hungry? I can have the nurse—"

"I'm fine," Sean said, his tone laced with frustration. "Would you please stop fussing over me?"

"Well, you don't look fine. Actually, you look like shit. And I'd appreciate it if you'd stop acting as if I'm torturing you. I've been worried sick. I just want to make sure...what is it?" she asked when Sean's face contorted and his eyes filled with tears.

He clenched his jaw. "Torture. That's what's going to happen to Josh."

Owen met her gaze from across the hospital bed, then he looked to Sean. "Did the sheriff tell you about Josh?"

"Sheriff? No, I haven't met him yet. I was either still unconscious or doped up on pain meds until about an hour ago."

"Then how did you know about Josh?" Rachel asked.

He reached for his sister's hand. As a tear slipped down his bruised cheek, he asked, "Has anyone found him?"

"No, honey, he's missing."

Sean rolled his head against the pillow and looked away. "Right now he's just missing. By the end of the week, he'll be dead."

Rachel touched Sean's shoulder. "How do you know this?"

"I...I thought the guys at the Zeta house were full of crap." Tears coated this cheek, and hit the pillow. "So did Josh. But they were right...they were right."

"Right about what?" Rachel asked.

Sean finally looked at her. "Every few years, a pledge is taken and never seen again. The guys at the Zeta house said the pledge is considered a sacrifice. You know, kinda like an offering."

Rachel gently dabbed a tissue along her brother's wet cheeks. "An offering to what?"

"Hell Week."

Even the Lexus's seat warmer couldn't stop the shiver of dread splintering through Rachel's body. What had happened to her brother could have been much worse. He could, like Josh, be missing. Maybe tortured. Maybe dead.

As Owen drove away from the hospital—which, in her opinion, was more like an urgent care center—she reached into her computer bag for a pencil. "When I was researching during the drive here, I came across a blog, written and maintained by Wexman students. In it, Wexman Hell Week was listed as a local legend, right next to Bigfoot and UFO sightings."

"Legend?" Owen repeated with sarcasm. "Fact: People have been going missing for twenty years. That's not a legend. That could be the work of a serial killer."

"I don't disagree. But, not one body has ever been recovered, and other than the missing persons, and the notes

41

left behind, I couldn't find any other evidence of foul play. Plus, people commented on this blog, as well as other websites, that some of the alleged missing people have been spotted throughout the years. Not in Bola, but I found reports in Florida, Ohio, California and Alaska."

"Yeah, and were these missing persons seen hanging out with Bigfoot, too?"

She half-laughed. "Right. Maybe having a beer with the Jersey Devil while the Mothman served them chips and salsa."

He chuckled, then grew serious. "Are you okay?"

"I'm fine," she lied. When she'd seen Sean lying in the hospital bed, it had taken everything to keep her cool. Her brother's injuries and knowing that he could have, like Josh, been abducted and still missing, had had her on the verge of a mental and emotional meltdown. For Sean's sake, she'd kept herself together and had shed only a few tears. But when she'd walked into the hospital hallway and saw Owen…she'd had the sudden urge to jump into his strong arms and bawl like a baby.

Never in her life had she been able to depend on someone else's strength to help her overcome a situation. Thanks to her flaky mother, she'd always had to play that role. Today, she wished she could have leaned on Owen. Pretend he hadn't kissed her, that he hadn't hurt her. While she might consider him the bottom feeder of the dating pool, she knew, deep down, that he was a straight up, good and decent man. He cared about his job, their coworkers, and when it came to the cases he investigated, each victim, as well as their families. Still, telling Owen the truth or even giving him a hint that she was currently experiencing some major emotional turmoil wasn't an option. Ian had given her lead on this case. Like the men on the CORE team, she needed to exhibit nothing but strength, especially if she wanted the opportunity for more field assignments.

"Although it might make our job easier, a part of me is relieved Sean doesn't remember what happened to him and Josh Saturday night," Owen said, then obeyed the GPS and turned right.

"I know what you mean. I asked his doctor if they'd done anything with his blood work. He already ordered a tox screen, and said he'd call when he had something for us."

"How big is Josh Conway?"

She rubbed her temple and brought Josh's image to mind. "He and Sean are the same height, but Josh probably has Sean by about thirty or so pounds. My guess is six foot, maybe a hundred and eighty pounds."

"Six foot? I didn't realize Sean was that tall. No offense, but what happened to you?"

"I know. Sean's all arms and legs, and walks slumped. If only Sean's dad had been my sperm donor. I could have been five five or even five seven."

He chuckled. "Height is overrated."

"Says the giant to the dwarf."

"Whatever. Okay, so you've got two young guys, who aren't small...one is kidnapped, the other is beaten and has no recollection of events. If they were drugged—"

"They had to be. How else could someone take the two of them without a fight? And Sean said he doesn't remember anything after leaving the dorms."

"Okay," he began, obeyed the GPS again and made another turn. "Sean said the last thing he does remember was eating pizza and—"

"Drinking a crap load of Mountain Dew."

"Do you have to finish my sentences?"

"Sorry, bad habit. Anyway, let's run with this. Specifically the Mountain Dew. What drug could be placed into a liquid, you can't taste it, and it makes you totally black out?"

"Rohypnol."

"The date rape drug. I've got to make sure Sean's doctor has their lab check for Rohypnol or anything similar." She quickly dialed the hospital and spoke with Sean's doctor.

As she ended the call, Owen pulled into the parking lot of a standalone, two story, brick building. While he parked the Lexus, and the GPS let them know they'd arrived, he said, "Hopefully that bottle of Mountain Dew is still in the dorm room. If whoever took Josh and hurt Sean had used the soda as a vessel for the drug, they might have left fingerprints behind."

"Doubtful. Whoever's behind this has been at it for a long time. They know what they're doing."

After shifting the Lexus into PARK, he killed the ignition and turned to her. "Or maybe it's your sheriff who doesn't know what he's doing."

She glanced at the Dixon County Sheriff's Department sign and shrugged. "Let's go find out."

Owen climbed out of the Lexus and followed Rachel into the building. When he stepped inside the small foyer, he felt as if he'd taken several steps back in time. From the look of things he guessed the building hadn't seen an update since the 1970s and probably hadn't been cleaned since then either. The stale smell of cigarette smoke and some flowery bathroom spray hung in the air. The walls, chipped, filthy, and stained brown from nicotine, had been painted dark mustard. The scuffed linoleum floor, an ugly olive and gold, actually matched the walls.

A young brunette sat behind a desk that had likely been built a couple decades before she'd been born. "Can I help you?" she asked.

"We have an appointment with Sheriff Tyler," Rachel replied and gave her their names.

Seconds later, a man Owen placed around his age, entered the foyer from a back hallway. Dressed in a light brown shirt, with the town and state insignia on the sleeve, and a pair of jeans, he approached them. "Miss Davis?"

When Rachel nodded, he extended his hand. "Jake Tyler."

As Owen introduced himself to the sheriff, he ignored Rachel's smug smile. He'd been wrong to assume the sheriff was a decrepit old man counting his days until retirement, and was certain Rachel would remind him later.

"Come on back," the sheriff said.

"Jake." The receptionist stopped him. "Abby's running late for her shift and I have a class in thirty minutes. What do you want me to do? I can go to class late."

The sheriff puffed his cheeks, then blew out a breath. "No, Melissa. School's important. Adjust the switchboard and have the calls go to my cell phone." Then rubbing the base of his neck, he led them down the back hallway and into a cramped office.

"Sorry about the mess. Our basement flooded around the first of the month, and there's not a whole lotta places for storage. You should see the jail cell." He moved stacks of file boxes off the chair in front of the desk, then retrieved a folding chair that had been hidden behind more boxes along the wall. "Please, have a seat."

Ever the gentleman, Owen gave Rachel the cushioned chair. Although worn and the upholstery cracked, the chair beat the hell out of sitting on metal.

"Is your receptionist a college student?" Rachel asked as she sat.

"Yeah. I have eight students who split all the shifts. It usually works out fine…" He shrugged, then said, "Honestly, I don't mind if I have to occasionally deal with the calls. When I took on this job, the woman who'd been running the front desk was a Townie—born and raised—and a real problem. With barely twelve hundred people living in Bola, you tend to know everyone. She spent more time gossiping than doing her job. I couldn't have her tying up the phone lines so she could call her friends and give them all the dirty details about how so and so was spending the night in jail for such and such."

Rachel smiled and shook her head. "Sounds like a nightmare."

"You have no idea. I'm down to three deputies when I should have six. The salary isn't enough to entice anyone with a law enforcement background to move to the area and I refuse to hire anyone from town. Long story, but I tried that route once and ended up arresting that deputy and throwing *him* in jail."

"How long have you been on the job?" Owen asked.

The sheriff leaned into the chair and folded his arms across

45

his chest. "Six years."

"And before that?"

"I was a Marine."

"You're not from Bola?"

"Pittsburgh." He held up a hand just as Owen planned to throw him another question. "Look, I'm sure you two are wondering what the hell the dumb hick sheriff has been doing while college kids go missing."

Owen looked to Rachel, who shook her head as if he were a jackass. Realizing he'd inadvertently been playing twenty questions with the sheriff, he said, "Sorry, Jake, I didn't mean to insult you. But understand it from my point of view. You were obviously in high school when the first student went missing, and ended up inheriting this mess. I still want to know your background and your capabilities as a sheriff. I want to know what you've done to stop this during the last six years."

"Oh my God," Rachel groaned. "For someone who didn't mean to be insulting…"

"It's okay," Jake said. "Actually, I appreciate your partner's bluntness. And he's right. I did inherit this mess. My first year as sheriff, a student went missing, and the Hell Week note was left in his dorm room. When I started questioning folks I discovered that, over the prior fourteen years, the same damned thing happened seven other times. The previous sheriff was dead, so he was obviously no help. The deputies claimed that the former sheriff exhausted every possible angle, which was a lie. My initial file on the first kidnapping victim I dealt with is thicker than all seven my predecessor investigated. So I called the Michigan State Police."

"You'd mentioned they're not interested in helping," Rachel said.

"Yeah, the first time they came to Bola, it didn't go well. I gave the two inspectors from the State Police Field Service Bureau the Hell Week note I found in the missing kid's dorm. In the meantime, I contacted the kid's parents, gathered a couple hundred volunteers from Bola and the university, along with trained search-and-rescue dogs loaned to us from another county. The inspectors even had divers come in to search the river. This search ended up going on record as the largest of its kind in this county, ever."

Rachel leaned forward. "But you never found the kid. That must have been rough."

"No." Jake shook his head. "We found him."

"But I thought you told me you've never found any of the bodies," Rachel said.

"True. None of the *missing* boys have ever been found. This kid wasn't missing though. He was in Niagara Falls with his girlfriend for the weekend."

Rachel frowned. "But the note."

Jake shook his head. "The State Police lab found fingerprints on it, and those prints ended up matching a couple guys from the fraternity the not-so-missing kid was pledging."

"I take it everyone knows about the kidnappers MO," Owen said.

"That's right. My predecessor and his deputies kept no secrets. Those two frat boys thought it would be funny to plant the note. Their hoax cost the county thousands of dollars it didn't have. The two boys lost their scholarships and were eventually expelled. And, their little prank ended up damaging my reputation."

Aside from assuming the sheriff had been days from retirement, Owen realized he'd pegged Jake Tyler wrong. It sounded as if, during his first year on the job, Jake had done everything by the book with this particular case. Unfortunately, that hadn't mattered. Although the circumstances weren't his fault, the sheriff had been the lead on the investigation, as well as the eventual fall guy. Owen could relate to Jake's frustration. Hell, a misguided and manipulative seventeen-year-old girl had cost him his career with the U.S. Secret Service. After his reputation had already been ruined, he'd later learned she hadn't meant to, just like he was sure those two frat boys hadn't meant for their prank to blow up in their faces, or Jake's for that matter.

"None of this was your fault," Rachel said. "I still don't see why, after that incident, the State Police—"

"It gets better. Two weeks later, another kid went missing. The kid's RA, his roommate, the guys from the fraternity he was pledging…they all thought he'd gone home to see his family. No one contacted me, or anyone at my department, about his disappearance. A month later, I get a call from this kid's parents, asking me to check on their son. When I went to his dorm room, and looked through his things, I found the Hell Week note. This time, because now I knew this Hell Week kidnapping had been legitimately going on for fourteen years, I checked the note against the others my predecessor had saved. They matched."

"Did you call the inspectors to help?" Owen asked.

"No. I set up a smaller search party. By nightfall, I sent everyone home with the intent to go back the next day. Which we did, only I knew we weren't going to find the kid."

"How?" Rachel asked.

The sheriff withdrew a file folder from his desk, then handed Rachel a photo. Her eyes grew wide, then she handed the four by six glossy to Owen. He stared at the decomposing body of a Caucasian male, who had likely been in his late teens, or early twenties, then looked to Jake.

"I found that in my mailbox the night we did the initial search. Except the two inspectors I worked with on the prank, I've never shown anyone that photo," the sheriff said, and gave a yellowing piece of paper to Rachel. "Or the note that came with it."

Rachel read the note out loud. "Quit wasting tax dollars. The pledge didn't survive Hell Week." She handed the paper back to the sheriff. "Do you know if the killer contacted the previous sheriff?"

"Not that I'm aware, and I've never been contacted since."

"What did the inspectors say about this?" she asked.

"That it could be another hoax, and the picture photoshopped. That's why they didn't want me showing the photo to the victim's parents. Plus, there wasn't one shred of evidence the kid *hadn't* disappeared on his own. I couldn't find his wallet, passport, cell phone, or laptop. And, according to his roommate, the kid's gym bag and some of his clothes were missing. I did call the phone company and asked them to see if they could "ping" his cell phone. They didn't find anything." The sheriff placed the note and photo back in the folder. "I did the same thing three years ago when another kid went missing. Set up a search party, looked through the missing boy's dorm room, contacted the phone company." He released a deep sigh. "I informed the State Police, but the inspector I spoke with told me to call him when I either have a body, or some evidence to work with...apparently the Hell Week note and all the other missing kids wasn't evidence enough."

"Except now you have a witness," Rachel said.

"Sean's doctor called me when your brother woke up, but that was about an hour before you were scheduled to arrive. I was at the university and the doctor said Sean wasn't lucid at that point," Jake said. "I apologize. I should have asked how he was doing."

"He's better than I expected."

"Were you able to talk to him?"

"Yes, but he doesn't remember anything. Owen and I are thinking that Sean and Josh may have been drugged. Sean's doctor is having his blood screened for Rohypnol. My brother said the last thing he remembers is eating pizza and drinking Mountain Dew. He also remembered leaving the dorms, then from there, everything's black."

"I've been in their dorm room," Jake began. "I did find a pizza box, but no bottles of any kind of soda. Empty or full."

"We're still going to want to check my brother's room. I'd also like to have a list of everyone you've interviewed."

Used to taking the lead during an investigation, but impressed with how Rachel handled the sheriff, Owen leaned into the metal chair and kept his mouth shut. For now. He'd sworn he had seen a flash of disappointment in her eyes when Ian had informed her that he would be helping her in Bola. Her desire to work in the field was no secret. While he honestly believed her talents lay with her computer skills, he didn't want to see her fail. There might come a time when he, or any member of the CORE team, might need her in the field, and she needed the experience.

Jake gave her another manila envelope. "This is everything I have regarding the Josh Conway investigation. I've talked with the RA, campus security, other kids from the dorms, kids from the frat house, and a few people from the university administration office. I planned on talking with the professor Josh and Sean were supposed to meet at the library the night they were taken, but he's been in class all day." Jake stood, then moved next to Rachel. After she opened the folder, he leaned in and pointed to a name on the list.

"Got it," Rachel said. "And Sean's clothes?"

The sheriff reached across the desk and grabbed a brown paper bag. "Everything he wore the night he was found is in here. Like I told you this morning, I can send it to the State Police."

Rachel set the bag on her lap. "No, that'll take too long. The lab CORE uses can give us results within a few days."

"Nice," Jake replied. "That's a hell of a turnaround time."

If only the sheriff knew the cost. But Ian had deep pockets and zero patience. With any case CORE took on, Ian wanted excellent, quick results. When one case ended, there was always another that needed to be solved.

"The perks of a private agency," Rachel said, then added, "When I was researching Bola and Wexman, I found a blog that claimed Wexman Hell Week was like Bigfoot...nothing but a legend."

The sheriff sat on the edge of the desk near Rachel. "There are a lot of superstitious people around these parts. Every Townie has a theory about what keeps happening to these students. Some are logical, others are ludicrous. There's one thing the Townies do have in common though, and that's...fear."

Owen frowned. "But all the victims have been college students."

"Not all." Jake turned to Rachel. "I told you this morning

that in twenty years we've had well over a dozen missing persons cases. Including Josh Conway, that exact number is nineteen."

"You'd said five had been solved."

"Right. Those cases involved missing campers and hunters who'd gotten themselves lost in the woods. As for the four that haven't been solved, I'm not sure if they're related to the Wexman Hell Week cases, but the Townies think so." He stood, grabbed a file box from the floor, then set it on the desk in front of Rachel. "This is everything I've got, dating back twenty years. Take it with you, these are all copies."

Rachel glanced at Owen, then back to the sheriff. "Thanks. This is a big help."

For the first time since meeting him, Jake smiled. "Don't thank me yet. I'm not sure how much this will help or not." Pulling a coat from his chair, he said, "I've got to go meet with the town council."

"Didn't you do that this morning?" Rachel asked, furrowing her auburn brows.

"It's a wonder I get anything done," he said with a rueful, half-smile. "The council consists of a bunch of business owners and retired busybodies. Although Wexman Hell Week isn't something new, we have something happening this weekend that is." He shoved his arm into the coat sleeve. "That professor Sean and Josh were supposed to meet...he and his students petitioned the Townies, then after receiving an overwhelming approval, have pulled together a festival. And it's going down this weekend."

"What kind of festival are we talking about?" Rachel asked.

"Well, this is where things get a little tricky *and* ridiculous. I'm almost embarrassed to say." Jake scratched the back of his head, looked to the floor for a second, then said, "It's a Bigfoot festival."

Rachel smashed her lips together, and closed her eyes. Owen had seen that same expression numerous times over the years and knew she fought to keep from laughing. To help her save face in front of Jake, he said, "That's the stupidest thing

I've ever heard...and I'm not just talking about Bigfoot. Why in the hell would this professor organize a festival now? Does he really believe Wexman Hell Week is a legend? I'd think missing kids would be enough to make anyone—"

Jake raised a hand. "Please. Don't get me started. I was against this festival from the beginning. The thing is, a lot of people around here believe in Bigfoot, just as much as Wexman Hell Week. Now here's the other thing. There hasn't been a single disappearance for the past two years. Because two years is the longest time between these missing persons cases, I think the business owners *did* worry another kid could possibly go missing this year, but I believe they also saw dollar signs."

Owen shifted in the metal chair. "So there's no pattern."

Jake shook his head. "None. Believe me, I've combed through the old sheriff's files and other than the note...well, maybe you guys will be able to come up with something solid."

"Are you expecting a lot of people to come to this festival?" Rachel asked.

"The local motel is booked, so is the campground—which has never happened in January. I just found out this morning that the motels and hotels in the neighboring county are also booked because of this festival. From what I understand, they're expecting about five hundred or so people, which is good business for Bola."

"But bad business for an investigation," Owen countered.

Jake nodded. "Right. So, between the festival and Josh Conway, the town council has been...um..."

Rachel smiled. "Up your ass?"

The sheriff released a low chuckle. "That's putting it mildly. Anyway, I've got to run. You might want to start with Josh and Sean's dorm room, then try meeting with that professor. I was told he should be available in a couple of hours. Before you head over to the university though, you better secure your rooms for the week."

"I thought you said the motel was booked," Rachel said, and stood.

Jake ripped a sheet of paper off a notepad, then handed it to Rachel. "It is, so I called Joy. She runs a boarding house and has two vacant rooms. Here's the address. I asked her to hold off on giving those rooms away, should any of the Bigfoot fanatics find out about her place. I wasn't sure if Sean would move back into the dorms after he's released." He nodded to Owen. "I also wasn't expecting Rachel to have company, but this should work out fine for now. Owen, if it turns out you need a place to stay, I've got a pullout couch."

While Rachel stuffed the information into her pocket, the sheriff moved toward the door. Owen grabbed the file box off the desk, then followed Rachel and Jake. As they exited the back hallway, a young, pretty blonde burst through the front door.

"Sorry, Jake," she said. "I got tied up in class."

"No problem, Abby," he said to the girl, then turned to them. "Let's meet up at River's Edge later. It's a local—"

"I know the place. They have the best pancakes," Rachel said, with a smile. "Does six o'clock work for you?"

Jake grinned as if they'd made plans for a hot date. "Works perfect."

"Works for me, too," Owen mumbled under his breath and pushed through the door. From the moment they'd entered Bola, things had started to become...whacked. There had to be a better word, but he couldn't think of one at the moment. Right now, all he could think about was the way Rachel had smiled—all sultry-like—at the sheriff. He hadn't even realized she could do sultry. He also hadn't expected his body to react with a sharp sting of jealousy.

As he walked toward the back of the Lexus, Rachel climbed into the passenger seat. Because she'd left her heavy coat in the car earlier, he was able to catch a nice view of her ass. Even in a pair of boring, black suit pants her butt looked...tempting. Round and tight. Unlike the women he normally dated, Rachel had the kind of ass he could hang onto while thrusting—

Good God, what the hell was wrong with him?

He wanted to slam the Lexus's gate shut, but refrained.

Knowing Rachel, she'd remind him of his *vehicle's* capabilities. At this point, he didn't need any smartass comments coming from her pretty mouth. He stopped short of the car door. Did he really just consider her mouth pretty? He thought about that smile she'd sent to Jake. The way her full, inviting lips had curved, then scrubbed a hand down his face. He needed to stop thinking about Rachel in any way other than a coworker. They had an investigation to run, and a missing kid to find.

Once inside the Lexus, he turned the key, then cranked up the heat. "Do you want to put the address for the boarding house in the GPS?" he asked.

"I don't think it's necessary. Jake wrote down the directions. It looks like we're only a few minutes away." She let out a sigh. "That was so nice of him to make sure we had a place to stay."

Yeah, Jake was just fan-frickin-tastic.

He drove out of the parking lot, and per *Jake's* directions, he turned left. "What do you think about this festival?" Bigfoot. Seriously? Although they'd been in Bola for only a couple of hours, this might prove to be one of his strangest assignments to date. They were literally walking into a fucking Bigfoot festival while dealing with an investigation that had Townies freaked out and superstitious. Now he had to stay at a boarding house.

"I don't know," she replied. "In a way, this could be a good thing. If people are heading into the woods hoping to catch a glimpse of the elusive Bigfoot, maybe they'll stumble across...sorry. Forget I suggested that. We have a week to find Josh. I don't want to write him off just yet."

Owen didn't, either. And once again, he thanked God that Sean hadn't been the one kidnapped. Based on the past missing persons cases, the chances of discovering Josh's whereabouts, as well as who's been behind the abductions, were slim to none.

After a few more turns, Rachel told him to slow the Lexus. "Four five nine seven Elmwood, this must be the boarding house," she said and pointed to a large, white colonial with a wraparound porch and a huge horseshoe shaped driveway. "Dang, this place looks like a mansion compared to the other houses we passed."

He eyed the house. Large, manicured, snow-covered evergreen shrubs lined the beds in front of the porch. Dark blue shutters framed all the windows. Dripping icicles hung from the eaves, while a stream of white smoke billowed from a red brick chimney. As he climbed out of the Lexus, he imagined walking into the inviting home, inhaling the aroma of fresh baked cookies, and standing in front of a warm, crackling fireplace.

When they reached the front door, Rachel nudged him and pointed to a wood plaque hanging over the threshold. "The House of Joy. Cute," she said, then knocked on the door.

Cute hadn't been the first word to pop in his head, but it worked for him. So did The House of Joy. During the drive to meet with the sheriff, they'd passed the local motel. In the 1960s, the place had probably been...nice. Now? Not so much. Only a third of the small, neon sign out front had been lit, the brick façade dingy, the paint around the old windows, peeling. He'd stayed at plenty of places like the Bola Motel, where the carpet was stained with God only knew what, the cleanliness of the sheets and room questionable, and the furniture nailed into the walls and floors. Yeah, he was grateful they'd be indulging in the comforts of the cozy boarding house for the next week rather than the crappy motel. He'd bet his next paycheck that Joy, whom he imagined to be an adorable, little old lady, would make sure they had delicious home-cooked meals and clean sheets. She probably like to fuss over her guests and—

"It's open," a woman yelled.

Rachel looked at him, then turned the knob.

He followed her into the colonial's foyer, then stopped when a large woman, wearing a menacing scowl rounded the corner.

Not only did they have to find Josh Conway before he succumbed to the Wexman Hell Week, they had to deal with a bunch of Bigfoot BS and, it appeared, live with Frankenstein's frickin' sister.

"Welcome to the House of Joy," the woman said, in a low, ominous tone, then spat into a Styrofoam cup. "I'm Joy. Follow my rules and we'll get along just fine. If you don't..." She ran a finger along the inside of her mouth, pulled out the hunk of tobacco, then dropped it into the cup. After setting the disgusting, phlegm-filled cup onto the wooden bench flanking the foyer wall, she cracked her knuckles. "Put it this way, I'll personally haul your asses out of my house."

CHAPTER 4

STANDING AT FIVE foot two inches, Rachel had grown used to people towering over her. Joy, big boned and probably almost as tall as Sean, could probably snap her in two. Between her crusty, don't screw with me attitude and her formidable size, Rachel believed Joy would, and could, haul their asses out of her house.

Rachel glanced from Joy to the gross cup of spit setting on the bench. Before she threw up in her mouth, she quickly looked away. "I'm Rachel Davis," she said, then offered her hand. "And this is Owen Malcolm."

Joy shifted her steel gray eyes to Rachel. "Joy Baker," she replied and shook Rachel's, then Owen's hand.

"Baker? Are you related to Hal Baker?" Rachel asked.

"He's my brother. And I hear tell from Jake that Hal quite possibly saved yours."

"I have no doubt that he did. Actually, I was hoping I'd have the chance to thank him."

Joy leaned against the wall and folded her beefy arms across her ample chest. "The bastard is always stopping by for a free meal. You'll get your chance." She gave Owen a once over. "You're a little too pretty to be a cop."

Owen flashed Joy a smile that Rachel suspected earned him plenty of notches on his bedpost. Despite being a dating pool bottom feeder, he really did have a sexy smile. The kind that not only distracted her, but made her toes curl.

"Good thing I'm not a cop," he replied.

With a roll of her eyes, Joy pushed off the wall and walked out of the foyer.

Rachel looked to Owen, then followed Joy. They moved past a state of the art kitchen filled with cherry cabinets and granite countertops, a dining area with a table big enough to seat ten, then into a large great room.

"This is the community room," Joy said. A ginormous flat screen TV hung above the mantle of the fireplace, where a beautiful fire blazed. Two huge, dark brown leather couches, along with a couple of beige over-sized chairs, and espresso-colored tables filled the room. An enormous, bronze and brick red area rug covered a large portion of the dark wood floors. With the walls painted mocha, the natural light streaming in from the windows overlooking the big backyard, and the artwork hanging on the walls, the room gave off a cozy and comfortable feeling.

The complete opposite of its owner.

"There's a bathroom over there," Joy pointed to the corner of the room. "That other door leads to the basement. There's a washer and dryer down there. I won't do your laundry, but feel free to use 'em." When they reached the staircase, she paused. "You see the door near the sunroom? That's my room. Don't even think of going in there." She eyed Owen, then Rachel. "Understand, Shorty?"

Shorty? Absolute fury whorled through Rachel's body as her mind spiraled with bitter, poignant childhood memories. Images of the kids at school and in her neighborhood suddenly took front and center, replacing the behemoth of a woman looming over her from the staircase. Ricky Lawrence and his pitiful crew appeared first. They had constantly teased her about her height, her small boobs, red hair and freckles. Then there was Ginny McAndrews, such a snobby bitch, and her equally snobby gang of mean girls. They loved to make fun of her for not having a dad around, for wearing the secondhand clothes her mom would buy from Goodwill, and they'd call her mom a slut because she always had a new boyfriend and Sean had a different dad. As she'd matured, Rachel had overcome her childhood insecurities, but she still harbored zero tolerance for bullies. Joy, plain and simple, was nothing but a bully who needed to be put in her place.

Stopping short of the staircase, she said, "Rachel."

Joy raised her dark eyebrows. "Right. You Rachel. Me Joy. Is this name thing too much for you to handle?"

"Not for me," Rachel replied.

"Well then, Shorty, quit with all this bullshit and let me show you your room."

"Call me Shorty again and we're going to find out if you can *really* haul my ass out of your house...ya know, personally."

After Joy sized her up, she snorted. "I could wipe my ass with you."

"Do it," Rachel said even as her heart raced with fear and outrage.

"Good God." Owen grabbed her arm. "What the hell is wrong with you?"

Without breaking eye contact with Joy, Rachel pulled free from his grip. "This doesn't concern you."

"Yeah, it does. Spending the week sleeping in my car doesn't work for me."

"You're right. You stay here with Miss Sunshine. I'll sleep at the hospital. There's a recliner in Sean's room. I've suddenly discovered that The House of *Joy* comes up a bit...short, even for me."

A shadow of a smile worked along Joy's lips. "No pun intended."

Ignoring Joy, Rachel said, "Let's go. We've wasted enough time." Hands clammy, heart still beating erratically, she walked out of the colonial.

Owen caught up with her on the front porch and touched her shoulder. "What are you doing? Who gives a shit what that woman thinks or says?"

"You're mistaken. I don't care about her at all." She really didn't. Being short, being called short...that was who she was and until there was such thing as limb-lengthening surgery, she'd remain—as Owen had aptly referred—vertically challenged. Joy, though, had touched a raw nerve. She'd treated them like crap the moment they'd walked into her house, threatened them, made fun of her height and Owen's looks. As a whole, Joy wasn't just a bully, she was a bitch. Between her mom, and the dozens of women she'd shared rooms with during her time in the army, Rachel had decided she'd lived with enough bitches. No need to add Joy to that list.

"If you don't care, then why the hostility?"

She stopped at the edge of the porch and faced him. "My brother is lying in the hospital. His best friend is missing and we have one week to find him. Bola, Wexman University could possibly have a serial killer roaming around here. I'm a bit…" The weight of what they needed to accomplish in a matter of days suddenly overwhelming, she reached behind her ear for the pencil. When she realized she'd left it in the car, she bit the inside of her cheek to keep her emotions under control. "I'm a bit stressed. I don't need any *Joy* in my life right now."

Understanding softened Owen's blue eyes. He gave her shoulder a light squeeze. "At the start, every case seems unsolvable. When they're personal…they can be downright daunting. I know it's easier said than done, but don't let the stress affect you negatively. Treat it like a tool you can use to hone in on your investigative skills."

She had no investigative skills, but didn't want to voice that to Owen. She'd already admitted enough. "Do you really walk into a case feeling like it's unsolvable?"

"Depends on the assignment."

"What about this one?"

"We've got a file box filled with years of missing person cases, a note, a missing kid, and the so-called legend of Hell Week…yeah, I'm a little worried."

His honesty, his admission to having doubts about the case, eased her to a degree. A very small degree. If Owen, a total badass with a one hundred percent case resolution, worried about figuring out this particular puzzle, Josh Conway could end up like the other missing persons from Bola and Wexman. An unsolved mystery.

"We still have Sean's clothes, which I need to overnight to DecaLab."

Owen took a step off the porch, and withdrew his cell phone. "I'll look up the nearest post office. We can stop on our way to the university. If you give me the sheriff's number, I'll call and see if I can crash at his place for—"

"Rachel," Joy called from the front door.

She ignored the bitchy bully and followed Owen.

"You don't seem the type, but maybe you prefer Miss Davis?" Joy asked.

Curious, Rachel turned.

Wearing only a thick, cable knit sweater, Joy hugged herself then moved down the porch steps until the two of them were eyelevel. "So which is it? Rachel or Miss Davis?"

"What do you think?"

Ten years fell from Joy's face when she smiled. "I think you're a real ball buster."

"You have no idea," Owen said.

Joy's smile grew. "That right?" She nodded. "Good. This place could use a ball busting bitch to spice things up."

"Is there room enough for two of us?" Rachel asked, still uncertain as to whether or not Joy was screwing with her.

What Rachel imagined a barking seal might sound like, if it was being run over by an ice cream truck with a dying sound system, suddenly echoed throughout the front yard. Holding her stomach, Joy continued to release the strangest laugh Rachel had ever heard, then she snorted and wiped the tears under her eyes. "Now that was fucking funny," Joy said, wrapped an arm around Rachel and grew serious. "No need to shack up at the hospital. I've got you covered."

Beyond confused, but grateful she wouldn't have to sleep in a chair, Rachel shook her head. "Okay. Um...can we take care of the paperwork and payment when we get back? We need to get to the university."

"No paperwork. No payment."

"Joy, we can—"

"Listen to me," Joy began and gripped Rachel's shoulders. "I've lived here my whole life. I didn't know any of those kids that had gone missing, but the four locals..." She looked away for a second. "This has to stop. Jake says you might be able to make that happen. Even if you fail, as long as you try to give us some answers, The House of Joy is open to you."

"So that Shorty BS was a test?"

"Nope. You *are* short, and neither one of you fit what I had pictured in my head as the people who were going to end this Hell Week shit." She shrugged. "It pissed me off."

"But we're good now?" Owen asked.

Joy pulled a key from her pocket and handed it to Rachel. "We're good. Dinner's at six. If you can't make it, leftovers are in the fridge. If you come home when I'm not up, room three and five are yours. Clean linens are in the closet in your rooms. Breakfast is at seven." She headed back up the steps, then stopped at the front door. "Bola might be a speck on the map, but it's a good place to live and raise a family...even if most of us are living in fear."

After shipping Sean's clothes to DecaLab, a private genetics laboratory CORE employed at a hefty price tag, Owen drove the Lexus down the only road leading to Wexman University. "How long before we hear anything from the lab?" he asked Rachel.

Without looking up from the list the sheriff had given her, she said, "Chihiro thinks, once they receive the package, it'll take about a day before they'll have any results."

"Chihiro?"

"Kimura."

"What? You've lost me."

Releasing an impatient sigh, she looked up from the list. "Chihiro Kimura is a forensic DNA tech for DecaLab."

"And I was supposed to know this how?" When she didn't

answer him, he said, "Joy's right. You are a ball buster." Truly. Other than Joy Baker, he'd never met a more hostile woman.

"Yes, I do have my moments."

He wished she'd have less of those *moments*. They were partners and needed to act as if they were on a united front. Although maybe he shouldn't discourage her from blowing him shit. Her volatile, sarcastic remarks might help remind him that he had no business thinking about her in any way other than coworker. Each barb she threw at him could keep this mind off her sexy ass and curvy hips. Her sassy mouth and tempting lips. Her big, green eyes...

He cleared his throat and shook all those enticing images of Rachel from his mind. "What do you make of Joy's parting comment?"

"About living in fear? Joy doesn't seem like the type who scares easy. Honestly, until Jake told us about the four missing locals, I hadn't given a whole lot of thought about the Townies. Well, except for considering that one of them is our kidnapper or killer or whatever we want to call him."

"Having a killer in their midst is bad for local business."

"True. But what if one of the locals, or a couple of them, has a grudge against the college students?"

"Possible. That doesn't explain the four missing Townies, though."

She tapped the pencil against her mouth, then slowly glided it along her full lips. Before he veered the Lexus off the road and into a tree, he looked away and brought to mind his nephew's poopy diapers. Anything to keep from thinking about what it would be like to have Rachel's lips and mouth slipping and sliding along...

"You have arrived," the GPS told them as the forest they'd been driving through parted and revealed the entrance of the university.

Thank God. He needed out of the Lexus and his mind focused on the investigation, not the woman running it. Besides, she didn't like him and even if she did, having an affair with Rachel might jeopardize his career with CORE.

While Ian hadn't issued a "no dating" policy, he couldn't imagine his boss liking the idea of potential relationship drama at the workplace.

After they passed between two immense brick walls with Wexman engraved on one and University on the other, Rachel pointed to the left. "We're on the campus's main drag. The dorms are up ahead."

Old style lampposts lined the narrow road. As he drove through the campus, similar sized lanes and dozens of narrower, paved paths splintered through the snow and led to various buildings. Naked trees, empty, snow-covered benches and stone picnic tables littered the area. In the fall, he'd bet the campus was a beautiful kaleidoscope of color. With the large gothic buildings, the barren trees, vacant paths and the surrounding dense forest, right now the university campus gave off a formidable vibe.

"This place is like a ghost town," he commented. "Where is everyone?"

She glanced out her window. "It's freezing. Plus it's almost four-thirty. It'll be dark soon and I'm assuming most classes are either finished or wrapping up for the day."

"What time do the administration offices close? We should probably talk with the university president and dean."

She flipped through the notes Jake had taken. "The president, Richard Lambert, is…well, this is random. He's in Wyoming for a funeral. Jake noted that the dean, Xavier Preston, is willing to fully cooperate with us, but it looks like his office hours are until five."

"Maybe we should meet with him first, then look at the dorm."

"I'd rather go to Sean's room. Jake also noted that campus security and the residence hall's RAs have warned students to leave the room alone, but I don't want to take any chances."

Considering Sean and Josh were taken *after* they'd left the dorm, and that the sheriff hadn't found any bottles—empty or full—of Mountain Dew, let alone any other evidence, he thought a search of the room could wait. "Your call. What about the professor?"

"I have his cell phone number. We can call him when we're finished." She tapped the dashboard. "Slow down. You see that building?" She pointed to a three-story brick building.

He read the sign out front. "Stanley Residence Hall."

"Right, Sean's room is in there. You can park in the lot behind it."

As he made his way to the parking lot, he said, "I really think we should speak with the dean. Maybe you should —"

"Call and at least set up an appointment for tomorrow?"

"Seriously. I really hate when you finish my sentences."

"*Anyway,* I spoke with his secretary. We have an appointment with him in the morning."

"When did you set that up?" he asked as he parked the Lexus.

"When you ran back into Joy's to use the boy's room."

"There's a sense of urgency for you," he said and reached for the door handle.

"Are you talking about hitting the boy's room or the dean?" she asked.

"Cute. Don't you think it's odd that the university dean, after one of his students was found beaten and the other is still missing, schedules us in for an appointment…the next day?"

"Absolutely, and I voiced this to his secretary. She gave me his home and cell phone numbers should we need to speak with him before tomorrow." Rachel opened the car door, then paused.

"What is it?" he asked.

"I…it's nothing. Let's go."

Before she asked or said something that might make her appear too incompetent to run this investigation, Rachel quickly slid off the Lexus's leather seat, then shut the door.

With daylight dying, and a brisk breeze whirling between the buildings, the temperature plummeted by the second. Tightening the collar of her heavy overcoat, she shoved her free hand into her pocket and dashed up the steps to the residence hall. Thankfully, Owen grabbed the door before she had to expose her hand to the frigid air. Once inside, she shook off the cold and released the lapel of her coat.

"This is a definite step up from the dorms I stayed in," Owen commented as he unbuttoned his coat and peered around the corner of the foyer. "Flat screen TV, pool table...I think those couches are nicer than the ones I have in my condo."

Based on Owen's designer clothes, tailored suits, and his eighty thousand dollar Lexus, she doubted his couches were anything but top of the line. She, on the other hand, could most certainly admit that her furniture had seen better days. The apartment she leased was the same one she and Sean had both grown up in, and the furnishings had all been her mom's, purchased from thrift stores or estate sales before Sean had even been born.

"You think this is nice, wait until we visit the fraternity house." Curious, she looked around the foyer. Specifically at the empty desk where a campus security guard should have been seated. Moving toward the desk, she said, "The last time I was here, Sean used a key card to get into the building. I was so cold, I didn't even think about it...we should have been buzzed in, met by a security guard, or at least an RA, showed our IDs..."

Owen moved close to her, close enough his arm brushed along hers. Still making contact, he leaned over the desk and pushed around some papers. She should take a step back and give him space. Instead, she stayed put. Even though they both wore thick, heavy coats, standing this close to him reminded her how good...how wanted she'd felt when he'd held her under the mistletoe last year. While she'd had a couple of brief relationships since then, not one of those guys could compare to Owen. They were nerdy and safe, whereas Owen was a tempting heartbreaker. And although she'd probably always consider him a bottom feeder, with the way he kissed, she'd bet he could supply her with multiple orgasms and the best sex of her life.

With that last thought in mind, she stepped back. "What

are you looking for?"

"A student roster, guard or RA schedule…"

She touched his shoulder. His muscles immediately bunched. When he turned to her she quickly dropped her hand. The scowl on his face surprised her. Over the years, she'd seen Owen irritated, but never truly angry. For whatever reason, he looked mad as hell right now. She didn't know if his sudden mood swing had something to do with her or the lack of security. She didn't care.

Liar.

She nodded toward the main hallway where a bullnecked, burly young guy approached. Wearing a navy security uniform, he walked with a little kick to his step, drawing attention to his scuffed black shoes and the white tube socks peeking from beneath the hem of his pants. He stopped at a water fountain, took a few slurps, then wiped his mouth with the back of his sleeve. When a pretty coed passed him, he nodded and smiled, then, as he checked out her rear, he ran a hand over the top of his short brown hair. Shaking his head, he continued toward the desk. Once he realized she and Owen were watching him, he grimaced and quickened his pace.

"Sorry, folks. Unless you have an appointment, this building is for students only."

She and Owen both handed him their IDs. "Sheriff Jake Tyler said campus security and staff would cooperate with us while we investigate the disappearance of Josh Conway," Rachel said as she slipped her ID back into her pocket.

"Sure, sure," the guard said as he moved behind the desk and flipped though paperwork. "Got your names…well, I know they're somewhere." He flashed them a smile. "It doesn't really matter. Come on and I'll take you up to Josh's dorm room."

"Hang on," Owen said. "You just told us only students were allowed, yet the desk was unattended and the door unlocked. Now you're going to leave your post again?"

The guard's face grew mottled as a heavy red blush stained his cheeks. "I…I…oh, man," he said on a sigh. "Please don't report me. I—"

"What's your name?" Rachel asked, and grew more irritated by the second. If this guy had been on duty the night Sean and Josh had been abducted, she'd do more than report him.

"Bill Baker."

Frowning she looked to Owen, who raised his dark blonde brows and half-smiled. "Are you related to Joy or Hal?" she asked.

"Hal's my dad, which makes Joy my aunt." Bill held the back of his head, then threw his hands in the air. "If they find out…man, oh man, I'm in real trouble."

Although annoyed with Bill for not taking his job seriously, especially in the wake of Josh's disappearance and her brother's beating, she couldn't help feeling a little sorry for the guy. If Hal was anything like his sister, Bill had a right to be worried.

"Let's talk this out," Rachel suggested. "Starting with the unlocked doors to the residence hall."

Bill nodded. "Yeah, it's been broken since Friday. I requested the work order and maintenance was supposed to take care of it. But they haven't gotten to my building because they've been too busy taking care of all the others."

"The others?" Owen prompted.

"Yeah, all four of the residence halls, the entrance to the grad student apartments, along with the main administration building, the athletic department, the library, the computer lab, not to mention three buildings used for classes—"

"Slow down." Owen half-chuckled and gave Bill a smile that would put anyone at ease, which right now included her. Something wasn't right at Wexman. "It sounds like the entire campus needs some major repairs."

"Not repairs, just the locks fixed."

"Do all the buildings require a keycard to get inside?" Rachel asked.

"Uh-huh, but maintenance and campus security have regular keys for emergency use." He looped his fingers through his belt and jingled his key chain. "Like I said, once I figured out the lock wasn't working, I called maintenance. They gave me the runaround, so I called my boss who told me to make sure the RAs and students knew about the problem."

"Was the sheriff aware of this?" Rachel asked. Going on the assumption the boys had been drugged, if the lock to this hall had been broken purposefully, that would have given whomever had spiked Sean and Josh's Mountain Dew easy access to the building. But wouldn't Jake have mentioned the broken locks?

"Don't know," Bill said. "When I saw him the night they found the beat up kid, he didn't ask."

"The beat up kid happens to be my brother, Sean."

"Oh man, sorry. I didn't mean—"

"It's fine. But you didn't think you should have mentioned the locks to the sheriff?"

"I…God, I'm such an idiot," he said, and slammed his fist against his thigh. "Ma'am, I'm so sorry about Sean. I really like him. He always gives me some of the awesome stuff his mom sends him. Cookies, muffins, brownies—"

She stiffened at the mention of *mom*. "I sent those things to him."

"Then *your* stuff is awesome."

Bill didn't need to know the awesome stuff was store-bought. While she knew the ins and outs of computers, the oven tended to be a technical challenge. "Thanks. Okay, let's stay focused. Were you here the night Sean and Josh went missing?"

"Yeah, yeah," he said, grabbed a log, flipped a couple of pages, then handed the binder to them. "They had a pizza delivered at five fifteen. I let the RA for their floor know and she brought it up to them."

"Was it just pizza?" Owen asked.

"And a two liter of Mountain Dew."

Beneath her heavy coat, goose bumps rose over Rachel's skin. Sean said they'd drunk the soda, Bill confirmed that it had been delivered with the pizza, yet Jake hadn't found the bottle. "Who was the RA?"

"Days kinda run together." Bill took the log back, turned it around, then flipped a page. "Abby Zucker."

"And she was here all night?" Rachel asked.

"I guess so."

"You guess?" Owen repeated. "Either she was or she wasn't. Which is it?"

The mottled, heavy red blush returned to Bill's cheeks. "Man, I'm in so much trouble."

"Bill, just give us an honest answer," Rachel said, keeping her tone soft and understanding. "What you consider a big deal might not be one at all."

"Okay," he said on a deep sigh. "So, Saturday I show up for my shift, like always, at three. I made sure I packed a bunch of food, a big thermos of coffee, and a couple of those five hour energy drinks. Normally I work three to midnight. But Gus, that's the guy who works night shift, asked if I could cover for him. I was one payment away from paying off my truck, and the extra cash would put me there quicker." He rested his elbows on the desk, then tugged on one ear. "The shift started out fine, but by six, I started to get real dizzy. My stomach was upset and I didn't know if I was going to throw up or...well, I'm sure you got the idea."

"Mixing those energy drinks with caffeine will do that to you," Owen said. "Unfortunately, I've been there."

Bill lifted a shoulder. "I wouldn't know. I never took the energy drinks. All I had was one cup of coffee."

"Maybe it was something you ate or the flu," Rachel suggested, even though she doubted Bill's sudden sickness had anything do with natural causes. Dizziness, nausea, vomiting, were all side effects of Rohypnol.

"Probably the flu," Bill said. "I felt like crap the rest of the night and didn't feel right until this morning."

"Who ended up covering your shift?" Owen asked.

Bill looked away. "No one. I tried calling a few guys, but couldn't get a hold of anybody. So I stayed and did the best I could...which wasn't much. If I wasn't in the bathroom, I was sleeping at the desk." When he finally looked at them, he said, "I know you probably don't believe me, but I really love my job and take it seriously. I tried to join the military out of high school, but my asthma stopped that from happening. Jake wouldn't hire me as a deputy because I've lived in Bola my whole life and a quarter of the Townies are somehow related to me. Jake took care of me though and got me this sweet job. I have health benefits, and even a 401k."

Rachel held up a hand. "Look, Bill, neither one of us wants to see you fired. You did what you had to do. Let me ask you this, did you see Sean and Josh leave Saturday night?"

"Yeah, it was about the time I started feeling sick. I remember making them sign out, then Josh told me a joke. At the time, I was so dizzy, I...I didn't even understand the punch line." He shook his head. "After they left, my night went downhill."

"Can I see the boys' signatures?"

Bill grabbed a different log, then opened to a page marked Saturday. "This is weird," he said, and handed the log to Rachel. "No one signed in or out after Sean and Josh."

She frowned and showed Owen. "And this is unusual for a Saturday night?"

"Absolutely."

"What about the RA, Abby Zucker?" Owen asked. "Did you ask her for help?"

"After Sean and Josh left, she stopped by on her way to...I don't remember. But I *do* remember telling her I didn't feel well and couldn't find another guard to cover my shift. She said something about having to write a paper and study for an exam, but that she'd check on me."

"Did she?" Rachel asked.

"She might have," Bill said. "I was pretty out of it."

"Did you go to the doctor the next day?"

"No. I went home, got into bed and didn't wake up for about ten hours. When I got up, I still felt bad, but nothing like the night before." He paused, then said, "So, should I quit or wait 'til they fire me?"

She offered him a reassuring smile. "Don't worry about losing your job. In the meantime, let us do ours."

Nodding his head, Bill reached for the keys attached to his belt. After unhooking one, he handed it to Rachel. "Like I said, the keycards aren't working right. Some of the rooms aren't having any problems, but this will get you in just the same."

After she thanked Bill, she nodded to Owen and together they left the main foyer and headed into the elevator. Once the doors closed, Owen leaned against the wall and gripped the metal rail. "Sounds like Bill might have been drugged, too."

Good. They were on the same page. "I know. Rather convenient that the entire campus is experiencing problems with the locks, and the security guard for this hall happens to end up with symptoms similar to someone drugged with Rohypnol."

"Too bad we can't have a tox screen run on Big Bill."

"If he's cool with it, and I'm sure he will be considering he *loves* his job, we can still have him screened. Rohypnol can be found in a urine analysis within sixty hours of being ingested. Bill said he started feeling sick around six Saturday night..." She shoved her coat sleeve aside and checked her watch. "It's a quarter to five now, so we're well within that sixty hour window. Bill can't wait until his shift ends, though. To be on the safe side, he's got to get over to the Dixon Medical Center immediately."

The elevator slowed, then stopped. Even with the doors still closed, Rachel heard the distinct sound of feminine laughter.

"Are the floors coed?" Owen asked.

"Unfortunately," Rachel said as the doors slid open, revealing the source of the laughter.

Four girls stood in the hall. Quiet now, they stared at Owen. Then, while each girl stepped past them and into the elevator, they looked between one another and burst into another fit of giggles. As the door slid shut again, one girl said, "Oh my God, was he hot."

"How special, you already have a fan club," Rachel said, and began walking toward Sean and Josh's room.

He hardened his jaw. "I don't want anything to do with

that."

"Please," she said, stopped in front of Sean's door and reached in her pocket for the key Bill had given her. "What guy wouldn't be interested in a bunch of cute college girls?"

He crowded the closed doorway. His nearness, his masculine scent made her hands sweaty. "They might be cute," he said, "but I have no interest in dating a college girl. I prefer a strong, intelligent woman who knows what she wants."

She almost dropped the key, but managed to slide it into the lock and open the door. She hadn't expected him to use strong and intelligent as a way to describe the women he preferred to date. Based on the women she'd seen him with, beautiful and easy seemed more on target. "Thank you for that interesting insight into the depths of your dating preferences."

"You're the one who brought it up," he said, and stepped into the room.

As she glanced around, Owen handed her a pair of Latex gloves. Damn, she hadn't thought about gloves, but would be sure to remember them in the future. Because Ian had sent Owen with her, she suspected their boss would want a full account as to how she'd handled herself in the field. If she wanted to escape life behind the desk, she'd have to be more on top of things.

After slipping on the gloves, they began searching the small room. As far as Rachel could tell, nothing was out of the ordinary. Actually, everything was neat and tidy. A little too neat.

"Sean's bedroom at home never looks like this. He always has clothes lying around and junk on his dresser." That was putting it mildly. Since he was a little kid, her brother liked to hoard and rat hole stuff. Either sharing a room with Josh had forced him to change his ways, or someone had cleaned up the place.

Owen opened the mini refrigerator she'd bought Sean before he'd started his first semester. "Empty." He closed the door, then looked through the trashcan next to the fridge. "Jake said he didn't remove anything from the room, correct?"

"That's right," she said, and closed the closet door. "Why?"

"There's not one piece of garbage in this room except for an empty pizza box."

"We knew about the soda bottles, but no garbage at all? That doesn't make any sense," She moved toward Owen. "Sean has a thing about napkins and baby wipes." When he glanced at her, she waved a hand. "I'd rather he be a little OCD than walking around with food on his face."

Owen stood and began peeling off his gloves. "Maybe they took the garbage out before they left for the study session."

"What about the pizza box? And why isn't there anything in the fridge?"

"Did Sean ever go into town and do any grocery shopping?"

"No, he doesn't have a car, and neither does Josh. They both eat at the school cafeteria. Wexman does have a small convenience store on campus. I give Sean a monthly allowance so he can buy sodas and snacks, or whatever toiletries he might need. He loves his junk food and uses every cent I give him."

"Which means we should have found something in this room." Owen shoved the gloves in his pocket. "We need to ask Sean if they emptied the trash and got rid of the empty Mountain Dew bottle."

"And what their room looked like when they left."

"Could be they cleaned up because they were planning on bringing a couple of those cute girls back to their place."

She winced. "I can't picture my brother bringing a girl to his room."

"Just because you can't picture it, or don't want to, doesn't mean it's not a possibility."

Needing to erase the mental image of Sean fooling around with a girl, Rachel focused on what they did know. "Okay, here's what we have so far. The building's lock was broken. Sean and Josh ordered pizza and Mountain Dew."

"Thanks to Bill, we know for a fact it was delivered."

"Then taken to their room by the RA."

"Right, we'll need to talk to Abby Zucker."

"Definitely. We suspect the boys, and maybe Bill, were drugged." She shook her head. "Sean and Josh disappeared after they left the building. Does drugging Bill make any sense to you? Maybe he did just have the flu."

"Too coincidental. My money's on Rohypnol. Could be whoever took the boys wanted to make sure Bill was out of it so they could go back to the dorm room and clean up any evidence they might have left behind."

She nodded. "That makes sense, but it doesn't work for me. The only people in and out of this building on a Saturday night would be other students. And that's what doesn't work. Wexman Hell Week has been going on for twenty years. This hall is filled with nothing but freshmen and sophomores. Some of them wouldn't have been born when the first Hell Week student went missing."

"What about a maintenance worker? The broken lock is also a little too coincidental."

"But it sounded as if more than half the campus buildings had, and still have, malfunctioning locks. Why would the kidnapper take the risk of disabling all of the locks, then grab the boys when they were walking to the library?" She moved to the door. "All of these possibilities won't matter until we get the tox screen results on Sean and Bill."

"Would a professor have access to the residence halls?" Owen asked after they left the room and she locked the door. "Specifically, a professor who pursues legends like Bigfoot and Wexman Hell Week?"

"Dr. Collin Stronach is next on our list." She pressed the elevator key. "Let's find out just how far he might go to keep the legend of Wexman Hell Week alive."

CHAPTER 5

TALKING BILL INTO going to Dixon Medical Center for a physical hadn't been an issue. Owen had been impressed with how Rachel had handled the security guard, giving him just enough info to prompt him to cooperate without telling him their suspicions. If Rohypnol had been used to drug the boys and Bill, with the little evidence they had, he didn't want to see that information leaked.

While Bill took care of finding someone to cover his post, Owen drove Rachel across campus to meet with Dr. Collin Stronach. The professor's office was located in Milton Hall, one of the many beautifully detailed Gothic buildings he'd seen during their initial drive through the campus. As he followed Rachel inside, Milton Hall immediately impressed him. With its grand foyer, numerous murals, and the imposing staircase framed with brass and mahogany rails, the building's interior rivaled its exterior.

After they checked in with the building's security guard, they headed up the staircase. "This building it beautiful," Rachel whispered. "Now I know why the tuition costs a fortune."

"It's nice." He glanced at her and smiled at the way she gaped at the tapestries and furnishings with childlike wonder. Considering he'd worked for the U.S. Ambassador to the Vatican, and their embassy was in the heart of Rome, he'd seen plenty of architectural and artistic wonders. Sure, Milton Hall impressed him, but it wasn't exactly the Sistine Chapel.

"Nice? I've never been in anything like it."

"Why are you whispering?"

She furrowed her brows. "Old habit," she said, now in a normal tone.

"Those Catholic nuns do like their discipline, don't they?" He didn't know if Rachel was Catholic or why he cared whether or not she answered him. But he did. Rachel made him curious. Again, he didn't know why. Outside of imagining what her great ass would feel like in his hands and beyond imagining her kissable lips against his mouth, he'd been trying to decipher this strange and complex woman from the moment he'd met her. Confident, yet insecure, brilliant, yet naïve, abrasive, yet considerate…he simply couldn't figure out what or who was the real Rachel Davis. He could care less about her religious preference or background, but if it led him closer to understanding this puzzling woman, then maybe he could stop thinking about her in ways he *really* shouldn't be thinking.

"I did eight years at St. Ambrose, then another four at Holy Name."

He chuckled. "You make it sound like you did time."

"You have no idea," she said, lowering her tone again and slowing her pace. She came to a halt in front of a door with Dr. Collin Stronach etched onto the clouded glass, then turned to him.

Her big green eyes held a hint of vulnerability as she drew in a shaky breath. He almost asked her if she wanted him to handle the interview, but remained silent. She was lead on this investigation. While he preferred her cosseted in the office, away from potential violence or the deadly results of some cases, several times he'd overheard Rachel ask Ian for a chance to work an investigation, and knew being in the field was important to her.

"Let's play nice with the professor," she finally said.

"Why wouldn't I?"

When she leaned toward him, he caught a hint of pink grapefruit, apples and…strangely, marshmallows. The combination made him want to linger outside the door, pull her close and find out if she tasted…

"Bigfoot," she whispered.

The single word knocked the image of kissing a trail along Rachel's slender neck from his mind. "Right." He nodded. "I won't make fun of him."

She gave the lapel of his coat a slight tug. "I would hope not. I was thinking more along the lines of the festival. If he's running the Sasquatch show, we might need his cooperation."

"If we need his cooperation, we have the sheriff."

"Wouldn't it be better to have the nutty professor on our side and avoid any possible issues that could hinder our investigation?" she asked, her tone coaxing, alluring.

"Of course," he said. He stared between her imploring eyes, her tempting lips, and her small hand tugging at his coat, wondering if maybe he'd been misreading Rachel all along. Maybe behind the sarcasm and insults, she harbored something—

She quickly turned and rapped the door with her knuckle. Whatever spell she'd held over him broke.

As they waited for Stronach to answer, Owen realized he had to be as delusional as the Bigfoot-loving professor. There was nothing between Rachel and him except whatever he'd been concocting in his own mind. Still, he did enjoy the quick moment. For some reason, standing close to her, close enough he could have easily hauled her in for a kiss that would leave them both…

Like déjà vu, a brief, fuzzy image swam through his head. Rachel looking up at him, her eyes on his mouth as he bent his head and brushed his lips against hers.

The door opened, snapping him back to reality.

"Ms. Davis, Mr. Malcolm, please come in," a man in his early forties said, and motioned them toward a leather couch.

"Thanks for taking time to meet with us, Dr. Stronach." Rachel took a seat. "Please call me Rachel."

"Rachel," the professor repeated. "Beautiful in form and countenance."

Owen remained standing and folded his arms across his chest. He shifted his gaze to Rachel, whose freckles were now indiscernible thanks to the pretty blush along her cheeks. She'd asked him to "play nice" with the professor, but if Dr. Dickhead continued down this path, things were going to become messy. Rachel was a professional, and deserved to be treated as such.

"I'm sorry," Stronach said with a nonchalant smile, and took the chair opposite the couch. "It's a thing I do."

"Hitting on women, you mean," Owen said, deciding, after the professor's blasé excuse, he really couldn't play nice after all.

"Owen, please," Rachel said.

"No, it's okay," the professor said. "Let me clarify. When I hear a name, I like to come up with the meaning. Rachel means beautiful in form and countenance, and aptly suits you."

"I thought it meant 'ewe.' At least that's what Sister Margaret had told me in second grade." With a lift of her shoulder, Rachel smiled. "Do Owen now."

Stronach adjusted his glasses, not the typical, thick, horn-rimmed glasses he'd expect from a nerdy professor, but stylish frames carrying the Prada logo. Actually, there was nothing typical about the professor. He didn't know why, but Owen had lumped Stronach with all the professors he'd experienced during his college years. Middle aged, paunch, nerdy. A bad stereotype to have as an investigator, but one, for whatever reason, he couldn't shake. Stronach was younger than he'd figured though, fit, athletic, and based on his Armani shirt— one Owen almost splurged on a few months ago—and his Italian shoes, he had expensive taste.

"Owen," Stronach repeated. "To the Greeks and Welsh, your name means young fighter or young warrior."

"Fascinating," Owen said with a sarcastic edge. "Now try Sean and Josh."

The professor shook his head, then reached over and

touched Rachel's knee. "I was so sorry to hear what happened to your brother and Josh."

"Thank you," Rachel said, and took his hand from her knee. She held onto him for a second, then with a slight smile released him. "Sean speaks very highly of you."

"So nice to hear. I teach anthropology at the graduate level, but students earning their bachelor's degree need to fulfill a list of general education courses outside their major. I think a lot of these students take my beginning course because they think it'll be easy, but it's not. I want to enlighten these young men and women. Give them a taste of the world around us. Your brother is a very apt pupil. He's doing well. The paper he recently turned in was excellent and earned him an A," he finished with an almost triumphant smile.

"Wow, that's great," Rachel said. "How about Josh?"

The professor's smile fell. "Josh...isn't doing as well. Academically, he's a bright student. When it comes to my teachings, he...resists."

He sounded more like a cult leader than a professor. "Your teachings?" Owen echoed. "What do you mean by that?"

Stronach's smile returned. "I like to give my students, especially those in my beginner's course, a well-rounded aspect of what different cultures, both past and present, believe, and how those beliefs affect our world as we know it. Josh's analytical mind can't seem to grasp those beliefs. Needless to say, he's currently carrying a low C in my class."

"Is that why he was attending your study group Saturday evening?" Rachel asked.

"Yes, I'm giving an exam later this week and offered to help my students better prepare."

"If Sean is doing so well in your course, why do you think he was attending this study group?" Owen asked.

"As I'm sure you know, neither made it to the library that night, so I can't answer that question positively. I do know the boys were roommates and friends. Perhaps Sean's attendance was moral support."

"That definitely sounds like my brother. He's always

looking out for his friends," Rachel said, then paused for a moment. "Do you know if any of the students who went to your study session saw Sean or Josh along the way to the library?"

"I honestly don't know."

Rachel's lip shot out in a pout as she looked to the floor. Then, with a wistful sigh, she glanced back to the professor. "I don't suppose you have a list of the kids that came to your session."

"There were less than a dozen. If you give me your number, I'll call you later with their names."

"Would you really?" Rachel asked.

"For Rachel, beautiful in form and countenance, I would gladly do just about anything."

Owen didn't know if he wanted to laugh or knock Stronach on his ass. The professor not only took himself far too seriously, but his arrogance and blatant flirtation with Rachel pissed him off. She was an investigator, here to help find a missing student, not his next lay.

To help him focus on the case and keep his mind off Dr. Dickhead and his inappropriate behavior, Owen moved around the office. A large, plaster imprint of a foot, encased in a glass box, caught his attention. "What's this?" he asked, even though he already had his suspicions. Stronach needed to refocus, as well.

"Beautiful, isn't it?" the professor asked.

"If you like feet," Owen responded, then looked over his shoulder and added, "Which I don't."

"Ah, but that's not just any foot, that's an impression of the elusive Bigfoot." He stood and moved to the glass box. "A local Bigfoot enthusiast found the footprint four years ago in the forests surrounding Bola. It's a wonderful treasure."

"We wanted to ask you about the upcoming festival," Rachel said, and instead of moving off the couch to look at the plaster foot, she meandered around the room checking out some of the professor's other treasures. "Before we get to that, can you tell me about the blog you and your students run?"

He nodded and leaned against the large, wooden desk. *"Wexman Wonders* has ended up being a huge hit and currently has over ten thousand followers. I can't take the credit. My students are the writers. I simply give them ideas and, of course, review the content."

"What does your class have to do with your *Wexman Wonders* blog?" Owen asked, wanting to redirect them closer to Stronach's take on the Wexman Hell Week. "It seems to me that your students are centering the blog around myths and legends."

Stronach pushed off the desk, then threw his arms in the air. "Yes, exactly." Steepling his hands now, the professor paced. "From the ancients to modern man, myths and legends are in every culture. Ancient peoples shared their knowledge with other ancient cultures and over time, that knowledge evolved. I believe many of our myths and legends are based on fact."

"But what about Wexman Hell Week?" Owen asked. "I guess I don't understand why you and your students look at this as a legend, when it's most certainly a fact."

The professor sat behind his desk. "Twenty years ago, a Wexman student goes missing," Stronach began. "From what I understand, the boy had been a misfit. He'd tried to gain entry into the fraternal system, but his efforts weren't well received. And on a frigid night in the middle of January, he disappears with only a cryptic note left behind in his dorm room. He's never seen or heard from again."

"But then the same thing happened nine other times," Rachel countered.

Stronach sent her a small smile. "Allegedly."

"Allegedly," she repeated. "I certainly wouldn't consider my brother's beating and his roommate's disappearance *alleged* by any means."

Behind his Prada frames, the professor's eyes softened. "You're right. And I apologize. Sean's case is…different." He wagged a finger. "But, I do believe legends and myths are based on something genuine. Isn't it possible that the first student who disappeared did so on his own accord? From what I understand, he'd been shunned—blackballed actually—from all the Wexman fraternal organizations, and ostracized by many of his fellow classmates for being...strange. Perhaps, as a way to garner attention, he faked his disappearance."

Not buying the professor's theory, Owen asked, "Then why, in twenty years, has he never turned up?"

"Twenty years ago society was on the verge of entering the age of the Internet. At that time, creating a new, false identity was easy compared to today's standards. This particular student's only claim to family was an eighty-year-old grandmother. And, by the way, a year after the boy disappeared, the grandmother died. What's interesting is that the money she left behind was claimed six months later *by* the missing boy. That was the only time he's ever been heard from again."

"Owen and I didn't know about that." Rachel leaned against the bookshelf. "Your suggesting that this kid walked away from his own life, created another, and in the process, initiated the legend of Wexman Hell Week. A very interesting hypothesis, but how does that explain the other disappearances?"

"Not to be repetitive, but again, this all goes back to legends and myths being based on something genuine. The last sheriff wasn't the most competent of individuals and didn't keep the Hell Week note a secret. Actually, six years ago, we had a Hell Week hoax that ended up—"

"Yes, we heard about that," Owen said, anxious for Stronach to come to a point that might actually matter.

"Good. Then consider this. Isn't it possible that one of the other missing students had a terrible accident? I've heard that students like to go to the river, drink alcohol and do drugs. Perhaps one of these missing boys fell into the river and drowned. Rather than face expulsion or worse, those who had witnessed the accident decided to use Wexman Hell Week as a cover."

Owen decided Dr. Dick was talking out of his ass. While

his theories for the Wexman disappearances held some validity, they didn't explain the other missing boys, not to mention the four people who had disappeared from Bola. "You're saying every person who disappeared over the last twenty years, including Josh Conway, could be explained away by either accident, hoax, or the desire to purposefully jump off the grid. To be honest, I figured you'd tell us Bigfoot took them."

Stronach's face reddened and his gaze hardened, but he remained in his seat. "I believe the Bigfoot is a gentle creature. He's likely more afraid of us than we are of him."

"Aliens then?"

"Owen, please. Dr. Stronach is trying to help us."

"It's okay, Rachel. And please call me Collin."

"Okay, Collin, back to Bigfoot," Rachel said. "Can you tell us more about this festival?"

"Yeah, like why you'd schedule it during a time when you had to know there was a possibility of another Wexman Hell Week disappearance." The festival didn't sit right with Owen. Neither did Stronach and his bullshit theories behind the legend of Wexman Hell Week. Something about the professor was...off.

Stronach glared at him before shifting his gaze to Rachel. "Statistically, it's during this time of year that we have the majority of our local Bigfoot sightings."

"Are you expecting a big turnout?" she asked.

"Yes," the professor said with enthusiasm. "Anywhere from five to seven hundred people. This weekend should be a huge success. With the events we have planned, there won't be a dull moment." He gave Rachel a toothy smile. "It's a great time to be in Bola."

Hungry and tired of listening to Stronach, who had given them no useful information, Owen moved toward the door. "I bet Josh Conway would disagree."

As he left the office, he heard Rachel apologize to Dr. Dick and give him her phone number. While he waited in the hall, he tried to put his finger on what bothered him about the professor. He'd dealt with men like him in the past, egotistical asses who considered themselves more knowledgeable than the rest of the world. So why did Stronach rub him wrong?

Jealousy.

He definitely didn't like the way the professor flirted with Rachel. At all. And while it had been obvious she held no interest in Stronach, he'd still wanted to knock the man upside the head for touching her.

Man, he needed to pull himself together. He'd never been a jealous person, but twice in one day he'd been ready to crack skulls over his woman. But Rachel wasn't his, and based on her sometimes hostile attitude, he doubted she'd ever be. Then again, he swore he'd seen something in her eyes before they'd entered the office. Something that said she didn't really hate him...much. Or maybe that was all wishful thinking. Maybe—

"Is the professor in?" A young, attractive woman asked as she approached.

Before Owen could answer, Rachel came out of the office. He nodded to the girl, who was already pushing her way through the door and greeting Stronach, then said to Rachel, "Let's get out of here."

"Yeah, it's almost time to meet Jake."

Jake. Jealousy reared its ugly head again.

"I'm glad he suggested we meet at River's Edge. For a bar, the food is awesome."

Well, wasn't Jake the man.

As they made their way down the staircase, he glanced at Rachel, at her sexy, sassy mouth. He was hungry, too. Unfortunately, what he had a taste for wasn't on the River's Edge menu. But alcohol was and at this point, he could use a stiff drink. To help take his mind off the case and the woman he had no business wanting.

"C'mon, Janie, your move." Lois, a fellow patient and my only friend, motioned to the chessboard. "You know you want to," she sang—off key—and grinned.

Lois knows I can't move my hands. If I could, I would have kicked her butt and won the chess match by now. Instead, all I can do is sit in this damned wheelchair and drool. I hate this chair. Hate living in a state nursing facility. Hate that no one has bothered to claim me. That no one here, not even Lois, knows who I really am.

If only I could make my mouth work. Tell Lois, my doctors and nurses the truth. I honestly think I would sacrifice my vision and sense of smell if I could at least talk. I'd rather not look at the other pathetic patients, the bleakness in their tired eyes as they stare at the TV or drab walls. And the smells...it's bad enough that I have to wear a diaper and, at times, sit in my own filth. I can tolerate my own odor. It's the other twenty, nauseatingly foul patients in the community room I could do without...except for Lois. She has an easy, pretty smile and upbeat attitude, which sometimes gives me hope even if in my heart, I know none exists. Plus, she always smells like chocolate.

"Stumped you again, huh?" Lois clapped, then wrinkled her nose as a nurse's aide wheeled a patient, who was in obvious need of a sponge bath, past our worn table. "Okay, then, I'll move my piece here and...checkmate."

In lieu of a smile, I forced a grunt, which only made me sound like Lurch from the *Addams Family*. Reduced to a diaper-wearing invalid, who can't even grunt correctly, caused my stomach to knot with frustration.

Lois smiled again. "So you think I cheated?"

I blinked once. I don't *think* she cheated, I *know* she did. Still, I don't care. Without Lois, her endless chatter, the way she's always making up our conversation and acting as if she actually knows what I'm thinking, I might have gone crazy by now. Before she had come into my life, nightmares and painful memories had been my only company. At night, when Lois and I are separated and I'm alone in my quiet room, those nightmares and memories rush through my mind. Because of them I'm afraid of the dark, afraid to close my eyes. I don't want to keep reliving the moment that had brought me to this place. The panic, the fear...the betrayal.

I shifted my eyes toward the windows. Icicles dangled and frost coated the exterior glass. Dusk had come and gone, leaving a black, starless sky. Glancing at the clock on the wall, relief settled my knotted stomach. The nightmares wouldn't come for at least another four hours.

After Lois put the chess game away, she stood and stretched. Her weight loss worried me. Her tired, grey long-sleeved t-shirt and equally worn black sweatpants hung from her small frame. "We can play again tomorrow. Maybe you'll redeem yourself," she said as she pushed her chair closer to mine, gave our table a little shove, then sat so our knees touched. "It's almost time for dinner anyway. I guess baked chicken is on the menu. Hopefully it's not too dry."

Breakfast, lunch and dinner have become a miserable time for me. During meals I'm bombarded with delicious, mouthwatering aromas, yet denied a taste. I can blink, move my eyes and make the occasional grunt, but chewing? God, what I wouldn't give for a piece of cheesecake.

"Today's Regina's birthday, so the nurses got a cake for her."

At the mention of cake, I quickly look at her.

"So you've got a sweet tooth?" Lois chuckled. "Too bad they can't shove a piece of cake into your feeding tube."

Or in my useless mouth.

"Yeah, too bad." Lois stared at the scars covering my limp hands. Scars that will forevermore serve as a reminder of the day I should have died.

"But what do I know about those things," she said, then her hazel eyes suddenly brightened, and she gave her leg a slap. "Hey, did I tell you what movie the nurses are planning on showing tomorrow night?"

I blinked once.

"No? Well, only one of my favorites...*Beaches*. You know the one with Bette Midler and Barbara Hershey? I always loved that movie. Makes me cry like a baby, but sometimes we all need a good cry. Don't ya think?"

After I blinked twice, Lois took my hand in hers. Her fingers and palm, calloused from manual labor, covered my scars, and I tried desperately to soak in her strength. From the moment I had woken from my coma, I've shed an ocean of tears. They welled in my eyes now and my throat tightened. Except for the time spent with Lois, pain, misery and my blind ignorance has haunted me.

Lois brushed one of my stray tears. "I'm sorry, honey. I didn't mean to upset you. It's just...I know our story isn't the same as the gals in *Beaches,* but as soon as I heard they were showing the movie, I thought about us."

She squeezed my hand tighter, and I loved the skin-to-skin contact, even if it played as a bitter reminder that I was still among the living, trapped in my body with no means of escape.

"Me and you," she continued. "I think we come from different worlds. I don't know how I know this, I just do. I sometimes imagine what it would be like if you could talk, how you'd sound, what you'd actually say to me." She started to laugh. "I'm thinking the first words out of your mouth might be 'shut the hell up, Lois, don't you ever stop talking?'"

I would never say that to Lois. She's right, though. We do come from different worlds. Had hate, a hunting knife and a tire iron not brought me to this place, I would never have known or associated with Lois. In my previous life, I had lived in a beautiful, custom built home in a quiet, safe suburb. Drove a BMW, wore designer clothes, ate at expensive restaurants and took exotic vacations with my family. Before her illness, Lois had worked as a cleaning lady for people like me. She'd lived in a dilapidated apartment building, walked or took the bus, wore Good Will clothes, and barely had enough money to pay her rent, let alone eat.

"Now that I think about it, you wouldn't say that to me."

Blinking twice, I inwardly smiled. My friend does know me.

"Anyway, I'm looking forward to watching the movie with you. We've been through a lot together. I don't think I would have lasted this long if it wasn't for you."

She's always saying things like that, which amazes me. I can't speak, and yet I've somehow given her the will to live? Her words are humbling. If only she truly understood the impact she's made on my life. Her humility, her selflessness, her uncanny ability to know what I'm thinking and feeling...she is the only reason I look forward to each day.

"This morning, my doc came to see me."

Heart racing, stomach balling into a knot again, fresh tears blur my vision. Anxious for the results of Lois' latest MRI, I wish I could squeeze her hand, and give her the same comfort she's given me day in and day out.

She rubbed her bald head with her free hand. "He told me the cancer moved to my brain."

Anger and overwhelming sadness punched a hole in my soul. Blinking, I fought the tears, fought to be strong for her. But hot trails trickled down my cheeks and I grunted—a real grunt this time—trying desperately to voice my pain and misery over her results. She has become my best friend. Without her in my world, I see no point in living.

"But don't you worry. I'm not going anywhere." She leaned in, kissed my cheek, then whispered in my ear, "Not until you tell me who tried to kill you."

CHAPTER 6

RACHEL WALKED ACROSS the small bedroom she'd chosen at The House of Joy and reached into the computer bag for a fresh pencil. At the rate she was going, she'd blow through the twenty-four pack by Wednesday. Better than smoking a pack of cigarettes. A habit she'd given up after her return from the Army, and one she missed, especially now. While the rush of nicotine certainly wouldn't make their investigation any easier, it might help battle her stress and frustration.

Gnawing on the pencil, she stared out the window. Dark now, there wasn't much to see, but she'd rather stare into the night sky than think about the investigation or...Owen.

Not true.

So she couldn't help herself. Even though she knew she shouldn't, she couldn't stop thinking about the press of his strong, hard body as he'd kissed her under the mistletoe. That night had happened a year ago, but it might as well have been yesterday. Even over a mouthful of pencil, she swore she could still taste his whiskey sweet kiss, the slide of his tongue, the touch of his firm, coaxing lips.

Being stuck in Bola with Owen, saddled to each other until they found Josh, might end up being both heaven and hell. For years she'd tried to convince herself that Owen was the kind of guy who used women for sex to feed his ginormous ego. Only he'd never shown an arrogant bone in his sexy body and he'd always treated her with respect.

She wanted to dislike him, had tried for years to keep their relationship distant and professional, but she couldn't shake what he'd awoken the night he'd kissed her. He'd made her…aware. Of her body, her desires, her longings. That brief moment under the mistletoe had also made her realize *something* had been missing in her life. To this day she still didn't know what that something was, or if she even wanted it. She just knew it was always there, on the fringes. Enticing her to explore her "Owen fantasies" and, ugh, her frickin' feelings for him.

One thing she knew for certain, for the past year, Owen, and whatever emotions he'd evoked, had been making her crazy. Which was stupid. She wasn't his type and he wasn't hers. She'd do well to remember that and stay focused on the investigation, not him. Not his smile, his blue eyes, his big, muscular body…his woodsy cologne that made her think of camping and stripping naked, then crawling into a sleeping bag with him.

She bit hard on the pencil. Before she chipped a tooth, she tossed it back in the computer bag.

Focus, Rachel. Think about Sean and Josh.

Shoving all of her confusing thoughts aside and shifting them on the investigation, she realized Owen had been right. Searching through Sean and Josh's room had been a waste of time. The only positive thing that had come from visiting Stanley Hall had been the security guard, Bill Baker. She hoped his tox screen came back positive for Rohypnol or some other drug that connected back to Sean. With the little concrete evidence they had, similar toxicology reports could prove a link to the kidnapper.

Dr. Collin Stronach had also been a waste of time. The professor had given them nothing useful. The highlight of the interview had been Owen. Other than that nasty look he'd given just before they'd met up with Bill, she'd never seen him so…confrontational and insulting. She had to admit, she'd liked the way Owen had provoked the nutty professor and how he'd come to her defense when he'd thought Stronach had been hitting on her. *Stop thinking about him. Think about Sean. Think about the investigation.* She glanced at the file box Jake had given them. After their interview with Stronach, Jake had called and cancelled their dinner, which worked out perfectly. She'd been up since four AM, been stressed about her brother's health and Josh's whereabouts, and didn't have any new, solid leads to share with the sheriff anyway. Plus, not having to meet with Jake had given her the opportunity to visit with Sean again.

Her brother had never been a good patient, and had been a crabby mess when she and Owen had stopped by his hospital room. While there, she did ask him about the Mountain Dew, empty fridge, garbage can and cleanliness of his dorm room. Sean had told them that when he and Josh left, the fridge and garbage can had been full, and the empty Mountain Dew bottle had been in the trash. As for the state of their dorm room, Owen had been right about that, too. Apparently the boys had kept their room clean hoping two girls from their anthropology class would come by after the study session.

They hadn't stayed long at Dixon Medical Center. Her brother's doctor was already gone for the day, and hadn't left the results for Sean or Bill's tox screens. Sean, who had been in obvious pain, needed his rest. Besides, she'd wanted to go back to Joy's, change into her comfy clothes, begin going through the old Wexman Hell Week case files, grab something to eat and pour herself a drink. Not necessarily in that order.

Instead of donning her fuzzy, pink and fuchsia polka dot pajamas, though, she'd opted for the lacy, formfitting, pale green camisole she'd accidentally packed and a pair of black yoga pants. She appreciated a warm, cozy room, especially when the temperature outside dipped into the teens. Unfortunately, this room had bypassed warm and cozy and had gone straight to desert hot. If she hadn't been waiting for Joy to stop by her room and fix the temperature, she would have lost the yoga pants and stripped to her underwear.

Too hot to eat the leftovers Joy had stowed away for her and Owen, she ignored the plate setting on the nightstand and drained the glass of water instead. With plenty of ice left in the glass, she poured a shot of vodka from the fifth she'd picked up from the liquor store on their way back from the hospital, then added some Sprite. After taking a sip, she plopped on the bed, then emptied the file box.

Before locking herself in her room, she'd given Owen half the files with the intention of discussing the information in the morning over breakfast. While she should have taken the box to his room or downstairs to the community room where they could work together, she'd needed some time alone. Who was she kidding? She needed time away from Owen. The more she was around him, the more she thought about that kiss and all the possibilities it could have led to if he hadn't walked away that night.

Instead of allowing herself the opportunity to consider those possibilities, she took another sip of her drink, then flipped open one of the missing persons' files. Derrick Rodgers had been the sixth student to disappear. He'd been eighteen, in his second semester at Wexman University, and pledging the Psi Upsilon fraternity. Ten years ago, on the night of January sixteenth, Derrick had disappeared after leaving a meeting at the fraternity house. The Hell Week note had been left on the pillow in his dorm room. All of his things had been accounted for, he'd been well liked, had a girlfriend, came from a good family.

She studied his photo. He'd been a good-looking guy, tall, blonde, athletic. According to his parents, he'd never been into trouble, didn't do drugs or drink, and had been a straight A student. The guys at the fraternity had concurred. According to the sheriff at the time, Tom Miller, he and his deputies had led a search party, consisting of a dozen men, through the woods surrounding the university. After one day, they'd given up and listed Derrick a missing person.

"That's it?" She sifted through the remaining files,

wondering if maybe some of the sheriff's notes regarding Derrick Rodgers's case had fallen out and mixed with the others. No such luck. Apparently, note taking hadn't been Sheriff Miller's strong suit.

As she moved on to the next file, a knock came at the door. "Thank God," she said, and crawled off the bed. Another hour in this hotbox and she might end up with heat stroke.

Opening the door she said, "Hey, Joy, sorry to bother..." She took a step back when Owen's big body filled the doorframe.

When he moved into the room she tried to ignore the way the worn, navy University of Virginia t-shirt hugged his well-muscled arms and chest. Except that ended up drawing her attention to the loose, grey sweatpants, which rode low on his lean hips and made his ass tempting enough to grab. Never in her life had she grabbed anyone's ass, nor had she had the desire. Until now. She wanted to grab him from behind, then reach around the front of those loose sweatpants. Slip her hand beneath the waistline until she stroked—

"Good God. It's Africa hot in here," Owen said, crouched and inspected the woodwork along the hardwood floor.

"No kidding. This room could rival a sauna."

"Yeah." He stood and angled the tall dresser. "Joy told me. She suggested I close the vents and kick the ceiling fan on high." He crouched again and shifted a latch on the floor vent. Standing, he moved around the small room, his focus on the floor. "She said there should be two of them...here it is." He moved the nightstand and revealed another vent. After he'd finished closing the vent, he reached up and adjusted the ceiling fan—which she couldn't reach—to high.

Within seconds, a blessed breeze ran through the room. "So much better," she said on a sigh. "Thank you."

"No problem." He glanced at the files on the bed. "Find anything interesting?"

She shook her head. "I've only gone through one case. There wasn't much there. Kid disappears, no evidence but the Hell Week note. What about you? Have you looked at any of the files?"

"Just a couple, then I needed to refill my glass with ice. That's when I ran into Joy in the kitchen and she told me about your room." He nodded to her vodka Sprite. "I brought up some extra ice. I can bring it over, we can bitch about Sheriff Miller and the way he'd handled these missing person cases over a drink."

When they'd stopped at the liquor store on their way back from the medical center, Owen had picked up a fifth of Jack Daniels and a six-pack of Coke. Although normally not one to drink alone, and tempted to engage in a bitch session, she knew spending the evening closed in a room with Owen could be a mistake. Considering she was having a difficult time trying to erase any thoughts of him that didn't have to do with work, she needed to maintain her distance when the opportunity, like now, rose.

"Thanks, but I'll pass. It's been a long day. I'm going to finish reading through these cases, then go to bed."

Nodding, he glanced at her breasts, then moved toward the door.

Due to the heat, she'd forgotten about the lacy camisole, and immediately folded her arms across her chest. She'd only worn the top once, then afterward, had shoved it in her underwear drawer never to be used again. In her opinion and experience, women with boobs as big as hers had no business going braless or wearing skimpy camisoles. Unless, of course, the intention was to seduce, or in her case, stay cool.

With his hand on the doorknob, he turned. His gaze drifted to her chest again and heat, having nothing to do with the wonky room temperature, rose to her cheeks. Even with her arms over her breasts, the breeze from the ceiling fan kissed her cleavage, which meant an ample amount of bare skin remained exposed and in plain view for him to see. She knew her breasts were one of her best assets. A part of her wanted to drop her arms and let him look his fill. Let him realize what he could have had if he hadn't blown her off after their kiss. If only she had the nerve and at least one slutty bone in her body.

When he met her gaze, she hugged herself tighter. His eyes had darkened and now matched the navy shirt he wore, and she swore he stared at her with something akin to hunger and longing. Then he blinked and whatever she *thought* she saw had disappeared. Or maybe she imagined the whole thing, which was likely the case. She might have a nice rack, but she didn't have the face and body to go with it. Based on the women she'd seen Owen with, unless he was desperate, she doubted he would be interested in her. Not that she want him to be interested in her.

Liar.

True. She couldn't help wanting what she knew she shouldn't or couldn't have—Owen Malcolm in her bed, naked and on top of her. Pining after a man who was not only way out of her league, but a serial charmer similar to the men her mom had been with, would only lead to resentment and feelings of inadequacy. She should know, because that was exactly how she'd felt after Owen had kissed her, then walked away as if it hadn't happened.

She glanced at his mouth. Memories of his lips on hers suddenly surged through her mind and body. The heat of his touch, the way his muscles had bunched under her hands as she'd clung to him, to his dominating lips...

"I know you're worried about Sean and Josh. If you change your mind and want to talk, I'll be up for a while."

She shook the kiss from her mind. "I won't," she said, too quick and curt. He had to leave. Her nipples were starting to ache and her other girl parts were beginning to come alive. She needed him and his big, sexy body out of her room. She needed to go back to the files on her bed and lose herself in the investigation, not the confusing thoughts and memories just being near him evoked. "I mean, we have an early day. Jake's going to be here at seven-thirty, and we're meeting with the dean at nine."

He clenched his jaw, then nodded. "Right. Jake. How could I forget?"

"What's that supposed to mean?"

"Nothing." He opened the door, then paused at the threshold. "There is one thing."

"And that is?"

"I noticed the way you and Jake...interacted."

Confused, she furrowed her forehead. "Meaning?"

"It's not my business who you...I mean, it's none of my, uh—"

"Just say what's on your mind."

"Fine. No offense, but you're new to working in the field. Trying to mix business with pleasure isn't advisable. Especially if the...ah...other party ends up not interested. It could make working the case uncomfortable."

How could such a brilliant investigator be so clueless? She had zero interest in Jake. Sure, the hunky sheriff wasn't hard on the eyes, but based on the weariness etched on his face and the despondency in his dark eyes, she suspected the man carried a lot of baggage. She liked to steer clear of guys like Jake. She had enough baggage of her own.

Rather than comment on Owen's ridiculous assumptions, she wished him good night and tried to close the door.

He stopped her. "So you admit you've got a thing for the sheriff?" he asked, his voice laced with accusation and irritation.

Highly offended, she dropped her arms and fisted her hands. "I'm not having this conversation."

His gazed dropped to her chest again. This time she didn't cover herself. She might not have the body and face to go along with the boobs, but she wasn't ugly. How dare he act as if she was the one who would end up rejected, not Jake.

"Fine," he said. "I just don't want to—"

"I don't care what you want," she interrupted. "Good night." After she closed the door in his face, she moved back to the bed. Although insulted, she had to admit that the timing of Owen's asinine bullshit had been perfect. Without trying, he'd not only reminded her why she should leave the mistletoe kiss in the past, but that fantasizing about Owen would prove pointless. He clearly had no interest in her outside of work, and undoubtedly found her unattractive.

But as she began to sift through the case files, her mind kept wandering back to Owen. To how hot he'd looked in his t-shirt and sweats. To his smile and how good he'd smelled. Damn it. To that stupid, sexy kiss and how badly she wanted one more taste...

He turned on the lantern. Light immediately illuminated the basement and reflected off the pledge, who hung from the wall, his position unchanged since early this morning. The small space heater remained in front of him, giving little warmth. Moving closer, he raised the lantern and shook his head. He might have to cut Hell Week short. The little puke's gauntness, his hollow, pale cheeks, and his shallow breathing worried him. His pledge couldn't die before his time. Not now. Not when he'd come so close to fulfilling his destiny.

"He doesn't look good," Junior said as she stepped down from the ladder.

"He'll be fine." He smacked the puke's face. "Rise and shine. It's time for dinner and calisthenics."

"You're unchaining him?"

"Yes. Get the bat." After setting the lantern on a bench, he pulled a bag of cold, cooked wild rice from his coat pocket. While he'd threatened to give the pledge maggots, producing the disgusting larva for consumption would have been too difficult, especially in the dead of winter. "I'm not about to feed the little puke. He can do it himself."

Metal bat now in hand, Junior hovered behind him while he released the pledge from his bindings. The pathetic puke fell to the ground, shivering and groaning, his naked back baring deep scratches from time spent against the rock wall.

"Get up. Now."

The pledge slowly moved to all fours, shook his head, then dropped to the floor with a grunt.

"I told you to get up," he said, then punctuated his demand

with a swift kick to the puke's stomach.

Back on his knees, coughing, mouth gaping, the pledge clutched his midsection. "Please," he begged. "No more. Cold. So cold."

"Ah, but you won't be after you've done your daily exercises. First, you need sustenance." He dropped the bag of rice in front of him, then pulled a plastic bottle, filled with salted water, from his other pocket. "I even brought you something to quench your thirst." He set the bottle next to the rice.

The puke looked up at him, his eyes wild, searching. Then he stared at the bag.

Wondering if the pledge remembered the maggots he'd promised for dinner, he smiled. Psychological torture had played a large part in the Hell Week he'd experienced twenty-five years ago. But he'd been mentally stronger than his tormentors had given him credit. He'd endured their infantile demands, ate items he and the other pledges were led to believe were grotesque. He'd do the same to his pledge and much worse as the days continued. Today was only Monday, after all. If he were to complete a reenactment of what had happened to him twenty-five years ago, he'd have to stay on course and exhibit an enormous amount of patience. This pledge was the most important of them all. He would close the circle. And his death...?

The ultimate revenge.

Junior lowered the bat. "How long are we going to wait on him to eat? I have to leave soon, but don't want to miss a thing."

Children, even when they're grown, should be seen and not heard. While he'd developed an infinitesimal amount of paternal warmth for his daughter, her whining grated on his nerves.

Raising the heel of his booted foot over the pledges hand, he said, "This pathetic pile of vomit has three seconds to begin eating. Otherwise, I'll crush his fingers. Afterward, I'll smash the maggots, dump them into his water and force the contents down his throat. Either way, boy, you *will* eat your dinner."

The pledge kept his focus on the rice, but he shifted the hand near the boot heel a fraction. Then another, and another until he touched the bag.

"Eat it."

While remaining on all fours, the pledge dropped to his forearms and scooted his knees until his bottom rested on his heels. Cupping the bag in one hand, he dipped three filthy fingers inside, scooped the rice, brought the food toward his mouth, then hesitated.

"You need your protein. And while not necessarily appetizing, maggots have as much protein as a chicken breast." He didn't know if that was true, and quite frankly didn't care. Even though what the pledge held in his fingers didn't move and it smelled like rice, the boy must think he was about to eat maggots. The horror one creates in ones own mind is sometimes worse than reality. Although in this case, that horror, something he'd experienced during his own Hell Week when he'd been eighteen, would eventually become a reality for the pledge. In order to complete the circle, to rid him of the demon that had haunted him for over two decades, he had no choice but to inflict terror, humiliation…pain.

The pledge's raw back, his bony spine, curved upward as he twisted his head and dry heaved. A moment passed. He looked back to his fingers, coated in rice, then quickly shoved the contents into his mouth. As he coughed and gagged, he scooped out more rice. Like a feral, undomesticated pig-child, he devoured the rest of the rice. When the bag was empty, he reached for the water bottle, then took a long swallow. Within seconds, he retched, splashing the salt water and rice on the ground.

"Disgusting," Junior said, and held the back of her wrist against her nose and mouth as she looked away.

"Agreed." He knocked the pledge in the head with the tip of his boot. "Clean it up."

Eyes red and watery, spittle hanging from his mouth, the pledge looked up at him. "W-with what?"

"Your mouth."

Crying now, the pledge used the tips of his fingers to pick up the rice from the floor, then cringed as he put several pieces in his mouth.

"If I throw up, will you make him eat that too?" Junior asked, while her pretty face contorted in an odd combination of both revulsion and amusement.

Not bothering to answer her ridiculous question, he checked his watch. Although he enjoyed playing with the pledge, he had work to attend to, and Junior needed to leave. "Watch him while I prep for his calisthenics. If he makes one wrong move…"

"Yes, sir."

Within minutes, he had the CD player and strobe lights placed in position and plugged into the extension cords leading from the upstairs electrical outlet. As he approached the pledge, he took the bat from Junior.

He handed her the lantern. "I need you to stand near the ladder for this. Stay there, and do not move. On my command, turn off the light."

"But I thought—"

Again, children should be seen and not heard.

"Silence. Don't think. Obey. Now go."

Her gaze flicked to the pledge before she did as he'd ordered. Once she was at a safe distance, he turned to the pledge. "Stand." When the puke didn't move, he kicked him in the stomach.

With a grunt, the pledge clutched his midsection, then slowly rose to his feet. He swayed, shook his head, then with defiance in his eyes, braced his legs.

Good. He wanted a fighter. In the past, some of his aspirant pledges had been weak, in mind and body. They'd given up too quickly, which had been disappointing. He liked when they fought, because when he finally broke them, and he always broke them, the reward had been that much more satisfying. Unlike those feebleminded weaklings, he hadn't cracked. He hadn't let them defeat him, not even that last day of his Hell Week when his demonic tormentor had defiled and violated him in the cruelest, most heinous of ways.

Based on the way the puke boldly glared at him with hatred and insolence, he knew he had no worries. Yes, this pledge had spirit and would not disappoint. But now it was time to show him who was in charge.

Nodding to Junior, he said. "Turn off the lantern."

Thick, black darkness swallowed the basement whole. The pledge's breathing accelerated into quick, short pants. The shuffling of his bare feet, as he likely dragged them along the dirt floor, echoed off the rock walls. Then the room went silent.

"What do you want from me?" the pledge screamed, his voice plagued with fear and panic.

Instead of answering, he pressed a button on the CD player. The speakers blasted a cacophony of electric guitars, bass and drums as Ozzy Osbourne began to wail Black Sabbath's, *Paranoid*. The same song they used on him, the same song he had continued to use on his own pledges. As much as he detested the heavy metal music, as much as it infused his mind with memories, he had no choice. Whatever had been done to him would be done to his pledges. From the moment he'd taken his first pledge, he'd discovered that mimicking that fateful week had become the only way to ease the nightmares.

And he wasn't finished yet.

When he pressed the next button, strobe lights flashed throughout the room. The white light sped quickly, bouncing off the pledge, the walls, Junior. As the light accelerated, he raised the volume on the CD player to a deafening roar. The pledge covered his ears. His mouth gaped, his scream silent against the raucous music. The strobe lights tricked the mind. Every move the puke made appeared as slow motion, as if he were an apparition, a ghoul who had been raised from the dead. Jerking, shuddering as if his arms and legs had been weighted with cement.

He glanced at Junior. She stood next to the ladder. Laughing, she stared at the pledge and tapped her foot to the heinous beat of the music. His daughter had come to him defeated, powerless...scared. She hadn't smiled much then, but as he'd introduced her to his world, he'd witnessed the blossoming of a unique and strong young woman. With further tutelage she would continue to grow and by the end of Hell Week, she would understand the true meaning of dominance, of supremacy, of total control.

Acquainted with every riff, every word of the Black Sabbath song, he knew he had only two minutes and fifty three seconds to terrify his pledge. According to the CD player, thirty-three seconds had already passed.

Time to have some fun.

Gripping the baseball bat, he approached the pledge. The puke's screams could now be heard and only heightened his need for vengeance. *He* had never screamed. Even when his tormentor had violated him in the cruelest, most degrading way, he had not cried or begged for release. He had been too proud to allow the demon to see the pain he'd caused. So unlike this, and the previous nine pukes. They'd always cried and begged. This one would, too.

Starting now.

Like a fencer lashing his sword, he thrust the bat, connecting with the pledge's stomach. The boy flung his arms wildly in a futile attempt to ward him away. But he came back, lunged and hit the pledge in the kidney. The puke dropped to a knee, then quickly scrambled to his feet.

Yes, this one would give him a fight.

Attacking again, he showed no mercy. While he had no intentions of breaking the pledge's bones—today—he would make sure the puke understood his place, maybe even his destiny. If not, he would come to that realization by the end of Hell Week. For now...

He swung the bat. Hit the pledge's shoulder, then spun and aiming for his legs, knocked the puke off his feet. On the dirt floor, writhing in pain, crying and screaming, the pledge held up his hands. As the last twenty seconds of *Paranoid* played, he hovered over his latest and last victim, and raised the bat over his head.

The pledge's eyes, eerily black from the strobe lights, grew big and round. He raised his knees to his chest and held up his hands. Shrieked and yelled. Then the music died.

Whimpering and panting hard, the pledge remained still. The crybaby's bellyaching made him want to take the bat and bash him in the skull.

Too soon for that.

Instead, with a guttural roar and all his might, he slammed the bat against the ground and only inches from the puke's head.

The pledge released a girly, high-pitched scream, then turned his head and stared at the bat. Wide-eyed, he slowly faced him. "Why?" he cried. "Why are you doing this to me?"

"Boo hoo," he mocked with a snort. "Stop your whining and act like a man." As he killed the strobe lights, he instructed Junior to turn on the lantern. The lighting back to normal, he looked at the pledge, at the puddle saturating the dirt, then shook his head in disgust. "The urine soaking your underwear might be warm now, but once you're hanging from the wall and the chill drapes itself over your body, your genitals will likely shrivel up." He moved closer and raised the bat. "Stand and assume the position against the wall. Calisthenics are complete for this evening."

The pledge obeyed without a fight. Which surprised him. The little puke's father had been a bully who had enjoyed terrorizing not only him, but the others who had gone through Hell Week with him. He'd expected the pledge to have inherited his father's aggression and hostility, his sick need to intimidate. As the boy raised his arms in compliance and waited for the shackles to return around his wrists and ankles, he realized his pledge was nothing but a pitiable, useless milksop pantywaist. While he'd shown strength prior to this first hazing, the pledge had easily succumbed to fear. And all over loud music and strange lighting. If the puke thought tonight was bad, then he was in for a big surprise. Tonight he'd treated him with fastidiousness and delicacy.

Tomorrow would only be worse.

Once he secured the pledge and replaced the space heater, he moved to the ladder.

"That's it?" Junior asked as she frowned at the pledge. "That's all you're going to do to him?"

At the end of spring, when he left Bola and Hell Week behind, he and Junior would go their separate ways. But she would carry more than blood in her veins. Without a shadow of a doubt, he would instill in her the knowledge of true vengeance, along with...patience.

"Yes. For tonight, this is it."

With a huff, she climbed the ladder. Dousing the lantern, he plunged the basement into darkness again. The soft cries and whimpers of the pledge a sweet melody as he followed behind his daughter. After he reached the top, then sealed the trapdoor, he turned to Junior.

Purse and keys in hand, she stood at the front door. "I think you were too easy on him," she said.

While he admired her hunger for power, he loathed her ignorance. Beyond irritated that she would question him and ruin the high he'd gained from playing with the pledge, he allowed his anger to snap. In three strides he pinned her by the lapel of her puffy coat and slammed her against the door.

"Put yourself in the pledge's shoes. Understand his fear, his terror." To punctuate the point, he shook her, then banged her against the door again. "Remember, it's only Monday. There was no need to beat the pledge or physically harm him, the fear I've instilled in him is enough for today." He shoved away from her. "Be careful what you wish for, Junior. Tomorrow will be worse, the day after that, dreadful. By the end of the week...horrifying."

Gripping the front of her coat, her eyes wide and wary, she nodded. "I'm sorry, sir. I shouldn't have questioned you."

"No. You shouldn't have," he responded, then realized he should enlighten Junior. He should tell her what had happened to him twenty-five years ago. Not tonight, though. Maybe not ever. Admitting that such atrocities had been bestowed upon him by a weak-minded bully, and that even after twenty years of Hell Week therapy, he still had nightmares, would reveal too much. Junior might be his flesh and blood, but she hadn't earned the right to know what no one but his pledge's father knew.

"Go," he said. "Meet me here tomorrow at the same time. I have a busy day and won't be able to talk."

"And the two people from the investigation agency?"

"I told you during dinner, I'm not worried. In my opinion, private investigators are buffoons who couldn't make the cut to be real law enforcement officials. As you are aware, I've dealt with the real deal in the past and managed to outwit them." He smiled. "Never fear, history will repeat itself. By the end of the week, the investigators will have run back to Chicago empty handed. The ignorant Townies and college students will have new fodder. They will spin tales that will only magnify the legend of Wexman Hell Week."

"And the pledge?"

A slow smile spread across his face. "He'll be dead."

CHAPTER 7

TUESDAY

OWEN SAT AT The House of Joy's large dining room table, ignoring the blueberry pancakes Joy had served him earlier, and instead stared at the staircase. Rachel should have been downstairs by now. Maybe she'd overslept. Or maybe he'd pissed her off enough that she'd opted not to join him for breakfast.

Shoving the plate aside, he reached for his coffee. He'd messed up last night. Bad. He should have never brought up Jake. But after he'd walked into her bedroom and saw her in that skintight top and form fitting pants, he'd lost all rational judgment. The most revealing thing he'd ever seen Rachel in had been a t-shirt. Last night, she'd given him an eye full. Her breasts had practically spilled out of the flimsy top. Tempting him. Teasing him. It had taken every ounce of control to not stare at her chest and imagine what it would be like to slip those skinny straps off her shoulders and shove her top to her waist. To palm her breasts, taste her nipples.

He knew it now, just as he'd known it last night when he'd stood in Rachel's bedroom. He had no business interfering in her love life. If she wanted Jake, and he wanted her, then that was that. Done. Only, the idea of Jake putting his hands on Rachel, of him kissing her, stripping her naked—

Coffee mug in hand, he left the table and walked out the front door. The rush of cold air didn't help cool his thoughts or libido. Standing at the porch rail, he tried to rein in his anger. His frickin' jealousy. Never in his life had he been jealous over a woman. Not in high school when his buddy had stolen his prom date away from him. Not in college when his girlfriend dumped him for a fellow fraternity brother. Not in his adult life, either. While he'd had a couple of girlfriends since college, he hadn't been in a steady relationship for a few years. He dated. Sort of. With his schedule, he couldn't find the time for a relationship. The women he did see understood this. These women were great, fun to be with, hot in bed, and knew the chances of him committing were slim to none. They also dated other guys, and he was cool with that. He never expected the women he slept with to wait around for him to commit.

So why did the thought of Rachel hooking up with Jake bug the living shit out of him?

"She's yours."

Owen spun to the right. A tall, gangly man, he placed in his early fifties, stood at the opposite edge of the porch wearing a red and black wool coat and a matching earflap hat. Good God, had the lumberjack been reading his mind? But Rachel wasn't his, even if he'd like her to be for just one night.

"Come again," Owen said.

"She's yours," the man repeated, then nodded toward the driveway.

Owen looked over his shoulder and realized the man had been referring to the Lexus. "Yeah, she's mine." Wouldn't that be a great thing to say when Jake arrived? Rachel's mine, so stay the fuck away. His stomach soured as the image of Jake touching Rachel emerged again. He had no business staking a mental claim on her, let alone a verbal one to Jake. Still, he wanted to. Last night he'd wanted to grab her bare shoulders and kiss her, then suggest...what? That they should have sex? Date? Do the whole "let's get to know each other" thing?

"She's pretty," the man said, then pulled a cigarette and lighter from his coat pocket. "You seen Joy?"

"She went into the basement to do some laundry."

"Good." The man slipped the cigarette between his lips, then lit it. After drawing in a deep breath, he released. The smoke caught on the chilly breeze and quickly dissipated. "I'm Walter Eastly."

"Owen Malcolm."

Walter took another drag, then said, "I know. Joy told me about you and Shorty."

For the first time since leaving Rachel's room last night, Owen cracked a smile. "I wouldn't call my partner that if I were you. Just ask Joy."

Chuckling, Walter shook his head. "Joy filled me in already. I'm looking forward to meeting the woman who had the nerve to stand up to Joy. Trust me when I say that don't happen...ever."

The front door opened. Walter quickly moved to the farthest corner of the porch, tossing the cigarette into the snow covered bush below the wooden rail.

"Have you seen Walter?" Joy asked from the threshold. "Tall guy, probably wearing a plaid coat and ugly hat."

From his peripheral vision, Owen caught Walter shaking his head. "No, haven't seen him. If I do, I'll tell him you're looking for him."

She nodded, then narrowed her eyes. "What the hell are you doing out here? And without a frickin' coat? It's balls ass freezing."

"Just needed a minute," Owen said while trying to fully decipher 'balls ass freezing.' "Did Rachel come downstairs yet?"

"Nope," Joy said, then shut the door.

The cold finally affecting him, Owen rubbed his arm. "She's pleasant in the morning."

"Don't let Joy bother you. Deep down, she's a sweetheart."

Sweetheart? Whatever Walter had been smoking, Owen decided he'd like some.

"Thanks for covering for me," Walter said, and reached for the wet cigarette, then shoved it into his pocket. "Can't leave any evidence behind."

"Do you live here?" Owen asked.

"For the past fifteen years."

"I take it Joy doesn't know you smoke."

"No, she does, but gives me shit when she catches me. I know it's cowardly, but I'd rather hide it from her than listen to her grief. Know what I mean?"

From the little he knew of Joy, Owen would probably take the coward's way out, as well. "But she chews tobacco."

"In her mind, it ain't the same thing." Walter moved past him and down the porch steps. "See ya' around."

An icy chill ran through him as Walter disappeared around the side of the garage. Glad he'd had Walter and Joy to distract him from thinking about Rachel and how he'd made an ass of himself last night, he headed back into the house. After dumping the cold coffee into the kitchen sink, he refilled his mug.

"I can use one of those."

He tensed. Rachel's sleepy, sexy voice aroused him. Made him think about what it would be like to wake up next to her, roll her beneath him and bury himself between her thighs. Trying desperately to shove the image from his mind before he embarrassed himself with a full-blown erection, he reached for a coffee mug.

"Morning," he said as he handed her the coffee.

With a nod, she took the cup.

"About last night," he began, hoping to right his wrong. "I shouldn't have—"

"Did you finish going through the missing person files?"

Sticking to business. He should be glad Rachel was blowing off last night, but he wasn't. A part of him wanted to explain why he'd said what he'd said. That he was a jealous jackass. That he couldn't stop thinking about her. Thinking about them. Instead, he said, "Yeah, I did."

"Good. Me, too. There's no one in the dining room. Why

don't we spread out there and go over what we've learned while we wait for...Jake," she said with a smile that he suspected was meant to be smug, only with the way her full lips curved, and the way he'd been thinking about her, the smile came off sexy as hell.

He followed her into the dining room, keeping his eyes on everything to avoid staring at her rear. In doing so, he still managed to conjure up last night's memory of how those black, stretchy yoga pants had hugged her ass.

"Are the files you looked at in your room?" she asked and took a seat.

"Yeah, I'll go get them."

Hesitating at the bottom of the staircase, he turned. "I want to—"

Morning, Princess. Was wondering if you were going to sleep the day away," Joy said as she kicked the basement door closed behind her. She set the full clothesbasket on the floor. "I saved you a couple of blueberry pancakes. If you want 'em, they're in the fridge."

"Thanks, Joy. I'm good," she said, and raised her coffee mug. "Do you mind if we work at your dining room table? The sheriff is going to be by soon and I thought it would be easier than using one of the bedrooms."

"Not at all." Joy picked up the basket. "Besides, the only bedroom I'd like to see Jake in is mine," she added with a wink, then chuckling, she headed into her first floor bedroom.

He glanced at Rachel. The corner of her mouth tilted in a wry smile. "Guess I've got some competition," she said, then pulled a file from the box.

Swallowing the apology he'd been ready to give her before Joy had interrupted, Owen went up the staircase, taking two steps at a time. Now, he realized, he could add vindictive to Rachel's list of *quality* traits. So he'd screwed up, had been a jerk about Jake. He wanted to right his wrong, but it looked as if she had no interest in hearing what he had to say.

After grabbing the files off the desk in his room, he slammed the door shut and headed down the hall. As he rounded the corner near the stairs, Rachel laughed. Curious, he snuck a quick peek, then quickly drew back and flattened himself against the wall, his earlier jealousy morphing into irrepressible bitterness.

Fucking Jake. The man sat close to Rachel, too close, his arm draped over the back of her chair as if they hadn't just met yesterday and had been intimately acquainted for years.

Irritation gnawing at his insides and making him regret that last cup of coffee, he stomped down the steps. *He* was the one who'd known Rachel for years. He understood her, and despite her abrasive approach and unforgiving temperament, he cared about her. Although at this moment he questioned why. She had a body he wanted to sink into, but an attitude that could use some serious adjusting.

"Morning," Jake said as Owen set the files on the table. "How do you like the House of Joy?"

While *shut the fuck up, asshole* sat at the tip of his tongue, Owen took the seat opposite of Rachel and said, "No complaints."

"Good to hear. I was just telling Rachel about last night's meeting with the town council and Bola business owners. Professor Stronach showed up and instead of talking about the festival and what we should expect, he gave us a crash course on Bigfoot."

"Because…"

"He's an idiot."

Owen couldn't agree more. Stronach had chosen to hold a festival at a time of year when everyone living in Bola and at the university expected Wexman Hell Week to happen. His stupidity and arrogance could cost them. With hundreds of people milling around Bola during the festival, chances of running a clean investigation could be jeopardized.

Rachel released a giggle. *A giggle? Seriously?* She wasn't the giggling type. This phony, flirty crap didn't work for her. Didn't she realize she didn't need to try so hard to gain a man's attention? She'd captured his interest the first day she'd walked into CORE. Her intelligent, green eyes had twinkled with amusement and confidence, an intriguing combination that had him constantly on alert whenever he'd been around her. Just like now, within the first few days of meeting her, he had wanted to explore something with her outside of CORE. During the years they'd worked together, she'd given him the impression she felt the same until about a year ago. That was when her tongue turned to barbed wire and she started giving him all kinds of crap, not to mention the ridiculous douche bag nickname. To this day he had no idea what had happened to change her mind or if she'd really been interested in him or not.

For four years now, he'd tried to pretend she had no effect on him. So he dated and kept himself busy with the job. Kept his mind off of Rachel and his tarnished past. Now, though, he was tired of pretending and worried that if he didn't overcome this strange obsession he had for her, their work relationship could become strained and awkward.

"Your insightful observation of the professor is spot on," Rachel said and flashed the sheriff a flirty smile.

Jake continued to hover too close and grinned back at her. Although he had no claims on Rachel, if Jake didn't back off, strained and awkward would become an understatement.

"We have an appointment at the university," Owen said, hoping to refocus Rachel and Jake's attention back to the investigation and off of each other. "Let's fill Jake in on what we learned yesterday."

"Already done," Rachel said.

When? He'd only been upstairs for a couple of minutes. If she'd managed to inform Jake about Bill Baker, Sean's dorm room and Professor Stronach in that short of an amount of time, he could only imagine what could have happened if he'd been gone any longer. They'd likely be married with four kids.

"Just now?" Owen asked.

Cocking an auburn brow, Rachel said, "No, last night."

When last night? Before he'd gone to her room? After?

Fucking Jake.

"You two had a busy evening," Jake said. "What Bill told

you has me wondering, though."

"About?" Rachel prompted.

"Why drug him, but take the boys after they'd left the dorm?" Jake looked to him. "Rachel said you two were thinking that the kidnapper drugged Bill in order to go back to the boys' dorm room to clean up whatever evidence might have been left behind. That seems awfully risky to me."

To Owen, too. He glanced at the notes he'd taken while going through the files last night. "I've been thinking about that, as well. Do you remember seeing a security camera anywhere at the dorms?"

Rachel and Jake both shook their heads.

"I don't either. After we meet with the dean, let's go to campus security and see if they have anything from that night."

Taking the pencil from behind her ear, Rachel put a line through an item on the list in front of her. Apparently they were on the same page.

"Can I see your files?" she asked.

After he pushed them toward her, she began to pull out all the photos of the missing students. She arranged them in a line, then did the same with the photos from her files. "What do you see?" she asked.

Owen already knew the answer and could once again cross the topic off his list. "All the missing students have the same hair color and build."

Jake studied the pictures, then with a sigh, leaned back into the chair. "I've been over this dozens of times. Besides having similar traits, the only other thing these missing kids have in common are that they'd pledged a fraternity—and not necessarily the same one—and the Hell Week note. They all have different backgrounds. Some came from money, others got into the university with the help of scholarships and financial aid."

"What about the first victim, Tim Simmons?" Rachel asked and pointed to a photo of a young man with longish blond hair. "Dr. Stronach told us that he'd been blackballed from the university's fraternities and that he was basically an outcast."

Jake snorted. "Stronach's an idiot who has his head so far up Bigfoot's ass he can't seem to grab hold of reality."

Owen couldn't help cracking a smile at Jake's assessment of the professor. Too bad Jake had his eye on Rachel, otherwise Owen could see the two of them bullshitting over a couple of beers.

"I've investigated Tim's case." Jake lifted the picture of Tim Simmons. "I've investigated them all. Other than a bad haircut, this boy had everything going for him. Grades, girlfriend, came from a good family…"

"Stronach said the only family Tim had was a grandmother and that a year after she died, he claimed the inheritance then disappeared again."

"That's the problem with the professor. His perception of legends and myths, namely our local Hell Week, is warped. Tim's grandma wasn't his only family. His parents were alive and well when he went missing, so were his four brothers and sisters. The crap Stronach fed you was just that…crap. He's taken some of these disappearances and distorted them to fit his lame theories about the Hell Week legend."

Nodding, Rachel said, "Based on the conversation we had with him, I have no problem believing that. Okay, let's forget about Stronach." She pointed to the pictures on the table. "One thing we can't deny is that the kidnapper is going for a certain type. The question is why tall, athletic blond males?"

Owen toyed with the handle of the coffee mug. "Maybe the kidnapper is taking these boys as a trophy or a replacement to someone or something he'd lost."

"Maybe a son," Jake suggested.

"Possible." Rachel took Tim Simmon's picture from Jake and began putting the photos away. "I like the idea of a trophy and/or replacement. Both of those theories make sense to me."

"Replacing a son, you mean," Jake said.

She shook her head. "Replacing an *experience*. Because he's taking them at the start of Hell Week, what if this guy is reliving his *own* experiences?"

"And the boy he's kidnapped is the trophy," Owen said.

"What about the four missing Townies?" Jake asked. "None of them match the description of the missing students. Plus, they went missing at different times of the year."

Rachel pulled out those photos and set them on the table. Three of the missing Townies were male and in their early to mid twenties, the fourth, an elderly female. "I've been thinking about that. And I don't think they're connected to this case."

He could cross that off his list, too. "I agree. Jake, a fellow agent had been a deputy in a town like yours, but in Wisconsin. He'd mentioned having issues with crystal meth. Said he and some of the other deputies from his county had busted several different operations and that many of them were found deep in the forest."

"Is it possible the three male Townies were either dealing or doing drugs?" Rachel asked the sheriff. "I noticed one of them had a record...DUI."

Nodding, Jake leaned forward and folded his hands. "Yeah, that'd be Wes Grabowski. He and his cousin, Keith, were a couple of hell raisers. They both disappeared at the same time two years ago and I wouldn't be surprised if they'd gotten themselves mixed up in drugs. I didn't know the first missing person. He disappeared a few years before I took over as sheriff. The one that still bothers me is the woman. Ethel Rodeck was eighty-six when she went missing. I doubt she was selling or doing meth."

Owen found her file, then opened it. "She disappeared six years ago."

"Yeah, about four months after my first Hell Week case."

"And she lived near the Menominee River, right?"

"Her house was built about fifty yards from the shore."

"Isn't it possible she fell in and was swept away?" Owen asked.

"That was our concern. She went missing during a rainstorm. We'd already had a lot of rain that spring, couple that with the melting snow and the river had swelled its highest in forty years. We did search the river, but the current was extra strong. She could have been carried into Lake Michigan."

"Okay," Rachel began. "For now, let's set aside the four Townies and focus on the missing Wexman students. After Jake and I talked last night, I did some more research on Wexman University. Sean told me that Wexman has a strict, no tolerance policy when it comes to fraternity hazing. I couldn't find out when that went into effect, and hope the dean we're meeting with can enlighten us."

"Hell Week is what's triggering this guy," Owen said.

"What about the local methamphetamine dealers?" Jake asked. "Maybe some of these students had gotten involved with the wrong guy and—"

"And maybe Bigfoot took them."

"Really, Owen?" Rachel glared at him.

"Sorry, I was having flashbacks to our meeting with the nutty professor," he said with a smile. "See, I buy the meth angle with regards to the missing male Townies, but not the students. If only a couple of these kids had gone missing, the meth dealers would top my list of suspects. But ten, and at the same time of year?"

"I told Jake how Professor Stronach had tried to blow off the missing students as either a hoax, or a deliberate jump off the grid. And I agree. I don't think drug dealers have anything to do with this."

"I obviously don't have the background you two have, and it's not that I don't agree..." Jake rubbed the back of his neck. "Is it normal for a serial killer to take a few years off before he attacks again?"

Rachel looked to Owen. "Absolutely," he said. "The BTK killer is a prime example. Over the course of seventeen years he killed ten people. At one point, he took off eight years between murders."

"Right." Rachel nodded. "Let's not forget Bola isn't exactly a sprawling metropolis. Taking too many boys, too fast..."

"So who are we looking for?" Jake asked. "Wild guess."

Owen wished he was a criminalist like CORE agent John Kain, or a profiler like his boss, Ian. Those two had an eerie knack of finding a way into a killer's mind and could generate a rough idea of who they were hunting. Although he didn't have their background, he'd been around enough investigations, both with the Secret Service and CORE to draw his own conclusions. "Male. Late thirties to early forties. Maybe even a little older, which would make the theory that the kidnapper is taking these boys as a way of replacing a son improbable. "

"If we went with the son angle, this guy would be closer to sixty than forty," Rachel said. "Let's stick with the idea that he's closer to forty. Hell Week has just begun its twentieth year. If he started when he was eighteen—"

"Maybe as a freshman at Wexman," Owen suggested.

"Exactly," she concurred. "He'd be thirty-eight now or maybe a little older. I'm wondering if he's local, or if he comes to the area in January...specifically for Hell Week."

"Whatever he is, he has some place private," Owen said.

Jake shook his head. "Unless he kills them, disposes of the body, then leaves. Maybe this is like a pilgrimage to him."

"No," Rachel said. "Owen's right. He has some place private. He's keeping these kids for a week. He states that in the note."

"If he's kidnapping and murdering, I doubt he's worried about anyone calling him a liar," Jake countered.

"True." Rachel grinned. "Only he sent you a photo of one of his decomposing victims, weeks after the kid was taken. Unless he's taking the bodies on the road with him, I'm betting he lives in the area—at least during the winter months."

"Gee, and what males in the age range we're discussing live in the area only part of the year?" Owen asked with heavy sarcasm.

Rachel's big green eyes grew round. "Males who work at the university. The only summer classes the university offers are online. A professor teaching a summer course could do so anywhere."

"The university might not have classes during the summer, but maintenance and security are there year round, and are locals from either Bola or the neighboring county," Jake said.

"I'm not one hundred percent certain, but I believe some administrators also maintain residences around here, too. The dean you're meeting with would have that information, or at least access to it."

Rachel jotted a note, then tapped her lips with the pencil. He stared at her mouth, and wondered if Jake thought about tasting her lush lips as much as he did. Shaking the thought from his head, he said, "So the plan for today..."

"Meet with the dean, campus security, the RA that had been on duty Saturday night—"

"Abby Zucker?" Jake asked.

Rachel frowned. "Do you know her? Never mind, that's right, you already interviewed her."

"Yeah, I talked to her. She also works for me. I'm not trying to stop you from talking with her, but to save you time, she was working on a paper that weekend and saw Sean and Josh when she dropped off their pizza."

"Is that typical?" Owen asked. "Does she always make deliveries?"

"That I don't know."

Owen glanced at Rachel, who met his gaze. "I guess there's only one way to find out," she said, then smiled at Jake. "Aside from meeting with Abby, we also need to speak with Sean's doctor. I'm waiting on the toxicology reports for both my brother and Bill."

Jake tapped the table, then pushed his chair back and stood. "Sounds like you two have a busy day."

"Would you care to join us?" Rachel asked, and stood as well.

With a smile, Jake looked to the floor. "Maybe for dinner," he said, then met her gaze. "I was sorry to have to cancel yesterday, but really enjoyed talking with you last night."

Fucking Jake.

"Me too." Rachel sent the sheriff a syrupy smile. "Same time, same place?"

Jake slipped into his coat. "Sounds good."

"Yeah, sounds great," Owen said. "I keep hearing about

how fantastic the food is at River's Edge."

They both looked at him as if they'd forgotten he was in the room. Then Jake pulled out his car keys and nodded. "I'll check in with you later," he said to Rachel, who followed him into the foyer.

He had no idea what they were discussing, which bugged the shit out of him. Were they making plans for after dinner, maybe trying to figure out a way to ditch him so they could be alone? Not going to happen. The jealousy that had been clawing at him since yesterday finally pierced his gut.

Although he knew he could be making a monstrous mistake, jeopardizing his professional relationship with Rachel, his career with CORE, he had to know if there was something, anything between them. He didn't mind her sassy mouth, or the abrasive barbs she'd throw at him. Actually, he loved the way she didn't hold back around him, how she didn't pretend to be anything but herself. Unlike a lot of the women he'd dated, Rachel didn't try. Her "what you see is what you get" attitude intrigued him, made him want to climb inside her head and maybe her...heart?

No. This wasn't about love. An intimate friendship with some hot benefits, that's what he had in mind. Did she? He'd caught her checking him out last night when he'd gone to her room. The moment had been so brief he could have imagined it. Still, there had been other times when he'd been certain she held...something for him. Or maybe he was delusional and she was really into Jake.

Until he knew the answer, Jake didn't have a chance in hell.

He rinsed out his coffee mug, then placed it on the top rack of the dishwasher. After drying his hand on the dishtowel, he put the toaster away, then reached inside the refrigerator for a bottle of water. In the time he'd been here, the pledge hadn't had much to eat or drink, and he needed to make sure his puke didn't dehydrate before the week ended. What fun would Hell

Week be if he couldn't make his pledge scream, cry and beg? No fun at all.

But he could have a little fun now. Not much, he did have his day job to consider. Yes, just enough fun and games to remind the pledge of his fate. That he was nothing but a little puke. If the pledge hadn't realized it last night, he'd understand by the day's end. He'd understand who held the control, that his supremacy and domination outweighed that of anyone else in the young pledge's life. Namely, the puke's father.

After shrugging into his coat, he took the now cold, burnt toast from the counter, then shoved it into his coat pocket along with the water bottle. Smiling, anticipation humming through his veins, he moved into the hallway, then opened the trapdoor leading to the basement. Once he'd connected the garden hose to the utility sink, then dropped it through the trap door, he made his descent into the basement. When he reached the bottom rung of the ladder, he stepped onto the rock floor, then turned on the lantern.

"Good morning, puke." He approached the pledge who flinched and winced, craned his neck away from the lantern's light. Even standing a few feet away, the foul odor of feces and urine emanating from the puke caused bile to rise in his throat. He tamped down the urge to regurgitate the delicious crepes he'd eaten for breakfast and said, "It's amazing how quickly our eyes adjust to the dark, isn't it? Personally, I find the dark easier than the light. Wouldn't you agree?"

The pledge kept his head turned, while his body shivered and his teeth chattered. "C-cold. S-s-so cold."

"Then maybe we should do another round of calisthenics. That seemed to warm you up last night."

"No. P-please, no."

"I don't have time anyway. Here." Ignoring the pledge's putrid scent, he pulled the burnt toast from his pocket, then shoved it in the boy's face. "Eat it."

The pledge's dry lips cracked with tiny beads of blood as he opened his mouth without hesitation. His thin, pale cheeks hollowed as his jaw worked. After a moment had elapsed, he swallowed, then finally looked at him. "More. Please."

"This isn't a buffet and I don't have any more toast, well, toasted. I do have some leftover maggots in the refrigerator. I could climb up the ladder and—"

"No." The pledge shrank against the rock wall.

"No, what?" he asked and cupped his ear.

"No thank you."

Smiling, he withdrew the water bottle. "Because you're chained to the wall of a cold, damp, dark, rat-infested basement doesn't mean manners should be forgotten. And because of your politeness, I've brought you this." When the pledge jerked his head away, he said, "No tricks this time. This is nothing but pure water. You have my word. You don't doubt me, do you?"

Eyes wide and alert, the pledge hardened his jaw and stared at the water bottle. Seconds passed, then he shifted his gaze to him and shook his head. "No. I don't doubt you."

"Good. Now open."

The pledge obeyed, then greedily drank the water.

"Slow down before you regurgitate it back up along with your breakfast. I'd hate to have to force you to clean your mess again."

Nodding, the pledge took his advice. He slowly drank until he emptied the bottle, then he licked his chapped lips and said, "Thank you."

"You're welcome. See, now. You've stopped shivering. All you needed was a little nourishment. I'll be sure to bring you something more substantial for dinner. Do you like fish? It's very good for you."

The pledge glared at him for a moment, confusion and uncertainty clouding his eyes, then he looked to the ladder.

"Ah, you must be wondering where Junior has gone to. Unfortunately she had a previous engagement, but sends her regards. Don't worry. She'll be with us this evening. She's looking forward to what I have planned, I know I am. I'd tell you all about it, but would rather keep it a surprise. I love surprises, don't you?"

He actually hated surprises. Hated happenstances. Hated not having control. He hadn't been able to control the circumstances of the Hell Week his pledge's father had put him through. Since that week twenty-five years ago, he'd had very few incidences that he hadn't been able to control. With the exception of fathering Junior, he'd always made sure to think through every decision, consider all worst and best case possibilities. He refused to ever allow another person to influence his life, his decisions, his destiny.

This pledge, this particular Hell Week, would define him and close the gap of what he considered the circle of his life. At the week's end, no one would doubt his legendary status. Not the Townies, the students at Wexman, or even those rent-a-cops from Chicago. They might never know his real name, or that of Junior's, but they would know and understand the true meaning of vengeance—without a shadow of doubt.

Wrinkling his nose, no longer able to bear the stench, he took a step back from the reeking pledge.

"Wait, please," the pledge said and yanked on his chains.

He glanced at the metal clasp secured to the wall, to the taut chain, then back to the pledge. "There is no more food or water at this point. You will have to wait until dinner."

"No…I…the woman, Junior. I know her."

"I expected as much."

"I know you, too."

"Of course."

The pledge's eyes clouded with tears. "You're not going to let me leave, are you?"

He tilted his head and considered how to answer. If he told the pledge the truth, the whiny puke might give up, refuse to eat, and become a useless pawn in this final match of Hell Week. He couldn't allow that to happen. Killing the pledge would be easy. After all, he'd killed ten others. With the exception of one, he'd held no regret. With this pledge, regret would not come into play, at least not on his part. The pledge's father?

Looking at the pledge, at the similar traits the puke shared with his despicable father, he lifted a shoulder. "You will eventually leave. In what fashion? That will be up to you."

"I don't understand," the pledge said in a rush and continued to pull on his chains. "If it's money you're after, my father is wealthy. He can give you—"

Gripping the stinking, pitiful puke by the throat, he slammed him against the rock wall. "I want two things from your father." Ignoring the disgusting odor, he leaned closer and tightened his hold. "His son and his...confession."

Eyes bulging and watering, skinny face purpling, the pledge's chains knocked against his arms as the boy tried to pry his hands away. Spittle frothed around his cracked lips. He opened his mouth and whispered, "Please."

Releasing the pledge, he took an immediate step back, then reached for the garden hose. "Understand something. Unlike your father, I am not a sadist. I abhor brutality and under normal circumstances, I'm not prone to violence." Against his palms the garden hose pulsated, the pressure of the water mirroring the mounting force, the overwhelming need for revenge straining every fiber of his being.

"My dad's not a sadist," the pledge shouted as tears streamed down his sunken cheeks.

"I've seen your academic records. I doubt you even know the definition of sadism." He shook his head. "It's a wonder you managed to gain entry to the university. I suppose having a father who had not only graduated from Wexman, but has extremely deep pockets, helped." Mentioning that he'd played a part in the pledge's admittance to the university seemed, at this moment...gratuitous. "Hmm, well, enough of that. Time for your morning toiletries."

The pledge opened his mouth as if to speak. Sure that the boy would defend his cruel father, he aimed the nozzle of the garden hose at the puke's face and sprayed. With the water pressure on high, he coated the pledge's head. The boy squeezed his eyes shut, turned his head from side to side. He kept the nozzle aimed at his head until the pledge finally opened his mouth and drew in a ragged breath. Water hit the puke straight in the mouth. He coughed and spat, threw his body against the wall.

Satisfied and certain the righteous puke would say nothing further with regards to his father, he directed the nozzle to the rest of the boy's body. After he'd sprayed his lower half, and hopefully washed away some of the stench, he turned off the hose.

The pledge continued to cough and sputter, but now shivered, his body shuddering with tremors. A shiver ran through him as well. The basement temperature had dropped overnight and he worried it might become too cold for his pledge. Death by hypothermia wouldn't work in this instance. The boy's death would have an effect no matter what, but if his death came from the abuses of Hell Week, the effect would be that much sweeter.

He pictured the agony, the utter desolation the pledge's bastard father would experience once he saw his only son dead. His rotting corpse showing the evidence of the horrors the boy would endure. The same horrors *he* had endured twenty-five years ago.

No, death by hypothermia wasn't an option. He moved the space heater a little closer to the pledge. Close enough to offer intermittent moments of warmth, but far enough that the pledge couldn't do anything foolish with the heater. Not that the boy could move his feet far, but erring on the side of caution had helped him sustain the last nine Hell Weeks.

Nostalgia wrapped around his heart. That this pledge served as his tenth Hell Week astonished him. The English proverb, time flies while you're having fun, came to mind. Like the powerful, fast moving current of the Menominee River, time had swiftly swept past him. He'd spent the five years after his own tortuous Hell Week planning his revenge, then the next nineteen years hoping his plans would erase the memories and give him the power and control he'd needed.

According to another English proverb, time heals all wounds. He'd gamble that the person who had fashioned the absurd proverb hadn't experienced what he had twenty-five years ago. Physically, he'd healed. Psychologically? The shame, the terror...the sheer degradation had never left him.

As he stared at the pathetic puke, imagining the father's revulsion, shock and overwhelming grief once he saw his son's corpse, he realized there might be some truth to that English proverb after all. This pledge, his death, would heal him. The father's tears would cleanse him. It might have taken twenty-five years, but he would have righted the many wrongs he'd suffered.

Smiling, he coiled the hose, then climbed up the ladder. After he placed it into the utility room and turned off the faucet, he snagged a towel, then he returned to the basement. "I'm afraid our time has come to an end," he said, drying his hands and moving toward the pledge.

While the boy continued to shake violently, he met his gaze. "P-please...I...won't t-tell."

"Silly puke," he chuckled. "I'm not going to kill you. Don't forget, fish is on the menu for this evening's dinner." He took the towel and wiped the pledge's face. "No, what I meant was that our time has come to an end...for now."

"You'll be back," the pledge said, not with fear, but with... expectancy.

He stroked the towel over the pledge's hair. "You're worried I'll leave you to rot in the basement. Strange. I would think you'd rather I leave you alone."

The pledge's chin wobbled and tears filled his eyes. "I don't want to die like this," he said and jangled his chains.

Smiling, he tossed the towel over his shoulder, then walked backward toward the ladder. "I told you I was a man of my word and you believed me, yes? Well, my dear puke, I promise that you won't die like this." He swept his hand around the former root cellar with the dramatic flair of a thespian, then turned off the lantern. The basement now bathed in blackness, he stepped onto the ladder and began his ascent. When he reached the top, he said, "No, you won't die like this. But after tonight, you will wish you had."

As the pledge screamed, he sealed the trapdoor.

CHAPTER 8

RACHEL LEANED INTO the leather seat, enjoying the Lexus's butt warmer, but loving the way Owen clenched his jaw even more. His "crabby face" gave her pleasure, especially with the way he'd treated her last night. Screw him. Who was he to say whether or not she could or should mix business with pleasure? Who was he to judge her or assume Jake wasn't interested? Again, she wanted nothing to do with Jake. Although not hard on the eyes, and a nice, intelligent guy, he just didn't do it for her. Why Owen did, she still couldn't be sure. He'd shattered her confidence when he'd left her under the mistletoe last year, and had knocked her ego down a few pegs last night with his assumptions.

Still, she couldn't help the deep satisfaction warming her more than the Lexus's seat. She might not have the skills of a field agent, but she could read people. Owen normally kept his emotions hidden behind a smile or joke. This morning, he hadn't hidden anything. He'd been clearly ticked off. She'd assumed his anger had something to do with her blowing off his advice about Jake. Once Jake had entered the House of Joy, she'd realized she might be wrong. With the way Owen had acted—surly came to mind—toward Jake, if she didn't know better, she'd think he was...jealous.

No. That made zero sense. Other than their make out

session under the mistletoe, which he'd abruptly blown off, he'd never showed any interest in her outside of CORE.

She chanced a glance at him. He sat straight, as if someone had slipped a yardstick down his sweater, clutching the steering wheel, his jaw shoved forward, and his eyes narrowed on the road. Back at Joy's, he'd narrowed his eyes at Jake, too. At the way the sheriff had draped his arm along the back of her chair.

Jake *had* been sitting a little too close. She hadn't thought much of it, though. He was a nice guy. They'd had a nice conversation last night. Maybe that was the problem with Jake. He was just too damned *nice*.

Slipping the pencil from behind her ear, she placed it into her mouth and bit, then reached in her computer bag for her notepad. Rather than worry about Owen and whatever might have him wearing his crabby face, she should be thinking about their upcoming interview with Dean Xavier Preston, and the questions they would ask him.

"*Must* you chew on that thing," Owen said, breaking the silence. "It's not only hell on your teeth, but annoying."

"*I'm* not annoyed by it," she said. "Besides, what do you know about teeth? Oh, wait. That's right. You went undercover as a dentist when you were in the Secret Service, so now you're an authority."

"Har, har. And I didn't go undercover as a dentist…I was an oral surgeon."

"Oral surgeon? Then in that case you must know what you're talking about." She gnawed on the pencil, exaggerating her bite. "Did you look over the list of questions I have for the dean?" she asked and flipped open the notebook.

"I did and added a few suggestions."

Thank God, she thought and slipped the pencil from her mouth. The interviews with Bill Baker and Professor Stronach had given her some confidence, but after they'd brainstormed some ideas this morning, the nervousness she'd felt yesterday had returned, knotting her stomach. They had little to no evidence, only "what if" possibilities. Like what if the kidnapper worked for the university?

She read his suggestions. *Why didn't the university hire extra security during Hell Week, or cancel Hell Week altogether?* "These are good questions." Why hadn't she thought to ask them? Probably because, last night when she'd written them down, she'd been too busy thinking about Owen. How sexy he'd looked. How much he made her want more than she should. And that kiss.

The kiss she should have completely forgotten about and purged from her memory.

Instead of traveling down that path again, she added a few more questions, based on ideas generated from their brainstorming session, to the notepad. If she ever expected to be promoted to a field agent she had to keep her concentration on the investigation, not some juvenile longing for a man who—

"So," he said.

"So, what?"

"So you could have let me apologize."

"For?"

He glanced at her, his blue eyes unreadable. "What I said about you and Jake. I…was out of line. I'm sorry."

He didn't sound sorry. At all. This wasn't an honest, heartfelt apology. She knew Owen, had witnessed the superficial persona he'd sometimes don when dealing with certain clients. Right now, he was being superficial. Could he honestly be jealous of Jake? Again, that made no sense to her.

"Hello, I just apologized," Owen said. "Aren't you going to at least say something?"

"You pulled a DB move, but I'm over it."

"Great, so now I'm back to being a douche bag."

She cracked a smile. Last year, after the mistletoe incident, she'd begun the whole DB, douche bag thing. Yes, absurdly childish on her part. In her defense, he *had* acted like a total DB. Any guy who kisses a woman, then turns around and walks out with another on his arm deserves the nickname. Not only was it rude, but…heartbreaking.

As she looked out the window, her smile fell. Up until that

night, she'd had the biggest crush on Owen. Hell, she'd been half in love with him. She'd looked forward to working with him whenever he'd been at the CORE offices, she'd anxiously await his calls whenever he'd been on assignment. Considering he tended to travel more than the other agents, she'd spent a considerable amount of time on the phone with him. Before, and even after, the mistletoe incident, he was usually the first person she spoke with in the morning and the last person at night. There had been nights, too numerous to count, where she'd lie in bed talking Owen through an investigation. She loved brainstorming, especially with him. They usually ended up on the same page, which had resulted in success.

Too bad he'd screwed with her heart. They made a great team. Based on the way he'd kissed her, the passion he'd ignited—passion she had no idea she'd been capable of experiencing—they probably would have made even better lovers.

"I told you I wouldn't call you a douche any more. While what you'd said was definitely out of line, I'm over it." A lie, but there was no way she'd tell him the truth. He wouldn't laugh in her face if she confessed she'd been crushing on him for years, or if she told him that he'd hurt her that night under the mistletoe. Owen had too much class, was too considerate of others. Still, opening herself up, exposing her emotions could strain their professional relationship. She loved her job and didn't want her juvenile crush to interfere with her career.

"Good. So…what did you and Jake talk about last night?"

Furrowing her forehead, she looked away from the passing trees and stared at him. "The investigation."

With a slight shrug, he asked, "Anything else? It sounds like you two were on the phone for a while. Plus with the way he was acting this morning…"

"And how was that?" She tapped the pencil against her lips, while her stomach did a huge somersault. He had her head confused, her heart hopeful and her body suddenly sizzling with anticipation. *Holy crap.* Owen was jealous of Jake. Why else would he drill her about the conversation she'd had with the sheriff, or comment on how Jake had acted at Joy's? Then again, she'd read Owen wrong before, had thought he wanted to take their relationship from professional to personal. She'd been dead wrong then, and was likely wrong now.

Rubbing the back of his neck, he said, "I don't know...friendly."

"What's wrong with friendly?"

"Nothing. Except if he'd gotten any friendlier, his tongue would have been down your throat."

"Oh my God," she half-laughed, while her stomach did another flip. "You seriously did not just say that."

As they drove through the gates of Wexman University, he smiled. "I was just joking. I mean, if you like Jake and he likes you..." He turned the Lexus onto the main drag, which led to the university's administration buildings.

Disappointment had her stomach knotting. She glared at him for a moment. So much for the jealousy theory. "The dean's office is in that building," she said instead of commenting on his 'if you like Jake and he likes you' crap. Apparently the whole business and pleasure BS he'd spouted off about last night had been his way of giving her advice. Now he was giving her his blessing. How freaking thoughtful.

After he parked the Lexus and killed the ignition, he turned to her. "I know it's none of my business, but—"

"You're right." She opened the car door. "It's none of your business who shoves their tongue down my throat or makes my headboard slam against the wall. So why don't we just pretend this and last night's conversation never happened. Now, let's go meet the dean. I want to wrap up these interviews in time to have lunch with my brother."

Owen caught a quick glimpse of her ass just before she slammed the car door. As much as he'd like to blame Jake for yet another wedge between Rachel and him, he couldn't. After she'd blown him off this morning, he'd told himself to let it go. To not bring up last night. With the image of Jake touching her, kissing her, coaxing moans from her sassy, sexy mouth, he couldn't leave well enough alone. And now he could add slamming headboards into that cluster of erotic images that didn't include him.

After he climbed out of the Lexus, he followed Rachel into the building. They signed in with the security guard, then took the elevator to the dean's the third floor office. As they traveled in the elevator, and then walked through the third floor halls, Rachel remained quiet. The tension radiating from her body thickened the air and served as a reminder that he'd screwed up again where she was concerned. He'd rectify things, though. Later. Right now he needed to regain the professionalism he'd lost when he'd questioned Rachel's intensions with Jake.

They approached the dean's secretary. "Good morning," Rachel greeted the other woman, then gave her their names.

The secretary rose. "Dean Preston is expecting you," she said as she escorted them to the dean's office. After delivering a soft knock against the closed door's etched glass, she turned the knob and motioned for them to enter.

Dean Xavier Preston sat behind an enormous, and incredibly neat, mahogany desk. With a nod and a wave of his hands, he silently invited them to sit in the two leather office chairs before him.

Once they'd settled into their chairs, the dean folded his hands, then raised his dark brows as if he had no clue as to why they were there bothering him.

"Thank you for taking time to speak with us," Rachel said, breaking the strange and uncomfortable silence.

To his way of thinking, he didn't see any reason Rachel needed to thank the dean for anything. The man should be on his knees begging them to make Hell Week go away.

"You're welcome," he replied, then leaned into his leather chair. "I'm not sure how much help I'll be with your investigation, but Richard has asked me to make sure that you're given top priority."

"Richard Lambert, the university president?" Rachel asked.

"The very same," the dean said with a slight tilt to his mouth. "I'm not only acting on his behalf while he's away, I do have my own duties to carry out. So, please, let us make haste with this..." He waved a hand. "Conversation."

Rachel glanced at him, then looked to the dean. "Of course. I'd like to start this *conversation* by asking why Mr. Lambert, or any of the past presidents for that matter, hasn't put an end to Hell Week? I would think that after the first few disappearances—"

"Ms. Davis, is it?"

She nodded.

"You have to have full knowledge of the workings of the university to comprehend all that is involved. It's not simply up to Richard, or even myself, to decide whether or not the fraternities and sororities can no longer hold their annual traditions."

"Then who makes that call?" she asked.

"The alumni," he said, his tone laced with disgust. "I've been with the university for eighteen years, first as a professor, and now as dean. Richard is the third president I've worked for. He and the other two had tried numerous times to cancel Hell Week."

"But the alumni wouldn't hear of it," Owen commented.

"Correct. And alumni support is important to this university."

"By support, I'm assuming you mean their donations," Rachel said.

The dean nodded. "As you know, this is a small, private university. Eighty percent of our students participate in either a fraternity or a sorority. That being said, many of our alumni are also former members of these *juvenile* organizations. If we went against the alumni and cancelled Hell Week...not to sound cliché, but it would be like biting the hand that feeds."

Owen understood the dean and president's dilemma. When he'd been a student at the University of Virginia, he'd had friends who had joined the same fraternities as their fathers. These fathers, all wealthy, prominent men, had played a vital role in some of the University of Virginia's fraternities and had also been hefty donors to the university itself. Donations from alumni, like these fathers, had helped keep the tuition down, enrollment up and the athletics department financially sound. "Am I wrong to assume the alumni are aware of the missing students?" Rachel asked.

"Your assumption is correct. I have been with each president when they addressed Wexman's alumni association on the subject. Unfortunately, the general consensus has always been against doing away with Hell Week. Personally, I'd love to go further and not only rid this campus of such a ridiculous, childish tradition, but close the doors of every fraternity and sorority."

Rachel leaned forward. "Yes, these missing students must take a toll on campus life. Honestly, I had no idea about the disappearances until they involved my brother."

"Yes. Missing students aren't advertised and never will be. The alumni, and even the president who had served prior to Richard, believed that eventually the disappearances would stop. Warning potential families of past occurrences that may or may not recur doesn't make sense. To that, I agree. After two years with no disappearances, I had hoped the university had seen the last of the Wexman Hell Week. Unfortunately..."

"What about campus security?" Rachel asked. "If you can't shut down Hell Week, couldn't the university supply extra security, for not only that week, but maybe the entire month of January? I would think that preventative measures—"

"Preventative measures have been taken." Dean Preston adjusted his navy and gold tie. "A generous alumnus donated all of the necessary equipment to upgrade many of the campus buildings door locks, as well as dozens of security cameras."

Rachel pulled out her note pad. "Can you give me the name of this generous alumnus?"

"I'll have my secretary phone you with that information."

"I find it hard to believe that you have no clue who donated the security upgrade and cameras. I also find it odd that nearly every one of these upgraded locks malfunctioned the night before my brother and Josh Conway were kidnapped."

Owen hid a smile as the dean narrowed his eyes at Rachel.

Even this blowhard had to admit that Rachel not only pointed out a damning coincidence, but that checking into the background of this *generous* alumnus was important to their investigation. With little leads, they needed to cover all conceivable angles. Could be this alumnus had attended Wexman twenty years ago and had intimate knowledge of the disappearances.

"Ms. Davis," Xavier Preston began in a placating tone. "I understand that you are emotionally vested in this investigation."

"Of course I'm *emotionally* vested," Rachel said, her voice rising. "I allowed my brother, my only family, to attend this school. If I had known about these disappearances...that would have never happened."

She cleared her throat, then looked at her notepad. Owen had the sudden urge to put an end to this interview, take her outside and hold her. He hadn't considered that she might feel guilt over her brother's beating. Which she shouldn't. The university didn't advertise the disappearances, so how could she know?

She was a hacker, CORE's forensic computer analyst and one of the brightest women he'd had the pleasure of knowing.

Shit. Yeah, he could understand the guilt and why she might hold herself accountable for what had happened to her brother. Rachel had been known to hack into places thought impenetrable. Knowing her hunger for knowledge, he'd bet she had researched the hell out of Wexman University. Why didn't these Hell Week disappearances pop up on her radar? He'd ask her later after they were through with the dean, which would hopefully be soon. Other than the alumnus who had donated the upgraded security equipment, the dean wasn't giving them anything new.

"You said you've worked at the university for the past eighteen years," Rachel began, her voice strong, the earlier emotional edge gone. "Is there anything you can add to help us find Josh Conway? Anything unusual that might have happened on or around the other disappearances?"

Xavier Preston leaned forward, set his elbow on the desk, then rested his chin in his palm. Seconds later he covered a yawn, then when finished said, "Didn't the sheriff share this information with you?"

Rachel sent him a quick smile. "He certainly did, but thanks to his predecessor, there wasn't much to share."

Still appearing uninterested in the conversation, Preston leaned back in his chair. "He wasn't a particularly good sheriff, or man for that matter. He tended to let incidents...slide. Wexman Hell Week wasn't of particular interest to him."

Rachel raised her auburn brows and half-smiled. "Given the little evidence we have prior to Sheriff Miller's retirement, that doesn't surprise me. Why do you think that was? I mean before Jake Tyler took over as sheriff, Miller had dealt with seven missing person cases. I would think this would hold top priority to him."

"Yes, one would think. Unfortunately Tom enjoyed the title of sheriff and the power and respect that went with it, not the actual responsibility of being an agent of the law." He checked his watch then said, "As for your initial question, I have never noticed anything unusual before, during or after the disappearances."

"Weren't the students nervous?" Owen asked. "With the university's history, I'd think every male freshman preparing to join in on Hell Week would have taken extra precautions and made sure—"

"Have you spoken with students or the Bola *Townies*?" Preston asked, the last word said with a hint of loathing. "If you haven't had the chance, you really must. I assure you that you'll find their answers both ignorant and amusing."

"How so?"

"I'm sure you're aware of the ridiculous Bigfoot festival slated for this week. If you're a believer, I apologize in advance for insulting you. Legends are unverified stories that are thought to be historical. Some people believe Bigfoot is no different than Wexman Hell Week."

"You're beginning to sound like Professor Stronach,"

Rachel said with a shake of her head. "Thank you for speaking with us. We won't take anymore of your—"

Dean Xavier Preston stood, pressed his fists against the desk and leaned forward. Although not overly tall, Preston's build surprised Owen. With large shoulders, arms and chest, the dean looked as if he lifted weights on a regular basis. He also looked seriously pissed and offended. Gone was the dean's earlier boredom. As he glared at Rachel, his face red and twisting in outrage, his lip rose in a snarl. If the dean's anger hadn't been directed at Rachel, Owen would have thought his reaction almost laughable. The man had gone from haughty and dispassionate to gnashing your teeth mad in a split second. All because Rachel had compared him to Stronach, another haughty ass.

"Hear me well, Ms. Davis. I am nothing like Stronach, and you will do well to remember that," the dean said, his voice low, threatening. He stared at her, his ice blue eyes hard and unwavering. Then he blinked, pushed away from the desk and smoothed his tie. "I believe that what has been happening these last twenty years is as real as you and I. My comparison to Bigfoot was made to prove a point. You'll find that once you talk to the students and town residents."

"I apologize if I offended you," Rachel said and rested the notepad on her lap. "And not to sound...obtuse, but could you explain what point you were trying to prove?"

If he wasn't mistaken, Owen swore Rachel had purposefully goaded the dean. And he liked it. For once, someone else besides him was in the hot seat.

"My point," the dean echoed. "The Townies are afraid. The students..." He shook his head and sent them a wry smile. "Young people think they are invincible. They also tend to make light of a serious situation. Like the Townies, they should be afraid. What if whoever is behind this changes direction? Kidnaps a sorority girl? A professor? A Townie?" He returned to his seat. "As I said, some people will compare what's happening here to legends like Bigfoot. But this is no legend or myth. This is a reality. Stronach foolishly believes otherwise."

Rachel picked up her notepad again and glanced at the small page. "Just a few more questions…would you be able to supply us with a list of university employees?"

"I'll have human resources give you what you need."

"Thank you. Would you happen to know how many employees live in the area year round?"

"Again, that would be a question for human resources," Preston said, then checked his watch again.

Owen suspected their time with Dean Xavier Preston was just about up, which was fine by him. They'd likely have better luck discovering something new if they talked with human resources and campus security.

Rachel slipped her notepad and pencil into her coat pocket, then looked to him. "I think that's just about all, right?"

Nodding, Owen stood. "Thank you for your time. Is human resources in this building?"

"Yes, first floor. I'll put a call to that department now. I'll also be sure to have my secretary give you the name of the alumnus who had donated the security equipment."

"Thanks," Rachel said as she moved toward the door. With her hand on the knob she stopped and faced the dean again. "One thing I forgot to ask…do you happen to know when Wexman University's no hazing policy went into effect?"

"Finally, one question I can answer without wavering doubt," the dean said and stood, then also moved toward the door. "Twenty-five years ago."

"Twenty-five…" Rachel furrowed her brows. "Do you know why? I mean, did something happen to prompt the policy?"

"Yes, Ms. Davis. Very bad things."

"Well, that was interesting," Rachel said as she closed the Lexus's door. "What did you think of the dean?"

"I like him about as much as I like Stronach."

She chuckled. "Right. At least Preston's secretary and the

guy in human resources were helpful." She waved the paperwork they'd been given on their way out of the building, then stowed it in her computer bag. "Thing is, I could have saved us the time and just hacked into their system."

"So why didn't you?" he asked as he drove the Lexus out of the parking lot and onto the campus's main drag. "I could have done without dealing with Xavier Preston. Even his name sounds pompous."

"I know. Can you believe how he snapped when I compared him to Stronach?" She shivered. Xavier Preston, though not much more than a half a foot taller than her, probably outweighed her by fifty plus pounds, which she suspected, based on the man's build, to be mostly muscle. The way he'd gone from calm, almost bored, to angry and threatening, had not only taken her by surprise, but scared the crap out of her, too. Yes, she'd gone through basic training while in the Army and had knowledge of hand-to-hand combat training. But that had been over ten years ago. Since leaving the Army, when she had the time, she'd hit the gym and taken Spinning classes and worked with free weights. Cycling and weight training weren't exactly going to help her with self-defense, though. The other CORE agents carried a gun, maybe she should, too.

"Yeah, the way he popped off on you surprised me. Preston has some obvious issues with Stronach," Owen said, while the unsettling thought of walking around with a loaded weapon, or the possibility of having to use a gun wrapped itself around her brain.

"There's an understatement," she said as an insecurity she wasn't prepared for coiled through her. Thinking about using a gun, defending herself, being placed in a vulnerable situation had her questioning her original goal of becoming a CORE field agent. If Owen hadn't been in the dean's office, would things have been different? While she doubted Xavier Preston would have gone a little bat shit crazy and knocked her on her ass, the possibility had been there. If she did begin to work in the field—alone—did she really want to place herself at risk?

Her brother's bruised and battered face flashed through her mind. Just as she couldn't imagine her life without Sean, based on their relationship, she was certain he felt the same.

Owen slowed the Lexus, then pulled into the parking lot of campus security. After he parked and cut the engine, he turned to her. "Are you okay?"

She glanced away from his probing gaze. "I'm fine. Why?"

"You haven't said much since we left the dean's office."

"It was a five minute drive."

"Rachel, in the last four years, I've spoken to you more than anyone else. I know how fast your brain and mouth work. You could probably recite *War and Peace* in its entirety in five minutes." He grinned. "Maybe even less."

She gave him a half-smile, then toyed with the three small earrings running up her right ear. He was right. Her mind and mouth did work fast. Unfortunately her mind wasn't presently on the case, but on whether or not she was even cut out to be a field agent. She could tell Owen this. He was right. The two of them knew each other well. Although he'd hurt her last year, and she made it a point to berate him whenever possible, strange as it sounded—even in her own head—she couldn't deny their friendship.

If she set aside her personal issues with him, and looked at Owen as a friend and agent, not a sexy guy she wanted to fulfill every wildest fantasies with, she was certain he wouldn't judge her for her insecurities, but would likely offer valid advice. Only she suspected Owen would report back to Ian once this investigation ended and give his opinion as to whether she could handle working in the field. She didn't want him to be in any position where he had to pass judgment on her or play a deciding factor should Ian consider unshackling her from her desk. Adventure had been the reason she'd joined the Army. Intrigue had drawn her to CORE. After working for the private investigating firm, witnessing what the other agents dealt with, if she could step away from the desk, she could have that thrilling combination of adventure and intrigue.

Drawing in a deep breath, she finally said, "Again. I'm fine.

I was thinking about the alumnus who donated the extra security equipment. I'm anxious to find out when he attended Wexman. I also think Preston's parting remark about the incident that brought on the universities no hazing policy is...interesting." She really hadn't been thinking about any of those things, but she should have been rather than deciphering the mixed emotions ping-ponging through her head.

"I'd definitely like to know what Preston meant by 'very bad things.'" He leaned his head against the headrest. "I didn't buy his BS about not being able to disclose what had happened."

"Right. It's not as if we're dealing with juveniles. Anyone involved in the hazing would have been at least eighteen. If the sheriff had been involved, they would have been treated as an adult."

"And if they were arrested, their record would be public." He smiled. "Well, they'd be easier for you to hack anyway."

She reached for a pencil to chew on, then thought better of it. Her habit annoyed Owen. Besides, her jaw had begun to hurt from the bad habit. "True," she said when she really wanted to tell him she wished she were back in CORE's evidence and evaluation room. Her domain. Her sanctuary. There she had access to CORE's state of the art equipment, multiple TV screens she used to manipulate video footage or photographs for viewing evidence, along with her good old-fashioned dry erase boards where she could list details as she brainstormed either solo or with fellow CORE agents.

"It'll take a little longer to hack into the necessary databases, but it can be done." She grabbed the pencil anyway, but stowed it in her coat pocket right beside her notepad. "I'll work on it when we get back to Joy's."

He opened the car door. "Let's get at it, then."

Moments later they stood in campus securities command center. While Rachel loved a bit of melodrama, describing the small room that housed two computers, three TV screens and a dispatching radio as a "command center" came off a little over-the-top, even for her. She'd spent many boring years working in the Army Major Intelligence Command Center and couldn't help being a little snobby over the term. At this point though, she could care less what Wexman's head of security, Adam Lynch, called this room. With so few leads to go on, she hoped the security cameras from her brother's residence hall had caught something useful.

"As you can see," Lynch said and motioned to the TV monitors. "Our system isn't much better than what you might see in a fast food restaurant, but it's better than what we had a few years ago."

"Dean Preston mentioned an alumnus had donated equipment to the university," Owen said.

Lynch bobbed his balding head. "That's right. We were able to add cameras to each building entrance and exit, plus we were able to give every building an electronic lock. Not every room, mind you. We could only stretch the donation so far. But we did make sure the dorms and graduate apartments had the electronic locks."

"With those electronic locks," Rachel began. "Can you tell when someone swipes their keycard?"

"I…ah…" Lynch rubbed the back of his neck.

"Yes," a short, portly man said as he entered the room.

Chuckling, Lynch said, "Well, there you have it. Charlie, here, is more tech savvy than I'll ever be."

She turned to Charlie. "We were told that the electronic locks began to fail—campus wide—Friday night."

"That's right. We've been able to restore seventy percent of those locks, but obviously still have work to do."

"Did those failing locks include the dorm rooms?" Owen asked before she had the chance.

"Only at Stanley Hall. It's a co-ed residence hall for freshman and sophomores."

And where her brother and Josh lived.

"The thing is," Charlie continued. "Not every lock at Stanley Hall failed."

"That's right," Lynch said. "Half of one floor went down along with the entire second floor."

Her brother's floor.

A chill swept through her as she asked, "Can we look at Saturday night's video footage of Stanley Hall?" There was no need to pull records of the time and number of keycard swipes made to Sean and Josh's room. If the kidnapper had been behind disengaging the locks, he'd done so the day before the boys had gone missing. Had the locks been working when they'd disappeared, they would have had evidence that someone had gone back to their dorm room to remove the two liter of Mountain Dew and empty any other valuable evidence from their trash can.

Charlie gave her a big smile. "Adam told me you were coming. I have it cued up for you on screen one," he said and pointed to the monitor.

She stood next to Owen and watched the screen. According to the date and time stamp, Charlie had begun the footage from Stanley Hall at five on Saturday evening.

"I've already gone through this," Charlie said and began to fast forward the video. "Nothing interesting happens until around six."

Like scurrying little mice, students quickly came and went. All the while, the security guard, Bill Baker, remained at his post. As the time stamp zipped through, anxiety rolled through her stomach, then slithered through the rest of her body when Charlie slowed the video.

Owen moved closer, his familiar scent comforted her, while his nearness alone had a calming effect. Something she needed right now as she watched her brother and Josh's images on the monitor. Just as Bill had explained to them, the boys stood in the foyer for a moment and spoke with the security guard. After they left, Bill swayed, then used the desk to steady himself. He shook his head, then suddenly covered his mouth, bolted from the foyer, running toward the hallway and out of sight of the security camera.

Seconds ticked by on the time stamp. As she was about to ask Charlie to speed up the recording, the handle of what appeared to be a broomstick filled the screen. It tipped and swayed, then fell out of sight.

Slowly, the view changed. With each second that passed, the residence hall foyer began to tilt and climb, the objects on camera fading away. First Bill's desk, then the bulletin board behind it...up the wall, past the clock. Then the slow ascent stopped and the screen filled with nothing but white stucco.

Her skin crawling with goose bumps, she rubbed her arms and whispered, "Oh my God."

Owen touched her elbow. She looked at him, at the concern in his eyes and nodded. "I'm good."

His jaw tightened as he turned toward Charlie. "When did you realize someone had tampered with the security camera?"

"Today, when I was cuing the video for you. I told the guard on duty at Stanley Hall to not touch it. Thought maybe you might want to check it for fingerprints."

She shook her head. "It's obvious they used something to move the camera."

Owen shoved his hands into his coat pockets. "Looked like a stick of some sort. Maybe a broom or a mop. Other than custodians, who would have access to supplies like that?"

Lynch leaned against the doorjamb. "Us and maintenance. But I can tell you that no one from custodial or maintenance services were in that hall Saturday evening."

"With the broken locks, I would think maintenance would be working overtime," Rachel said.

"They weren't able to repair any of them without certain parts, which were placed on special order late Friday night and didn't arrive until yesterday morning. So, no. Maintenance wouldn't have been there to work on the locks, and there were no other service orders placed that day. As for custodial, Saturday's they're gone by three in the afternoon."

"Does your custodial service include cleaning dorm rooms?" Owen asked.

"No," Lynch answered. "We had an issue with students claiming things were being stolen from their rooms. So, now the students take care of their own cleaning. Even their bathrooms."

After thanking the security guards, Rachel followed Owen out of the building and to the Lexus. Once inside the car she finally succumbed to her bad habit and pulled the pencil from her pocket. "This isn't good." She chomped on the pencil. "At all."

"Nope," Owen agreed as he backed the Lexus out of the parking spot. "If custodial and maintenance weren't at Sean's residence hall that night, and the camera didn't pick up anyone other than students entering the building, that means only one thing."

"Right. Either a student is copycatting Wexman Hell Week or—"

"Our kidnapper has himself a new recruit."

"Meet our longest resident," the occupational therapist, Olivia, said to a young, pretty brunette as they entered the room. "Jane Doe has been with us for approximately eighteen months." Olivia glanced my way and offered a pleasant smile, her plump cheeks dimpling.

The brunette shifted her dark eyes over my limp body as she moved closer to the bed. "Hello, Jane. I'm your new speech therapist, Elizabeth Cormack, but everyone calls me Bunny." With a wry smile tilting her lips, she said, "Long story. I'll fill you in another time. For now..." She turned back to Olivia. "I'm anxious to find out all I can about Jane so we can begin our therapy. It's my understanding that you've taken care of her from the start."

"Yes," Olivia began while I wondered how the pretty speech therapist ended up stuck with what sounded more like a pole dancer's nickname. "Even when Jane was in a coma I was working with her, exercising her limbs, stretching her muscles." Olivia's pale, green eyes softened as she looked at me. Other than Lois, she was the only other person I've come to care for in this shitty, smelly, drab institution. She'd shown me nothing but kindness and based on her patience, her compassion, even her frustration at my lack of progress, I honestly believe she cares and wants to see me walk out of this place.

"Can we pretend I've never seen Jane's case file?" Bunny asked. "I'd love to hear about her from someone who's familiar with what she's been through."

"Her file is missing things anyway."

"How so? All of the medical records—"

"Right, all of the medical information is in there, but the rest..." She patted my numb leg. "My brother's a Marietta cop, but he's got a good friend who's a deputy with the Washington County Sheriff's Department."

With the way the bed had been raised, I was able to watch the confusion crossing Bunny's face, along with Olivia's sympathy and disgust. She should be disgusted. Not for what had happened to me, but the reasons it had happened in the first place. My father had once told me that you make your own bad luck. While bad luck hadn't brought me to southern Ohio and this dreary institution, blind ignorance, self-absorption and vengeance had. Unknowingly, I had brought this on myself. And while I'd love nothing more than to walk, talk and take a huge bite of a greasy cheeseburger, sometimes I wonder if maybe I deserve my fate. That being mute, paralyzed and forced to wear a diaper was the universe's way of meting out the ultimate punishment.

Bunny nodded and sent Olivia a sly smile. "So, you know her story."

Olivia stepped away from the hospital bed, peered into the quiet hallway, then closed the door. "This stays between us, understand?" she asked, her tone hushed, conspiratorial.

"Absolutely," Bunny replied with a firm nod.

My stomach jumped and anticipation burned through my veins. I knew what had happened to me, but have never heard anyone actually discuss it. Of course there had been moments when things weren't exactly clear. Black, fuzzy passages of time that to this day made zero sense. To be able to hear every gory detail...

"Eighteen months ago, my brother's buddy, Dave, got a

call from a farmer. Apparently the farmer was brush hogging his fields when he found our Jane. At first, the farmer thought she was dead. I guess she was covered in—oh my God, Jane," Olivia cried and pounded on the nurses call button.

The room tilted. Olivia and Bunny's voices became tinny. Panic caused my vision to blur and distort. For the first time since they'd removed the ventilator, every breath suddenly became a struggle. Suffocating, constricting, as if an anvil sat on my chest.

"Where's the nurse?" Olivia shouted, gripped my shoulders and pulled me upright.

Choking. I couldn't draw enough air into my lungs. Tears streamed down my cheeks, sweat coated my face. The tips of my fingers tingled, itched to claw at my throat, to shove the weight off my chest. Gasping, panting, I wildly shifted my eyes, searching for help, for a lifeline to ground me, to keep me sane.

"I'll go find her," Bunny said and moved for the door.

Desperation clawed inside my belly, coiled like a spring, then snapped. A low, guttural groan escaped from my parted lips, stopping Bunny. I didn't need the nurse or doctor. They would only dope me up on some sort of potent, prescription cocktail that would render me comatose. A panic attack. I've silently suffered through a multitude of them since waking from the coma. It would pass. They just needed to give it time. They couldn't let them drug me. I needed to hear—

The door burst open and a nurse rushed into the room, followed by the doctor. My breathing grew ragged and my chest constricted even more when I saw the needle. Searching the room, my gaze locked onto Bunny's. Jaw clenched, her dark eyes clouded with concern, she hugged herself, then winced when the doctor stabbed the needle into my arm.

Never breaking eye contact with her, I fought to keep awake. But as the medication filtered through my veins, my heart rate slowed, my chest lightened making it easier to breathe, and my eyelids drifted shut.

The doctor said something inaudible, the nurse and Olivia

responded, their words completely lost from the buzzing in my head. Then the sweet scent of lavender cocooned me, followed by a warm puff of air against my cheek.

"You're safe, Jane. I promise," Bunny whispered against my ear. Her soothing voice, a subterfuge of comfort and hope, washed over me like a hot, summer rain with the expectation of a powerful, destructive thunderstorm to follow.

As I began to surrender to the mind-numbing drug the doctor had given me, Bunny's gentle, calming voice mingled with my would-be killer's familiar, hate-filled eyes. In the dark, foggy recesses of my mind, they coagulated, then congealed. Bunny was wrong. I would never be safe.

I was supposed to be dead.

CHAPTER 9

RACHEL MADE HER way down the second floor hallway of Dixon Medical Center carrying a bag filled with sandwiches they'd bought from a local deli. She'd brought her brother his favorite, and while the tangy aroma of his corned beef Rueben mixed with the pungent odor of antiseptics, her stomach still growled. A reminder she'd skipped breakfast this morning.

"Hungry?" Owen asked as he fell into step beside her.

She absently touched her stomach. "Starved."

"You should have had Joy's blueberry pancakes. I swear they're like crack. I couldn't get enough of them."

Half laughing, she stopped at Sean's hospital room. "Crack, you say? Interesting. Omelets are on the menu for tomorrow morning. If there's any mushrooms in them, you might want to think twice. Otherwise you could end up on a trip down the rabbit hole."

He chuckled, then motioned toward the door. "After you."

Ignoring the tingle in her belly that had nothing to do with her need to eat something, she glanced away from him, from his sexy smile and entered Sean's room. Then froze. "Oh my God." She rushed to the bed. The linens had been torn away. Fluids of some sort soaked the remaining sheets, while sensors that had been attached to her brother dangled from the machine in the corner like limp spaghetti noodles. The chair she'd sat on during her last visit rested haphazardly on its side as if it had been kicked out of the way.

Panic weakened her knees, yet her instincts, her love for Sean, forced her feet to move. She rushed back to the doorway where Owen stood. "Something's wrong. Something's very wrong." That earlier tingling in her belly morphed into a spasm of dread. The room was a mess, her brother was missing. Now that she thought about it, she hadn't seen his doctor, let alone any nurses. Terror clenched her by the throat. She rushed past Owen.

He gripped her by her upper arms and pressed her against the wall before she could make it through the threshold. "Look at me," he demanded with a slight shake. "Focus on me."

She stared into his blue eyes, into their calm, serene depths. Composing herself, she fed off his strength.

Thank God he was here with her. The last time Sean had been in the hospital, she'd been on her own. Young, scared, her mother nowhere to be found. Like that night fourteen years ago, she could use a friend, a shoulder to lean on, someone to help ease her fears.

"Are you with me?" he asked, loosening his grip and rubbing her arms.

With a nod, she drew in a shaky breath.

"Good. I'm sure there's a logical explanation. Come on. Let's find some help."

Holding her by the elbow, he escorted her back down the corridor toward the nurse's station. A woman, dressed in scrubs, exited a nearby room. Taking the lead, Owen approached her and asked about Sean. The empathy softening the nurse's eyes took Rachel's fears to new heights. She leaned against Owen and ran a trembling hand across her forehead.

"My brother..." He was all she had left in the world. No other family. Very few friends. What would she do without him?

"Is stable," the nurse said and touched Rachel's shoulder. "He's been moved to ICU, which is located—"

Without allowing the nurse to finish, Owen took Rachel's

hand and led her into another wing of the medical center. He didn't speak, didn't slow his pace until they reached ICU. When they spotted Sean's doctor, Owen tightened his hold on her hand.

"I was about to call you," Dr. Gregory said when he reached them.

"What happened?" she asked, fighting the tears, the fear.

"He was doing fine...I spoke with him this morning. We were supposed to have lunch together." She raised the bag of sandwiches to emphasize, then dropped it on the nearby nurse's station.

Dr. Gregory nodded. "I know. He told me earlier. But about an hour ago, he started to experience severe chest pain. Although he has broken ribs, where he was experiencing the pain concerned me. I immediately ordered a CT scan and—"

Never letting go of Owen, she stepped forward. "Please, what's wrong with him?"

"He developed a blood clot in his spleen. I can't be sure, but I'm assuming the clot is a result of his injuries."

"Blood clot," she echoed. "How serious?"

"He's stable and the medication we have him on will help shrink the clot. I do want to keep him in ICU for the next twenty-four to forty-eight hours, though. After that, I'd still like him to stick around for another day or two. Run additional scans to be sure there's no other complications."

She glanced at Owen, who gave her hand a gentle, reassuring squeeze. "Can I see Sean?" she asked the doctor.

"Of course." Dr. Gregory motioned toward a room kept private by a dark gray curtain. "He's sleeping though. If you'd like, I can have someone call you when he wakes."

"I'd appreciate that," she said. "I don't want to disturb him, but I do want to peek in on him." As she began to move toward the curtain, dragging Owen with her, she paused and turned to the doctor. "Can you stick around for a few minutes? I want to talk to you."

After Dr. Gregory agreed, she pulled back the curtain and stepped into the small, dimly lit room. Sean lay prone on the hospital bed, sensors stuck to his chest, an IV dangling from the top of his hand. The glow of the heart monitor cast eerie shadows across her brother's pale, bruised face. She finally let go of Owen, took her brother's hand in hers, then leaned over him. After kissing his forehead, she whispered, "I love you." And as she stared down at him, images of Sean flipped through her mind. Like a slideshow of snapshots, they came and went. Bringing a smile to her face and tears to her eyes.

So many memories. So many good times.

In that moment she realized there had been more good times than bad, despite living with or without their mother. That she should embrace those wonderful memories, shove aside the resentment she held against her mom and move forward. And as she gazed down at her brother, gently touching his red hair with the tips of her fingers, she also realized that today was the first time she'd told him she loved him in…she couldn't remember. She also couldn't figure out why she hadn't bothered to say those three little words that spoke volumes.

With a sigh that bordered on relief, she stepped away from the bed and looked to Owen.

"If you want to stay with Sean, I can handle the investigation."

With a slight shrug, she shook her head. "I'd rather keep my mind busy. And find whoever did this to my brother."

After giving her brother a final glance, she stepped out of the room. Dr. Gregory waited for them at the nurse's station and offered a small stack of papers as they neared. "Sean's toxicology report," he said and handed them to her.

"What were the results?" she asked, not in the mood to try and decipher the report.

"He had Rohypnol, as well as trace amounts of chloroform, in his system."

She stared at the first page of the report, the letters and numbers blurring as fury settled deep in her soul. Sean had been drugged and beaten. Now he was in the ICU of some Podunk hospital recovering from a blood clot. They needed to find the man behind her brother's kidnapping and beating. More importantly, they needed to find Josh Conway before he suffered a much worse fate.

With renewed determination, she squared her shoulders and cleared her throat. "What about Bill Baker? Do you have his results yet?"

Dr. Gregory furrowed his brows. "Bill Baker?"

She hid her irritation. "I called you about him yesterday. We wanted a tox screen done on him, too."

"Yes, that's right." The doctor nodded. "I haven't received anything on him yet. Let me check with the lab." He leaned over the nurse's station and grabbed the phone.

While Dr. Gregory made his phone call, she pretended to review her brother's test results. Now that the initial shock of Sean's blood clot had somewhat abated, she couldn't help the embarrassment rolling through and making her cheeks burn. The way she'd clung to Owen, physically leaned on him...what had she been thinking? She'd treated him like crap for the past year. Yeah, while fantasizing about all the things he could do to her body. And sure, they *were* what she'd considered friends before the mistletoe incident.

Still.

She glanced at him, then quickly looked back to the tox report. The concern, the tenderness in his eyes cranked up her heart rate. Even with Sean lying in a hospital bed with a blood clot, Dr. Gregory standing a few feet away trying to find Bill's toxicology report, nurses buzzing around ICU, and a killer/kidnapper on the loose, she couldn't help but wonder if she'd been wrong about Owen. If maybe he wasn't a douche bag bottom feeder of the dating pool. She thought about Jake. About Owen's actions and reactions every time the sheriff was around, and wondered. What would it be like to have Owen? Not just in her bed, but in her life as more than a coworker or platonic friend. Before her mind could wander down that path, Dr. Gregory hung up the phone and turned to them.

He shook his head. "Bill never came in yesterday."

"Are you sure?" Rachel asked, confused. Bill had been

more than happy to agree to the testing and they'd watched him make a call to have his shift covered. Plus, he'd been so worried about losing his job. She might not know the man, but she doubted he'd blow off the testing and risk being fired. "Maybe the lab tech made a mistake."

"No. They were slow yesterday. The tech I just spoke with was there all day and knows Bill. I guess they went to school together."

"Well, maybe something happened that prevented him from making it in," she said, now beyond irritated with Bill and also a little...suspicious. Maybe Bill was somehow involved and had faked his symptoms the night the boys had been taken. Maybe *he* had laced Sean and Josh's Mountain Dew with Rohypnol and knew that the drug would be undetectable after a certain period of time. If that were the case, and he had pretended to have been under the influence, then purposefully skipped the blood test, he would have gotten away with aiding and abetting a kidnapping. Even if he showed up for testing today, and had truly been drugged, the Rohypnol would have already worked through his system, which ruined any possibility of linking Bill to the boys.

Based on her perception of Bill, she didn't truly buy her own suspicions. Until they found him, though, considering Bill a possible suspect topped her empty list.

After thanking Dr. Gregory, and one last check on her brother, they left Dixon Medical Center. Once they were in the Lexus, Owen shoved the key into the ignition, but dropped his hand on his lap.

"What?" she asked, embarrassed to meet his gaze. She'd been too clingy earlier and had crossed the line from coworker to intimate friend.

"Why don't I take you back to Joy's."

"Because?"

"Rachel, look at me."

When she did, her heart tripped. The concern brightening his eyes and hardening his face made her want to crawl onto his lap, have him cradle her in his strong arms and sleep the day away. Pretend her brother wasn't in ICU and that Josh Conway wasn't still missing.

"What's on your mind?" he asked, then reached over and lightly touched her jawline with the back of his fingers.

After swallowing the lump in her throat, she said, "I'm wondering about Bill."

Dropping his hand away, he shook his head. "I don't want to talk about Bill, or Hell Week. I want to talk about you. That was a big scare and I want to make sure you're okay."

She stiffened. "If you're worried my head isn't in the investigation, don't. I'm fully capable of handling this case despite Sean's injuries."

He placed his head against the headrest and looked to the Lexus's ceiling. "I've never doubted you." He momentarily shifted his gaze to her. "Ever." His eyes back on the ceiling, he released a deep sigh. "I don't know what changed between us. But I still...care."

Care? A soft flutter flitted through her stomach. She went back to her earlier thoughts, imagining her and Owen as more than coworkers. Then quickly shoved them aside. If he'd cared about her, then why had he dismissed her after their kiss? As disbelief, insecurity and self-doubt crept in, she crossed her arms over her chest. "I don't know what you're talking about."

She really didn't. He'd stood by her side in ICU, offering his comfort and strength when she'd needed it the most. Other than that moment, he'd been...different memories from the past year moved through her mind. Owen teasing her with an endless supply of number two pencils, bringing her back cheesy, yet sweet, souvenirs from his trips, and gift cards for her birthday and Christmas. Then there was Jake. How Owen acted toward the sheriff every time he was around or they'd discussed him. Like he was...jealous?

She stared at his profile. At his strong jaw and firm lips. An emotion she couldn't name bubbled to the surface and tightened both her throat and chest, along with remnants of the hurt and anger he'd caused a year ago. She'd considered herself half in love with Owen up until the mistletoe incident.

After that, she'd tried to hate him. Tried to stop the fantasy, the hope. And she'd succeeded. Or so she thought. Being here in Bola, stuck together, dealing with not only Sean's injuries, but the investigation, had all of those emotions—whatever they were—jumbled, uncontrollable, indiscernible.

When he finally looked at her, the intensity in his eyes made her breath hitch. She'd caught that same look from him before, just before he'd kissed her under the mistletoe and also last night, when she'd worn that skimpy camisole. A flurry of awareness burst past the anger she'd tried to harbor against him. Past the fear of losing the one person she could depend upon—her brother. Even past her self-doubts about running her first investigation and finding Josh Conway. All of those things, while still raw and fresh, and still at the forefront of her mind, suddenly didn't compare to the one thing she selfishly craved the most. Owen. His touch. His friendship and, God help her, his love.

Damn it. She'd never stopped loving him. And for the first time in her life, she wanted to pretend she had no one else depending on her or measuring her capabilities. She no longer wanted to be the brainy geek seeking action and adventure. She wanted to be wanted, needed and yes…loved. But love was an emotion she had a hard time understanding. The love of a sibling or a child—which she considered Sean more of a son than sibling—wasn't the same as the love shared between a man and woman. Her mother hadn't given her the best example of what a solid, loving relationship looked like. If anything, her mom had tainted her outlook on relationships, and had made her cynical, wary and completely ill at ease when it came to opening herself up to not only the opposite sex, but people in general.

A slow smile spread across his lips as he swept his gaze over her breasts, then mouth before meeting her eyes. "You really don't know what I'm talking about, do you?" He leaned forward, eating the distance between them, but then stopped inches from her face, her lips. "I care about you and everything that matters to you." With the pad of his thumb, he caressed her lower lip. "I…miss your smile, Rachel. You don't show it off as much anymore. Now you have more to worry about with Sean in ICU."

He eased back, leaving her lip tingling and her body craving for more of his touch.

"I want you to know that I'm here if you ever need me. You don't have to deal with all the crap life throws at you alone." He turned the key and the Lexus hummed to life. "Okay, where to?"

As he moved to shift gears, she touched his hand and stopped him. "When Sean was five, my mom had decided she'd met the newest love of her life. His name was Elvis, and yes, that was his given name, and he was a Baptist minister." She shook her head at the memory and ignored the sadness that seeped into her heart every time she thought about that period in her life. "Elvis invited my mom to go on *tour* with him." She half-laughed. "That's what he called his preaching schedule. His *tour*. So, while my mom and Elvis spread his word, I took care of Sean."

"You were what? Seventeen?"

Boy, did he have an excellent memory. "Yeah, but it wasn't a big deal. I was already used to taking care of Sean and the apartment, it didn't matter if our mom was around or not. Honestly, I don't think it mattered much to Sean, either. Except, while she was playing the role of the minister's mistress, Sean ended up in the hospital with appendicitis."

He flipped his wrist and held her hand. "That had to have been scary."

"Scary and awful. He'd been up all night vomiting. It was Halloween and I figured he'd eaten too much candy. Thank God I didn't slough his symptoms off as a bad case of pigging out on too many sweets. His appendix had already burst when I finally got him to the ER."

"I'm so sorry you had to deal with that," he said and tightened his hold.

She looked at their joined hands, shocked at how natural the small, yet intimate gesture felt, and even more shocked that she'd decided to share this story with Owen. Something she'd never shared with anyone. Sure, her mom eventually found out when she'd remembered to call and check on them. But she'd had no one. No other family, no close friends to call. She'd been alone, her only companions hopelessness and fear. Today, while she'd been scared when she discovered Sean had developed a blood clot and was placed in ICU, she hadn't been alone. She'd had Owen by her side, taking the heavy weight of that same hopelessness and fear off of her shoulders.

He'd waved the white flag. Told her he cared. To what extent, she couldn't be sure, but he was willing to help her ease some of the burdens she normally faced alone. Because of this, or maybe because she was still half in love with him, she'd wanted to share a part of herself with him. Give a brief example and explanation as to why she found it difficult to unload all of her emotional crap.

"I know. If I had waited through the night and took him to the pediatrician the next day..." A shiver ran through her as she remembered how small and fragile Sean had looked lying in the hospital bed all those years ago, followed by another as she pictured him currently lying in ICU. "That was a very dark time in my life," she said, before she lost her nerve. "When Sean was born, I looked after him as if he were my baby. My mom would joke about it to her boyfriends, but the reality was...*is*, that I am the only constant in his life, just as he's mine."

"And right now you're struggling with whether you should stay by your brother's side, or do your job." A statement, a fact, not a question.

She looked at him and realized she hadn't given him enough credit. He was more intuitive than she'd thought. Then why hadn't he acknowledged the kiss that had, in her mind, destroyed their friendship and flattened her ego?

"I am," she answered honestly.

"But what do you think Sean would want you to do?"

"Find Josh, which is exactly what I intend to do."

He smiled and gave her hand another gentle squeeze.

"Then let's do it."

Nodding, she returned the smile, then looked to their joined hands again. "Thank you." She wanted to expand, explain her gratitude, but her throat had tightened and her eyes stung with tears, making it difficult to speak. Besides, she'd already exposed too much, and saw no need to bring on the waterworks.

Owen released her hand, then shifted the Lexus into reverse. He wasn't quite sure how to respond. Saying "you're welcome" would ruin the point he'd tried to make. Although, she'd exposed a bit of herself, he still didn't think he'd made that point clear. That he cared about her in ways that went beyond friend and coworker.

As he drove into town, Rachel called the sheriff and told him they'd meet with him at his office. While she made the call, he replayed their conversation, wondering if he should have been more assertive. Then again, he'd shocked himself when he'd told her he cared about her. He hadn't planned on saying anything about his feelings for her, but she'd looked so defeated and scared. The protective side of him had taken possession of his mouth and wanted her to know that no matter what, he had her back and would always be there for her.

When they'd been inside the hospital and she had leaned on him, something strange had swelled inside his chest. Whatever it was had surged through his body and mind. Making him more aware than ever that this pint-sized, abrasive woman had done more than heighten his sexual interest. He still wanted to touch her, hold her, bury himself between her sexy legs, but he realized that might not be enough. There were a half dozen women back in Chicago he could have sex with, but the thought of them didn't do anything for him. Sex was sex, and he'd had plenty of it in his lifetime. But to make love to Rachel...

He needed to maintain a grip on reality. Despite being the one to bring up the caring thing, jumping from caring to love, or sex to love, was more of a leap than he was prepared to own. Hell, for all he knew, Rachel could be into Jake, not him. Before he'd even considered showing or telling her just how deeply he cared, he needed a sign, some confirmation that she felt the same. He'd been burned once.

Those last days with the Secret Service tore through his mind as he pulled into the parking lot outside the sheriff's office. His job, his career with the Secret Service had been blackened, tainted by the lies of a promiscuous teenager. Ian Scott had given him the opportunity to rebuild his career. Owen loved working for CORE and although he had an overwhelming need to be with Rachel, in every sense, he wasn't sure if he was willing to risk his career. If he made an advance, and she rejected him, their work relationship could be jeopardized, maybe even his career with CORE. Rachel didn't realize she wasn't expendable. Her skills were beyond measure, and over the years, Ian had made that fact clear to the rest of the team. He, on the other hand, could easily be replaced.

A dark blue Yukon pulled up alongside the Lexus. As Owen glanced over, Jake exited the SUV, then walked around the front toward the Lexus's passenger side. Rachel quickly climbed out and closed the car door. While she exchanged words with Jake, who stood way to close to Rachel, Owen's earlier thoughts about jeopardizing his career over a woman evaporated.

Fucking Jake.

Owen slammed the Lexus's door harder than he'd intended, and not bothering to hide his irritation, he approached Rachel and Jake. As he moved, each exhale caught on the frigid air in bursts of white puffs. He probably looked like an angry, snorting bull preparing to skewer his victim, but he didn't care. The sheriff and his *friendliness* toward Rachel needed to stop. The only thing Jake could offer her was a few days of...pleasure.

That last thought made his head throb. Consumed him with an immense amount of jealousy and anger. Who Rachel chose for her pleasure wasn't up to him, but he certainly wasn't about to step aside and allow Jake to be the frontrunner. Not that this was a race to see who would wind up in her bed. As much as he wanted to strip her naked and bury himself inside of her, she meant more to him than just another sexy woman to ease his lust. From the moment he'd met her, Rachel's big, green, teasing and inquisitive eyes had captured his attention. Her sassy mouth, tempting lips and feisty attitude had intrigued him. Her intelligence and quick wit floored him. Over the years, he'd come to know her, care about her, and unlike Jake, he lived in Chicago and only minutes from Rachel. He could do more than simply warm her bed. He could offer her stability and friendship, maybe even more if she let him.

"It's freezing out here," Jake said as he gave Rachel's shoulder a squeeze. "Let's head inside. Sounds like you two have had a hell of a day and it's only lunchtime."

A spark of satisfaction rolled through him when Rachel slipped away from Jake and held her coat tight against her throat. When she shivered, that spark fizzled and turned as frosty as the icicles hanging on the eave of the building. In the short amount of time they'd been exposed to the cold, her ears and nose had grown red and he wished he could kick his own ass for putting his jealousy and anger before her needs.

By the time they entered the sheriff's cluttered office, Owen managed to refocus on the reason why they were here. Although Rachel, the way she messed with his head and body, wasn't far from his thoughts, and he still wanted to knock Jake on his ass, he honed in on something he and Rachel hadn't had a chance to discuss. Bill Baker.

"Sean's going to be okay, right?" Jake asked as he took a seat.

Rachel nodded. "Dr. Gregory also had Sean's tox screen, which contained Rohypnol and trace amounts of chloroform."

"And Bill?"

"That's one of the reasons we wanted to meet with you. Bill never showed up at the lab yesterday."

"Which makes me wonder if he's somehow involved," Owen said, then shrugged when Jake shook his head. "Think about it. If he had helped drug Sean and Josh—"

"No way," Jake said. "I know Bill. He might be a little flighty at times, but he's no killer."

Rachel stared at him for a moment, then a small smile tilted her lips as she turned her attention back to the sheriff. "We obviously don't know him like you do, but I have to agree with Owen." She raised a hand as Jake opened his mouth. "Hear me out. Just this morning, we all agreed that the kidnapper likely has access to the residence hall where Sean and Josh live. Now, Bill's age doesn't fit. I'm thinking he's what? Twenty-five?"

Jake nodded. "That's probably about right."

"Okay, so Bill isn't the mastermind, but maybe he's an...assistant."

"Or patsy," Owen said.

She snapped her fingers. "Exactly. To me, Bill seems like the kind of guy who wants a position that comes with respect, authority or even power. He couldn't get that with the military, and he said you wouldn't hire him on as a deputy."

"That's right." Jake folded his arms across his chest and leaned into his chair. "He's related to half the town. Bill's a good guy, but I couldn't run the risk of his family taking advantage of him. I still don't think Bill would involve himself with a kidnapping."

She sent Jake a small smile. Owen knew that smile, knew what it meant because he'd been on the receiving end more times than he cared to admit. She wanted Jake to shut his mouth and let her speak.

"As I was saying," she said, her tone cool, clipped. "I got the impression Bill was looking for respect." She turned to Owen. "Remember he mentioned picking up the extra shift because he needed the money?"

"Right, to pay off his truck."

"Then when he ended up sick, he couldn't find anyone to cover his shift."

Owen knew where she was going with this because he'd had the same thought. "Rather convenient. When we're done here, I want to call campus security and find out who was originally scheduled to work the Saturday night shift at Stanley

Hall, along with the names of the other security guards."

"Right," she said. "Let's find out how much of an effort Bill actually made to cover his shift."

Jake looked between them. "I can't believe you two seriously think Bill is involved." He pulled out his cell phone. "Instead of playing a 'what if' game, I'm going to call him and find out why he didn't show up for the tox screen."

Rachel arched a brow and looked toward Owen. He suppressed a smile, along with smug satisfaction. With the way Rachel had acted toward Jake just now, maybe he'd allowed his jealousy to cloud his judgment. Maybe Rachel just wasn't into Jake, period.

Frowning, Jake set the phone on the desk. "Went right into voice mail. Hopefully he'll call me back."

"Do you have the number for campus security?" Owen asked Rachel, wanting to move this conversation along and leave. Time was ticking. They had several more people to interview this afternoon, and he figured Rachel would want to stop at the hospital when they were finished.

She pulled the notepad from her coat pocket, flipped through the pages, then rattled the number off to Jake. While the sheriff spoke with someone from campus security over the office landline, Owen leaned toward her. Ignoring her citrusy sweet scent and how it made him want to kiss the slender column of her throat, he said, "I think the receptionist working here today is the RA we wanted to interview."

"Abby Zucker?"

He nodded, lingering close longer than necessary. "Might as well get that out of the way while we're here, then we can head back to the campus and make our meeting at the fraternity house."

Before she could respond, Jake said, "Bill didn't show up for his shift today. While I've got Adam Lynch on the phone, do you want to ask about Saturday night's schedule?"

"Absolutely." Rachel leaned across the desk and took the phone from Jake, stretching the curly cord taut. Minutes later, she handed the phone back to the sheriff. "Well, it turns out that Bill didn't lie about picking up the Saturday night shift. He also *did* try calling other security guards to help him cover that same shift when he took sick."

"Bill's a legit guy," Jake said.

"Then why didn't he show up for the tox screen or go to work today?" Rachel pinched her chin between her finger and thumb, then leaned forward and rested her elbow on the desk. "Jake, do you know his family well enough to call and ask them if they've seen Bill?"

"He's Joy's nephew," Owen reminded her. "We could ask her to make some calls. But the reality is, he's a grown man. Could be he left work yesterday, stopped at the liquor store before heading to the lab, then maybe tied one on. He might be sleeping off a hangover as we speak."

"Maybe, but that doesn't sound like something Bill would do. I've never known him to be much of a partier." Jake stood and pocketed his cell phone. "Unless there's anything else, I've got to run. Professor Stronach and some of the local business owners are butting heads over where they're going to set up the stage for the bands scheduled to play during the festival." With a roll of his eyes, he shook his head. "The temperature is supposed to be in the thirties during the day and the teens at night. Why the hell they need bands playing...anyway, I'll call Bill's dad and cousin. They all live on the same street, so they'd know where to find him."

"Do you mind if we talk with your receptionist?" Rachel asked. "We don't want to interfere with her job."

"Not at all." Jake shrugged into his coat, then frowned and shook his head. "I'm sorry. I've been so caught up in the stupid festival...you obviously spoke with campus security. Did they have a security tape from Stanley Hall?"

Rachel quickly filled the sheriff in on what they'd discovered, then finished by telling him the potential lead they'd gained from when they had spoken to the dean.

"I remember when the university updated their security system." Jake leaned against the doorjamb. "That was about a year ago."

Standing, Rachel moved toward the door. "I'm still waiting for the dean's secretary to send me the donor's info. Did you meet the man or know the name of his company?"

"Sorry, I didn't meet him and can't help you out with that one. Preston might be a little pompous, but he's good about getting back to you. At least in my experience."

Rachel looked as if she planned to say something more, but instead took the lead and headed down the hall toward the main foyer. Abby Zucker sat at the aged desk, the phone to her ear. As Jake waved good-bye to them, and Abby remained on the phone, Owen pulled Rachel to the far corner of the foyer.

"What is it?" she asked him.

"Jake."

Fidgeting with her earrings, she glanced away. "I told you I'm not going to discuss—"

"No. That's not where I was going...back in his office, what were you going to ask him?"

After looking over his shoulder toward where Abby sat, she moved a little closer. Her scent teased him, made him ache for a taste of her.

"Preston said Wexman put their no hazing policy in effect twenty-five years ago. I was going to ask Jake if we could look through files dating back to then, hoping Tom Miller actually filed a report."

"Then why didn't you? I can't imagine you'll find any records online. Then again, I can't imagine the former sheriff bothering to leave much of a file behind, either."

"No kidding. But I wasn't going to try and hack into Dixon County's system anyway. Well, at least not yet. It's been my experience that very few counties have arrest records dating back that long, available online." She looked to Abby again, then keeping her voice quiet, said, "But Wexman University might have what we need."

"How so?"

"Wexman might be located in the backwoods of a small town, but they have an excellent engineering program. They also were one of the first universities to develop a Computer

Engineering program. When Sean and I were researching colleges, I found out that Wexman was actually ahead of its time. Case Western Reserve offered the first computer engineering degree program in the early 1970s. Other colleges followed suit years later and by—"

"Rachel, focus."

With a quick smile and nod, she said, "Sorry. Right. Okay, Wexman had their program up and running by 1975. I'd bet your next paycheck that if I happened to go into Wexman's system, I might come across *something* that could shed some light on what happened that was *so* bad that they issued their no hazing policy. I bet I could also get a list of male students who were enrolled at the university between fifteen and twenty-five years ago, as well as faculty members."

"That's a lot of people to check up on, don't you think?" While he liked fitting pieces of a puzzle together, what she suggested sounded more like time consuming busy work.

"Not if we match those people to local addresses or those living within a relatively short driving distance to the university. We can also cross-reference those names against seasonal residents, too."

"I still like the idea of a faculty member or another university employee being behind this."

"Me, too." She pursed her lips. "I want to go to the bar."

"A little early in the day for a drink, don't you think? Not that I'm judging," he added with a smile.

Grinning, she looked over his shoulder again. "A drink does sound good...looks like Abby is getting off the phone." When she met his gaze again, she whispered, "Joy made it clear that she and other locals are afraid. Jake said the same thing. I was thinking we should start talking to the Townies, especially before Bigfoot rolls into town with his groupies and things get too chaotic. Maybe someone remembers hearing about what happened at the university twenty-five years ago."

He liked that idea more than the time consuming busy work. What he'd like even more was to pretend Sean had never been beaten, that Josh was safely tucked away in his dorm room studying for an upcoming test, and that he and Rachel were exploring something other than possible kidnappers.

She nudged him with her elbow. "You take the lead on this one. Seems like these college girls like you."

Owen stared at Rachel's backside as she approached the desk. He could care less about those college girls. There was only one woman he wanted.

CHAPTER 10

RACHEL'S EYES SLOWLY adjusted to the dim room, her nostrils flaring on a deep inhale. "Heavenly." The mouthwatering aroma of fried bar food hung heavy in the air, along with the hint of musty, stale beer. The only thing missing was hazy cigarette smoke. Obviously the owners of River's Edge had upheld Michigan's no-smoking law. Not that she'd fire one up, but the secondhand smoke might have helped settle her nerves.

"Do you want to sit at a table or the bar?" Owen asked.

She looked to the bar and immediately recognized the tall, gangly man she'd seen hanging around outside of The House of Joy. "Do you know who that guy is? The one wearing the earflap hat."

Nodding, Owen leaned closer. The smells from the bar were immediately replaced by his woodsy, outdoorsy scent. She thought about camping again. Something she really didn't enjoy, but would consider if Owen were her tent mate. Even though she continued to tell herself to let it go—this emotional turmoil she experienced every time he was near her or she thought about him—that was proving difficult. He was constantly around and she constantly thought about him.

"That's Walter Eastly," Owen said. "I met him this

morning. He lives at Joy's, has for the past fifteen years."

"Don't you think that's strange? I mean, living at a boarding house for that long?"

"I think *we* look strange just standing in the doorway."

Smiling, she shoved a hand in her coat pocket. "You're right, people are staring. Come on. Introduce me to Walter. Maybe he can help get a few of the Townies to talk to us."

As she followed Owen through the crowd, she caught her reflection in the mirror hanging behind the long bar. An assortment of liquor bottles and neon beer signs hid parts of the mirror, but not enough to block her and Owen's images. Seeing herself next to him had self-doubt creeping into her head. Owen had already removed his heavy, wool coat and carried it on his arm. He'd dressed casually today. Jeans, black boots, and a dark gray sweater, which unfortunately didn't hide his muscular chest, arms and wide shoulders. Nope, that sweater just kept her imagination wandering down a road she had no business taking. And as she walked behind him, periodically checking their reflection in the mirror, she realized they, in no way shape or form, looked good together. Owen had the kind of physique and good looks that deserved a woman with similar qualities. She pictured a few of the women she'd seen him with over the years. Tall, leggy, super slender, gorgeous women. As much as she'd like to deny it, those women had looked good on Owen's arm and were definitely what people would call eye candy. Whereas if she were the one on his arm, she'd be the opposite. Whatever that might be...eye fungus? Eye broccoli?

Smacking into Owen's wide back, she rubbed her nose and fought the heat rising to her cheeks.

He quickly turned and grabbed her arm. "Are you okay?"

"I'm fine, just wasn't paying attention." Because she was too busy thinking about him and opposite terms for eye candy. Pathetic.

He eyed her for a moment, then took a small step back, revealing the gangly man in the earflap hat. "Walter, this is my partner—"

"Shorty," Walter said on a raspy chuckle and offered his hand. "Heard all about you from Joy. Wish I could have been there when you told her what's what."

Shaking his weathered hand, she smiled. Not the least offended by the nickname. With Walter's teasing, hazel eyes and easy grin, "Shorty" came off like a term of endearment.

"It wasn't all that exciting," Rachel replied, then began slipping out of her bulky coat.

Owen pulled out an empty barstool and offered her a seat next to Walter. As she placed her coat on the back of the stool, the patron next to her scooted over to allow her more room. Before she could thank the man, he said, "You one of those investigators from Chicago, then?"

She glanced at Walter, who raised his beer mug to his lips. "It's no secret," he said, then sipped his beer. "People been wondering when someone was gonna come here and try to figure out what the hell's going on at that school."

Standing behind her, Owen draped his arm on the back of the stool and insinuated himself between her and Walter. "We heard it's not just the school that needs some figuring." He caught the bartender's attention, a big, meaty man with a beer belly and more hair on his arms than his head, then turned to her. "Drink?"

She nodded, but before she could tell him what she wanted, Owen rattled off the order to the bartender. As she waited, the man next to her leaned into the scuffed, yet shiny wooden bar and said, "One don't got anything with the other."

"The hell you say." Walter shook his head. "Hey, Percy, you might want to cut off Duke. The whiskey's gone and burned the last of his brain cells."

The bartender—Percy she assumed—set a drink in front of her. "Vodka tonic with a splash of Rose's lime juice." Then after giving Owen his whiskey and Coke, he turned his attention to the man on her right. "Walt's right, Duke. Gramma didn't walk herself into the river."

A chill snaked along her neck, leaving goose bumps in its wake. Ethel Rodeck was the eighty-six-year-old Townie who had gone missing three years ago, and apparently Percy's grandmother.

Using the skinny black straw, she stirred her drink. "Are you referring to Ethel Rodeck?" she asked, wanting to back her assumption.

"That's right."

"And you think someone kidnapped your grandma?"

Percy tossed a rag over his shoulder. "Nope. I think someone killed her."

Next to her, Duke groaned, along with the man sitting to his right. "Here we go again," Duke scrubbed a hand down his face, then tapped his empty glass. "I'll have another. Hell, if I gotta listen to this story again, I'll need it."

Percy drew his dark, bushy eyebrows together and glared at Duke while he poured whiskey into the glass. "It ain't a story. It's a fact."

"What makes you think someone killed her?" Owen asked.

"A few months before she died—"

"Disappeared," Duke said.

Percy leveled Duke with an "I'm going to kick your ass" scowl, and said, "Gramma started complaining about seeing someone in the woods. At first she assumed it was a hunter, which pissed her off. She didn't allow no hunters on her property."

Walter chuckle. "Ain't that the truth? If Gramma Rodeck caught you poaching on her land, she wasn't afraid to pull out her shotgun and let you know you were trespassing."

Smiling, Percy nodded. "The old woman was a piece of work."

"Bat shit crazy, more like it," the man next to Duke said.

"Terry." Percy slammed a fist against the counter. "You mock my Gramma again and I'll show you how bat shit crazy we Rodecks can get. Understand?" He turned his attention back to her and Owen. "Now, I'll admit that Gramma was about ankle deep into dementia. But she was still taking care of herself just fine."

"*Did* she see a hunter on her property?" Rachel asked.

"Don't know what she saw for sure. But, one stormy night she couldn't sleep and said she took a cup of tea and sat out on her covered porch." Another smile, but one Rachel noticed didn't quite reach Percy's eyes. "That was a few days before she went missing."

"We'd gotten an early warm spell that spring," Walter said. "Remember? Snow melted, started flooding some areas…"

"That's right," Percy continued. "Her house didn't sit far from the river, but was far enough away she didn't have to worry about being flooded. That wasn't why she was sittin' out that night, though. Along with her tea, she had her shotgun. As Gramma told it to me, she sat on that porch sippin' tea and watching the woods. Waiting."

Percy's story was starting to sound like a tall tale. Praying he wouldn't say Bigfoot, she asked, "What was she waiting for?"

"The Hell Week killer."

Owen reached for his drink. "Do you know why she thought this killer was roaming her property?"

Sliding his gaze to Walter, he pulled the rag off his shoulder and leaned forward. "Cuz a few months after a kid goes missing, she always sees the killer wandering in her woods."

"I absolutely do not want you to show me how bat shit crazy you can get," Owen said with a half-smile. "But I'm wondering…how could she see him at night? And how was it that she was certain that what she saw was the person who killed the kids?"

"I was wondering the same thing," Rachel said. "Did she ever consider that maybe it wasn't the killer, but one of the missing kids? Or maybe an animal?"

Laughing, Duke nudged Terry. "Or Bigfoot."

"Walt's the expert," Terry said, a big grin splitting under his graying mustache.

"Yeah, him and that asshole professor," Duke added with a shake of his head. "Hey, Walt. Didn't you track Bigfoot onto Gramma's property?"

"Watch your damn mouth," Percy snapped. "There's a lady present."

After Duke apologized into his drink, Percy said, "I understand how all this probably sounds. Thing is, my Gramma lived on that property for over sixty years. When kids started going missing, she and my Granddad started seeing…things." He shot Duke and Terry a look before either man said a word. "Always the same thing. A few months after a kid goes missing, they'd spot someone or something on their property. Usually late evening or on a clear night. My Granddad would always go and check it out in the morning, but never found any tracks."

"Did your grandparents tell the sheriff?" Owen asked.

With a snort, the bartender shook his head. "Yeah, they told him. But Tom was useless. Never followed up on anything. Jake did that first year he was sheriff. Unfortunately, Granddad was dead for five years by the time Jake came to Bola. Gramma always kept watch, though, and she called Jake when she saw the man on her property."

"Strange time," Walter said. "That was the year those idiot boys pulled off the hoax that ended up costing the town the new traffic light and the high school the bleachers for the football field."

"Yeah." Percy nodded, his mouth set in a grim line. "Jake caught all kinds of hell when it wasn't even his fault."

"I'm still wondering how your grandparents knew whether what they were looking at was a man and not an animal." Rachel toyed with the napkin under her drink. If this was the type of story they were going to end up with from other Townies, then they were wasting their time. They needed real evidence.

A big grin spread across Percy's face as he looked to Walter. At that point, Rachel suddenly realized they were the butt of a joke. Furious, she picked up her glass, chugged her drink then slammed it on the bar. She looked to Owen. "I'm leaving."

Owen touched her shoulder and gently pushed her back onto her seat. "What's the problem?" he whispered into her ear. The vodka clearly had gone straight to her head. She had the sudden urge to tell Percy and Walter, even the two dicks, Duke and Terry, to go fuck themselves. She also had the urge to turn her face, ever so slightly and brush her lips along Owen's. Just a taste…

She jerked away before she did something she'd completely regret. "We're here to run an investigation, not be the butt of a joke." Reaching behind her, she fumbled around until she found her coat pocket, then she pulled out a business card. After handing it to Percy, she said, "If you have any *real* information that might actually help, give us a call."

Frowning, Percy looked at the business card. "That *was* real information."

"Really, then why were you all smiles to Walter when I asked how your grandparents knew they were looking at a man and not an animal?"

"Because Walter sold me a pair of night vision binoculars and happened to be there when I gave 'em to Granddad and Gramma for their wedding anniversary."

"Yep," Walter grunted, then chuckled. "You should have seen them two. They were hilarious. Shutting off all the lights and having people trying to hide around the house and yard."

She couldn't help smiling as she pictured an old couple playing with night vision binoculars. "Sorry. I seriously thought you were messing with us."

"Not a problem," Percy said and reached for her glass. "Ready for another?"

Although tempted, she shook her head. "Not yet…so after your grandpa passed, your grandma kept searching the woods with her binoculars?"

"Wasn't like that." Percy leaned against the counter holding all the liquor bottles. "She only did that after a kid went missing."

"A few months after, you mean?" Owen asked.

"That's right."

Rachel rested her elbow on the bar. "You said Jake only searched your grandma's property that first year he was sheriff. Why didn't he do anything after the last student went missing three years ago?"

Percy frowned. "Gramma went missing before Jake had the chance."

Interesting. If Percy's grandparents weren't bat shit crazy like Duke had implied, then could it be possible that they were witnessing the killer dispose of his victims? If so, why hadn't anyone found any evidence? And why kill the grandma? Did she see something she shouldn't have? Better yet, did she actually know the killer?

In the meantime, they'd gotten a bit off track and while Percy's story had taken a curious turn, she wanted to hear about the interactions between Wexman students and the Bola Townies. With so little to go on, they could use a good, *solid* lead.

"So, Walter," she began. "How long have you lived in the area?"

"Goin' on sixteen years." He nodded to Duke and Terry. "Those two and Percy have lived here all their lives." He lifted his beer mug. "I'd say the majority of the people around here have, wouldn't you guys?"

The three men grunted in agreement.

"How do people around her feel about the university?" Owen asked.

"Wouldn't want to see it shut down, if that's what you're asking," Duke said, then draped his arm over the back of his barstool. "I work at the mill, so it's not like I benefit from the school, but a lot of businesses in Bola do. Percy gets college kids in here on the weekends."

"That's right," the bartender said, with a nod. "Other than the missing kids and this festival coming up, I don't think any of us have an issue with the school."

She loved how Percy grouped the missing students with the Bigfoot festival. As if the festival was as bad as disappearing kids. Priceless. "What do you think happened to the kids?"

"Yeah, we're curious about any kind of theories the people in town might have," Owen said.

Duke pushed his empty glass toward Percy. "I know some

folks think these frat boys are doing some weird hazing crap. Things go bad...they try covering it up with this whole Wexman Hell Week thing."

"What do *you* think?" she asked.

"Might be some truth to that."

"Why do you say that?" Owen asked. "Wexman has a strict no hazing policy."

"Years ago there was a big mess at the school. Hazing gone bad. No one knows for sure what happened, it was all hush-hush."

"How many years are we talking?" Rachel asked, hoping Duke could shed some light on the elusive reasons for the original no hazing policy. The dean sure as hell was no help.

Duke glanced to Terry. "When was that...twenty...twenty-two years ago?"

Terry shook his head and looked to the ceiling. "That was the year—the same time of year, actually—that the boat dock caught on fire. Remember?"

Percy absently wiped the bar. "That's right. With everything happening in town, whatever happened at the university didn't matter much to us."

Which could also explain why the former sheriff hadn't done much about the bad hazing. "Do you remember exactly when this fire happened?" Rachel asked, hopeful they were moving in the right direction.

Percy's eyes widened. "Hell, now that I think about it, twenty-five years this January." He stopped wiping the counter. "That's weird, don't ya' think?"

Weird didn't begin to describe this case.

"What's weird is that professor pulling together this stupid Bigfoot festival," Terry said. "No offense, Walt."

"None taken," the other man said, then went back to his beer.

Rachel looked to Walter. "Why would you be offended?"

"Because in my spare time I look for Bigfoot."

Yes, weirder and weirder. "And what do you think happened to these kids?"

"I don't think any of them are alive, if that's what you're asking. And I believe Percy's grandma and granddad saw something they shouldn't. I also think that's why Ethel went missing."

"Because she saw something she shouldn't." Like maybe the killer disposing of his victim. But then where was the body?

"Right. I think someone's got it in for the university and taking those kids is their way of getting even."

The other men grunted, while the woman next to Walter said, "Sorry, don't mean to eavesdrop, but I think that's all a bunch of crap. My son lives overseas and he was telling me about these sex slave operations. I wouldn't be surprised if that's what's going on. Someone is taking those boys and selling them to the highest bidder."

"C'mon, Karen," Duke said. "You watch too many movies. That kind of thing don't happen 'round here. That's big city stuff."

The man next to Karen leaned across the bar and said, "You know what I think?"

"Oh, God. Here we go," Walter muttered, while the other men and Karen laughed.

The man stood and shot Walter a dirty look. "What? Everyone's okay with Walt claiming he's seen Bigfoot, but no one believes me when I tell 'em about the night I saw a UFO?" He threw down some dollar bills. "That's bullshit."

"No, you thinking you saw little green men is bullshit," Duke said, as the man waved a hand behind him and walked out of the bar.

Rachel looked to Owen who smiled and shook his head. "Interesting theories," she said.

"Very." Then Owen nodded to Percy. "How about another round, and put their next drink on my tab." Owen motioned to the three men and Karen.

"So." Rachel began to tick off on her fingers. "We have Duke's hazing gone bad theory, Walter thinks this is about revenge, Karen thinks we could be dealing with sex slave traders, and the guy who just left believes UFOs are involved.

Did I cover it?"

After a round of nods, she focused on Percy. "And you think your grandma disappeared because the killer believes she saw something she shouldn't."

After placing fresh drinks in front of her and Owen, Percy folded his hairy arms across his chest. "Exactly."

The only theory she could agree with was Walter's. Just this morning she, Owen and Jake had considered that the kidnapper/killer could be out for revenge. But why? What had happened to make him go after innocent students? She glanced at Duke and thought about his theory. Hazing gone bad. This morning she'd also suggested the idea that maybe whoever was behind the kidnapping had had a bad experience at the university. And maybe that experience was related to the reasons behind the no hazing policy.

She glanced at her watch. Nearly six. Jake should be by soon. She decided to ask him more on the subject over dinner, then head back to Joy's. Anxious to open her laptop and do some research, she was tempted to suggest to Owen that they skip dinner and leave. Based on the previous sheriff's shortcomings with well-documented case files, she doubted Jake could help them anyway.

A disturbance at the door caught her attention. Instead of focusing on whatever Percy was saying to Duke, she glanced toward the front of the bar. Jake shook a man's hand, then slapped another on the back. Wearing a big grin, he leaned in and said something to the two men, then laughed. Jake really was a good-looking guy. Nice, too. She shifted her gaze to Owen, who was engaged in conversation with Walter. Owen definitely didn't have any problems in the "looks" department, either.

She wasn't stupid, and could tell Jake held a smidgeon of interest in her. A dollop, at the very least. If she gave him a hint that she reciprocated, the results could be interesting. Only, she had no desire to reciprocate anything when it came to Jake.

Why?

Why couldn't she just let go of the fantasy and move on? Find herself a nice, sweet, geeky tech guy and settle down. Push out a couple of babies and maybe rescue a dog or cat. Why the obsession with Owen?

She looked to Jake again and this time tried picturing him naked. Her cheeks grew warm as she imagined what his bare, muscular chest might look like as he hovered above her, poised to insert his penis between her thighs. Poised. Insert. Really? Poor guy, she probably could have done better than that, but unfortunately she'd come up empty.

Redirecting to Owen, she did the same thing. Imagined what his naked, muscular chest might look like as he spread her legs with a rough hand, then settled his hard, hot arousal between her thighs. He'd brush her lips with his, cup her breasts, toy and tease her nipples, his hot breath caressing her mouth before he drove deep inside her.

She shoved the vodka away. While she hadn't had a sip of the second drink, she'd grown dizzy. With lust and need. And right now she needed to pull herself together. Nudging Owen, she said, "Jake's here. Maybe we should get a table."

Owen acted as if his drink was the most interesting thing in the world. "Whatever you want to do."

If you only knew.

Jake saved her from making a decision. He approached the bar, smiling and shaking hands with patrons along the way. When he finally reached them, he jerked his dark head toward Percy and ordered a bottle of Budweiser. "How'd the rest of your day go?" he asked Rachel as he reached for the beer Percy set on the bar.

"Like you thought, Abby didn't have much more to add to the original statement she gave you. She did confirm that, Saturday evening, she was heading to her room to study for a test and get to work on a paper due that week when Sean and Josh's pizza arrived. She brought the pizza and Mountain Dew to their room and that was the last time she saw them. She also said that Bill told her he wasn't feeling well. That he looked awful, but she only checked on him once."

Jake scraped the beer label. "When was that?"

"About nine. At that point, Bill was half asleep at the desk. She told us she planned to check on him again later, but ended up falling asleep with her head in her books."

After taking a sip of his beer, Jake said, "I'm wondering why she never mentioned Bill being sick the first time I talked to her."

Owen finally acknowledged Jake. "We wondered the same thing. Abby said she felt sorry for Bill and worried he might lose his job if she told anyone about him being too sick to man his post."

"What about the frat house?" Jake asked. "I went there the night we found Sean, but only talked with a couple of kids."

Owen shook his head. "Man, that place was ridiculous."

"What? Were the kids out of hand?"

"No. The opposite. Those Zetas keep a clean house. I swear I smelled Pine-Sol when I walked inside."

"I know," Rachel said with a smile. "Sean told me each member has certain daily cleaning duties. If I hadn't been there, I would never believe forty plus boys could be so clean."

"Did you happen to see their game room?" Jake asked with a wistful sigh.

"Sixty inch flat screen, pool table, foosball, gaming systems..." Owen shook his head. "I wasn't in a fraternity when I was in college, but I've been in plenty of frat houses. None of them ever looked or *smelled* like this one."

"Yeah, it's pretty pitiful that these kids have better furniture and electronics than most adults." Jake brought the bottle to his lips, then added, "Me included."

Rachel toyed with the edge of the damp beverage napkin and considered another sip of her drink. "Aside from Owen drooling over the Zeta's game room, we didn't get a whole lot out of that stop, either. The older Zetas said they remember the last two disappearances. Those guys, along with the boys who are just a year or two behind them, said they warn every pledge about Wexman Hell Week." She picked up the sweaty glass. "Sean told us that the Zetas said the missing students were sacrifices to Hell Week. When I brought that up, every one of those kids agreed." She rolled her eyes. "Gullible."

"Sacrifices for what?" Jake asked. "That sounds like one of Professor Stronach's ridiculous legends."

"I know, and Owen brought that up to them. All we got was a roomful of blank stares." She took a sip of the now watered down drink, then set it back on the bar. "What about you? Any luck with Bill?"

Jake rolled his empty beer bottle between his palms. "He's not home. I checked with his dad and cousin, they haven't seen or heard from him since yesterday morn—" His cell phone rang. "Sorry." He took a step back and answered.

She noticed Walter's cell phone vibrate against the bar. At the same time, Percy silenced the ringing restaurant phone by picking it up and placing it against his ear. Looking around, she realized half of the people in both the bar and restaurant were on their cell phones. Weird.

"Noticing anything unusual?" Owen asked her and jerked his head toward Duke and Terry, who were both shoving their phones into their pockets and shrugging on their coats.

"Yeah." She shifted her gaze toward the main restaurant. "Look how many people are leaving."

"Either happy hour just ended or something's going down."

Jake reached between them, then set his bottle and a few dollar bills on the bar. "We gotta go. Now."

While Owen paid their tab, she grabbed her coat and rushed after Jake. "What's going on?" she asked when they reached the parking lot.

Jake stopped at his SUV. When he faced her, the distress in his dark eyes created a knot in her stomach.

Please let Josh be alive.

"It's Josh, isn't it?" she asked, just as strong hands gripped her by the upper arms. *Owen.*

"We'll meet you by the river, Sheriff," a man shouted as he ran from the restaurant and to his truck.

Jake waved to the man, but kept his attention on her. "Not

Josh. Bill."

Frowning, she watched cars, trucks and SUVs scramble out of the parking lot.

Owen snatched her coat from her hand and wrapped it around her shoulders. "What the hell's going on, Jake?"

His gaze unwavering, Jake continued to stare at her. "They found Bill's truck submerged in the river." He finally looked at Owen. "And there's no sign of Bill."

CHAPTER 11

HE STOOD IN front of the pledge. A shiver wracked the boy's body as he raised his head and glared at him. Since this morning, the puke's face had taken on an ashen hue and his lips were slightly blue. He'd survive...at least until the weekend. At that point his health, body temperature, lack of hydration and sustenance, would no longer matter.

The pledge would be dead.

"The faucet is leaking," Junior said as she dropped from the last rung of the ladder, her booted feet hitting the rock floor with a muffled thud. "I wrapped a towel around it, but I'm worried it'll come loose and spray all over the utility room."

"Useless," he muttered under his breath, then lightly slapped the pledge's face. "Dinner will be momentarily delayed. Never fear, I'll be right back."

After instructing Junior to not engage with the pledge, he climbed the ladder. With each rung his irritation grew. Maybe he'd been wrong about Junior. When she'd first come to him, she'd been energetic and eager, anxious for his tutelage. But she'd made a ghastly mistake the night she'd brought the pledge to him. By bringing the other boy, she'd almost changed the dynamics of his Hell Week. And when she'd tried to fix her mistake, the sheriff ended up bringing in the two buffoons from Chicago to help find his pledge. Then there was this morning. While he understood the reason behind her absence, for her to comprehend, to gain the upmost satisfaction that Hell Week imparted, she needed to be on the premises for each and every interaction with the pledge.

He stepped into the utility room and quickly moved to the sink. The towel Junior had wrapped around the faucet and hose connector was soaked and dripping. With a curse, he shut off the water, fixed the connector, then turned the water on again. No leaks.

With an impatient sigh, he dried his hands with a paper towel, then made his way to the trapdoor. As he moved down the ladder he wondered how someone as bright as Junior could be—at times—incredibly inept. Granted, kidnapping the pledge was a difficult, risky task. Although she'd brought him two boys when he only needed one, she'd proven herself worthy as an accomplice. If only she could master these smaller tasks and not waste his time.

"Did you fix it?" Junior stood where he'd left her, hands in the deep pockets of her puffy coat. "I hope it didn't make a mess. If so, I'll clean it up before dinner."

His stomach grumbled at the mention of dinner, and his aggravation with Junior grew. Because Junior had been running late, he'd decided to postpone their meal until after they were finished with the pledge. Rushing through the scrumptious pheasant he'd prepared for their supper in an effort to play with the pledge wasn't an option. He'd rather savor his meal and then linger at the dinner table while drinking a couple fingers of his aged cognac.

"Everything is fine," he replied and eyed the pledge who kept his gaze on the floor. "But we've wasted enough time. My pheasant will be ready within the next thirty minutes and there's nothing I detest more than dry, tough meat."

"Thirty minutes?" Junior shook her head. "That's all the time we're going to spend down here?"

He glanced at her. "If you'd rather stay in the basement with the pledge than dine in front of a warm fire, be my guest. I'll keep your plate warm."

"I'm sorry. I didn't mean to question you. It's just..."

"Go on," he encouraged. Although she needed to know her place, that she would always and forevermore be subservient to him, she also needed to learn she wasn't powerless and gain confidence. While her opinions and ideas might not intrigue him, and he could care less what she thought about how he handled his pledge, his daughter needed to realize she had a voice in this world. The whole point in inviting her into his Hell Week was to help give her that voice, confidence...power.

"It's okay," she said. "You're right. Dinner will be ready soon and we're wasting time. Besides, it's freezing down here."

A momentary flash of disappointment rushed through him and he hoped by the end of the week, Junior gained a backbone. Otherwise, there would be no point in having her with him. Knowing the ins and outs of his Hell Week, if she didn't step up and take ownership, she could become less of an accomplice and more of a liability. He thought of his neighbor. How he'd ended her life with a spade shovel. Yes, liabilities definitely didn't work for him, either.

"It *is* freezing down here," he said and approached the pledge. The boy's odor more tolerable than this morning, he moved closer. "Did you find the temperature unbearable?"

With a grunt, the pledge glared at him.

Good. He wanted him fighting for his life. When past pledges had given up, seven days of Hell Week had seemed more like seven weeks. The time had dragged. He'd ended up thinking too much, questioning himself, his intentions, his motivations and dwelled on his own past rather than his bright future. Even if this pledge didn't fight, and the week dragged, there would be no dwelling. Not with the ultimate vengeance creeping in the shadows.

"Are you going to hose him down?" Junior asked.

"Not just yet. I'm debating whether to feed him now, or wait until we've finished with our evening entertainment." He'd already decided to feed the pledge first, but enjoyed the melodramatics and making the pledge wait in suspense. From his own experiences, he'd learned that horrible thoughts and assumptions the mind could create were sometimes worse than reality.

Sometimes.

With a grin, he drew a strip of black fabric from his pants pocket. "Let's combine dinner *and* entertainment." He tied the fabric around the pledge's head, making sure his eyes were covered. "Hand me that container," he ordered Junior.

After she gave him the plastic container, he lifted the lid and eyed its contents. "We're going to play a little game."

He drew out a hardened hot dog that had been cooked, but sitting in a bun on his countertop for the past five days. The bread had grown stale and moldy, while the hot dog had become more like beef jerky. Before he'd allowed that to happen, he'd stuffed a very thin, hard bread stick—he'd personally made and found extremely bland for his taste—in the middle. He held the hot dog to his nose and sniffed. Excellent. It had lost its original scent.

"What's grosser than gross?" he asked the pledge.

Blindfolded, the puke twisted his chapped, cracked lips and furrowed his forehead. "Sir?"

"What? Have you never heard of this joke?"

The pledge's Adam's apple shifted as he gulped. "I...I'm sorry, sir. I...I've never heard it before."

He turned to Junior, who shrugged and said, "I haven't either."

Apparently he was dating himself. Although now that he thought about it, his last two pledges had acted as if they'd never heard the joke, either. Nevertheless, he would educate both the pledge and Junior on the juvenile antics of his own youth. After all, this was part of Hell Week and to complete the week properly, everything had to be exactly as it had been done to him. Only one time had he deviated, and he'd been left unsatisfied. Tormented by the demons of his past and forced to take another pledge too soon. If the former sheriff hadn't been incompetent, he could have been caught. His destiny and plans for vengeance left unfulfilled.

"Hmm," he hummed and faced the pledge. "Well, it's an old joke and I have one I'd like to share. So, let's try this again.

What's grosser than gross?"

The pledge's chin trembled. "I don't understand this and don't know what you want me to say," he whined and hung against his chains, his torso bowing forward making him look like a bird in flight.

"When you join a fraternity, you must trust your brothers. Without trust, there is nothing. Do you trust me?"

After a moment, the pledge nodded.

"Good. Now, again. What's grosser than gross?"

"I don't know," the puke answered.

"Open your mouth," he said, raised the hot dog to the boy's mouth and inserted it. "Now take a bite."

As soon as the pledge bit into the hot dog, he said the joke's punch line, "Biting into a hot dog and finding a bone."

At that moment, the boy gagged. From the back of the cellar, Junior coughed, then laughed. He didn't understand how she thought that was funny. The joke implied that a finger was in the bun, which was disgusting. Although the contents were, in fact, an actual hot dog, the point of the joke, the point of this part of their *entertainment*, was to instill trust. At eighteen, when he'd been a freshman and going through his own horrifying Hell Week, he'd learned that these juvenile antics had been put in place to inspire faith in his fellow fraternity brothers. At the beginning, their mission had been accomplished. Unfortunately, the puke's very own father had taken that trust and faith to a level of no return. Imparting him with doubt and suspicion.

Then horror. Utter, degrading horror.

His skin prickled. He shook off that last thought and refocused on his ultimate revenge. Though the pledge had twisted his face in disgust, and he occasionally gagged, he chewed the hot dog, then swallowed.

"Very good," he told his pathetic puke. "What did that taste like?"

"J...jerky."

"Excellent." He fed the boy another bite. "You've passed this test. But I'm curious. What did you think I was feeding you?"

The pledge swallowed, then answered, "A finger."

He laughed and fed him more of the disgusting hot dog. "Now, where would I get a finger?" When the pledge didn't answer, even after he'd finished chewing and swallowing, he shouted in his face, "Answer me!"

Gasping, the boy jerked against his chains. He licked his chapped lips, then sucked air through his nose. "They...the guys from the fraternity told us there was a Hell Week sacrifice."

He turned to Junior, who took a step closer, her gaze intent on the pledge. When he faced the pledge again, he grinned. "Hell Week sacrifice? Believe it or not, I haven't heard that one yet. But I like it." After brushing his hands along his pants, he reached into the container and pulled out a small, Styrofoam cup, then removed the plastic lid. "In a way, I suppose my pledges are a sort of sacrifice. Without you, and the others just like you, these last twenty years might have been..."

Junior moved to his side and stared at him like a hawk might stare at a mouse. Intent. Ready.

While he'd eventually told each one of his pledges about the pain and humiliation he'd suffered when he was eighteen, now wasn't the time. He'd tell his puke when they were alone. Place the blame for every one of his Hell Weeks on the pledge's father's shoulders. He looked forward to that moment. What would his pledge think of Daddy once he had learned the truth? Would he curse the man for ultimately putting him in his current position? Would he still defend him? Or would the pledge's hatred and disgust run deep?

His smile fell, the final day of Hell Week at the forefront of his mind. The desecration of trust, the defilement of the body and soul...

Yes. The pledge would come to hate his father as much as he did.

"We really don't have time to discuss the past. My dinner will be done shortly, and I'm sure you're anxious to finish yours." He raised the Styrofoam cup and peered at the single goldfish wriggling in the shallow water. After the childish "grosser than gross" joke, he'd rather move on to what he'd planned next. But, he did promise the boy fish for dinner, and he never went back on a promise.

He brought the cup to the pledge's mouth. "Remember. Being part of a fraternal organization is about trust. I need you to drink this in one swallow."

The puke parted his lips and did as he was instructed.

"Excellent." He chuckled when the pledge choked. But he gave the boy credit for keeping the contents down and not regurgitating all over himself and the floor. His past pledges hadn't been as strong stomached, and had to learn the hard way that he didn't tolerate weakness of any kind. Removing the boy's blindfold, he ruffled his hair. "You did good. Ate an old hot dog and swallowed a goldfish."

The pledge didn't return his smile, but he did relax against his restraints. "Thank you, sir."

He clapped his hands, then rubbed them together. "Now that you've been fed, time for something new. Junior, I need you to move back to where you were. Take the bat with you. If he's a bad pledge, crush his knee cap."

After she obeyed, he removed the pledge's restraints, then ushered him toward where he'd hosed the puke's urine and excrement earlier that morning. "Drop and give me twenty."

With only a few seconds of hesitation, the boy obeyed. After little physical activity and sustenance, the pledge's arms shook as he dipped his body toward the floor. Still, the puke must understand that one of the benefits of Hell Week was to show strength despite any given circumstance.

Resting the sole of his boot along the boy's raw, filthy, bony back, he pressed. "Dig deep, Puke. One down, nineteen to go."

The pledge pushed along, occasionally dropping his entire body to the ground and landing in his own waste. Finally, he made it to the end. Huffing and puffing, he stood, shoulders bent, head hanging, sweat and filth coating his skin.

With a small stab of pride, he cupped the only clean part of the boy's shoulder. "Very good."

At that moment, Junior released a sigh.

He led the pledge back to the wall where his chains dangled. As he restrained the boy, he looked over his shoulder at Junior. "Are we boring you?"

She opened her mouth, then mashed her lips together without uttering a word.

Once sure the boy's chains would hold, he approached Junior. "If you have something to say, say it."

She looked to the ground and leaned against the baseball bat. "I just don't understand what you're doing," she said, her tone hushed. "No offense, sir, but I expected more from you. Not these kid's games."

"Kid's games," he repeated. "You think how I'm handling the pledge is childish?"

She met his gaze, then quickly nodded and looked away. "I'm sorry. I just don't see the point in any of this. Last night you told me today would be worse for him, that the next day even more horrible. If anything, I thought you were too easy on him."

Because she'd never gone through the hell he had, she wouldn't understand. While her questioning aggravated him, he knew he couldn't fault her for wondering the point of his Hell Week. He also knew that he'd gone easy on the pledge today. Not out of sympathy. No. This morning he realized he needed *this* pledge's trust. The others had never trusted him. Without that trust, there would be no betrayal. And the betrayal was what he craved the most. The degradation and treachery bestowed upon him by the demon who had spawned his current pledge had nearly destroyed him. The duplicity of several of his fraternal brethren, as they'd turned a blind eye to what had happened to him at the hands of a monstrous bully, had been just as bad. Trust was a precious thing. Something earned and never taken for granted.

Something he held for no one save himself.

He eyed his daughter. In the shadowy light her nose and chin appeared sharper, pointer. He never considered her pretty, but average. Right now, with her mouth twisted in disapproval and her pale, blue eyes glittering with condemnation, she looked positively ugly. "What would *you* do to him then?" he asked, curious to discover if she'd suddenly grown a backbone. She looked to the pledge, then to the metal bat. "You wouldn't mind if I showed you?"

Unease and a touch of apprehension settled in the pit of his empty stomach. He realized he'd been mistaken. The glitter in her eyes had nothing to do with condemnation, but perverse pleasure. She wanted to take his Hell Week in a different direction. Up the ante, make the pledge suffer. He saw it in her eyes, felt it in his gut. While he did too, now wasn't the time. He needed the boy's complete and utter trust first, otherwise the end result wouldn't be as rewarding.

Junior needed to learn this. Unfortunately, the pathetic puke hanging from the basement wall would serve as Junior's *learning* curve. Although he wasn't sure what she planned to do to the boy, he doubted whatever she had planned was anything near what he intended to do by week's end.

With regret, he nodded. "No, Junior. I don't mind. Go ahead and show me."

The corner of her mouth tilted in a half grin. She popped the bat in the air, caught it in her hand, then quickly moved to the toolbox against the far wall. After rummaging for a moment, she turned and held up the hammer as if it were a trophy.

With a huge smile on her face and her eyes dancing with excitement, she practically skipped toward the pledge. She gave the boy's nose a playful pinch, dropped to one knee and slammed the hammer against his toes.

Howling in obvious pain, the pledge arched his back and pulled against his restraints.

She hit him again.

Then again.

As she raised the hammer a fourth time, he rushed to her side. "Junior, stop!"

Hammer still raised and panting hard, Junior shoved off the

ground and stepped away from the crying pledge. "Now that's what I'm talking about," she said and propped her hands on her hips.

As the boy screamed and moaned, he looked to the pledge's foot, to the toes Junior had just crushed. Hiding his rage for what she'd done to *his* pledge, he took the hammer from her. "Satisfied?"

"Are you kidding? I'm exhilarated." She pointed to the boy's swollen, purpling toes and began laughing. "*This* is what I've been waiting for you to do."

Junior's cackling, the pledge's cries and pleas all mingled with the fury he'd been trying to keep at bay, and pierced his ears as if someone were drilling an ice pick into the orifices. The grating shrieks and wailings crawled into his brain. Junior's eerie laughter shook his countenance. Her sheer disrespect of Hell Week made him want to lash out at both of them. Stop the maddening noise from festering in his head.

Hammer in hand, a large part of him wanted to smash Junior in the face. Crack her pointy chin and teach her a valuable lesson. He raised his free hand, instead, and smacked the pledge in the face. "Stop. Man up, Puke." He gave Junior the hammer and instructed her to put it away, then to go upstairs. Once he and the pledge were alone, he took the hose and ran it over the boy's body. When he finished, he took a towel and dried the pledge's hollow, tear-filled cheeks.

"I didn't know Junior planned to smash your toes." He gripped the boy's shoulders. "That's not how I normally conduct Hell Week. Do you understand?"

Wincing, the pledge swallowed and nodded his head.

"Once Hell Week is over, we will be brothers. United. Bonded by trust." He stepped back and tossed the towel over his shoulder. "Do you still trust me?"

Choking on a sob, he stuttered, "Y…yes, sir. B…but, Junior—"

He waved a hand, then set up the space heater. "Don't worry about Junior. That won't happen again. Now get your rest. I'll see you in the morning."

After darkening the basement, he climbed the ladder and met Junior in the kitchen. "Looks like dinner is done," she said as she pulled the pheasant from the oven. "Mmm, smells delicious."

The pheasant's aroma filled the room. Too disgusted by Junior's actions, his mouth didn't water, but turned sandpaper dry. "Set the bird on the stove and join me." He moved into the foyer, then grabbed her coat from the closet.

"What's going on?" she asked, staring at the coat. "Are you angry with me?"

Fighting the urge to beat her face to a blood pulp, he cleared his throat and helped her into her coat. "What did you accomplish by smashing the pledge's toes?"

Her questioning gaze met his. "I...I wanted to spice things up, that's all. Give the pledge something to fear. Something to think about while he's hanging from the wall tonight."

He fisted his hands, but didn't raise them. If he struck her, he doubted he could stop. Her stupidity could cost him what he needed from his pledge. Trust.

Taking a step back before he lost control, he nodded. "Yes, no doubt you instilled fear in him. But don't you think he was afraid before you crushed his toes?"

"Well, I'm sure he was—"

"Don't you think he hangs from the rock wall waiting and wondering what will happen next?"

"Of course, but—"

"The pledge will not be touched by you unless I've instructed. Do you understand?"

The confusion in Junior's eyes turned to contempt. Instead of defying him, she said, "Yes, sir."

"Good. I will dine alone this evening and I don't want you to come for breakfast tomorrow. You need to think about what you've done."

"I'm sorry, sir. I know I hurt him, but I assumed that's what you'd do anyway."

Chuckling, he shook his head. "Don't doubt it. What the pledge will suffer will be beyond what you could ever imagine.

But I need his trust before that moment arrives. Today, you could have possibly damaged the fragile bond the boy and I share. We have only five more days of Hell Week. I don't want to waste time repairing the damage you've done." He opened the door. "Go."

Junior hesitated at the threshold. "I…I'm confused. Why do you need his trust?"

With a slow smile, he faced her. "So that I can shatter it."

CHAPTER 12

DOZENS OF HEADLIGHTS illuminated the riverbank. Mist rose from the water in an eerie, shadowy haze, enveloping Bill's large pickup truck. Men wearing fishing waders and hip-high boots stood at the shoreline or in the water, securing the hooks and chains from an enormous tow truck to the back end of Bill's pickup.

Despite the hat and gloves, nothing could stop the chill slicing through Owen, or the dread as he and Rachel watched the locals do their best to fish Bill's truck out of the river. She stood with her gloved hands stuffed in her coat pockets. When the beam of a flashlight briefly chased across her face, he caught the fear in her eyes and he resisted the urge to haul her trembling body next to his.

According to Bill's family, the security guard was last seen leaving his post at Wexman University. That was over twenty-four hours ago. Today's temperature had reached a high of twenty-one, while last night it had dropped to eleven. Tonight was supposed to be just as cold. Even if Bill had survived the crash into the river and managed to make it to shore, without dry, warm clothes or shelter, hypothermia would have been his next obstacle. But if Bill hadn't survived the crash, then where the hell was his body?

"Here comes Jake," Rachel said and nudged him with her elbow.

He glanced to where Rachel had been looking. Jake made his way toward them, capped head down, shoulders slumped and his boots crunching over the trampled, icy snow. They now had two possible missing persons in a matter of a couple of days. Was what happened to Bill a simple coincidence, dumb luck or something more disturbing?

"How's it going?" Rachel asked when Jake finally reached them. "Are they about ready to pull the truck from the water?"

Nodding, Jake looked back to the riverbank just as the tow truck's engine revved. "Yeah, as we speak."

Water rushed over the partially submerged hood of the pickup as the driver inched the tow truck away from the river. Men shouted directions at the driver, who popped his head out of the driver's side window and looked over his shoulder. The engine suddenly roared. The tow truck lurched, and quicker than Owen had anticipated, Bill's pickup was dragged from the water.

Other than the tow trucks guttural purr as it sat idling, and the rush of the river water, the Townies who had crowded along the riverbank remained unnervingly silent.

"Empty," a man wearing hip-high boots shouted as he moved a flashlight over the interior of the truck's cab. "What do you want us to do with it, Jake?"

Jake glanced at Rachel. "Something's not right," she said. "You told us Bill lived in town and the last time anyone saw him was when he left the university. This..." She twisted her body and looked at the river, then the woods. "This isn't even close to a main road. Why would he be out here?"

"The only people who come out here at this time of year are illegal hunters and die hard fishermen. Bill wasn't either." Jake took a step back. "Are you suggesting foul play?"

Rachel nodded. "Can you have his truck towed to a garage? It's too dark out here, even with headlights and flashlights, to look for evidence."

"Yeah, I'll take care of it."

"And the man who found the truck?" Rachel asked.

Jake stopped, then looked toward the tow truck again.

"Looks like Evan is finished helping them. I'll send him over."

"This isn't good," Rachel said after Jake walked away.

"Nope."

"I mean, we ask Bill to get blood work done, then he *coincidentally* disappears?"

"Into a river."

She leaned closer. "Even if we found him...dead, if he'd been drugged with Rohypnol and died Monday afternoon, the drug would still be in his system. We'd still have our link."

"If that's the case, then it also means whoever took Josh is watching us." He didn't like that idea. At all. If the killer/kidnapper knew about them, what if, to retaliate, he went after Sean again? Worse yet, what if he went after Rachel?

The thought of Rachel falling victim to a nameless, faceless serial killer caused a tightening in his chest. He had the urge to go all he-man on her. Toss her over his shoulder and haul her sexy butt back to Chicago where she would be safe. He wouldn't, though. Not yet. Having this opportunity to work in the field was important to her. Even if he didn't like the uncertainties of this investigation, he wanted her to succeed. He wanted her happy. Hell, he wanted her, period.

Wearing camouflaged fatigues and tall, matching rubber boots, the man he assumed was Evan approached. Adjusting his bright orange knit hat, he gave them a curt nod. "I'm Evan Hart. Jake said you wanted to talk to me."

"How did you find Bill's truck?" Rachel asked after she introduced them. "Were you hunting?"

Evan looked to the snow covered ground. "That wouldn't be legal. I was...thinking about testing out the new fishing rod my wife got me for Christmas."

While Owen suspected Evan was bullshitting them, he could care less. With the dozens of people and cars trampling the area, Evan was the only person who saw the *possible* crime scene when it had been fresh.

"Did you see tracks off the road?" Owen asked. "You know, like Bill might have lost control of the truck. Maybe skidded on some ice or something."

"Nah, nothing like that. I parked up on Miller's Run," he said and pointed to the road running parallel to the river. "Got out of my truck and walked down that slope. That's when I saw tire tracks."

"And that's unusual?" Rachel asked.

"For this time of year." He motioned to where they were standing. "This isn't exactly what you'd call a road. No telling how deep the snow is in the winter, and in the summer you wouldn't want to drive down here unless you've got yourself an all terrain four-wheeler."

"Would Bill know this?" Owen asked.

"Shoot, that boy grew up here. He'd know better."

"Okay," Rachel began. "So you saw tire tracks…"

"Right. Saw the tracks and followed 'em. That's when I saw the back end of Bill's pickup stickin' out of the water. The only reason I knew it was Bill's was because of his Ohio State bumper sticker. This is Wolverine territory. Bill's the only fool I know that likes those damned Buckeyes."

Considering Rachel knew nothing about football, Owen could guarantee she had no idea that Evan was talking about a college rivalry. "After you realized it was Bill's truck, you obviously called the sheriff, but did you look for Bill?" Owen asked. "Maybe find any footprints in the snow?"

"Right after I hung up with Jake," Evan said. "I called some of my buddies who hunt and fish around here—when it's legal, of course. While we were waiting on Jake, and for Bernie to bring his tow truck, we went about a fifty or so yards into the woods looking for Bill."

A minute amount of hope prickled his interest. "So you did find footprints."

"No. But when my buddy first got here, he roped me up and I waded out into the river to see if Bill was trapped in his cab. When I didn't see anything, I was hoping that maybe he'd made it out. I just…I didn't want to give up on him. He's a good kid." He looked at the river. "It's too late tonight, but tomorrow we'll check further down the river. The current might've grabbed him."

"When they pulled the truck out of the water, I noticed the doors and windows were shut," Rachel said.

Evan shook his head and crossed his arms. "You couldn't see it from here, but the driver's side window was cracked open about four inches."

"Which isn't enough for a man Bill's size to escape."

"No." Evan half-chuckled, then grew somber when a tall, heavyset man rushed past them and toward Bill's truck. "That'd be, Hal, Bill's dad. If there's nothing else…"

After Rachel thanked Evan, and the man jogged after Hal, she hugged herself. "They're not going to find Bill in the river." She muttered something under her breath, then said, "And if this is a crime scene, it's been completely contaminated. We still need to come back in the morning and—"

Bill's dad yelled and screamed. Kicked the wheel of the pickup truck. Jake rushed to his side, but Hal shoved him away and throwing his hands in the air, paced.

Jake headed toward them again, his strides long and with purpose. At the same time, Bernie fired up the tow truck. Men cleared, giving the driver room to navigate the narrow path back to the main road.

"Come on," Jake said and motioned for them to follow him. "I want to follow Bernie back to his garage and take a look at Bill's truck. I'm assuming you two want to come along, right?"

"Absolutely," Rachel said.

When they reached his Lexus, which Owen had parked next to Jake's SUV, the sheriff paused. "When I asked about foul play, you never answered my question, and I want an answer." He slapped the hood of his SUV with a gloved hand. "Actually I want a shit-ton of answers. I'm sick of having this Hell Week bullshit hanging over my town."

Owen caught a flash of sympathy in Rachel's eyes. "I wish we had some definite answers for you, Jake," she said. "Let's head to the garage and start there."

Jake didn't respond. He climbed into his SUV and flipped

on the headlights.

Owen and Rachel did the same. And as they followed the sheriff back to town, Rachel said, "Jake's pretty pissed off right now."

"Can you blame him?" As much as he didn't like the sheriff, Owen could imagine Jake's frustration. The man lived here, was sheriff, was supposed to be protecting and serving his community. Instead he was spinning his wheels with the Wexman Hell Week that had been plaguing Bola for twenty years.

"No, I can't. Especially because I think he suspects what we do."

"Yeah, what's that?"

"Someone wanted Bill dead."

Two hours later, carrying her computer bag over her shoulder, Rachel made her way downstairs to Joy's dining room. After Owen brought her back to the boarding house, she'd changed into her yoga pants and a thick, fleece sweatshirt. She wished she'd remembered to pack slippers. Even though the temperature in the house was comfortable, she couldn't shake the chill still shivering through her body.

When she caught Joy sitting at the table, her head in her hands, a Styrofoam cup, a magnum of white wine and a coffee mug in front of her, she paused. Sensing Joy probably wanted time alone to deal with her missing nephew, she took a step backward. The floorboard creaked. Joy raised her head, but kept her chin in her palm.

"Hey, Shorty," she said, her tone quiet, melancholy. "Go grab a mug. I don't want to drink alone."

Rachel did as Joy requested, then sat next to the other woman. Joy unscrewed the bottle cap, then poured Rachel a mugful of wine. "How'd it go at Bernie's garage? Hal isn't answering his phone and I…" Her chin wobbled. "Damn, I don't know what the hell to do with myself." She topped her own mug off, then raised the cup to her lips.

She understood what Joy was going through. After working at CORE for four years, she'd met plenty of distraught, helpless clients searching for answers, for closure, for justice. Unfortunately, she didn't have any of those things to offer Joy right now.

"The window of Bill's truck was partially open when it went into the river. The entire cab ended up filled with water." She took a sip from the mug, then masked her surprise. Joy had excellent taste in wine. "Inside, we found the keys, which were still in the ignition, a duffle bag filled with Bill's clothes and a lunch pail."

Joy stared at her, her red-rimmed eyes heartbreaking. "He always takes a change of clothes with him to work." She cracked a smile. "My brother doesn't know it, but Bill's sweet on a graduate student at the university. She also works at the school library in the evenings." Her smile grew. "I swear that boy has read—or pretended to read—more books in the last few months than he has his entire life. Anyway, he knows her schedule and if it works with his shift at the university, he likes to get himself all dolled up and pay her a visit." She raised the mug to her lips again, her smile falling. "This isn't good, Shorty. Hal's wife died last year, cancer. Bill's all he has left. If something happened..." She shook her head and drew in a shaky breath. "I love that little shit," she said on a sob, then dropped her face into her hands.

An angry, bitchy, bullying Joy, she could handle. But a wounded, saddened, grieving Joy? She didn't know what to do. Hug her? She glanced at Joy's wide, trembling shoulders. Pat her on the back? She raised her hand, then curled her fingers. No. She didn't know Joy, but from what she could tell, the woman wouldn't want coddling from her. She'd want honesty.

"We plan on going out in the morning to search the river and woods again."

Joy raised her head, then wiped her tears and nose with a napkin. "Even if you found him, he's been exposed to the cold for twenty-four hours. Do you have any idea what happens to a wet body when it's out in temperatures below freezing?" She shook her head. "I'm so frickin' worried. And pissed. I'm fucking pissed." She threw the napkin across the table.

Thank God the other Joy was back. She needed the woman angry rather than weepy. She needed her help, and didn't think she'd have it if Joy went off the emotional deep end. "I'm pissed, too." She took a long swallow of the wine, then slammed the half empty mug on the table. "I know you're concerned and grieving over Bill and what your brother is going through, but here's what you don't know—and it *better* not leave this room—Bill was my link to whoever beat my brother and kidnapped Josh Conway."

Joy leaned back in her chair, her face turning as red as her runny nose. "You think Bill is connected to Wexman Hell Week? My Bill? Why in the hell would he be a target? I mean this out of love, but that boy isn't the brightest bulb in the chandelier, if you get my meaning. He does good as a security guard, but I can't imagine why anyone would go after him. What could he have done to even—?"

"His truck."

Rachel looked up to find Owen standing at the bottom of the steps. As he approached the dining room, wearing the same t-shirt and sweatpants he'd worn last night, there was the hint of excitement brewing in his eyes.

"What about his truck?" Joy asked.

And then Rachel remembered. Bill telling them he'd picked up the extra shift at the university to make the last payment on his truck. Bill coincidentally becoming ill when the boys had been kidnapped. The security camera in the residence hall's foyer being moved. Now Bill was missing and his truck water logged and devoid of any possible evidence. "Oh my God," she gasped. "He used Bill's truck."

Owen nodded and took a seat. "That's exactly what I'm thinking."

"Who used Bill's truck?" Joy grabbed the magnum of wine. "And what in the hell are you two talking about?"

Rachel removed the laptop from the bag, then found an

outlet. "Whoever took my brother and Josh," she said and fired up the computer.

The front door closed and seconds later, Walter strolled into the room, clutching his earflap hat. He immediately looked to Joy, who visibly relaxed. Her face softening with what Rachel considered relief.

"Was wondering when you were going to be home," Joy said, her tone quiet, tentative. "Were you with Hal?"

He pulled a flask from his black and red coat pocket. "Yeah. Just dropped him at home. After we left the garage, we went back to the river."

Joy swore and shook her head. "Fools. It's five degrees. I'm guessing you didn't have the proper gear on or right equipment when you decided to roam around the frickin' woods, right?"

Walter's face remained impassive. "Hal's grieving, Joy. He's worried sick. If I didn't go with him, he'd gone alone. And *that* would have been foolish."

"Jake's setting up a search party for the morning," Rachel said and connected to the Internet. "He even said a couple of men volunteered to search the river."

"He ain't in the river." Walter set the flask on the table, then shrugged out of his coat. "The driver's side of his truck was catching the force of the current, which was quick today. Bill's a big kid, but I can't see him being able to push the door open."

"The passenger side?" Joy asked, her tone hopeful. "Or, what about the rear window?"

Owen shook his head. "Both were locked."

Joy smacked a hand on the table. "Then where the hell could he be?" she asked, her voice rising. "None of this makes sense. That boy wouldn't purposefully dump his truck in the river and walk away. And even though Evan can't track for shit, there should've been footprints by the shore and in the snow. Bill's *or* this whoever you two are talking about."

Rachel looked to Owen. "There wasn't any evidence of a struggle inside the cab of Bill's truck," he said. "Which means he either was immediately incapacitated or he knew the killer."

"Whoa, whoa, whoa." Walter sat in a chair. "Killer? Are you talking about the Wexman Hell Week?"

When Owen nodded, Walter rubbed a hand along his scruffy jaw. "Why would the Hell Week killer go after Bill?"

Before she or Owen could answer, Joy snorted. "For his truck, if you can believe that one."

Walter reached for the flask. "I'm not sure what to believe at this point."

Rachel connected her cell phone to her laptop to pull up the pictures she'd taken at Bernie's garage. "Let's go back to what I started to tell Joy just before you got here. And again, this stays in this room."

After Joy and Walter nodded, she checked her computer screen. The pictures were still loading, so she reached into her bag for notecards and a pencil. "Damn it," she mumbled when she realized she didn't pack any notecards. More than ever, she missed CORE's evidence and evaluation room, all of her gadgets, extra computers, TV screens and her beloved dry erase board. Going old school, writing information, clues, leads on notecards wouldn't have been ideal, but it would have worked for a mini brainstorming session.

"What's wrong?" Owen asked.

"I didn't pack any notecards."

"So?" Joy took a drink from her mug.

"So, I'm used to displaying ideas and images when I'm helping with an investigation."

"Rachel likes whiteboards and computer screens," Owen said. "She's a visual person and it helps when she can have all the details surrounding her."

Stunned, Rachel stared at him. Damn, he knew her well. For a split second, she wondered what else he knew.

"I can't help you with a whiteboard, but I've got some notecards." Joy went to the kitchen, then returned with a stack of blank recipe cards. "Not exactly what you're probably looking for, but it'll work."

After she thanked Joy, she took the pencil and wrote 'Sean' on the recipe card. "First my brother is found on the side of the road. The Hell Week note stuffed in his pocket. Jake and Dr. Gregory think some of his injuries were due to being thrown from an SUV or a *truck*." She finished jotting the information, then place the card at the center of the table.

Joy grabbed the pencil and cards from her. "You talk, I'll write."

Rachel nodded her thanks. "Okay, new card. Now we have Josh Conway. He's been missing since Saturday night. He's also my brother's roommate and the person we suspect the Hell Week note was intended for. His parents have been notified of his disappearance, but are overseas."

"If my kid was missing, I'd do everything in my power to get back to the states," Joy said as she wrote.

"The father is working in Afghanistan, and the mother is with him," Owen explained. "They're having some issues getting out of the country, but told the sheriff they'd be in Bola by the end of the week."

"Let's stay focused." Rachel opened her small notepad and flipped to the beginning. "New card…Rohypnol," she said and spelled the word.

After Joy jotted it down, she asked, "What's that?"

"Date rape drug," Owen answered. "Sean's toxicology report showed traces of it in his system. We also think Bill was drugged with the same stuff."

Joy paused the pencil over the recipe card, and looked up at him. "Are you suggesting that someone was planning on…?" She shook her head. "That doesn't make sense to me."

Rachel understood her confusion. "Rohypnol *is* commonly known as the date rape drug, but in this case, we think the killer used it to incapacitate Sean and Josh in order to kidnap them." She explained about the Mountain Dew and the missing trash in the boys' dorm room, and Joy wrote down the information. "We think Bill was given the drug to knock him out."

Walter screwed the cap back on the flask. "So the killer could use his truck."

"Right." Owen drummed his fingers on the table.

"Whoever was behind this also moved the security camera in the foyer of the residence hall where Bill works."

As Joy quickly wrote on a fresh card, Rachel added, "The last time anyone saw Bill was yesterday afternoon. After we interviewed him and checked out the boys' dorm room, we asked him to go the lab for blood work. His symptoms were similar to someone drugged with Rohypnol and we wanted to be sure. Because if that were the case, Bill is linked to Sean and Josh's initial kidnapping."

Joy looked at her. "Hal said Bill came down with the flu over the weekend. Are you sure it just wasn't—?"

Rachel shook her head. "We're not sure of anything. But, everything we've seen so far is just too coincidental to ignore. And now Bill's missing."

Owen rubbed the back of his neck. "Because someone didn't want him to have that tox screen."

His biceps flexed, momentarily distracting her, but she refocused. "But why? If you think about it, what difference would it make if we found the drug in his system. That's no reason to get rid of him." Realizing she should have thought before she spoke, she touched Joy's forearm. "I'm sorry, I didn't mean to imply—"

"It's okay, Shorty." Joy gave her a wry, half-smile. "You're just doing your job. Now keep going. Because if something did happen to my nephew, I want whoever did it to him. My daddy was a hunter and he taught me how to skin a deer. It's been a while, but I plan on practicing those skills again, if you get my meaning."

Oh, I got it, all right.

"What if the killer started to worry that he left behind some evidence of the kidnapping in Bill's truck?" Owen asked. "He finds out Bill's going to be tested, thinks that when they find the Rohypnol in his system, we might start nosing through Bill's things, his truck included."

Rachel took a sip of wine and realized they had a bigger issue than finding Bill. "Someone is watching us."

Owen snapped his gaze to hers and caught the frustration

and fear in her eyes. "It's a small town," he said to help alleviate her fear and maybe a bit of his own. If they had a leak, or the killer had strong ties with the community and this investigation, they could be in danger if they came too close to the truth. The killer had been at it for twenty years, he couldn't see him stopping now.

Rachel picked up a pencil and tucked it behind her ear. "Small town or not, the only ones who knew Bill was going for the tox screen were me, you, Dr. Gregory and Jake."

"Maybe someone overheard you talking," Walter suggested.

Who? Owen drummed his fingers again. They'd specifically asked Bill to not tell anyone, not even his boss with campus security.

"Joy," Rachel began, "you said Bill was sweet on a girl. Do you know her name?"

"I wanna say it was Kaylie." She frowned. "Or was it Kylie? Anyway, it was something like that. Like I said, she works at the university library, so someone there would probably know her."

"If Bill told his girl and she blabbed about it..." Rachel shook her head and reached for the pencil behind her ear. Owen could practically feel the frustration radiating from her, and expected her to bite the pencil in half. "Okay." She blew out a breath and set the pencil—unbitten—onto the table. "Let's get back to our notecards. I still have some research to do and we've got a search in the morning. By the way, Joy, do you have a printer I could borrow?"

At this point, Owen would rather suffer the cold and search the woods by the river for Bill. He knew what Rachel wanted with that printer. And by midnight, he'd been right. The short stack of reports she'd printed off sat in front of him. After Joy and Walter went off to bed, he'd gone through them all and had grown tired of sitting hunched over, scanning names, dates and addresses. Hell, he'd grown tired of this no-win investigation, period.

"One step forward, two steps back," he muttered, dropped the neon, yellow highlighter, and rubbed his tired eyes.

"What's that?" Rachel asked, but kept her focus on the laptop screen.

"Nothing." But it wasn't *nothing*. The busywork Rachel had him doing made him restless and edgy. He'd had a hard time focusing on the lists of current and former university faculty and staff that lived in or near Bola. Damn it, he had a hard time focusing because *she* distracted him. Even in a baggy sweatshirt. Because he knew what was underneath all that fleece. Images of Rachel wearing that skintight tank top she'd had on last night popped into his head—again. Her large breasts practically spilling from the top. Erect nipples piercing the flimsy material.

He cleared his throat. *Focus.* On the reports, not on Rachel.

"Are you at least finding anything useful?" she asked, the glow of the laptop screen reflecting off her pretty face. Off her full, kissable lips.

Business. Stay focused on business.

"I don't know how useful any of it is..." Picking up the stack of reports, he glanced at the top page where he'd made notes. "Going back twenty-five years...nothing. No students, faculty or staff—which includes maintenance, janitorial, security—still live in the area. I didn't see a cross reference until eighteen years ago."

Her eyebrows rose, and her tired eyes lit with excitement. "Really? Who?"

"Xavier Preston, the dean."

She visibly deflated. "Oh."

They'd both been working hard at pulling together something solid to help with the investigation, and he hated hearing the defeat in voice. "But there's a dozen guys—maintenance—on the payroll who started working at the university between fifteen and ten years ago," he said, hoping to lighten her disappointment.

"No former alumni living in the area?"

"Sorry, no. But one thing we didn't consider is the possibility of a visiting professor. Based on the dates I've been looking at, it looks like that might be a separate list that we don't have."

"I'll check the university data base again tomorrow and see what I can come up with on the visiting professor route. That might give us a lead." She began shutting down her laptop. "Well, we didn't come up with a whole lot tonight, but we can interview the maintenance guys and see if they fit the pathetic profile we came up with for the killer."

"It's not pathetic," he said and stood. "Pinning him to be in his late thirties to mid-forties makes sense. So does our thoughts about him living in the area during the winter months."

"I suppose." She shoved the computer into the bag. "What's pathetic is that I can't find anything on why Wexman initiated their no hazing policy. I can't believe—considering the size of the town and university—that no one knows anything about it."

"Yeah, but you heard what Walt, Percy and the others said about that."

"The dock caught on fire. I remember." She slung the bag over her shoulder. "I can see where the Townies would be more concerned about that than what was going on at the university. Still…"

"You'd think there'd be some kind of record," he finished with a nod.

When she moved next to him, they began to walk up stairs.

"You'd think. I'm going to ask Jake if he can do some digging. Maybe he has a list of deputies who used to work with the former sheriff and *they* remember something."

"Good plan," he said as they made their way into the dimly lit hallway.

When they reached her door, she let the bag slip from her shoulder and set it on the floor. "He's coming by in the morning, we can run everything we worked on tonight past him. We can also see what else he remembers about Percy's grandma. That whole story is a little too coincidental to brush off, even if it sounded like some wannabe spooky campfire story you tell to a bunch of Girl Scouts."

209

Glad Rachel hadn't lost her sense of humor after they'd spent hours spinning their wheels and coming up empty, he cracked a smile. "So, do you believe what the guys at the bar said about Walter being a Bigfoot expert?" he asked, keeping his voice low. He hadn't seen any other tenants traipsing through Joy's and he wasn't sure which room was Walter's. He didn't want to risk anyone overhearing them. Besides, he liked Walt, and didn't want to have any issues with the man.

She grinned, and leaned close. Her unique scent teased him, making him want to draw her closer. "After spending two days in Bola, it wouldn't surprise me," she whispered. "The people around here are definitely...unconventional. I don't know how Jake handles it. He's so normal."

Fucking Jake. How many times was she going to mention the man's name?

"I feel sorry for the guy," she said, keeping her voice low.

He did, too. But at the moment, he could give two shits about Jake. Right now, his mind was on the woman standing in front of him. Her citrusy sweet scent and the way it made his mouth water for a taste of her lips, her soft skin. How her baggy sweatshirt brushed against him as she leaned in to whisper. Knowing that beneath the sweatshirt was a tiny waist and full hips he could hang on to while his drove himself deep between her sexy thighs. And her breasts...Damn, if he didn't want to touch them, bury his face in her cleavage, skim his mouth along her nipples.

"Jake doesn't seem happy here," she continued, obviously oblivious to his wicked thoughts and current state of arousal. "Not that I know him, but I just get that feeling...you know, that he'd rather be someplace else."

Jealousy settled in the pit of his stomach. He needed to walk away and go to his room. If she mentioned that man's name one more time, he swore he was going to give her a reason to forget the sheriff existed. And that could be a colossal mistake. Knowing Rachel had hand-to-hand combat training, he could end up with a broken nose and in the process jeopardize his career with CORE.

"Yeah, well, Jake's a big boy," he said quietly and tried to mask his irritation. "I'm sure he has his reasons for staying in Bola." Not that he cared.

She stared at his chest for a second, and then looked up at him. "Don't you think it's strange that a man with his background would waste his time in a small town? I bet Jake could—"

Owen cupped the back of her head and kissed her, silencing anything else she had to say about the sheriff. He didn't want to hear his name again. And as she softened her mouth, separating her lips, inviting him to deepen the kiss, he refused to consider the consequences of the kiss and how it could ruin their professional and personal relationship. He refused to think about anything or anyone but Rachel. The way she tasted, faintly like apples and pears. The way her small body and sexy curves melted against him.

Then she speared her fingers through his hair and gripped his head. Slanted her mouth against his and intensified the kiss. Making sexy throaty moans as she tangled her tongue with his.

Her aggressiveness, the way she boldly held him, surprised and excited him. The need to strip her naked and kiss every inch of her had his heart pounding and his brain sex-muddled. Sliding his hand beneath her sweatshirt, he gripped her hips, pressed her against his erection. He wanted her to know exactly what was on his mind.

She broke away. Panting, her breath fanned across his lips. Her eyes were big and round, and held hints of shock and desire. Letting go of him, she pressed the back of her trembling hand against her swollen lips, but kept her eyes locked on his.

His breathing labored, he tried to tamp down his needs. He'd obviously stunned her. Hell, he'd stunned himself. He'd fantasized plenty about how and when—if there'd even be a when—he'd attempt to seduce Rachel. He hadn't planned on a hot and heavy make out session, at least not tonight. They were in the middle of an investigation and staying in a boarding house filled with strangers. Still, he couldn't help the smug satisfaction surging through him at the way she'd responded. He'd always thought of her as a quick-tempered firecracker, but Rachel had just shown him how hot-blooded and explosive things could be should they take their next make out session any further. And he planned on another one.

She dropped her hand away, then straightened and tilted her chin as if she were unaffected by what had just transpired. With the way her pulse beat hard at the base of her throat, and how her eyes still glittered with sensual excitement, she didn't fool him. But he could understand her wanting to take things slow. They worked together, and he'd bet that thought was on her mind, just as it had been on his.

"Well," she finally said, her tone husky. She cleared her throat and looked over his shoulder. "That was...interesting."

Interesting? How about frickin' amazing?

She turned toward the door. "On that note..."

He took her hand before it hit the doorknob and spun her to face him. "That's all you've got to say?" There was no way he could be wrong about what just happened between them. She'd kissed him back with an aggressiveness and eagerness that had matched his own. Maybe she was trying to play it cool. If so, he understood. Again, they worked together. Things could become messy if they moved too fast.

"I'm sorry, did you want a critique?" she asked.

Critique? What the hell? He released her hand. "I don't think that's necessary considering you seemed to enjoyed it."

She sent him an infuriatingly sarcastic smile. "I'll give you one anyway. It was okay." Turning the knob, she opened her bedroom door, then slipped inside. "A definite improvement over the last time," she finished, then shut the door in his face.

CHAPTER 13

WEDNESDAY

THE NEXT MORNING, Rachel put her head under the shower spray. As the shampoo rinsed from her hair, she closed her eyes and wished she could go back to bed and catch a couple more hours of sleep. But Jake would be there soon and they had a lot on their plate today. Beginning with the search for Bill.

Metal scraped metal as she whipped open the shower curtain. While she'd love to stand under the hot water for a few more minutes and let the heat work at her tense shoulders, she'd learned yesterday that hot water was a precious commodity at The House of Joy. Either Joy had the hot water tank on some sort of timer—if that were possible—or there were more phantom boarders staying at Joy's than she'd realized.

After toweling off, she zipped through her morning toiletries, then changed into an old pair of jeans and a heavy sweater. Never having participated in a search and rescue, she had no idea how long they'd be out in the cold, and she wanted to be prepared. She turned in front of the mirror and eyed her reflection. These jeans were her favorites, hugging her butt in just the right way so it actually looked sort of firm. The sweater? Well, it wasn't the most flattering thing she owned. The thick material made her big boobs look even bigger, and hid her waist. But she wasn't dressed to impress, she was dressed for the elements.

Liar.

So what if she was lying to herself? She refused to allow thoughts of Owen and his stupid, sexy kiss to penetrate her brain. *He* was the reason for the bags under her eyes. *He* was the reason she'd stayed up late, messing around on her laptop with the hope that she could block him from her mind. Later, she'd tossed and turned, tried to erase the way he'd kissed her and the way she'd kissed him back. What had she been thinking? Shoving her hands through his hair and practically swallowing his tongue.

"You're such a dumbass," she muttered to her reflection as she tried to conceal the dark circles under her eyes. Mortification reddened her cheeks when she thought back— for the umpteenth time—to the way she'd blatantly grabbed Owen's head and kissed him back like a sex starved crazy woman. In her defense, she hadn't had sex in a long time. So, technically, she was sex starved and would have probably reacted the same way if some other hot guy kissed her, right?

Wrong.

If she couldn't even lie to herself, how was she going to maintain the "I could care less that you kissed me" attitude once she saw Owen this morning? As she finished messing with her hair, she wondered—also for the umpteenth time— how Owen could have acted shocked over her parting shot last night. The last time he'd kissed her, he'd walked off with another woman. Other than her and Joy, there weren't any other women around to warm his bed. Was *he* sex starved? Was he that hard up that he'd think she'd stupidly have sex with him after the way he'd so easily dismissed her last year? He obviously didn't think much of her.

What was unfortunate? She couldn't stop thinking about him. The press of his hard chest, the way his thick arousal tempted her to throw her principles aside. The way he'd glided his tongue against hers, his firm lips demanding, coaxing, igniting something inside of her she couldn't name, and last night, couldn't control. His rough hands, the way he'd gripped her hips, caressed her bare skin, had made her want to do more than throw her principles aside. For a few heartbeats, Owen had made her feel alive, passionate...wanted. But reality had reared its ugly head and thankfully knocked some sense into her before she'd made a monstrous mistake.

She made a mental note to herself. No more creeping around dim hallways with Owen, especially if a bedroom was only a few feet away. From here on out, she would maintain nothing but a purely professional relationship with him. And when they returned to Chicago, she would make sure they went back to business as usual.

She frowned at her reflection. Things had never been "business as usual" between them. Of course she gave each CORE agent equal time when it came to whatever they needed during an investigation. But she didn't talk to the other agents daily, not like she did with Owen. She didn't look forward to their calls or anticipate their return to Chicago. How did she *not* notice this before? Well, she knew she spent a ridiculous amount of time on the phone with Owen when he was away on business. Still. Suddenly embarrassed, she closed her eyes. What if the other agents or Ian had noticed, too?

She packed up her toiletries, telling herself that the late night phone calls would come to an end, too. The favoritism she'd been absentmindedly showing Owen would also stop. She was a professional and needed to act like one, especially if Ian were to give her more opportunities to work in the field.

After stowing her things back in her room, she grabbed her computer bag, then headed downstairs. When she reached the bottom step, she came to an abrupt halt. Stunned, she stared at the dining room wall. The beautiful painting had been removed and replaced with a dry erase board, along with a corkboard. Taking another step, she realized all of the recipe cards Joy had written on last night were pinned to the corkboard. Next to it, the photos of all the missing students were taped to the wall, Josh Conway at the top of the collage.

Jake stepped into the room carrying a cup of coffee and wearing a grin. "Good morning," he said, then nodded to the wall. "What do you think?"

"Morning," she managed, then looked back to the wall. While it was a bit rudimentary compared to what she had in CORE's evidence and evaluation room, she was beyond ecstatic. While she loved her computer and having access to unlimited information with a few strokes to the keyboard, having everything pinned or taped to the wall now gave her the opportunity to better organize and streamline her thoughts, look at the clues, leads and evidence with a fresh perspective.

"I love it," she finally answered and moved to the wall. After picking up the dry erase marker and removing the cap, she inhaled the poignant, distinct scent. "Smells like home."

"Hey, Shorty. I think I've got some glue if you want to sniff that, too." Joy moved into the room carrying a couple of plates filled with waffles and eggs. "After you're done getting high, I've got some breakfast for you."

For all her gruffness, Joy was a wonderful person. The woman had gone through a lot of trouble to try and match what Rachel had back at CORE. A tenderness she hadn't thought she'd ever feel toward Joy warmed her heart and brought a prickle of tears to her eyes. This small gesture meant the world to her. Joy had thought about her, had taken the time to listen and understand her earlier frustrations, then took it upon herself to try and mimic the tools she needed to work an investigation.

"Thank you so much, Joy." She moved to the other woman and touched her shoulder. "This means so much to me."

"What? Breakfast? Damn, girl. If you're this grateful over waffles and eggs, wait until you try my beef brisket."

"Ain't that the truth," Walter said as he walked into the dining room and took a seat. "Joy's brisket is the best I've ever tasted."

Rachel chuckled. "I am grateful for your waffles and eggs,

and I look forward to your brisket." She thumbed toward the wall. "But I'm exceptionally grateful for this."

"I didn't do it," Joy said, then went back into the kitchen.

Rachel looked to Walter. "Did you?"

"Nope," he said, then picked up his fork and dove into the eggs.

She glanced at Jake, who had also taken a seat. "Don't look at me." He raised his hands. "I wish my office wasn't so cluttered. I'd love to have a setup like this."

That left only—

"Owen," Walter said as he poured syrup on his waffles. "How's the morning treatin' ya?"

Her stomach did a nervous flip as she turned toward the staircase. Dressed in jeans, boots and another heavy sweater that hugged his broad shoulders, Owen moved into the dining room. The memory of his kiss, the taste of his lips, the feel of his strong hands wrapped around her waist and grazing her bared skin collided together, and sent spastic tingles of excitement straight between her thighs. So much for keeping it professional, she thought and tried to ignore the traitorous sensations skidding through her body.

"Morning," Owen replied just as Joy entered the room again with more platefuls of waffles and eggs.

"You look like shit," Joy said to Owen, and set a plate on the table. "Here, start eating. I'll get you some coffee. It's good and strong. It'll wake you up and if you don't have any, it'll put hair on your chest."

Walter raised his coffee mug. "Ain't that the truth."

Rachel stared at Owen, who remained standing, his gaze locked on hers. "The wall," she said, despite the lump in her throat. She'd been so grateful when she'd thought Joy had gone out of her way to create a mini evidence and evaluation room. Now that she knew Owen had been the one to give her this gift, even after she'd ruined the afterglow of the hottest, sexiest, most arousing kiss of her life, she didn't know how to react. Actually, she knew exactly what she wanted to do, but was glad the large table stood between them and there were three other people in the room. Because right now, with all of the foreign, overwhelming emotions bombarding her head and body, she could picture herself launching into his arms. Kissing him, stripping him naked, backing him onto the stairs and straddling him, riding him until they both came.

She didn't want to want him. She didn't want to care about him. He'd hurt her. Had walked away after their first kiss, leaving her confused when he went home with a prettier, taller, skinnier woman. If she allowed him to touch her again, she wasn't sure if she could resist him, even if her mind knew having sex with him could be a huge mistake. And sex with Owen would be a disastrous mistake. He'd fuck her, then that would be it. Off to find the next conquest, no doubt a former or current beauty queen, or maybe a super model.

With that last thought in mind, she realized the entire room had gone silent and that she and Owen were locked in some sort of unspoken staring contest. Ignoring the heat burning her cheeks, she said, "Thank you for setting this up for us. It's a big help."

Eyes still on hers, he moved into the dining room. "Not for us, for you." He broke eye contact and sat next to Walter.

"Real nice." Walter nodded while wiping his mouth with his napkin. "Thoughtful." He looked to Joy. "Don't you think?"

Joy raised a brow. "It's not like he brought her flowers. *That's* thoughtful. But I guess it makes a statement."

Oh. My. God. Seriously?

Rachel glanced at Jake, who had paused mid-bite, and had his eyes on her. "It kicks ass," he said, then took a bite of his waffle.

"Yes." Rachel took a seat. "What Owen did was thoughtful, made a statement and definitely kicks ass." She met Owen's gaze from across the table. "Thank you."

"Where'd you find this stuff?" Walter asked as he added more syrup to his plate.

"I drove to the next county and found a twenty-four hour Wal-Mart."

Holy crap. It had been around midnight when they'd gone

their separate ways. For Owen to do all of this, he had to have only ended up with a few hours of sleep. Was this his way of apologizing for the mistletoe kiss? Then again, he looked as if she were talking Chinese last night when she'd told him his kisses had improved from the last time. Had the way she'd kissed been that forgettable? Or had he been drunk at the CORE Christmas party? She had tasted and smelled whiskey on his breath that night, but he hadn't acted drunk.

Her mind spun with too many unanswered questions, while her hardened heart cracked with a tiny sliver of hope. Even before they'd come to Bola, Owen had been nothing but kind and considerate. Since they'd been here, he'd shown her compassion, patience and with what he'd done to the wall, he'd proven how well he knew her, that he'd paid attention to her wants and needs. Maybe last night's kiss was his way of offering comfort after a long, stressful day. Or maybe she should stop thinking about all of this and focus her energy on what they had to do next.

Find Bill Baker.

Not hungry, but also unsure when they'd eat again, she picked up her fork. "Again, I really appreciate what you've done. I also have a few recipe cards to add to the board." She went on to tell Owen and the others that they still were waiting on the DNA results from Sean's clothes—which she expected today or tomorrow—plus they still needed the information the dean had promised regarding who had donated the security equipment that had *coincidentally* malfunctioned before Sean and Josh had been taken.

"Did you ask Jake if he might have something in the archives about the twenty-five-year old Hell Week?" Owen asked her.

"Twenty-five-year old Hell Week?" Jake repeated. "What are you talking about?"

"When Owen and I met with the dean yesterday we asked when and why Wexman initiated their no hazing policy. He told us the policy began twenty-five years ago, but wouldn't give us a reason why."

"Yeah." Owen reached for his coffee mug. "He gave us a line of BS about not being able to discuss what had happened because of privacy issues. All he'd say was that some very bad things happened."

Jake arched a brow and shook his head. "If there'd been an arrest, it would've been public record…assuming the kids involved in this particular Hell Week were at least eighteen."

"That's what we thought," Rachel said. She then told Jake what Percy, Walter and the others at the bar had said about the fire that had occurred in Bola the same night of the mysterious Hell Week drama that had started the no hazing policy.

"I remember that," Joy said, and began gathering empty plates. "The whole dock caught on fire. Burned a few buildings to nothing, took out a handful of boats, too. I'd say seventy-five percent of the town was at the docks trying to put out the flames."

"But do you remember hearing about something bad happening at the university around that same night?" Rachel asked.

"Sorry, no. But I do remember a bunch of students coming into town to help." Joy paused and glanced at the wall. "It was late, around eleven when the fire broke out. We worked throughout the night and finally had it stopped by dawn. If anything else happened that week, I didn't hear about it. All me and anyone else could think about was rebuilding the town."

"I heard about the fire a few months after I took over as sheriff," Jake said. "Never heard about anything bad happening at Wexman, though. Well, other than the Hell Week disappearances. I'll call the office and have our receptionist dig through the archives when she has the time." He looked at his watch. "Speaking of time…are you about ready to head out? The search party is meeting in about thirty minutes."

Rachel wanted to ask Jake about Percy's story regarding his grandmother, Ethel Rodeck. But he was right. They needed to leave, and she could ask him later. She stood and gathered her plate.

"Leave it," Joy said. "I got this, you go find my nephew."

Nodding, she raced up stairs to grab her coat, boots, hat and gloves. By the time she made it downstairs, the dining room was empty. As she slipped on her coat and headed for the foyer, she ran into Joy just outside the kitchen doorway.

"Put these hand warmers inside your gloves and boots. Make sure Owen does the same." Joy handed her a small bag and two thick scarves that looked handmade. "Nothing pretty about chapped skin, so make sure you wrap your face up, same with Owen."

"Thanks, Joy. I really appreciate it. I'm sure Owen will, too."

"I think Owen would probably appreciate a better thank you than the one you gave him this morning," Joy remarked as Rachel opened the front door.

Pausing, Rachel looked over her shoulder. "I don't know what you mean," she lied.

"You're a smart woman, but apparently not too bright when it comes to men." Joy held up a hand before Rachel could defend herself. "Let's just hope you're smart enough to figure out what the hell is going on in this town. I want my nephew home."

Owen now understood the true definition of Joy's eloquent phrase, "balls ass freezing." Despite wearing heavy layers of clothing, every part of his body had begun to grow numb from the cold. And they'd only been exposed to the freezing temperatures for little over an hour. If Bill had survived crashing his car into the river, without proper shelter, Owen doubted he'd lasted through the night.

At least the cold and futile search for Bill had taken his mind off of Rachel. His boot sank into a snowdrift when he glanced in her direction. He swore under his breath as icy, wet snow slipped inside his boot. The snow and cold were miserable, the gray skies gloomy, and knowing the man they were searching for was likely dead...dismal and depressing as hell.

He looked at Rachel again just as she slid the scarf Joy had given her under her chin. After removing one glove, she wiped perspiration from her upper lip then blew out a stream of breath that caught on the frigid air and then quickly dissipated. Jake said something to her, and touched her shoulder. She nodded and smiled. As she replaced the scarf, she glanced his way. Their gazes locked. He thought about her lips, the way her breasts had pressed against his chest last night, how soft her skin had been when he'd gripped her hips.

Jake touched her shoulder again, then pointed to the left. She blinked and quickly turned away, then began following Jake's new direction.

Fucking Jake.

As he trudged through the snow, he thought about all the different ways he could tell Jake exactly what he thought of him. When the wind kicked up with wicked intent, causing him to shield his eyes and then his head when a chunk of snow plopped from a pine tree, he realized Jake wasn't the problem. The stubborn, caustic, sexy, sassy woman with killer curves was the issue.

She confused him, running hot one minute, then icy cold the next. He didn't understand her. Didn't understand what the hell she'd meant last night when she'd said the kiss had been a definite improvement over the last time. *Last time?* He'd been aching for the chance to kiss her and more for nearly four years. If he'd kissed her, he would've damn sure remembered. If Walter hadn't been in the Lexus with them during their drive to the river, he would have asked her about her *last time* bullshit.

Last time my ass, he thought and scanned the open field they were approaching and the line of woods beyond it.

"Walter," Jake called. "Let's split up from here. Have your men fan out ten feet from one another and take them east toward the old state park hunting post. Call if you find anything."

As Walter moved the six men he'd been leading, Jake had

them continuing west. When they'd first arrived, they'd done another search near the river, checking the shoreline and the woods within one hundred yards of the water. When they'd found nothing, not even a single footprint, Jake had them split into two teams. They'd been walking for about twenty minutes and while he wasn't sure how far they'd gone, he could no longer hear the rush of the river. Actually, with all the cawing crows flying overhead, he was lucky he could hear himself think.

Maybe that was a good thing. Because all he could think about was last night and Rachel's cryptic parting remark.

Last time.

After she'd slammed the door in his face, he'd gone to his room. Between having sex on the brain and her sarcastic, confounding barb, he couldn't sleep. Restless, horny and pissed, he'd left Joy's. Initially he'd planned to go for a drive to clear his head. When he'd wound up in the next county and had spotted the Wal-Mart, he'd thought about Rachel's frustration with not having the equipment she was used to back at CORE. He'd bought what supplies the store had, not as a peace offering—hell, he wouldn't know what to apologize for anyway—and not as a way to charm her out of her yoga pants, either. He'd made those purchases because he'd wanted do whatever possible to help wrap up this investigation and go back to Chicago. Once home, Ian would give him a new assignment, hopefully a thousand miles away from Chicago, and he could put some distance between him and Rachel. She drove him crazy, and he could use the time away from her to figure out how to shake whatever hold she had over him.

"Everyone spread out in a line," Jake called. "Once we cross this open field we'll head into the woods."

"The edge of the university property is about seventy-five yards through those trees," Percy said and pointed to the woods in the distance. The bartender, along with about two-dozen Bola residents, as well as a handful of guys Bill worked with at the university, had also joined the early morning search party. "Do we need permission to continue the search once we hit that land?"

Jake looked over his shoulder. "I'm not worried about it, considering Bill works for them. Come on, let's go."

Fifteen blustering minutes later, they reached the woods. The naked trees and their thick trunks gave a small reprieve from the biting wind, but Owen suspected that wouldn't last long. Another small clearing loomed in the distance, which meant they'd be out in the open again.

With the back of his gloved hand, he pushed his knit cap up a little to rub his throbbing temple. Exhausted, cold and irritated, he wanted the search to end. He wanted to find Bill—alive—head back to Joy's, take a hot shower, then sleep. Unfortunately, sleep would have to wait. After they finished with the search, he and Rachel had to head back to the university for a couple more interviews, then they'd likely visit Sean at the hospital. Plus, knowing Rachel, she'd probably have more busy work for him.

The ache in his temple grew just thinking about reading through more lists of names and all that other cross-referencing bullshit she had him doing last night. And he swore if those fucking crows didn't stop all their squawking, either his head would explode or he'd pull out his gun and use the birds for target practice once they reached the next clearing.

"Damn." Percy stumbled over a rotted log, then righted himself against a tree. "Look at the way those crows are circling."

Owen dropped his head back and looked through the naked treetops. About a dozen or so black birds dipped and dove, but remained, eerily, in the same mid-air location. A chill swept through him that had nothing to do with the cold temperatures. He looked to Rachel who was about twenty feet from him. As she picked her way through the woods, she kept her eyes on the ground. Because she didn't acknowledge what Percy had just said, he assumed she hadn't heard him.

Taking advantage, Owen rushed to the bartender's side. "Why would crows circle?"

Without pausing, Percy lifted a shoulder. "Probably feeding

off a dead deer or whatever the coyotes could've left behind."

He gripped the sleeve of Percy's heavy-duty hunting coat, then glanced at Rachel, who continued to navigate the wooded terrain. "What about Bill?" he asked, keeping his tone quiet. If Bill ended up being the crows' current meal, he didn't want Rachel witnessing something so horrendous.

Percy jerked his head and stared at him, his eyes growing round with either understanding or horror. Owen couldn't be sure which, and at this point it didn't matter. Bill might not be the crows' focus. The missing man might not be out here, period. "Sorry." Owen let go of Percy's sleeve. "That was morbid. I'm sure you're right about the deer or whatever," he said, even as his gut twisted with unease.

"Walter found footprints," Jake shouted, his voice bouncing off the tree trunks. He waved his phone. "Sounds like he's heading back in our direction. Let's get to the clearing up ahead, then head east and intercept his group."

Still wide-eyed, Percy stared at him and shook his head. "This ain't good." He looked over his shoulder to where Rachel hiked. "The women in my family grew up hunting, but what you're suggesting isn't something even I think I can stomach. How about your partner?"

The only murder victims Rachel had ever seen were from photographs or video footage. No doubt he considered her tough and—mentally and emotionally—one of the strongest women he knew. Still, he'd rather shelter her from what he suspected lay beyond the trees. Then again, working in the field was important to her and she needed to earn her stripes. "She'll be fine," he said and quickened his pace.

As he neared the edge of the tree line, he caught sight of where the crows circled, and took off in a full sprint. The icy air burned his lungs as he ran through the clearing toward the next set of trees. Toward where dozens of crows gathered on the ground and in the sky.

His heart sped, and adrenaline and dread rushed through his veins. Percy and Jake shouted behind him, but between the cawing and wind, their calls were muffled and indistinct. Then he heard Rachel cry out, the alarm in her voice had him slowing. He turned, slowly jogged backward, then freaked by the horror crumpling her pretty face, stopped dead. She'd shoved the scarf under her chin and was running full steam, waving her arms and calling for him. Worried he'd missed something while sprinting to the crows, terrified by the way she was panicking, he retraced his steps and took off toward her. Running as fast as he could through the layers of snow until they stood face-to-face.

"Oh my God," she panted, bent and placed her gloved hands on her legs. "You scared the shit out of me."

He grabbed her upper arms and gripped her thick coat sleeves. Torn between shaking her and hauling her into his arms, he asked, "What the hell happened? Why are you—?"

A shot exploded behind him.

He hauled Rachel into his arms, covered her head and used his body to shield her. Keeping her protected, he quickly looked over his shoulder just as a thick black cloak rose from the ground then scattered in a wave of beating wings and piercing shrieks.

"It's just Walter firing a warning shot," Jake said as he slowed to a jog and approached them. "Didn't want you getting in the way."

Men's shouts replaced the crows' caws. With reluctance, he released Rachel, and turned back toward the tree line. The moment he did, he wished he hadn't let go of her. Wearing his security guard uniform, Bill Baker sat on the snow-covered ground against a tree. And it didn't look like he was sleeping.

Taking Rachel by the hand, he put himself in front of her and slowly approached. Walter and his men had already surrounded Bill. By the haunting expressions paling their faces, Owen knew this wasn't going to be pretty.

"What do we have?" Jake pushed his way between the men. They parted ways, giving the sheriff ample room and in the process revealed a sight Owen could have gone without seeing.

The crows had picked at Bill's eyes, leaving behind hollow cavities that made the man look less human and more like something out of a grotesque horror movie. The birds had torn the skin away from his mouth and fleshy cheeks, giving Bill a monstrous grin. Thick ropes intersected and twined around Bill's neck, wide chest and stomach. His arms had been wrapped behind his back in a way only a limber contortionist could manage. In a way meant to keep Bill from protecting himself from the harsh elements, the birds…from escaping.

When Rachel gasped, he turned and realized she'd moved next to him. As she stared at Bill's lifeless body, her face grew alarmingly ashen. Her eyes watered with unshed tears, but she quickly blinked and held a gloved hand to her mouth. Knowing this was likely the first victim she'd encountered, he had an overwhelming protective urge to shelter her. Actually, he wanted to shake some sense into her. She might be brilliant and have a knack for coming up with different angles and leads, but she shouldn't be in the field. She shouldn't have to see this. Then again, maybe now she'd realize her position as CORE's computer forensic analyst wasn't such a bad thing, after all. She could go back to her regular job, to the safety of the office and not have him worrying. About her, about how cases like this one would affect her emotional, mental and physical well-being.

Worried she might vomit, he ushered her away from the body and other men. "Do you have the camera?"

Her gaze remained on Bill as she nodded and pulled the small camera out of her pocket.

"I'll take some pictures. Why don't you hang tight and—"

"No. I can do this," she said, but the uncertainty in her tone told him otherwise.

"Are you sure?"

"I'm sure," she said, and still holding the camera, added, "I'll take the pictures. Just give me a head's up if it looks like I'm missing anything."

His earlier anger subsided. He still didn't want her exposed to this, but he couldn't help but admire her determination. She'd set out to do a job, to lead her first investigation and she planned to see it through, despite the outcome. Despite the possible body count.

When they reached the group of men again, Jake took a step away from Bill's body. "Did anybody call the other team yet?" After receiving a unanimous no, he nodded. "Good. Let's hold off. I don't want Hal here for this."

Bill's dad was part of the other group that had splintered off after searching the river. Like the sheriff, Owen was also grateful those men hadn't been notified of their discovery yet. He could only imagine the distraught father's grief. Until they had a better look at what exactly happened to Bill, he didn't want Hal compromising their possible crime scene.

"I'm not a medical examiner," Jake said. "But I think Bill died of hypothermia."

Rachel squatted and began taking pictures. "The rope around his neck is loose. He could twist his head, but couldn't slip out of it. Look at the skin around his neck."

Rope burns lined Bill's blue skin. Bits of flesh had been removed along the abrasion, likely from the crows.

"More of the same here," Walter said from behind the tree. "Looks like he tried to work his way out of the ropes around his wrist." He craned his neck around the tree trunk. "He had to have been in a lot of pain. Got some nasty frostbite. I'm guessing his shoulders were dislocated, too."

Owen had suspected the same thing. Replacing his warm gloves for Latex ones, he bent and examined Bill's neck and face. Due to the freezing temperatures and rigor mortis, he had a hard time twisting his neck. Leaving the body exam for the ME, he moved to stand, but something sticking out of Bill's front shirt pocket caught his attention. Plucking the folded piece of paper free, he flexed his hand to ward off the numbness, then opened the note.

Dread gripped him, held him by the throat and shook him to the core.

"What does it say?" Rachel asked, her voice quiet, uncertain, as if she might not want to really know.

He glanced at her, then back to the note. "Now look what you made me do. Enjoy the rest of Hell Week. I know I will."

CHAPTER 14

RACHEL BLEW OUT a deep breath after Walter closed the back passenger door of Owen's Lexus. They'd dropped Walter off at Dixon Medical Center where he planned to meet with Joy and Bill's dad, Hal. Personally, she thought Walt should take Hal back to Joy's. She didn't see the point in the three of them sitting in a waiting room drinking crappy coffee while the medical examiner discovered what they already knew. Bill had been murdered.

Her nauseated stomach rolled, her heart raced, her head ached. With the image of Bill Baker seared to her memory, she fought the urge to vomit, cry, complain and whine. The sudden impulse to jump out of the now moving vehicle had her fisting her hands in her lap before she reached for the door. The roomy Lexus grew rapidly stuffy and suffocating. She didn't want to be here. In the car. In Bola. She wanted to be home, lying on her ratty sofa, wearing her favorite PJs and drinking a gallon of vodka. What had happened to Bill was her fault. If she hadn't involved him...

Tears prickled her eyes and her throat tightened. She drew in a shaky breath and wiped her sweaty palms on her jeans. Damn it. She needed out of this SUV. If she couldn't magically transport to her apartment in Chicago, she would at least like to go back to Joy's. Needing to be alone, needing to unleash the pain and grief tearing her from the inside out, she ached for the solitude of her room.

"You doing okay?" Owen asked as he turned the Lexus toward the direction of the university.

"Yes…no. I feel horrible about Bill," she admitted, but stopped from saying anything more for fear she'd have an emotional conniption fit if she continued down that path. While she knew in her gut—in her heart—Owen wouldn't hold a crying jag against her and would probably give her some well-needed words of wisdom, she refused to break down in front of him. Once they were back in Chicago, Ian would probably expect Owen to give him a detailed report with regards to how she'd handled the investigation.

How could she expect Ian to let her work in the field if she couldn't hold it together? She couldn't even view a dead body without the urge to puke. Curling into the fetal position and crying probably wasn't proper field agent behavior. What was she even thinking? At this point, she wasn't sure she wanted to be a field agent. After seeing Bill, frozen and tied to a tree, his eyes and parts of his flesh plucked away by crows, the interior of CORE's evidence and evaluation room was proving more her speed.

"The killer wanted him to suffer." Owen removed a glove and turned down the heat. "That's something I don't understand. Are we wrong to assume the killer murdered Bill because he used the pickup truck and wanted to destroy evidence? Or could it be that Bill was working with the killer and he somehow became a liability?"

She didn't want to talk about Bill. Every time she heard his name or thought about him, she pictured his face. His hollowed out eyes, the way his teeth had shown because the birds had removed his lips and parts of his cheeks. Cringing, she shifted in her seat. The urge to grab a pencil and do some serious gnawing struck her fast and hard. But her jaw already hurt from grinding her teeth and Owen hated when she chewed on pencils.

Shoving her hands inside her pockets, she looked out the

window. At the gloomy gray skies, the snow covered ground and barren trees. "I'm not sure what to think. Tying Bill to a tree and leaving him to…ah…freeze to death seems personal. Cruel." *Unnecessary.*

He touched her shoulder. Even though she wore a heavy coat, the contact brought comfort and at the same time, made her tense. While she'd longed for his comfort, for so much more of him beyond the physical, she'd learned a long time ago not to depend on anyone but herself.

"Do you want me to take you back to Joy's?" he asked as he pulled his hand away.

Yes. "No. There's too much to do. By the time we're finished with our interviews at the university, hopefully the ME will have something for us. Which reminds me. I need to see if Jake wants us to ship Bill's clothes and the rope used on him to Chihiro. Same with the note. We should have a handwriting analysis done to compare to the previous notes and also see if we can pull a print. Or maybe he'll want to involve the Michigan State Police now that…you know."

"Chi-who?"

When she turned to remind him that Chihiro Kimura was the forensic DNA tech at DecaLab, she caught him grinning. With that sexy smile of his momentarily wiping Bill's image from her mind, she half-smiled. "Har, har. I'm serious about the state police. Especially with the Bigfoot festival starting tomorrow. Jake doesn't have enough men to patrol the area. With an unpredictable killer running free, I think he needs to ask for help."

"We *are* the help."

Right. Some help she'd turned out to be. Because of her, Bill was dead. "If you say so."

"I do. But I agree. It's not a bad idea."

He drove through the gates of Wexman University. The school no longer appealed to her the way it had when she'd first visited with Sean two years ago.

Funny how murder taints a place.

After Owen parked in front of the library, he killed the

ignition. "First stop, Bill's girlfriend."

And after that, they had ten more interviews with the Wexman maintenance employees that had been with the university for at least the past ten to fifteen years. Damn. If she wasn't on the fence about working in the field she would have taken Owen up on the offer to go back to Joy's. They still had a long day ahead of them and all she wanted—needed—was time to digest and deal with what had happened to Bill.

The security guard's gruesome image filled her mind. Overwhelming grief gripped her, took root in her heart. She gripped the door handle, but hesitated.

You wanted action and adventure. Now you have it. You can to do this.

She opened the door and caught her breath as the icy wind rushed through her lungs. Yeah, she wanted action and adventure, and she could do this. But the question remained...would she ever want to work in the field again?

Four hours later, Rachel slammed the Lexus's passenger door shut. She couldn't remember having a shittier day, and it was only four in the afternoon.

"Don't take it out on the car," Owen said as he closed the door.

"Sorry." She crossed her arms to ward off the cold. "I'm frustrated. That last guy we talked to was a total jackass." Instead of showing any signs of sympathy for Bill, the last maintenance worker they'd met with had not only acted as if Hell Week was a bunch of bullshit, but that Bill was an incompetent fool. If the man hadn't had a solid alibi, she'd have loved to bring him in for more questioning. Hell Week was real. And Bill...she hadn't known the man, but incompetent or not, no one deserved to die the way he had.

"I get it. But you need to shake assholes like him off and stay focused." He held open the door to Dixon Medical Center. "Hopefully Jake and the ME will have something for us."

As they walked through the basement hallway of the hospital, her queasy stomach did a flip. She hoped to God she wouldn't have to view Bill's body again. Actually, she hoped Joy, Hal and Walter had already left. Seeing Bill on a metal slab was bad enough. Witnessing the pain his death caused his family would be worse. She might not know Joy or Walter well, but she'd come to like and respect them both. And Hal had found her brother the night he'd been left for dead. These were good people who shouldn't have to deal with murder.

Before they reached the morgue, Jake rounded the corner from a different hallway. "Hey. Perfect timing. I was starting to worry you two weren't going to make it. How'd the interviews go?"

Rachel unzipped her coat, then pulled her notebook and pencil from her pocket. "Longer than we planned. Is the ME ready for us?" Although she kept her tone even, her mouth grew dry and her heart raced with dread. She wasn't ready for the ME and wasn't sure if she ever would be, for that matter. After this case, she'd have to do some serious soul searching. Working in the field had major drawbacks. She stared at the word 'Morgue' etched on the frosted glass of the door at the end of the hall. Yeah, some serious drawbacks.

Jake knocked on the door. "Let's find out."

A young man, who looked as if he'd just graduated from high school, shut off the faucet he'd been using to wash his hands. Frowning, he dried his hands with a paper towel as he approached them. "Good to see you, Jake. Just sorry it's under these circumstances."

Jake shook his hand. "No kidding. Where were you this morning? I was expecting to see you, not your old man. You should be ashamed of yourself for making him hike through the snow."

The ME sent Jake a sheepish grin. "Dad insisted. He said the people of this county expect to see him, not his punk ass kid." He turned and motioned to Rachel and Owen. "The investigators from Chicago, I assume?"

Rachel shook his hand and introduced herself and Owen. "Henry Cline," he said. "If we were at River's Edge, I'd buy all of you a drink. I know I could use one. Unfortunately, we're not. So why don't we get at it and let me tell you what I've found."

She'd been so focused on Henry and his interaction with Jake that she hadn't bothered to look around the room. Now that she did, she caught sight of a body on a metal table, a white sheet pulled up over the head.

Bile rose in her throat, but she swallowed it down and followed the others across the room. Henry stopped in front of an x-ray view box, turned its light on, then reached for the clipboard sitting on the nearby counter. "Here are a couple of shots of the head."

Rachel forced herself to look at the x-ray, and held back a gasp. The two different x-rays showed large cracks running along the front and back of Bill's head. Relief slightly settled her nervous stomach. Maybe Bill had been dead when he'd been tied to the tree, after all. She hoped so, because she couldn't imagine the fear and pain he would have gone through if he had been left bound and conscious, with no way to free himself, and no hope of rescue.

"He had a couple of skull fractures," Henry continued, "but whatever was used to cause them didn't break the skin. I did find slight swelling and signs of bleeding around the brain."

"Would that kill him?" Jake asked.

"No. Cause of death is hypothermia. Based on his stage of frostbite, I estimate the time of death to be somewhere between ten and twelve Monday night."

"I noticed part of Bill's nose was blue and it almost looked like he had blood blisters. Is that...ah...?" She tried not to picture Bill's face. "Frostbite?"

"Yes. He had it on his fingers, ears and I found signs on his cheeks. The crows removed a lot of the damaged skin and then some." He sighed and shook his head. "My dad has been the county coroner for forty years. I've been in and out of the morgue since I was kid. I've seen a lot of things, but this...this doesn't settle well. At all."

"Aside from the obvious, what do you mean?" Owen asked.

The only other pre-mortem injuries are his dislocated shoulders." Henry turned off the x-ray view box. "Mr. Baker weighs two hundred and forty pounds. According to my dad, he was found about a half mile from the river. Right?"

"That's right," she said, her mind zeroing in on what she suspected Henry was thinking.

"How long did it take your search party to walk a half mile in the snow?" Henry asked, and folded his arms and clipboard against his chest.

With the way the ME frowned, add on the weariness lining his eyes, she realized he was older than she'd originally thought. Perceptive, too.

"A solid hour," Jake answered.

"If it took us an hour and we were walking on our own, uninjured, how long would it take to drag Bill?" Owen rubbed his chin, then looked over his shoulder. "The ligature marks around his neck and hands...could be his wrists were tied and he was forced to walk."

"Could be he knew the person he walked with," she added. "Not that it matters. Faint tracks were found in the snow and none of them indicated someone was dragged."

"Between the frostbite and the crows it's difficult to say whether he was bound before reaching the tree." Henry shook his head. "In my opinion, the ligature marks around his neck were of his own doing. Like he was trying to loosen the ropes. I found abrasion along his chin that led me to that conclusion." With a long exhale, he looked at the clipboard, then flipped a page. "Our lab rushed the toxicology report. No alcohol or drugs of any kind."

"Did they screen for Rohypnol or chloroform?" Rachel asked. Again, not that it mattered at this point. Even if Bill had the drug in his system—a drug that would link him to Sean and his kidnapping/beating—the killer had left a note behind. *Why?*

"I'm friends with Dr. Gregory. I know about your brother and am no stranger to all this Hell Week crap. So, yeah. They checked for those drugs and didn't find any." He set the clipboard on the counter. "Did you want to view the body?"

She glanced between Owen and Jake, then offered her hand to Henry. "We're good." As she exited the morgue, she felt as if they were leaving with more questions than answers. Could it be that Bill had known the killer? Could he have been involved in the kidnappings? And the note stuffed in his pocket. Was the killer taunting them?

"We could have used that steam coming out of your ears when we were out in the freezing cold," Owen said as he snagged her arm. "You're obviously thinking hard about something. What do you have?"

She leaned against the whitewashed, basement cinder blocks, and stuffed her hands in her pockets. "Too many questions and not enough answers."

Jake mimicked her pose against the opposite wall. "Did something happen during your interviews at the university?" he asked, his voice quiet, distant.

Owen ran both hands through his hair, then linked his fingers behind his head. "Yes and no." He dropped his arms and looked to Jake. "Bill's girlfriend, Kaylie Gallagher, isn't a girlfriend at all."

"So, Joy misunderstood."

"No." Rachel shook her head. "I think *Bill* misunderstood."

Jake nodded and winced. "Gotcha."

"We caught up with her just when she was finishing her morning shift at the library," Rachel continued. "Kaylie works part time at the library, but is also Professor Stronach's teaching assistant."

Jake pushed off the wall. "I can't stand that guy."

Owen grinned. "You and me both."

"So what did the girl have to say?" Jake asked.

Rachel swallowed hard while trying her best to keep her emotions in check. But she couldn't stop Kaylie's tear-streaked face from popping into her head. She cleared her throat and looked to the tiled floor. "She said she saw Bill Friday afternoon. He stopped by after his shift to let her know the security system had malfunctioned. That was the last time they spoke."

"And the other interviews?" Jake asked.

Owen quickly told him that they'd met with ten university employees. "These men began working for Wexman ten to fifteen years ago. The other two men on our list retired from their jobs. One moved to South Carolina and the other died three years ago."

"None of them fit our profile," Rachel added.

"You said two of the guys retired. What about the ones who retired around the time Hell Week started?"

Rachel frowned. "If they retired twenty years ago, they'd be too old."

"Maybe your profile is wrong."

She bit the inside of her cheek. Jake was being a jerk and she didn't need it. "Maybe you should tell us if you made any progress on the incident that started the no hazing policy."

"Fair enough," the sheriff said with a curt nod. "I got nothing."

"Not one thing?"

"That would be the definition of nothing."

"Why so combative, Jake?" The way Owen clenched his jaw belied the calm, quiet tone he used on the sheriff. "Something on your mind you want to get out?"

Irritation flashed in Jake's eyes. He rubbed a hand down his face. "No."

"Good," Owen said. "Have you thought about our suggestion?"

Between their interview with Kaylie and the university employees, she'd called Jake and recommended he ask the Michigan State Police to become involved. He'd said he would think about it, but based on the way the investigators with the state police had treated him and the community he represented, she'd worried he wouldn't be on board.

"I thought about it, and I think you're right. We need some

extra manpower during the festival. State police also has a lab in Neguanee. It's about an hour and half from here. Their facility doesn't have all the technical services like the Lansing lab, and probably won't be as quick as the lab CORE uses, but it's close, and worth a shot. I'll make the call when I get back to my office. Which is where I'm heading now." He started down the hallway, then stopped, and looked over his shoulder. "Bill was a friend." Then with a slight nod, he continued on until he disappeared around a corner.

"He's not mad at us," she finally said, then started to walk down the hallway.

Owen walked alongside. "Nope. He's pissed off at the situation. Can't say I blame him."

Nodding, she shoved her hands into her pocket before she did something stupid. Like reach for Owen. Just like Jake, she was angry with the whole situation. What happened to Bill didn't make sense. "Why leave a note?"

Owen pushed the door open and held it for her. The cold wind practically took her breath away.

"Now look what you made me do," he said, repeating a line from the note, and unlocked the Lexus. Once inside the SUV, he started the ignition and cranked the heat. "It's as if the killer is *blaming* us."

"Or taunting." She looked out the window, then rubbed her temple. "Let's say Bill's an innocent victim."

"Do you think he is?"

She thought about Bill, her initial interpretation of him, what Joy and others had said about him. "Honestly, yes. He might have slacked a little on the job, but he doesn't seem the type who would get involved in kidnapping and murder. I think he had too much integrity."

"Agreed. Okay, so Bill's an innocent victim..."

"Right. Friday, the killer somehow causes the malfunction of the majority of the campus's electronic locks. Saturday, he not only drugs my brother and Josh, but Bill, too. While Bill is out of it, he moves the security camera at the residence hall, takes Bill's pickup, kidnaps Sean and Josh, then..." Damn it, she didn't know.

"Then he returns the truck. Bill's too sick to notice it's been moved," he finished for her. "If Sean had been tossed from a truck Sunday night, then it couldn't have been Bill's. He told us he went home after his shift and stayed in bed the rest of the day."

"Unless the killer went to his house and borrowed it again," she suggested. "But that doesn't ring true. Too risky."

"So the killer uses his own truck or SUV to get rid of Sean. He did it late on a Sunday night when the traffic is down to nothing and the risk of being seen isn't as high."

"Then why use Bill's truck at all?" She drummed her fingers on her thigh. "Okay, back to Bill. We ask him to go to the lab for blood work, he leaves and disappears. Someone either overheard us, or Bill might've let it slip...I can't help thinking that if we didn't ask him—"

He grabbed her hand. "We didn't kill him."

She stared at their joined, gloved hands and wished they were skin to skin, his strength and confidence seeping into her. Although she knew in her heart that Bill's death wasn't her fault, she couldn't stop the guilt. She couldn't help thinking about how they could have done things differently, like escort Bill to the lab themselves.

Bill's horrifying image entered her mind again and her stomach knotted. Before she burst into tears, she let go of Owen's hand and said, "Anyway, if the killer was concerned about Bill's blood work coming up positive for Rohypnol, it makes sense that he would go after Bill before he made it to the lab."

"Then why kill him the way he did? Why tie him to a tree and force him to freeze to death?"

She shook her head at her stupidity. "Because the killer wanted the drug to run its course," she said with exasperation. "And because Rohypnol could stay in the system for up to sixty hours, if he murdered Bill too soon, a tox screen would still show evidence of the drug. Tying Bill to the tree gave the killer extra time, but also ensured him that Bill wouldn't be talking to anyone."

"Great theory, and I don't disagree." He parked the Lexus in front of Bill's house. Hal, Joy and Walter had promised to meet them there to give them a chance to look through Bill's things. Rachel hoped to find items from Saturday night. Anything, something that might put them in the right direction.

"But?" she asked.

He killed the ignition. "Again. Why leave the note? Unless it was meant to blame or taunt us, it seems like overkill to me."

She stepped out of the Lexus. A crow cawed from above, and as she watched the ugly bird soar, the image of Bill's crow-bitten, frozen face emerged. She shook the memory from her mind and focused on what Owen had just said.

Meant to taunt or blame us...overkill...

Her mind raced with everything they'd just discussed, along with the interviews they'd done today, as well as the leads and clues they'd organized last night. Glancing away from the gray, cloudy sky, she caught sight of the bumper stickers on the backend of Walt's truck. One said, "Gone Sasquatching," while the other had the words "I Believe" etched onto a Bigfoot footprint. She thought about the Bigfoot festival starting tomorrow, about the hundreds of people who would be infiltrating the town and campgrounds, about the need for extra security, and how the festival might distract from the initial Hell Week.

She drew in a shaky breath and stared at Bill's house. "Why do I feel like he's setting us up?"

Naked rage clawed at his throat. That pure emotion, so strong, so vile, so unlike anything he'd experienced since that fateful night twenty-five years ago splintered. Raising his tear-soaked face he stared blindly out the kitchen window. To the woods. To where all his pledges rested. Their young bodies decimated by the elements and muriatic acid. Their short lives a token of

Hell Week. *His* Hell Week. His shame, anger and hatred.

Chin trembling, he raised the brandy snifter. With his nose too clogged to enjoy the aroma of the aged cognac, deeper frustration rose and shattered. *Why?* Why did Junior have to be such a fucked-up piece of shit? He'd thought she had half a brain, but clearly had been wrong. She couldn't follow simple directions. She couldn't do as she was told. Had she no respect for him? For his authority? Didn't she realize whom she was dealing with? The white trash Townies knew. They knew to fear him and so did the little shitheads prancing around campus in their designer clothes mommy and daddy had bought for them, flashing their fancy phones and latest digital devices as if they didn't cost what most Townies might make in a month.

Obviously Junior had never learned to respect authority. She would. He gripped the snifter, furious the phlegm gathering in his throat and the snot in his nose made drinking the expensive liquor pointless. Turning away from the window, he moved into the living room where a roaring fire crackled. He stared at the flames, envisioned tossing Junior into the hearth. Imagined her hair igniting, her face melting, her mouth open as she screamed and writhed in pain.

But he couldn't touch her. He couldn't do a fucking thing to her. At this point, she needed to remain…unmarred. If she moved around campus with bruises on her face, people would question. They would demand answers.

Despite not being able to taste the cognac or feel the delicious burn slide down his throat, he tossed back a swallow, then threw the glass into the fireplace. The snifter cracked and splintered into pieces, just like his patience. He might not be able to punish her now, but the time would come. Maybe the little bitch should experience Hell Week first hand. He couldn't help smiling as he pictured his daughter bound and hanging from the rock wall in the basement. His smile grew as he fantasized. Beating her. Torturing her. Making her feel and understand the pain he'd gone through twenty-five years ago.

His smile fell. He looked across the room, to the foyer. To

where the trapdoor remained closed. Junior would have to wait. Because of her, because of what she'd done to that fat, useless, hillbilly security guard, he now had no choice but to deviate from his plan. Fresh tears emerged, but he quickly brushed them away. He was a man, damn it. Not a weepy little boy. No. Never again.

"Never again!" He took the fireplace poker and smashed it against the curio cabinet. Ugly, glass figurines, once belonging to his mother, crashed to the floor. Not satisfied, he raised the poker again and swung. Over and over. "Never, ever, ever!" Chunks of wood flew across the room and hit him in the head and face. Ignoring the sting of glass and splinters of wood, he didn't stop his tirade until the curio cabinet had become nothing but kindling for his fire.

Breathing hard, sweat dripping down his back and temple he stared at the mess he'd made, then looked to his hands. To the poker. His heart and mind still in turmoil, an eerie calm settled in his soul. He knew what needed to be done, and it needed to begin now. Glancing at the closed trapdoor, he marched into the foyer.

He whipped open the trapdoor. Wood smacked wood as the door bounced from the impact. Holding the poker in one hand, he rushed down the ladder and when he reached the bottom, rested his head against a rung. *You must begin tonight. Must. Must. Must.* But he didn't want to. He was so close to earning the pathetic puke's trust. How can there be betrayal without trust? Without that trust all of this...this Hell Week would have no meaning.

Torture without meaning.

Pushing off the rung, he reached for the lantern. But torture he must. *Be a man*, his mother had told him after...after his Hell Week happening. That had been what she'd called it. *The Hell Week happening.* She'd nurtured him back to health, had tended to his wounds while his oblivious, incompetent, simple-minded father assumed his son had developed the sort of affliction one might contract when living with a houseful of filthy, young, teenaged boys. No, his father hadn't known, but his mother knew, she knew what they'd done—every heinous detail. And as he'd lain in bed, suffering both physically and mentally, she hadn't an ounce of sympathy.

"Vengeance," he whispered, and turned the light on his pledge. That had been what Mother told him as she'd nursed him back to health. As he stared at the puke, he realized the boy could use a little nursing, as well. But that would be pointless. Thanks to Junior's fuck up, the pledge would be dead in less than two days.

Fresh tears prickled his eyes. He wanted to hurt the pledge. He needed to hurt him in order to keep the demons at bay. Today was only Wednesday, though. If he rushed through Hell Week, would there still be satisfaction? There had to be. This was supposed to be his last Hell Week. His *coup de gras*. He didn't want there to be another. How could any other Hell Week top this one? After all, his pledge was the son of the demon who had tortured him.

Be a man. Don't let what they did to you change you. Find a woman. Use her. Prove you're still a man. And when you're done, when you're more successful than your pitiful father and his father before him...get your revenge.

Those words had been his mother's mantra as she'd applied a warm cloth to his wounds that cold, icy Sunday night twenty-five years ago. As he stared at the pledge, he saw himself. Stumbling naked from the fraternity house, running, tripping and sliding through ice and snow as he'd fought to find a way home. Even slightly delusional with the onset of hypothermia, he'd managed to find his parents' home, *his* home. Beaten, naked, multiple parts of his battered body in the first stages of frostbite, his mother had found him on the doorstep. Instead of reporting the incident, she forced him to suffer in silence. No one could know what had been done to him. The Townies might think he was a sinner who'd brought upon him the wrath of God in the form of a twenty-year-old demon. They might think he *liked* it. His mother had suspected as much, but she'd been wrong.

There is no pleasure in rape. Only pain.

But he'd reported the incident, and had sent an anonymous letter to the university president before transferring schools. Not all the gory details, nor did he name names. He'd feared his tormentor, and had worried the demon would seek vengeance against him. A tear slid down his cheek. "Vengeance," he repeated as he slowly approached the pledge. With his free hand, he ran his palm along the boy's bony cheek. When the puke's head lulled to the side and rested in his palm, a fresh wave of sadness and rage overwhelmed him. He had sought that same comfort from his own mother the night he'd returned home defeated, demoralized and haunted by what he'd endured. That same need for a tender hand, to know he was safe. While she had performed her motherly duties and healed his wounds, she'd done so clinically, coolly. There had been no love in her healing touch. There had been nothing but disgust.

The metal poker slipped from his other hand and dropped to the rock with a clank. Gripping the boy's face with both hands now, he rested his forehead against the pledge's. "That's what Mother said was important. Vengeance." His tears burned a path down his cheeks, and as he rested his face against the puke's, he realized the boy cried, too. Their tears mingled and bathed each other's faces.

Awareness caused him to draw a sharp intake of breath. He raised his head and stared at the pledge. Never had he touched a pledge in this way. He'd never once allowed any of them to see his weakness, to see the pain that still haunted him. For some inexplicable reason, this new cognizance didn't bother him. He touched his wet cheek, relished that he couldn't tell the difference between his tears and the pledge's. And, as if he'd been baptized by the chosen one, by his savior, his heart and soul lightened with hope.

"Yes," he hissed and gripped the pledge by the shoulders. "You will save me, won't you? You will take me out of Hell Week and make me whole again." Grinning, he wiped the boy's wet cheek. "I will owe you for an eternity."

The pledge's watery, bloodshot eyes shifted nervously with

confusion. "I...I don't understand, sir."

Reeling at the thought that all was not lost, that Junior's fuck up might have been a blessing in disguise, he stepped away from the pledge. No doubt, his anger for her remained and she would be punished...eventually. For now, though, he'd tap into some of his mother's mantra.

Be a man...get your revenge.

"All in good time, Puke." His step a little lighter, his world a little brighter, he moved to the corner of the cellar. He picked up the can of yellow paint he'd purchased months ago, along with a paint tray and roller. "Has anyone ever called you a coward?" he asked as he poured the canary yellow paint into the tray.

"Yes," the puke answered quickly.

After wiping the paint can clean of any drips, he looked at the pledge. The boy stood tall now and no longer dangled from his restraints. There was a fierce glint in his eyes that he admired. No. This pledge was no coward, not like the others who sniveled, whined and begged for release.

"Who?" he asked, curious.

The pledge raised his chin. "My father."

He smiled. "That doesn't surprise me. But you do realize that your father is the coward. He preys on those he deems weaker than him rather than battling those who are his equal or stronger. He's pitiful."

The internal struggle the puke suddenly dealt with was evident in his eyes. He'd bet the boy, who had defended his father just the other day, didn't know whether to agree with his assessment or support the demon who'd spawned him.

"You know my dad?"

He dipped the roller in the paint tray until every inch had turned yellow. "Yes," he admitted. "Quite well. You can thank him for your current situation." Standing, roller in hand, he approached the boy. "And while I do not find you cowardly in any way, I must keep up with tradition."

Using the puke's body as his canvas, he painted. Rolling over his concave stomach, his bony ribs, skinny legs and arms, his mangled foot, then across his face. When he forced the pledge to turn, which must have put a tremendous strain on the boy's shoulders based on the pain crossing his face, he painted the puke's back. Covered all of the open sores and abrasions as he ran the roller over his knotty spine. After he righted the boy again, he looked at his artwork. "*Voila.*"

He returned the roller, tray and paint can to the corner. "Normally, this is where we would have stopped for the night, but something has come up that has forced me to shorten Hell Week." He paused. "I believe, technically, we won't be able to call this Hell Week considering a week consists of seven days." He shrugged. "We'll just call this…Hell."

"Sir?" Junior's voice drifted from the upstairs foyer. "Can I come down?"

"*May* I come down?" He shook his head. "My daughter is showing signs of her idiocy left and right today," he muttered to the pledge, who stared at him with a strange mixture of confusion and hatred.

"Yes, Junior. You *may* come down." When she reached the bottom rung, she looked first at the pledge, then to him. "So glad you could join us," he said. "Thanks to you, I've been forced to add more calisthenics to this evening's agenda."

She frowned. "I don't know what you mean."

"Doesn't know what I mean?" Guffawing, he approached the pledge and pressed a finger to his painted chest. "Still a bit tacky, but I see no sense in waiting."

"Sir." She took a step forward. "I *really* don't understand."

In a heartbeat, he knocked her back, pinning her against the ladder's rungs. Holding her by the throat, her thick coat no protection against his ire, he slammed her head against the rung. "Don't." Breathing hard, he tightened his grip. Satisfaction oozed into him when her eyes bulged and her face reddened. "Don't lie to me, Junior. I know what you did. I know all about the security guard."

Mouth gaping open, she clawed at his hands. He could easily kill her. He could easily dispose of her like he had with the others. There was plenty of room at the bottom of the old well, and he owned plenty of muriatic acid and lye. But she did serve a purpose and he might still have use for her. His reach was far, but she could infiltrate areas with inconspicuous ease. Should things become…complicated, he would need to quickly dispose of the pledge and leave Bola. Permanently. When this was over, he'd kill her. She didn't deserve to carry on his legacy. Her ineptness, her lack of respect for Hell Week, for him, was the proof.

Releasing her, he stepped away and moved toward the pledge. Her wheezy inhale, her coughing and pathetic sputtering echoed off the rock walls. The sounds were quite nice, triumphant, really. Hopefully his daughter would remember this moment should he give her another assignment. He refused to tolerate another one of her fuck ups.

Rubbing her throat, she leaned against the ladder. "I'm sorry, sir," she rasped, then cleared her throat. "I…I should have told you, but I wanted to prove my worth to you. Show you I can clean up any mess."

"Fool," he shouted and reached for his belt buckle. "*You* created this mess. You should have never involved that stupid Townie in the first place." He whipped the belt free from his pants, held both ends together until the leather strips were taut. "The sheriff and those buffoon, rent-a-cops are going to be more determined than ever to stop Hell Week." He struck the wall with the belt, and both Junior and the pledge flinched. "Damn it! If you left any evidence—"

"I didn't," she said on a grating whine. "I swear."

He stalked toward her, slapping the leather belt against his palm. "What did that security guard do to you?"

"I…what do you mean?" she whispered and stared at the belt.

"Did he sneak into your room and try to molest you? Rape you like—"

"No," she yelled. "I used his truck to bring you your pledges. I drugged him and borrowed his truck. That's it."

Rage simmered under the surface. "You drugged him?"

"Yes, like I drugged him and the other guy," she said and

pointed to the puke. "How else was I supposed to bring them here?"

"How else?" he asked, and smacked the belt against his palm. "How about the way I told you? The way I *thought* you did. You lied to me."

"No."

"You lied to me and now I'm wondering how many other lies you've told."

"I swear. Sir. Dad," she pleaded. "You've been nothing but good to me. You took me in when I had no place else to go. You're giving me an education...you're giving me my life back and along with it, confidence and strength I've never felt before." She dropped to her knees and hugged his legs. "Please believe me. I didn't mean for this to happen. I wanted so badly to prove to you that I'm worthy enough to be called your daughter. Please."

Tears streamed down her face as she looked up at him. Part of him wanted to kick her hard enough in the jaw her teeth would pierce the back of her skull. Pride held him back. While he was used to whining and pleading from his pledges, this was different. Junior wanted acceptance. While he'd never publicly accept her as his daughter, and he would likely kill her when everything was said and done, he admired her spirit.

"Stand up," he ordered. "Why did you use the security guard's truck instead of luring the pledge here the way I instructed?"

"It was dark and I was afraid I'd get lost in the woods."

"Try again. You know that path like the back of your hand."

"Fine," she shouted. "I was afraid, okay? I didn't want to be alone with them in the woods. After...after the last time I was alone with a man like that...I was afraid the two of them would..." On a sob, she turned away.

Stupid girl. She should have been upfront with him. He would have found another method to obtain his pledge. "Understood," he said and kept his voice quiet, gentle. "But why kill him?"

Wiping her nose with her sleeve, she looked over her shoulder. "Those agents from Chicago wanted him to get some blood work done. If he made it to the lab, they'd know he was drugged with the same stuff I used on the kid I left on the side of the road, and him." She jerked her head toward the puke. "So, I pretended I wanted to fool around with him, took him out into the woods where I told him I knew of a great spot, and knocked him out. Then I tied him to a tree, went back to his truck and put it in the river to get rid of any evidence I might have missed."

Good God, maybe his daughter wasn't as stupid as he'd thought. Still. "Why tie him to the tree, why not just kill him?"

"I needed to make sure the drug was out of his system," she said. "Please don't be mad at me. I know I should have told you…"

"Yes. You should have, but what's done is done. Unfortunately I still need to move Hell Week along faster than I'd like. Rather than ending on Sunday, our puke will be initiated Friday evening."

"Friday? That's so soon."

"I know. Not enough time to fully enjoy myself. As much as I hate to deviate from my plan, I must improvise." Belt raised, he approached the pledge. "Starting now."

The leather whistled through the air just before it cracked along the boy's abdomen. The puke howled in pain and twisted his body to avoid the next blow. And as he wielded blow after blow, just as the puke's father had done to him twenty-five years ago, he released his rage on the pledge. The boy might not deserve the pain and torture, but he couldn't quite whip Junior.

Yet.

The darkness normally scares me. Most nights I lie in this hospital bed watching the shadows of vengeance creep along the wall, waiting for it to reach out and snare me. Drag me into a living nightmare that just won't quit. And while those shadows linger, tonight they're not dragging me into the fringes of madness. Excitement has replaced fear. Tonight sleep eludes me, but not because I refuse to give into the nightmares, but because my thoughts are solely on tomorrow and the hope the new day will bring.

I love my new soft-spoken speech therapist and her positive attitude. From the moment I awakened from the coma, my attitude has been anything but positive. Unable to move and talk, unable to forget the past and the pain I'd caused...I couldn't find a sliver of hope in my broken heart. All I could do was endure this institution I've been forced to call home. Live in a shell with no means of escape. But now I not only have my dear friend, Lois, I have Bunny.

Embarrassment momentarily knots my belly, but I quickly shove it away. I didn't quite make the best first impression with her. At least, not in my mind. But when Olivia started to tell Bunny about what had happened to me...I couldn't handle it. I wanted to. I wanted to hear everything they had to say, everything they knew. What the police knew. Unfortunately, if anything had been said, it had happened after I'd blacked out. But that no longer matters. Yesterday, the day before, the weeks and months before that...none of it matters.

A fantastic flutter unknots my stomach, then zips and weaves its way into my chest. The heart rate monitor to the left accelerates with a series of beeps. If I could smile, I would— big and toothy. Tomorrow things will change. I believe it. I feel it.

Bunny had left early today with the promise she'd see me tomorrow. She also promised she'd bring something with her that would give me what I haven't had in over a year and a half. Mobility. Control. Speech.

The beeping monitor rang in rapid sequences. If I don't settle down, the nurses will burst into my room and possibly sedate me. I don't want that. Clear headed is what I need to be if I'm going to work with Bunny tomorrow.

Closing my eyes, I picture steering my wheelchair

throughout the ward. Knowing Lois, she'll probably joke about racing her, which would be completely inappropriate and immature. It also might be the first thing *I* suggest we do when I finally have the chance to talk. Bunny explained that my voice would be synthetic for now, but that's okay. I'll be able to express myself. Tell Lois what a wonderful, beautiful person I think she is, and that I love her and need her to fight the cancer. Tell Lois, tell them all, that my name isn't Jane, or Janie. Tell them to call me...

I snap my gaze to the ceiling. I'd thought my earlier hope had chased those shadows of vengeance away, but they're here. Looming over me in a thick, foggy cloud of fear and despair.

A warm tear slips down my cheek as anxiety and dread settles in my chest and tightens my throat. I'm supposed to be dead. My killer *thinks* I'm dead. If I can talk, if I tell the police my name and who brought me to this place, my killer's vengeance will be tenfold. It used to be I didn't know enough, now I know too much.

If I talk, I'm as good as dead.

CHAPTER 15

BACK AT JOY'S, Rachel slumped on the bed and grabbed her ringing cell phone. If she hadn't been waiting for the call from Chihiro regarding the DNA evidence—if there was any—left behind on Sean's clothes, she would have let it roll into voice mail. She wanted, needed time to process everything that had happened today. What she needed was a good, long cry.

Before she could attend her pity party, she needed to take care of business first. Clearing her throat, she answered the phone. "Hey, Chihiro. Please tell me you have some good news."

"Bad day?" the other woman asked.

Bill's image didn't pop into her head right away, but Hal's did. When she and Owen had met him, Walter and Joy at Bill's house, the man hadn't bothered to hide his grief and anger. Her throat tightened and she swallowed hard as she remembered how Hal, a tough, gritty man who had served two tours in Vietnam, broke down in a way she hadn't expected nor wanted to see again. Watching the big man openly weep over the loss of his son had torn her in two. Witnessing the way Joy had cried along with him, cradling him to her as if he were a child, had been more than she could bear. She'd been uncomfortable standing in the same room with them, surrounded by their sobs and signs of Bill. His pictures, trophies, the afghans his mother had knitted for him before she'd died, his sweet, sad Golden Retriever who had lain curled in a corner as if he knew...

"Yeah," she finally answered. "Today was pretty bad."

"Sorry to hear," Chihiro said, her tone quiet, empathetic. "I emailed you the results, but wanted to go over a few that I thought might be pertinent."

Rachel glanced at her closed laptop, but didn't have the energy to move across the room to retrieve it. "Great, what do you have?"

"Let's start with what I don't have...other than Sean, there was no other human DNA on his clothes, meaning the kidnapper left no traces of himself."

"Damn."

"But, here are some interesting things I *did* find," Chihiro said. "Dog hair—specifically from a Golden Retriever. I confirmed that with one of our techs who's an expert on animal DNA. There were also traces of limestone and dolomite, both of which are commonly found in the area where you're investigating, especially along or near rivers. What really intrigued me? I found components of loose, pigmented mineral powder."

Rachel regretted answering Chihiro's call. The dog hair wasn't any help at this point. Bill had been known to drive his dog around town. The limestone and dolomite weren't much help, either. Especially if the two substances could be found all over the area. Now mineral powder? She'd been hoping for blood, or some sort of body fluid that could result in a DNA profile of their killer. Instead Chihiro was giving her a geology report.

"Okay," she said, disappointed, and now in real need for a pity party. "Thanks for the quick turnaround. I'll look over your email and—"

"Wait," the tech said. "Do you realize what the pigmented mineral powder is?"

Rachel sat straighter. "I assumed it was along the lines of the other traces of minerals you found."

"No. It's makeup."

"As in cosmetics?"

"Exactly."

Moments later, after she disconnected the call with Chihiro, she stared out the window. Darkness had swallowed Bola several hours ago, but had also settled in her heart and soul. As much as she wanted to process Chihiro's findings, she couldn't. Not now. Not yet. Never good with emotions, she had a hard time putting her finger on the ones making her want to scream and cry. The overwhelming sadness and grief consuming her, she understood. She'd come to like Joy, and while she didn't know Hal, he'd saved her brother. Sympathy didn't begin to encompass the sorrow and heartache she harbored on their behalf.

A tear slipped down her cheek as she remembered watching Hal pick up a framed photograph of him and Bill. In the picture, they'd both been wearing hip-high fishing waders, and dangling large fish from hooks. Hal had lovingly stroked the photo, then turned away, his shoulders and back moving as he wept.

Swiping at her face, she moved toward the window and stared at her reflection. Who was she to think she could do this? Bill was dead. Josh was missing. They were no closer today than they were two days ago, to finding him and stopping a killer.

Her chin trembled and more tears spilled down her cheeks. She let them. Hoping to God they could somehow cleanse her, wash away everything she'd seen today. But as she stood in front of her reflection, her vision distorted and blurred by her tears, Bill's image emerged.

Squeezing her eyes shut, she smacked her palms to her ears and shook her head. Trying desperately to ward off the memories, to shake off the sounds of cawing crows. But Bill remained. Lifeless. Eyes plucked, skin torn...

She quickly reached for the blind, and pulled it shut, blocking her reflection. Breathing hard, she turned around, looking, searching for...something, anything to stop the maddening thoughts and emotions. She needed a punching bag. If the temperature hadn't been nearing zero, a long, hard run might have worked. The energy seething throughout her body needed a portal of release.

Grabbing a tissue, she blew her nose, then paced. With each pass through the small room, she tried to convince herself that she'd done everything right, that the investigation was solid, but also seriously messed up. That she wasn't the one messing it up, either.

No. I just got Bill killed.

Her stomach cramped and knotted. Sobs wracked her body as she dropped to the floor. Pressing her forehead against the soft area rug, she exorcized the high hopes and optimism she'd felt at the beginning of the investigation. She purged her goal of being a field agent. And with it, she banished her ridiculously silly dreams of action and adventure.

This life wasn't for her. She couldn't handle death up close and personal. She couldn't—

A warm hand rubbed her back. She froze, but didn't bother to look up and over her shoulder. Through her crying frenzy she hadn't heard Owen walk into the room, but she knew it was him. He'd only intimately touched her a few times, but she'd relished those brief encounters to the point she'd memorized every nuance.

Bringing the tissue to her nose, she drew in a deep breath, then whispered, "Please. Go."

Instead of obeying, his knees hit the area rug. In an instant he had her in his lap and cradled to his solid chest. He smoothed his hand over her hair, then kissed the top of her head. "I can't."

The anguish in his voice forced her to look up at him. He half-smiled, touched her cheek and swiped away her tears. "You're so strong. I can't believe you've managed to keep this locked inside you all day."

"I don't feel strong. I feel weak, and guilty, and so...sad."

Shifting her body so she sat squarely in his lap, he pressed his lips to her forehead, then hugged her. "I understand." He rubbed her back, his firm fingers working the knots along her shoulders and spine. "Weakness, guilt, sadness…if you don't feel those things, if you don't let them out now and then, they'll destroy you." He placed a finger under her chin and tilted her face. "That would kill me."

Confused by his admission, and unsure how to react, she did what she did best. Sarcasm. "Nice word choice."

Disappointment showed in his eyes as he studied her face. "I've always loved your sarcasm and jokes." He cupped her cheek in his palm. "But sometimes I wish that maybe once in a while you'd stop hiding."

If she had the energy, she might have stiffened at the remark. She didn't hide, she kept herself protected. For years she'd watched her mother destroy her life with one messed-up relationship after another, openly wearing her emotions on her sleeve, inviting people—and not just the useless men in her life—to knock her down until she'd become needy and pitiful. At a very young age, Rachel had decided she would not be anything like her mom. And if that meant being alone, without many friends, so what? "It beats the hell out of being hurt," she admitted, then closed her eyes with regret. They weren't talking about relationships. They were talking about how to deal with an investigation, the murder victims and all that other horrible crap.

"I have no intention of hurting you. Say what's on your mind," he murmured, his voice soft yet filled with so much conviction, she opened her eyes.

He already *had* hurt her.

But she shoved that thought aside and again reminded herself what they *were* talking about…Bill and how she was handling his death. Owen had plenty of experience with murder victims and their families. She trusted him. Beyond that, she could use someone to lean on. She could use a friend to help her deal with her doubts and insecurities. And despite her shitty attitude toward Owen, despite the hurt she'd endured since that mistletoe kiss, he'd been a good friend to her.

"I…it's more than that," she said. "I've wanted Ian to give me a chance to work in the field for a long time. But now that I'm doing it, I don't think I'm ready. Seeing Bill today…I've analyzed crime scenes through photos and videos, but I've never actually seen one." Tears filled her eyes. "I let it become personal, especially later, when we went to Bill's house. Seeing how hard this is on his dad, Joy and Walter." She choked on a sob. "The way Bill's dog just lay on the floor as if he knew…Owen, I just don't think I'm cut out for this. I'm having second thoughts and at the same time, I'm second guessing myself."

"What do you need?" he asked, his tone coaxing, the caress of this thumb along her cheek soothing, his familiar scent enticing.

He tempted her to take what she wanted and needed right now. Him. His touch, his strength, the comfort and relief she knew she could find in his arms. The intensity, the undeniable concern and desire in his eyes didn't help. Neither did the way he tilted his head, drew his mouth close enough so his warm breath burned a path along her lips.

Knowing how they would feel against hers, she stared at his parted lips. The earlier tension that had coursed through her body throughout the entire, messed-up day began to slowly subside. Encouraging flutters grew deep within her belly, while her heart raced with indecision and longing. She wanted to let go. She wanted to melt into his kiss, into his hard body and replace all the bad with something good. She wanted—

His lips brushed against hers. Firm. Warm. The tentative touch, the simple caress sent sparks of desire straight to her core. When he grazed his mouth against hers again, she parted her lips. And when he ran his fingers through the back of her hair and held her head close, she lost all sense of right and wrong. Swept her tongue along his. Lips melded together, they kissed. Last night's kiss had been a clumsy passionate rush. Tonight, he took his time, kissed her with gentle finesse, seduced her with slow, languid strokes of his tongue. He stoked the fire, and the love she'd tried to deny.

Snapping her eyes open, she drew back, the "L" word an icy, cold reminder that he *would* hurt her again. "You should go."

His forehead lined with frustration. "I...what am I not getting?" he asked while keeping her head locked in his hand and his lips still temptingly close. "Yesterday you said something about the last time we kissed. I still don't know what you're talking about. What I do know?" He swiped the pad of his thumb along her lower lip, which sent goose bumps along her skin. "From the moment you walked into CORE I've wanted to kiss you. I've fantasized about tasting you. So unless I have a clone running around Chicago, I think you owe me an explanation."

"You really don't remember, do you?" The confusion contorting his face might have been comical if guilt hadn't suddenly swallowed her whole. She'd pegged Owen as the bottom feeder of the dating pool, a charmer who would do anything to talk his way into a woman's bed. But she'd labeled him after the mistletoe kiss when he'd quickly dismissed her for another woman. Prior to that, she'd considered him a solid, honorable man filled with integrity. She still did. "Oh my God," she whispered. "Last year's company Christmas party...you, me, the mistletoe."

"I didn't make it to the party. I was flying back from Germany. Remember the Shmelter case? The one where I—"

"Yeah, I remember the case. But you *did* come to the party. I saw you there. You kissed me under the mistletoe, then suggested we leave and go for a drink. I went to the bathroom to freshen up my makeup, only to walk out and find you leaving with another woman." She gripped the front of his shirt. "You're telling me you don't remember one thing from that night? Sorry, but I might have to call bullshit on that one."

"You of all people know I don't lie." She gasped when he gripped her hair and brought them nose-to-nose. Powerful determination filled his eyes as he tightened his jaw. "By the time I left Munich I had a total of eight hours of sleep over the course of three days. I took one of those prescription sleeping pills, but it didn't work. So I had a couple of drinks, hoping I'd eventually sleep. I...ah." He eased his grip. "Shit." He shook his head, then completely disengaged their bodies and stood. "I remember getting my luggage and I remember Amber. Was the woman you saw me with a tall blonde?"

She nodded, stunned. Because she had a feeling that what had infuriated and humiliated her for over a year could easily have been solved over a cup of coffee.

"Yeah, she picked me up from the airport, but I swear I went home." He paced for a few seconds then stopped and faced her. A wry smile tilted his skilled lips as he ran a hand through his hair. "I woke up the next morning, alone and feeling like hell. Amber left a note by my coffee pot telling me to lose her number. That she doesn't date guys who call her by another woman's name." In a heartbeat, he knelt in front of her and gripped her shoulders. "She ended the note by saying, 'I don't know who Rachel is, but I hope she was worth it.'"

Her head grew dizzy with hope, while her heart raced out of control. He really hadn't remembered that night. And...Oh. My. God. From the sound of it, he'd called another woman by *her* name. Instead of unadulterated satisfaction, a sense of loss also filled her. For the wasted year. For all of the horrible things she'd said to him. For the way she'd treated him like some bottom feeding douche bag.

"I'm so sorry, Rachel. I...I honestly didn't know." He looked away. "Um," he began when he met her gaze again. "Did you...like the kiss? I mean. Was it what you wanted? I'd never—"

She slammed her mouth against his and twined her arms around his neck. He fell back on his rear, but she didn't let go. Instead, she climbed on top of him and kissed him with reckless abandonment. Her confidence soared as he kissed her with equal fervor. It soared even higher as his words continued to sink in.

From the moment you walked into CORE, I've wanted to kiss you. I've fantasized about tasting you...

Over the past four years, she'd had quite a few fantasies of her own. Despite those fantasies, despite the throb building between her thighs, she also knew this could be a mistake. They worked together, and sex would change everything. But she ached for him. Body, heart and soul, she needed him for at least tonight. She needed his touch. She needed to erase the misery brought on by today's events, the guilt, the horrible images.

As she tangled her tongue with his and he gripped her bottom, forcing her against his erection, she knew she was spinning half-truths to herself. Today had been terrible, but that wasn't the only reason for giving her body to him. She'd been half in love with Owen for nearly four years. While she'd liked the men from her past, she'd never given herself—her whole self—to any of them. Fear of rejection, fear of dealing with uncomfortable and unfamiliar emotions had always forced her to keep her heart guarded. Tonight, this moment would live with her. She would give and take, keep those strange emotions to herself, but enjoy the pleasure of sinking her body onto his.

With that thought in mind, the tension in her belly coiled, and the ache between her thighs intensified. Tearing her mouth away, she pushed herself up, straddled his thick arousal and whipped her bulky sweater over her head.

A hiss escaped from between Owen's parted lips as he pressed his palms over her bra, holding, cupping her breasts. He stared at her, lust darkening his eyes to denim blue. "Gorgeous," he murmured, then lazily slipped the bra straps over her shoulders until her breasts spilled forward. Eyes still on hers, he grazed her hardened nipples with the back of his knuckles. Then, holding the small of her back, he leaned forward and circled one areola with his tongue.

She gripped his biceps, stared at his mouth. At the way he curled his tongue along one nipple, then the other. The sight so erotic, she sought some sort of release and ground herself along his erection.

With a low groan, he gripped her hips and sucked. She tossed back her head as delicious tingles radiated from her breasts and zipped throughout her body. Holding his head steady, she encouraged him, until she thought she'd explode if he didn't strip off his sweatpants and bury his hard length inside her.

When she squirmed against his arousal, he chuckled, his hot breath fanning across her sensitive breasts and nipples. "Am I going too slow?" he asked and sent her *the* sexiest grin.

"Yes." She unclasped her bra and quickly shucked if off, then reached the hem of his t-shirt. After pulling it over his head, she looked her fill. Holy crap. Used to dating guys whose closest call to the gym was programming the facility's computers, she had never seen a man, never touched a man with such a sculpted body. She'd always suspected Owen would have an admirable chest, but…damn. She ran her hand through the dark blond hair lining Owen's thick slabs of muscle, then trailed her fingers along his hard, flat abs. "Work out much?" she asked, then using her palms against his chest, pressed him back to the area rug.

When she had him the way she wanted, skin to skin, she rubbed her breasts along his chest. Loving the way the soft hair tickled and teased her nipples, she kissed him again. He slid his hands down her spine, cupped her rear, then shocked her when he rolled her on her back.

On his knees and between her thighs, he unzipped her jeans, then yanked them and her panties down. Raising her legs so they balanced on one shoulder, he slipped the clothes off and tossed them aside. Then he parted her legs, let them rest on both shoulders, and bent his head. He stared at the apex of her thighs, at where she ached the most, then snapped his gaze to hers. "I told you I've fantasized about tasting you," he said, and keeping his eyes on hers, dipped his head and slowly licked her labia.

She sucked in a breath and arched her hips, wanting more, wanting it now.

Another low chuckle rumbled from his chest. From between her thighs, he smiled. "Have you no patience?"

Pushing herself onto her elbow, she reached for his head.

"At the moment, no."

"So this…" He gave her another slow, torturous lick. "This is too slow for you?"

"Yes," she hissed.

"Then how about this?" Owen smashed his lips against her folds, and pushed his tongue deep, curling it inside her slick opening. Loving the taste of her, her throaty moans and demands, he left finesse behind and focused on her pleasure. When her inner thighs shook against his cheeks, he worried he'd come in his pants. Based on her fiery temperament, he'd always suspected Rachel would be a hot lover. But he hadn't expected her to be so sensual and passionate. He also hadn't expected his body to react the way it was now.

Fierce need coursed through him. Hell, it scared him. He'd had plenty of women, and he'd cared about them, but not like this. Beyond wanting to give her pleasure, he wanted to bind her with trust. He wanted to show her, prove to her they could be partners in and out of bed.

Now wasn't the time to tackle all of that. Not when he was loving her body and on the verge of embarrassing himself. Determined to coax an orgasm from her, he spread her lips, sank his thumb between her folds and honed in on her clit. He licked and sucked. Her wetness coated his thumb while her throaty moans filled the room.

She suddenly gripped his head and arched her back. Releasing a husky groan, her flat belly trembled, her inner thighs shook. As he tasted her orgasm on his lips, pride and need consumed him. While he quickly lost his jeans and underwear, caution lights went off in the back of his mind. He'd already tasted her, and knew he'd want to again and again. She intoxicated him more than he ever thought possible. But once he filled her, once he sank into her warmth, felt her heat around him…there might not be any turning back. No denying they'd made love. No room for regrets if things went south and they had to continue to work together.

And that's what scared the hell out of him.

She lay on the area rug, a small, sexy smile playing along her lush lips as she stared at his naked body. When she swiftly pushed herself upright, he knew her intention. He intercepted her hand just as she wrapped it around his erection. Covering her small hand with his, he helped her stroke him, then he closed his eyes and gritted his teeth when she pressed her lips against the tip. When her tongue slid along his sac, he abruptly pulled away, scooped her in his arms and set her on the bed.

Fuck it.

He pressed himself between her slick folds. He'd spent too many years regretting the past and avoiding the future. Right now, with Rachel's inner muscles gripping him, her sexy legs wrapped around his ass, he was too far gone to care about tomorrow. Now was all that mattered. And making her come again.

Holding her hips, he rocked into her body. Loving every little, throaty moan, the way she bit her bottom lip and stared at him. As if he mattered. As if what they were doing mattered. Before his mind went down another road he wasn't prepared for, he pumped harder, faster. She pushed onto her hands and braced her upper body with her arms. He held her rear off the mattress and guided her over his erection. Over and over, the pressure, the stimulation…it was too much. He needed her to let go before he did.

"Come for me," he murmured, his breath labored, his heart racing.

She wrapped an arm around his neck. Bucked her hips and met each of his thrusts. Her breasts tempted and teased him. Desperate for another taste, he dipped his head and caught a nipple between his lips and sucked. Her inner walls suddenly clenched and milked him. Releasing her nipple, he sought her lips. Their noses bumped as he captured her mouth, mimicked each thrust with his tongue until she cried out against his lips.

Primal satisfaction tore through him as her orgasm peaked. Before he lost all sense of control, he set her rear on the bed, pulled out and came in a rush across her stomach. Caging her with his arms, he rested his cheek against hers, then couldn't stop smiling when she wrapped her arms around his neck and peppered his shoulders with hot, open-mouthed kisses.

Moments later, his breath still slightly labored and his mind less sex-dazed, he planted a quick kiss to her lips, then reached for his t-shirt. As he wiped his passion from her stomach, he met her gaze. He swore her eyes had never been as green as they were now. She smiled and he looked to her lips, which were fuller, moist.

Damn, he could do this again, and it had nothing to do with lack of sex for the past six months. Something about Rachel made him want to throw caution aside, forget about consequences, take risks, search for adventure. When he'd been with the Secret Service he was controlled, watchful, but ready to take action when necessary. He did his duty, served his country, but always with restraint. He'd liked his career and had never been one to rock the boat. Tonight, he'd done some serious rocking and the hell of it was, he didn't care about the consequences. Being with Rachel was more than he'd fantasized. She'd cracked a part of himself he hadn't realized he kept guarded. While that didn't bother him in the least and instead gave him a strange euphoria, he still worried.

What was going through her mind?

"Thanks." She broke the silence. "I appreciate that."

Thanks? He didn't want her *appreciation.* He wanted her again. He wanted her to want *him* again.

Crumpling the t-shirt, he tossed it back on the floor, then immediately covered her body with his. She gasped and widened her eyes when he pinned her arms over her head. "You appreciate what?" He gave a tempting nipple a quick taste. "Sex? Orgasms?" He latched onto her other nipple, and gave it attention. "Was this just a release? A way to ease the tension from a bad day?"

She stared at him, her eyes narrowing and a slow smile spreading across her lips. "No. That's not what I meant, but thank you for the orgasms anyway." Angling her head forward, she reached for his lips, but he remained still, waiting for more. "Kiss me," she whispered.

"What did you mean, then?" he asked instead.

With a sigh, she dropped her head against the mattress. "I meant that I appreciated that you had enough sense not to come inside me."

Of course. He should have known. Logical, rational Rachel would look at this situation and instead of basking in the afterglow of awesome sex, she'd thank him for making sure he didn't accidentally knock her up. Talk about consequences. There would be no way to keep their relationship secret if she ended up pregnant. Plus her plans for working in the field would be placed permanently on hold. He would never allow her to endanger herself or their child.

He released her arms, then rolled onto his back. What the hell was he even thinking? They'd had sex. One time. Besides, a few days ago she was calling him a douche bag. He understood why, now. He would have been pissed off over being ditched after a kiss, too.

"Did I say something wrong?" she asked, rolled onto her side, and ran her hand along his bicep.

Realizing he was being a dick, he turned his head to look at her. "No. You're good." Reaching over, he grabbed her rear. "*Very* good."

She gave him a quick kiss, then smiled. "You're not so bad yourself."

As he caressed her hips, his arousal swelled. "Does this mean no more name calling?"

"Cross my heart," she said, and did just that, drawing his attention to her breasts. "Hold up." She placed a hand over her chest as if to cover herself. Didn't work. He still had a beautiful eyeful. "Before things get out of hand again, there's something I want to tell you."

His gut clenched. He wasn't sure he wanted to hear what she had to say. If she were to tell him this was a one-time thing, that once they returned to Chicago she wanted them to go back to being platonic coworkers, he didn't want to hear it. While he valued their friendship, and he wasn't exactly sure where or how their relationship would go, he was tired of living with regrets. He at least wanted a shot at *something* with her. If it didn't work, then he couldn't say he didn't try.

"I spoke with Chihiro before…you know." A pretty blush stained her cheeks as she looked away. Meanwhile both relief and irritation settled in the pit of his stomach. Relief she hadn't planned to blow his ass off—yet. Irritation because she'd rather talk about the investigation than them. Damn, growing up with a gaggle of girls sometimes made him think like one.

"It's late, almost midnight." He cupped her breast and loved the quick intake of breath she took when he tweaked her nipple. "I'd rather talk…later."

"Really?" She closed her eyes as he massaged her breast. "Because based on what she told me, I think either a woman is behind Hell Week or is working as an accomplice with the killer."

Torn between her tempting body, and the curious, new lead, he stilled his hand. And while intrigued by the DNA results, he also wondered if maybe bringing up business was Rachel's way of avoidance. In the four years he'd known her, she hadn't had many boyfriends. Maybe this was her way of digesting what they'd done, and the consequences they could potentially face. Maybe he should let her off the hook, and give her space.

That primal side of him rose to the surface again. Fuck it. She was a tough, ballsy woman. And he planned to stick around. She'd just need to get over it.

"Interesting." He slid his hand down her belly until he reached the apex of her thighs, then sighed when he slid his fingers along her slick folds. "I can't wait to hear all about it." He rolled on top of her, nudged her legs open, then settled himself between her thighs. "Later," he murmured and kissed her entrance with the head of his erection.

Her cell phone rang. She snared his gaze, alarm brightening her eyes. "I have to get that. It could be the hospital."

He grabbed the phone for her, then sat next to her on the edge of the bed. When she looked at the caller ID, her face immediately softened with relief. "It's just Jake."

Fucking Jake. The man had the worst timing.

"Hey, Jake," she answered.

While Rachel spoke with the sheriff, he moved and settled himself comfortably on her bed. Whatever Jake had to say could wait until the morning. He had no plans of leaving her room tonight. But, when she ended the call, the distress and confusion clouding her eyes had him rethinking.

"What is it?"

She set the phone on the nightstand, then crawled into bed with him, snuggling in the crook of his arm and resting her head on his chest. "A photo was delivered to Jake's office."

"A photo of what?" he asked and ran a hand along her back.

"Josh Conway. Beaten, tied up and hanging from a rock wall."

CHAPTER 16

THURSDAY

EARLY THE NEXT morning, Owen stared at the photograph of Josh Conway, wondering what the hell kind of game the killer was playing. According to Jake, the only other contact the killer made had been six years ago when he'd sent the sheriff a picture of the decomposing body of one of the missing kids. Yet during this Hell Week, the killer had made contact twice. First, the note that had been stuffed in Bill's pocket, then the picture of Josh Conway. Now they had DNA evidence proving a woman might somehow be involved.

He set the photo, which had been printed off a standard photo printer, onto the dining room table. "How'd you make out with the Michigan State Police?"

Jake pushed off the wall. "My deputy dropped all the evidence off yesterday afternoon. I spoke with one of their lab people and explained the urgency of the situation, but the guy couldn't guarantee me anything. He thought they might have to ship some of the items to Lansing, which would push the timeline well past Sunday."

Owen cracked his neck. "Shit."

"Right. An inspector with the Michigan State Police Field

Service Bureau will be here sometime this evening. Latest, tomorrow morning. He's bringing a handful of men with him."

Rachel tossed a pencil on the table. "It's Thursday," she said with exasperation. "If we don't figure out what's going on, Josh could be..." Looking to the ceiling, she drew in a deep breath. When she met Jake's gaze again, she looked as if she might rip off his head.

"Tell Jake what Chihiro found," Owen said to Rachel before they wound up wasting the morning away with arguing.

When she glanced at him, there was a quick moment of understanding. Below that, a slow burn that held promise. But now wasn't the time to think about touching her. Besides, if they were going to continue a relationship while working together, they'd have to become used to separating their personal and professional lives.

After Rachel finished explaining Chihiro's report, Jake finally took a seat. "So you're saying a woman is behind this?" He shook his head. "I don't buy it. Are you sure your brother doesn't have a girlfriend you don't know about?"

"I called the hospital before you got here and spoke with him about it. Nope. No girlfriend." She grabbed the pencil, then started tapping the eraser. "Josh didn't have one, either. Plus, Sean said the clothes he wore that night were clean."

Jake blew out a frustrated breath. "This changes everything. We were looking for a man when we should've been looking for a woman."

"No." Owen shook his head. "We're looking for an accomplice. Rachel and I discussed this and we think the killer is using a woman to help him. Actually, we think he's using a female student."

The sheriff looked at the two of them as if they'd lost their minds. "Why would a young girl hook up with a forty-something man and help him with a kidnapping and murder? Sorry, I'm not buying it."

"Why do women marry men who are in prison for life?" Owen countered, then thought about his last assignment with the Secret Service. How the seventeen-year-old daughter of the ambassador he'd been assigned to had consistently sought out older men. And not just him, he'd discovered after he'd been detained for questioning, then given the option for reassignment. Apparently he hadn't been her only target, just the only one that had been falsely accused. "I don't think it's a stretch to consider that a girl—a college-age girl—could be easily influenced by an older man."

"Especially if that man held a position of power," Rachel added. "Could be she has daddy issues. When I was in the Army, I knew a girl who only dated guys twenty plus years older than her." She wrinkled her nose. "We were young, I'm talking twenty-one, and I thought it was strange that she was attracted to men old enough to be her father. Oh, and by the way, that girl's dad died when she was around thirteen. From what I gathered, they were very close. Which made me think she was looking for a daddy replacement."

"What kind of position of power are we talking about?" Jake asked.

Rachel lifted her shoulder. "A professor, guidance counselor...business owner."

"You said you cross referenced past and present university employees and came up empty. Now you're suggesting the killer could be a Townie?" Jake shifted in the chair. "Killing is bad for business and I know all the business owners in this town. Like me, some of them hire college students, but not many."

"Can you check out those particular business owners?" Rachel asked. "That'd help save us time, and they know you."

"Besides the fact they've hired college students, what am I looking for?"

"Male owners in the age range we've profiled for the killer, if they own a truck or SUV, and if they've hired a female student who lives at Stanley residence hall." Rachel tucked the pencil behind her ear. "Owen and I are going to head there now. I've put a call into the dean and asked him to enforce that all female students living at Stanley residence hall meet in the hall's gathering room for questioning at nine. He agreed and assured me an extra security guard would be on hand to help."

"I think having Jake with us would be better," Owen suggested. Now that he and Rachel had taken things to a new level, the jealousy he'd had over the sheriff no longer existed. Besides, he actually liked Jake. The guy had proved to be a solid, intelligent cop. And he knew some of these girls, maybe even their friends. The RA who worked for Jake, Abby Zucker, came to mind.

"Agreed." Rachel reached for the photo of Josh. "Jake, you in?"

The sheriff scratched the back of his head and winced. "That pain in the ass Bigfoot festival starts today. The town council wants to have *another* meeting at eleven. Screw 'em. I want to maintain order here during the festival, but I want that killer more." He shrugged into his jacket. "Let me reassign and rearrange my deputies' schedules, and I'll meet you there."

Rachel held the clear plastic bag containing the picture of Josh. "The photo..."

"Can you do anything with it?" the sheriff asked.

"I...no," she said, her voice laced with disappointment. "I don't have the right equipment."

Jake took the bag from her. "I guess I know what one of my deputies will be doing again today. I'll meet you in the residence hall at nine."

After Jake left, Rachel stood then headed into the kitchen. He followed behind and caught up with her at the sink. Sensing the tension rolling off her shoulders, he touched the small of her back. With defeat in her eyes, she turned and leaned against the counter. "Talk to me," he said, and fisted his hands at his sides. They might have made love several times last night, then again at dawn, but he knew that didn't give him the freedom to touch her wherever and whenever he wanted. Not when he had no idea where their relationship was heading, and not when they were in the middle of discussing the case. Neither of them needed sex clouding their judgment.

She pressed her lips together, shook her head, then pushed off the counter. "I'm so frustrated, Owen. You know what I need?" She paced the kitchen. "I need me. I need a clone of me, sitting in CORE's evidence and evaluation room. Do you realize that I could have already scanned that photo and evaluated it? The note we found on Bill? Yep. I could have done a handwriting analysis on that the day we found it. I could have personally handed all of this evidence over to Chihiro and got it back within twenty-four hours or even sooner. Instead, I'm at the mercy of the state police. I have to hope that they'll drop any red tape bullshit and get us immediate results, which you and I both know isn't going to happen." She stopped pacing and looked to the ceiling. After a second, she met his gaze. "I'm sorry. I didn't mean to pop off on you. It's just…"

Despite telling himself to keep their relationship professional during business hours, he pulled her into his arms. Whether she realized it or not, she wasn't alone in her frustrations. He wanted her at CORE, too. He wanted her in that evidence and evaluation room doing what she did best. Pulling pieces of this crazy-ass puzzle together until something fit. When she melted into him, a sense of pride swelled inside of him. Chink by chink, he'd break past the barriers she'd set up around herself. Sex was one thing, but having her open up to him, confide her frustrations and insecurities, was a step in the direction he hoped they'd eventually take.

Rachel reentered Stanley Residence Hall's gathering room. She'd just finished interviewing one of the girls, her thirteenth. She was about to call the next girl on her list when Owen and Jake came into the room, followed by the girls they'd both just interviewed. With the list of all the residents' names in hand, she met them at the door, then nodded her head toward the foyer. "Well?" she asked, once they were outside of the gathering room. "How'd you two make out so far?"

Jake puffed his cheeks, then exhaled. He glanced at his own copy of the list of residents. "I've met with fifteen girls. All of them check out fine. None of them work in town, only one of them is in Stronach's class, but she's practically failing. They all knew Sean and Josh, but didn't see or hear anything the night they were taken."

Owen rubbed the back of his neck. "Minus Stronach, the dozen girls I've interviewed all said the same thing."

As she stared at his hand, a rush of desire coiled in her belly. *Focus.* But focusing was hard to do when she couldn't stop thinking about last night and the way he'd touched her with that same hand. The way he'd affected her mind, body and...heart. Clearing her throat, she looked to the list. "I've met with thirteen girls and don't have anything, either."

"Well," Jake began, "we have what? Another seventy or so to go?"

"Unfortunately." She looked over her shoulder just as a familiar looking brunette exited the hall. "Melissa, right?"

The girl smiled. "Yeah, hi." She looked at Jake. "Um...Jake, I don't know where I am on the list, but can you either take my statement now, or maybe we can talk later? My tutor is going to be here any minute and I have an exam in an hour."

As if on cue, the front door opened, sending in a chilly breeze. The security guard manning the front desk looked up from his paperwork and grinned. "Hi, Kaylie."

Kaylie returned the grin, but her smile fell when she noticed them. "Melissa," she said as she signed the guest roster. "Are we still on, or is this a bad time?"

Melissa gave Jake some pretty effective puppy dog eyes. "I'll be at the Sheriff's Department this afternoon. I'm relieving Abby at two. Can we talk then? Please? I'm not doing well in my anthropology class and Kaylie..." She glanced at the other woman. "She rearranged her morning to work with me."

Jake nodded. "That's fine. We'll catch up later. Good luck on your test."

Beaming, Melissa turned to Kaylie. "Come on. Let's study in my dorm room."

After the two women exited the foyer, Rachel turned her attention to Jake and Owen. "Okay, about those seventy girls…"

Jake shook his head. "I'm starting to wish I'd skipped this. Dealing with another pain in the ass council meeting is sounding better and better."

"What's wrong?" Rachel asked. "Were the girls asking you for relationship advice? I know I had a few. Either some of them haven't heard about Bill yet—which I find shocking considering he used to work here—or they're just that self-centered and clueless."

Smiling, Jake nodded. "Actually, two did. And I'm going with self-centered. How about you, Owen?"

Owen looked toward the gathering room where the door stood open. Several of the girls craned their necks and Rachel knew they were looking at Owen. Those pretty, young co-eds could look their fill. She certainly had last night, and while she knew it probably wasn't a good idea, she hoped for an opportunity to do it again later. The chances of anything more than sex happening between them were probably slim to none.

She'd never had a relationship based solely on sex. Just the thought of it didn't sit well with her. She might not be the greatest catch, but she knew she deserved better than being a man's fuck buddy. All she had to do was look at her mother. The woman had been and always would be a serial dater. Jumping from one slick talking man to another, using her body to hold them, trap them and when they grew tired of her and had tossed her aside…she'd be off to find her next conquest.

No. She might be half in love with Owen, and despite the tragedy they'd dealt with during the day, last night might have been one of the best nights of her life. But she wanted more from him than just sex. The question was… did he?

He looked away from the gathering room and met her gaze. The heat in his eyes brought back a rush of memories. The way he'd held her, glided her over his thick erection, made her come apart…made her come alive.

"Nope. No one was asking me for relationship advice," he said, his eyes still on hers. "A couple of them did try to give me their cell phone number."

Jealousy momentarily tightened her chest. "Really? I mean, huh. That's...forward, but I guess that shouldn't surprise me. You're single and well, you look...well, like you." She'd wanted to say he looked hot, sexy. That his smile was enough to make a woman melt and his eyes had a way of making her heart trip. Add on all those muscles hidden beneath his sweater and he was the perfect male specimen. Fortunately, she caught Jake practically gaping at her and she'd managed to stop herself from looking like one of Owen's many adoring admirers.

"He is kind of pretty," Jake said with a grin. He brushed past them and entered the gathering room, calling out the next name on his list.

To avoid the awkward situation she'd stupidly brought on herself, she began to follow Jake. But Owen moved past her, then paused at the doorway and looked over his shoulder. "Who said anything about being single?"

As he went inside the gathering room, she remained in the foyer. Too stunned to move, too shocked to gather her thoughts and focus on the next interview.

Who said anything about being single?

Hope and longing pulsated throughout her body, making her legs weak and her mind thick and foggy. She didn't know what to think or how to react. The man she'd wanted, been half in love with for nearly four years just implied that they were...*together*. As much as she'd fantasized about being with him—on every level—her skin grew clammy with panic and anxiety. Men didn't stick around, her mother's love life was the proof. Would Owen? And if he didn't, how could they continue to work together? She loved working for CORE, for Ian, and had no intention of going anywhere else.

"Ma'am, are you okay?" the security guard asked her.

She nodded. "I'm good," she lied. Because Owen's cryptic remark had just rocked her world. Her safe, boring world. She might have craved action and adventure, and being in a relationship with Owen would definitely be action packed and adventurous, but safe and boring would at least keep her heart intact.

****

Bunny fluttered around my room, a big smile on her pretty face. "I'm so excited," she said, then glanced to the table. When she'd first arrived, Bunny had burst into my room with an orderly carrying a computer. It had taken her the past forty minutes to set everything up, and during that time she'd explained that this computer would become my lifeline to the world.

I'm still not sure what she's talking about, but her excitement is infectious. Instead of dwelling on the worry and anxiety of finally revealing my name, anticipation runs through my veins and has my belly burning with a sensation that has been hard to maintain. Hope.

"Okay," she said, propped her hands on her slender hips and eyed the table and equipment. "I think we're all set." She looked at me, her eyes bright and eager. "Are you ready?"

I released a pitiful grunt and blinked my eyes.

"Excellent." She maneuvered my wheel chair until I sat directly in front of the computer. From behind me, I heard her snap something onto the back of the wheel chair, then she moved to my side holding a couple of cords. "I'm just going to plug this into here…turn this on, and…yes," she said with a triumphant hiss. "Okay, Jane. And I hope this is the last time I'm going to call you that, unless of course your real name is Jane." She grinned, then raised a thin, mechanical arm from the wheel chair. Fastened to the arm was a small box with what looked like straws sticking up from the center.

"Now, I told you you'd be talking today, but I'm not going to lie. You'll have to work for it."

Despite last night's worries, I'd do whatever she asked. To be able to talk, to voice my thoughts…until I'd come to this point in my life, I had taken the value of communication for granted. How without it, life could be lonely, desolate, bleak.

"This is a sip and puff, mouse controlled joystick. It's going to take some practice, but once you get the hang of it, you'll be reciting the Pledge of Allegiance in no time." She moved the straws to my mouth. "Think of these as a sort of mouth stick. When you move the stick to the left, it'll direct the mouse to the left side of the computer monitor, move the stick down, and the mouse will move to the bottom of the monitor." She pointed to the monitor. "This is an online keyboard. All you need to do is move the mouse to the letter you want and click. To click, you just need to sip or puff into the stick. There's a voice synthesizer attached to the computer, but we'll hold off on that for now and save that for when you're ready to talk up a storm." She put one stick in my mouth. "Okay, give it a shot."

Only recently I've been able to drink from a straw. My therapist, Olivia, along with my last speech therapist forced me to practice several times a day. While I loved coating my mouth with whatever cool, refreshing liquid they'd given me, the process had ended up being clumsy, messy and embarrassing. The liquid had dribbled down my chin and soaked my hospital gown, leaving me feeling like a drooling idiot. But there was no liquid at the other end of this "straw." Only hope.

"Use your tongue to nudge the stick," Bunny encouraged.

As I did what she suggested, my heart pounded hard and I swear my fingertips tingled as if they wanted to toss the stick aside and tap the keyboards. But that wasn't a possibility right now, if ever. With that daunting thought in mind, I forced my tongue down. The cursor moved downward and settled on the letter G. I nudged the stick again and the cursor landed on the letter V. Excitement had my chest tightening and my lungs constricting. I drew in a deep breath to slow my racing heart and waylay my anxiousness.

"Very good," Bunny praised. "One letter down."

Glancing at the screen, I realized that in sucking in a deep breath, I'd inadvertently "clicked" the mouse stick. Encouraged and determined as hell, I nudged my tongue again. Up, up, then over a few times until the cursor hovered over the letter I. As I continued with the tedious tongue-nudging task, my name—my real name—suddenly hovered on the screen above the letters I'd painstakingly typed. It had been so long since I'd seen my name, I gasped, which caused the stick to "click" on the letters and finish my name for me.

"Vivian," Bunny whispered, then crouched next to me. "Your name is Vivian?"

My throat tightened as tears momentarily blurred my vision. Grunting, I blinked.

"Your name is beautiful." Tears swam in Bunny's eyes as she gave me a watery smile. "But if we're to do a proper introduction, we'll need a last name. Are you ready, or do you need to take a break?"

Only a power outage could stop me. Seeing my name, knowing I would no longer be Jane or Janie to the world, gave me encouragement. It put a fire in my belly that would not be doused. Inner strength that I'd thought no longer existed, surfaced. A week ago, I wanted to die. Trapped in a useless body, I wanted to fall asleep and never waken. But as I moved the straw, my tongue flexing and more controlled now that I was exercising it, I started typing my last name.

"Keep up the good work," Bunny urged me on while staring at the monitor. "Once we have your last name, we can contact your family. I can't imagine how much they've worried about you."

I momentarily paused and shifted my eyes toward her, wishing I could type faster and tell her the truth. No one was looking for me. My fanatically religious parents had disowned me when I'd had a child out of wedlock, and both had passed on years ago. I had no siblings. No extended family. Until eighteen months ago, all I had was my husband and daughter.

Now, one was dead and the other…a cold-blooded killer.

"Good afternoon, Puke. I trust your day is going well."

The pledge glared at him with hatred and disdain. Regret momentarily crept into his chest. Before last night, before he'd taken the belt to the boy, there had been a glimmer of trust in his pledge's eyes. But that was gone and it would never come back. What he planned to do this afternoon would assure that.

Without a backward glance, he crossed the basement and opened a small, metal toolbox. An assortment of ropes and cords greeted him. He sifted through the box until he found the thin spool of twine necessary for today's calisthenics. Normally, at this point, eagerness would fill his body giving him a euphoric high. But his week hadn't gone as planned. Being forced to rush through the hazing left him hollow. He'd looked forward to this particular Hell Week the moment he'd discovered his puke would attend Wexman University. Last spring, when the boy's name had showed up on his radar, he'd thought of nothing else. He'd daydreamed about the moments they'd share together. The trusting bond he would build with his puke, and how he'd destroy it.

Last night, he'd allowed his emotions to gain the best of him. When Junior had set foot into the basement, he'd sobered. He'd allowed his rage to surface and with it came the realization that all would not be lost. Besides, even God had taken a day off, why shouldn't he take two? Disposing of the pledge earlier than planned gave him the weekend to rejoice. Maybe he'd join his fellow Townies for a drink, don one of the ridiculous Bigfoot masks he'd seen students wearing around campus in celebration of the festival.

He pulled the twine taut. Or maybe he'd kill Junior. Once the pledge was gone, rotting in the bottom of the well with his fraternity *brothers*, he would have no use for her. She'd served a purpose, and he now realized that she also, inadvertently, had given him something else. With her fuck ups, he'd been forced to deviate from his plans. Change was something he'd never been able to accept. Twenty-five years ago, after he'd recovered and his physical wounds had healed, he'd changed. He could no longer go with the flow. Everything had to be precise and orderly. Everything had to be in his control.

Junior had forced him to overcome and adapt, to improvise when things hadn't gone as expected. These were good traits to own, and ones he would carry with him when he left Bola to begin anew. That, and the knowledge that he'd come full circle. With the death of his pledge, vengeance would be served. The demon who had tormented him would suffer a fate much worse than if he'd tortured and killed him twenty-five years ago.

Guilt.

Yes, guilt would eat at the demon's blackened soul. Because of that sick, twisted, immoral demon, because of what he'd done to him, the deaths of his son and the other pledges were on that bastard's hands. The puke's father had put Hell Week into motion twenty-five years ago, now he would finish it.

Holding the stretched twine in his hands, he approached the puke.

"Where's that crazy bitch?" the boy asked, then spat.

He backhanded the puke, knocking his head against the rock wall. "She might be a crazy bitch, but you have no right calling her one. Understood?" When the boy didn't answer he went nose to nose with him. "Understood?" he shouted.

The pledge nodded, and licked the blood trickling from his chapped lips.

"Good. Now to answer your question—not that it's really any of your business—Junior is busy. Just because it's Hell Week doesn't mean we can walk away from our daily obligations." He pulled the twine taut again. "Besides, I didn't *want* her here for this session of calisthenics. Do you know why?"

The puke shook his head.

He leaned close to the boy's ear. "Because *I'm* a crazy bastard and I'm worried I might do something to her."

"L...like what?"

He wrapped the twine around the boy's neck. "Like this." Pulling the twine tight, he choked the puke. The boy's mouth hung open, he jerked and twisted his body. His eyes grew big and watery, his face, even in the dim lighting, took on a lovely purple hue. Not ready for the boy to expire yet, he loosened the twine.

The puke suddenly drew in wheezy gasps, then began

coughing. When the boy's breathing became somewhat normal, he gave the pledge's cheek a light slap. "Better?"

After the boy gave him a quick nod, he raised the twine, then wrapped it around his throat again. The pure shock and outrage in the puke's eyes made him giddy and reckless. A part of him wanted to simply kill the pledge now. What he had planned for tomorrow, although necessary if he were to maintain consistency, had always been his least favorite part of Hell Week. Now that he thought about it, the demon wouldn't know if he'd defiled his son the same way the bastard had defiled him twenty-five years ago.

The pledge's eyes rolled back. He quickly loosened the twine and gave the boy another slap, this time hard enough to keep him conscious. "Sorry," he said over the boy's wheezing. "I shouldn't have let my mind wander like that." He took a step back to give the puke a moment to recover. They weren't finished...yet.

"You're probably wondering the significance of this test. I know I did when it was administered to me." He cocked his head and thought back to that night. The fear had been unbearable and overwhelming, but the demon had explained the reasons behind the choking. "Trust," he said to the pledge, repeating a revised version of what the demon had told him twenty-five years ago. "I've asked you several times if you trusted me, and each time you've said yes. Last night I betrayed that trust when I whipped you with my belt. Today I will attempt to regain it."

Holding the twine stretched, he approached the boy. "Do you trust that I won't kill you...today?" When the boy didn't answer, he asked, "Would you *like* me to kill you?"

The puke met his gaze, pure hatred brightening his narrowed eyes. "No."

He cupped his ear. "No...what?"

"No, sir."

"Good. Do you trust me?" At this point, he knew the trust was gone, along with the hope of a climatic betrayal. While he liked the newfound ability of adaptation and improvisation, tough habits were hard to break. This had been a question he'd asked every pledge. Of course they had all lied to him and told him what he'd wanted to hear. What else would they say to a man who held their lives in his hands? "Well, Puke. Do you?" "No."

"No? Why is that?" he asked, eager to hear the boy's reasoning. Never had a pledge been honest. With the boy's honesty, a small part of his damaged heart softened and he wondered if the puke's demon father had any idea of his son's strength. Any father would be proud to have a son like this. *He* would have been proud to have him for a son. Unfortunately, he'd ended up with *Junior*.

"You said you knew my dad."

"That's right."

"Were you friends?"

He raised the twine and wrapped it around the boy's neck again. "No."

The puke's Adam's apple bobbed, moving the loose twine. "He…ah…my dad is pretty quick with his fists. I've taken plenty of beatings. But I always knew he'd stop. I *trusted* that he would stop." The boy glared at him. "You, *sir*, might stop today, but I don't trust that you won't kill me."

He gripped the boy's shoulder and smiled. "You're tough. I truly admire your strength. Truly." Twine in both hands now, he squeezed the puke's neck.

The boy writhed and yanked against his restraints. The shock in his bulging eyes gave him no satisfaction. He hadn't lied. He admired his puke and if they'd met under different circumstances, he could see the boy as his protégé. But fate had given him Junior instead.

Thinking about his idiot daughter had him tightening the twine. "You're quite intuitive, Puke. You're also correct. I won't kill you today." He leaned closer and pressed his mouth against the boy's ear. "I'm saving that and so much more for tomorrow."

CHAPTER 17

"I'M SO THANKFUL Sean's been moved out of ICU." Rachel dropped her head against the Lexus's headrest as Owen pulled out of the Dixon Medical Center parking lot. Relief eased the tension in her shoulders and neck, while exhaustion made her boneless and longing for a bed. "At least one positive thing has finally happened," she added, and glanced at Owen.

He veered the Lexus and turned down the road that would take them to the Sheriff's Department. "It'll be great to see him out of the hospital." He drummed his thumbs along the steering wheel. "But I wouldn't say it's the *only* positive thing that's happened."

"Oh, really? Prior to visiting Sean, we spent half the day interviewing over one hundred girls. I swear, I think they scarred me. If I ever have kids, I want all boys. I can do without girl drama."

"I grew up with three older sisters. Trust me. I get it." The drumming grew more rapid. "And I still don't think that's the only positive thing."

When he looked at her, the tension returned. The heat and promise in his eyes caused a deep ache between her thighs as memories of last night resurfaced. "I suppose you're right. The tech from the Michigan State Police lab did say he thought he'd have something for us later today or tomorrow morning."

"You're a piece of work," he said with a grin. "Seriously. A real piece of work."

"Yeah, well, you're a nice piece of ass."

He laughed and shook his head. "Guy's aren't a piece of ass. Women are."

Was that true? "Whatever. I think you like correcting me when you have the chance...because you're usually the one who's wrong," she teased, her mood lighter than it had been since she'd received Jake's call Monday morning about Sean. "And besides, correct or not, I enjoyed...ya know."

"No, I don't know. Maybe you should enlighten me."

The sexy grin he wore and their teasing banter made her want to be reckless and playful. "Well...I enjoyed the way you...um...kissed me."

"Where?"

Oh, boy. He'd just taken reckless and playful to another level. Unused to this sort of...dirty talk, she kept her mouth shut.

"Chicken," he said with a half smile and pulled into the parking lot next to Jake's SUV.

"I am not."

"Bawk, bawk."

She gave his arm a light punch. "Okay. Fine. I'll tell you—"

He grabbed her hand, and pulled her close. "Where?"

"Yeah." She gripped the front of his sweater with her other hand, and leaned closer. Possessing a sexual confidence she'd never had before, she brushed her lips against his. "I enjoyed the way you kissed my lips." Releasing his sweater, she reached for his hand then brought it between her thighs. "I especially enjoyed the way you kissed me here. Having your tongue—"

He quickly drew back and raised both of his hands. "Okay. You win."

"But I thought you wanted to know."

Resting his arm on the steering wheel, he looked out the front window. When he met her gaze again, another jolt zipped straight between her thighs. The look in his eyes was filled with lust and desire, sensual promises that, after last night, she didn't doubt he could keep. "You can tell me later, after I wine and dine you at the Bigfoot festival."

"Bawk. Who's the chicken now?"

He chuckled. "Better than walking into the Sheriff's Department with...never mind."

Remembering how good he'd felt inside her, rocking his hips, thrusting his thick arousal until she came, she dropped her gaze to his lap. And smiled.

"I gotta get out of this car," he said and quickly opened the door.

"Don't you want your jacket?" she called after him.

"Nope. I'm good for now."

Once she closed the passenger door, she grabbed a handful of snow. "Would this help?"

Laughing, he sidestepped her before she could toss the snow at him. "I swear you're going to pay for this later."

Although unsure what her punishment might be, anticipation hummed through her body. If the punishment had the same results as last night, around Owen, she was going to have to start behaving badly...all the time.

When they reached the glass doors of the Sheriff's Department, an air horn sounded off in the distance, followed by cheering. "And so it begins," she said and turned toward the center of town. Although only late afternoon, the winter sun had begun to dip and the lampposts lining the sidewalks were already illuminated. A handful of two and three story buildings blocked her view of the town square, but based on the cars lining the street, along with the loud cheering, she had a feeling the Bigfoot festival had drawn a large crowd.

"Jake said the festival will shut down by ten tonight." Owen held the door open for her. "Hopefully it won't be too bad."

"Killer on the loose, missing kid, a party for Bigfoot in full swing...yeah, shouldn't be too bad."

"A real piece of work," he said and followed her inside.

Melissa sat at the old receptionist desk. "Hi. Jake's waiting for you in his office."

"Are the state police with him?"

"Just the inspector. The troopers he brought with him are

already working the festival."

As they headed toward Jake's office, Rachel stopped. "How'd the exam go?" she asked Melissa.

The girl rolled her eyes. "I think I did okay. I'm just glad it's over."

"Having a tutor had to have helped."

"No doubt. Kaylie is awesome. She's been working with me since the semester started. I wouldn't want Professor Stronach to know this, but I swear I've learned more from her than him."

"Yeah." Rachel smiled. "That might take his ego down a notch."

Melissa half-laughed. "No kidding. Don't get me wrong. He might be egotistical, but he's a decent teacher. I just think this dumb Bigfoot festival has him distracted. He's been kinda jerky lately." The phone rang. "Sorry. Gotta take this."

While Melissa answered the call, Rachel started walking again. Owen moved alongside her, his big body crowding the narrow hallway. "A part of me would love to pin all this on him."

She smiled and shook her head. "Because he's guilty of being an ass? If only it were that easy."

He stopped short of Jake's office door. "We need a list of visiting professors to make sure none of the faculty has been here at any point prior to their current position."

"I know. The only info I found dates back to last year. When the dean's secretary called earlier, I told her I'd need a list from their human resources people. But there's no certainty she'll have it for us. She needs *approval* from the dean." She sighed. "I've got work to do when we get back to Joy's. I'll add looking deeper into their database to my to do list. Maybe I'll find something new."

"Are you two going to come in or were you waiting for an invite?" Jake called from inside the office.

"Sorry," she said as they stepped inside. "We were just finishing up something."

"No problem. I want you to meet Inspector Marty

O'Reilly." After introductions were made, Jake stood and grabbed his coat. "I'm taking Marty over to the morgue. He wants to talk with Henry about Bill's autopsy. I also thought that maybe later we could meet over at Joy's. Marty might want to see everything we've come up with over the past few days."

"I'm good," the inspector said. "All up to speed. The medical examiner is all I'm interested in for now. Once our lab gives me their findings from the evidence collected at the crime scene, we'll take it from there."

"Take what from where?" Rachel asked, her temper spiking. Who the hell was this guy to blow into town and take over? "Did you look at the reports from *our* lab? Considering that's all we have to work with now, I'd think you—"

"Ms. Davis, I appreciate your enthusiasm, especially with this particular investigation. It's always tough when family is involved. I also know all about CORE and the agency's excellent record of case resolution. But, the sheriff asked for *our* assistance. Now that we're here, I'll be conducting the investigation."

"If you're familiar with CORE, then I would think you'd rather utilize our—"

The inspector held up an infuriating hand, silencing her. "I'm not saying I won't utilize you two, I'm saying I'm the lead. Let's touch base in the morning. I'll consider your full report then. Ready, Sheriff?"

"Right behind you." After Marty walked out of the room, Jake shook his head. "Sorry. I wasn't expecting that to happen." He ran a palm over his mouth, then dropped his hand to his side. "Fucking prick doesn't realize this is my county, he's just a guest. I'll handle it."

"Let it ride," Owen said. "I'm used to guys like him. What does he know?"

Jake moved to the door. "Like he told you, he's up to speed. Are you two heading to the festival?"

"That's the plan," she said. "How many extra men did the illustrious Marty bring with him?"

The sheriff cracked a smile. "Five. They'll stay until it ends on Saturday. After that…I'm not sure what Marty has in mind. Gotta run. I'll catch up with you in a bit. Percy's been slow roasting ribs and big, honkin' turkey legs all day. I want some. Too bad I'm on duty. I could use a beer." He glanced out the front door to where Marty stood, checking his watch. "Or four," Jake added.

"Any luck with the business owners?" Owen asked.

"No. Between my deputy and me we found only two business owners who own either an SUV or a truck and have a girl from Stanley Hall working for them. Problem is, the two owners are both in their late sixties and both of them are women."

"Maybe we could look into their husbands or sons," Rachel suggested.

"Already done. One is a widower, the other is married, but her husband is seventy-two. The widower doesn't have kids, the other lady has two daughters, one living in Ohio and the other in North Carolina."

Marty rapped on the door.

Jake glanced over his shoulder and held up a finger. Not the one Rachel would have preferred, either. "I better go." He moved toward the door. "By the way, I also found the only living deputy who'd been working with Sheriff Miller twenty-five years ago. He's in a nursing home and has Alzheimer's. Oh, and Josh Conway's parents are scheduled to be here in the morning. Can you two meet me here at eight? I'd like you part of that meeting."

"Of course," Rachel said, even though she dreaded meeting Josh's parents. While she knew dealing with the families of victims would be part of working in the field, she now realized she'd rather hide behind her computer. She hadn't been prepared for how emotionally involved she'd become with this investigation. After watching how hard Hal and Joy had taken Bill's death, she'd gained new respect for Owen and the rest of the CORE team. It amazed her that they could remain immune on the surface and stay focused on their jobs.

After Jake left, and they said good-bye to Melissa, Rachel

pushed open the door. "Shall we go and get ourselves a big, honkin' turkey leg?"

"Joy."

"What's the problem? You're a guy. I thought manly men liked eating—"

"No." He nodded his head to the left. "There's Joy."

Joy held Walter's hand as they walked toward them. Guilt, sadness and despair came at Rachel in a rush. While she'd spoken with Joy yesterday, their conversation had been brief. Joy's main concern had been for her brother and helping him cope with Bill's murder. Between the deep lines of exhaustion etched on her face and the purple smudges under her eyes, Rachel worried how well Joy was coping with the loss of her nephew. Thank God Joy had Walter.

"How are things?" Rachel asked, then gave Joy an impulsive hug. "How's Hal doing today?"

Joy hugged her back, nearly crushing every one of her rib bones. "He's the same. Depressed. Been lying on the couch with Bill's dog. Dog's depressed, too. I couldn't even bribe him to eat some leftover meatloaf." Her chin trembled. "We...ah...just left the funeral home. Hal's in no shape to make arrangements."

Rachel rubbed Joy's arm. "When will the funeral be?"

"Monday. The frickin' festival's screwing everything up around here."

"That's where we're heading," Owen said. "Want to join us? Dinner and drinks are on me, if you're interested."

God, she loved him. No. Wait. She loved that he was thoughtful and perceptive, and knew just the right things to say and do at the right time. Besides, she was only half in love with him. And in her mind, there was a big difference, because if things didn't work out between them, it would only hurt half as much. An irrational rationalization, but in her mind, it worked.

"We're going to pass." Walter put his arm around Joy's shoulder. "We've got an empty house to ourselves, so I thought I'd make a fire and pamper my girl." He squeezed Joy closer. "She needs a little pampering."

The adoration in Joy's eyes filled Rachel with warmth. Joy and Walter were a strange couple. Loud, potty-mouthed and gruff, Joy was the polar opposite to Walter's quiet, laid-back personality. But they worked well together, and despite how they usually acted around each other, over the past few days it had been clear to Rachel that they were a solid couple with a relationship built with love.

"Sounds like a great idea," Rachel said.

"I'm wondering," Owen began, "you said the house is empty. I haven't seen any other tenants since we've been here. Are they working odd hours or something?"

Joy looked away, a surprising red blush staining her cheeks that had nothing to do with the cold.

"Ah...you two are the only tenants," Walter answered. "We...Joy..."

"We like our privacy," Joy finished for him, then looked at Walter. "I hate for you to miss the festival because of me. You've been searching for Bigfoot for nearly twenty years. If you want to go for a bit, I'm willing to walk around with you."

Walter touched Joy's chin. "It ain't nothing but a bunch of fools running around in Bigfoot costumes, fair food and loud music. I'm not buying into, or willing to support that professor's BS. Besides, I'd rather be home with you."

Joy cleared her throat, and offered a tentative smile. "I think Walt's become a Bigfoot snob."

"You're right on that one." Walter grinned. "I don't like dealing with wannabe Bigfoot fanatics, and don't need to go to no festival. I've got proof Bigfoot exists."

Owen raised his eyebrows. "What kind of proof? Wait, did you give Stronach a plaster mold of a Bigfoot footprint?"

Walter's grin turned into a huge smile. "It's a copy, I got the real deal at home. I've also got pictures, videos, feces, and—"

"You have Bigfoot poop?" Rachel laughed and turned to Joy. "Seriously?"

Joy nodded. "You don't want to know."

Walter tugged on Joy's hand. "You kids have fun. No curfew tonight," he finished with a wink, then the two of them continued along the sidewalk.

Owen offered his arm. "Shall we?"

A sudden giddiness took over. After Owen retrieved his coat from the Lexus, with a grin, she hooked her arm through his and began walking. This almost felt like a date. Not exactly the kind of date she'd imagined going on with Owen, but it didn't matter. They were spending time together. Once they left Bola, and Owen began traveling again, she wasn't sure how much they'd see each other. And while his earlier comment about not being single remained on the forefront of her mind, she also wasn't sure how serious he was about being with her. Would this be a brief affair? Or would he be willing to jump head first into a committed relationship? She didn't want a brief affair, and stood behind her earlier thoughts. She would not be in a relationship based solely on sex. She wanted what Joy and Walter had, minus the Bigfoot feces. She wanted love and commitment, a partnership. She wanted to matter to someone. She wanted to matter to Owen.

"When did you realize Joy and Walter were a couple?" Owen asked as they crossed the street where the center of town loomed ahead.

"Tuesday. I'm not saying I knew for sure, but based on the way the two of them looked at each other, I got the impression Walter was more than a tenant and groundskeeper."

"They do act like an old married couple. The morning I met Walter he was sneaking a cigarette out on the front porch."

"Joy chews tobacco."

"So they're kind of a strange couple."

She half-laughed. "Strange and sweet. They run a boarding house, but don't want to have any boarders."

"They made room for us."

"Yeah, only because of Hell Week."

He stopped in front of a wooden roadblock barrier that had been placed in the middle of the street. Behind him, the snow-covered square was crowded with vendors and people. Smoke rose from a variety of food stations, and bright lights from the vendors' booths, as well as the stage and gazebo, lit the square. "For the next few hours, let's pretend Hell Week doesn't exist," he said, and reached for her gloved hand.

"That's kind of hard to do when we're supposed to help patrol the area along with the state police and Jake's deputies," she said, even though she loved the idea of pretending they were on a date. Caution wouldn't break her heart.

He nodded, and scanned the crowd behind him. When he met her gaze, he smiled. "We'll do both." He led her toward the square. "I promised I'd wine and dine you. Besides, you're not carrying a gun and I don't think putting the state police to use will do any good, except give the Townies some piece of mind."

"True. Kidnapping a victim from a large crowd isn't the killer's MO."

He gave her hand a tug. "You're not pretending very well."

"Sorry." She smiled. "Play acting was never my thing. But for you, I'll try."

"Promise? Because I've got a few fantasies we could role play."

She half-laughed. "And you keep saying I'm a piece of work? Look in the mirror."

When they reached the thick of the crowd, he tightened his grip on her hand and moved them toward the fringes where the vendors were lined up in a row. They perused each vending station. One sold Bigfoot bumper stickers and t-shirts. Another had a variety of Bigfoot masks for sale. She laughed when they found a guy selling Bigfoot slippers and gloves.

"I should buy a pair of these for Ian." She raised the furry slippers. "Think he'll wear them?"

He chuckled. "I'd pay to see that, especially if he wore them with one of his Armani suits."

Unable to resist, she bought a pair. Considering Ian didn't have much of a sense of humor, she probably wouldn't give the gift to her boss. Her brother might get a kick out of them though, and she was always on the lookout for unique stocking stuffers.

As they moved past more booths, a sweet and tangy aroma caused her mouth to water. She looked ahead and spotted Percy in front of an enormous grill. "We should stop by and say hi to Percy."

"You just want to check out his turkey legs," Owen whispered in her ear, his tone seductive.

She laughed. "You're the one who keeps saying you're going to wine and dine me." She held up her empty hands. "No wine. No dine."

"Then let's rectify that."

Hand in hand, they walked to Percy's stand. After joking with the bartender for a few minutes, they left with two Henry the VIII size turkey legs, a half rack of ribs, and a couple of cans of beer. They managed to secure a small section of a picnic table, and sat.

As they noshed on the food, the band took the stage. "I was wondering what type of music they'd have for a Bigfoot festival," Rachel said. "Polka was not on the top of my list."

He used a wet wipe to clean his hands. "Maybe Professor Stronach's students confused Bigfoot for Oktoberfest." He picked up his beer. "Either way, this band isn't any good. My first year with the Secret Service, I was working in Germany. At the time, I was low level, but the US ambassador's elderly grandmother had come to visit and needed some babysitting. The woman was born in Germany and left during World War II. She was determined to see everything. So me and another agent were put on granny detail for an entire week. Good ol' Aggie dragged us to every festival she could find and made us dance and eat right along with her." Grinning, he shook his head. "She was a lot of fun."

"Do you miss it? The Secret Service, I mean."

He stared at the crappy band. "Honestly, no. Don't get me wrong. I've been to amazing places and along the way, met very powerful people."

"But that sounds so exciting," she said, and imagined going to fancy dinner parties, or driving in a limo through the streets of exotic countries. After spending her childhood and teenage years caged in Chicago, looking after her brother, she'd craved action and adventure. Owen had experienced the things she'd longed for, and she couldn't help envying him the opportunities he'd landed.

"It was." He rolled the can between his palms. "Shortly after the granny detail, I asked to be reassigned to criminal investigations, which is what my background is in. Now *that* was exciting. I love fitting pieces of puzzles together, and that position gave me the opportunity."

"What changed?"

"I was in the wrong place at the wrong time." Smiling, he lifted his beer in a mock toast. "I spent ten months in Italy working with a team to bust up a counterfeiting operation. Turns out the operation was coming out of our embassy."

"What? As in the *U.S.* embassy?"

He nodded. "So I went undercover as an agent assigned to the ambassador's family. We suspected the ambassador's brother, who was attending John Cabot University in Rome and living with the ambassador and his family. The kid was young, but far from dumb. We discovered he and some of his university buddies were involved in credit card fraud. It was small time, but one of our agents found a red flag linking the kid to a counterfeiting operation we'd been trying to bust. The long and short of it...I collected enough evidence to arrest the brother and everyone else involved." He crushed the beer can and set it on top of the paper basket filled with discarded rib bones. "But in the process, the ambassador's seventeen-year-old daughter accused me of...inappropriate behavior. Of course *that* ended up being my legacy, not the criminals I brought down during the years I was with the Secret Service."

Nosey by nature, she already knew what Owen had done during his time with the Secret Service. When she'd met him, she'd been so intrigued by his background she couldn't help doing a little...snooping. Hacking into the U.S. Secret Service had been out of the question. There were certain challenges she refused to take, and breaking into their network to research the man she had been infatuated with from the very first meeting wasn't worth jail time.

Ian's computer had contained a wealth of knowledge, though. While her boss was a brilliant profiler and businessman, he wasn't necessarily computer savvy. If he'd had a clue that she'd looked through his files, he'd never said a word. But his files had been light and sketchy. She'd always suspected Ian might be a little old school, keeping certain information and files as hard copies in his safe or locked in his brain. Now her suspicions were confirmed, because while she knew about Owen's Secret Service background, she didn't know anything about a seventeen-year-old girl.

She toyed with the fringes of her scarf. "This girl...is she the reason you resigned? Not that you have to tell me. It's not like it's any of my business."

"Let's walk around before our bottoms freeze to the picnic bench." He gathered their trash and dumped it in a nearby garbage can. She grabbed the bag with the Bigfoot slippers, then after hooking her arm through his again, they strolled around the festival. "The girl, Molly, was a pretty, spoiled wannabe socialite. She had no ambitions other than shopping, partying and...me." He gave her a sideways glance and shook his head. "Even if she was of legal age and not part of an assignment, I wouldn't have gotten involved with her. Quite frankly, I just didn't like her."

"But she liked you."

"I don't know about that. I think she liked when men gave her attention. Her father didn't give her any, so maybe this was her way of filling a void. I don't know if that's true or not. What I do know is that I wasn't the first agent she tried to seduce."

"If that's the case, then why did you say what happened with her ended up being your legacy?"

"Because I was brought up on charges for statutory rape."

She stopped dead. No way. Owen might like the ladies and he might be a serial charmer, but charges like that were ludicrous. He was too moral and had too much integrity. "That's ridiculous."

"No kidding. I never touched her and was only around her when necessary. My sole focus was on the ambassador's brother, not a bratty girl."

"I'm assuming the charges were dismissed."

"Yeah, a few months later, I was reinstated. Molly confessed to making the whole thing up, and after questioning, other agents and acquaintances of the ambassador made the same claims about the girl. But the damage was done." He gave her a wry smile. "I'm talking serious damage to my reputation. The whole thing left a bad taste in my mouth." He looked over her shoulder toward where the polka band played. "So, I quit. Twenty-four hours later, I get a call from Ian asking if I'd take his private jet to Chicago for an interview."

"Subtle."

Owen half-laughed. "Tell me about it. Ian has eyes and ears everywhere. Doesn't bother me, though. He made me an offer I wasn't about to refuse. I love working for CORE and can't imagine doing anything else."

Which made things between them more complicated. She loved working for CORE, too. If they continued sleeping together or took their relationship to a level that went beyond the intimacy of sex, their work rapport, their careers with CORE, could be affected.

"Sorry." He nudged her with his shoulder. "That was a downer story. I didn't mean to get into all that tonight."

"Don't be sorry. I'm glad you told me. I've always wondered why you left the Secret Service."

"Come on. You didn't do a little...looking? I know how you are and what you're capable of when you get in front of a computer. You're brilliant when it comes to technology."

"Egomaniac." She nudged him back. "My brilliant skills are only used for the good of CORE."

Chuckling, he pulled her closer. "Liar. I bet you've got the scoop on all the CORE agents. You probably have a spreadsheet detailing—"

"Spreadsheet? Seriously?" She laughed and held a gloved hand over her heart. "I do not, nor have I ever, snooped into anyone's *personal* files."

She did know quite a bit about the men who worked for CORE, but just basic background information. Although nosey, she drew the line at digging into her coworkers' personal lives. A firm believer in karma, she didn't want her actions to come back and bite her on the ass.

"All right. I believe you...sorta."

She dragged him toward a vendor selling cookies, chocolates and fudge. "If we really don't need to be here, let's go. I have work to do and my nose is about to freeze off my face."

"Then why are we stopping here? Is chocolate going to stop your nose from freezing?"

"I wish." She bought fudge, cookies and several chocolate suckers shaped like Bigfoot and the footprint similar to the one they'd seen in Professor Stronach's office. Bag of goodies in hand, she turned to Owen. "I noticed Joy and Walter have a sweet tooth. I thought they might like these."

Grinning, he shook his head. "Well, aren't you sweet."

"Of course. You're just now realizing this?"

"You've been calling me a douche bag on a daily basis for nearly a year. So, yeah."

A little tremor of guilt caught in her belly. "I didn't exactly have the chance to say this last night, but I'm sorry for the way I treated you. Looking back, I wish I'd confronted you about the Christmas party right after it happened. You made it hard to keep up a bitchy front, plus it was exhausting trying to come up with new ways to be nasty," she finished with a grin. Based on his honesty about his former job, how he'd treated her throughout the day...making love last night, she knew they were in a tentative, but good place right now. She could be honest and teasing, without offending him. "And for the record, I didn't call you a douche bag every day, at least not to your face."

He threw an arm around her shoulder, steered her away from the crowd and toward the street. "No. That inventive mind of yours came up with other choice nicknames. What I'm wondering? Why exactly didn't you have a chance to apologize last night?"

"Because Jake called." She suspected what he was hedging at, but wasn't about to take the bait. She still couldn't believe how brazen and reckless she'd been in the car earlier when she described where she enjoyed his kisses. A welcoming heat warmed her cheeks just thinking about how he'd loved her body with his mouth, and how much she'd love for him to do it again.

He veered her onto the sidewalk and led them back to the Lexus. "You could have told me after you got off the phone."

"No. We talked about the case."

"You could have told me after that."

She could have if he hadn't been so distracting. Massaging her back, then her bottom. Kissing her until she'd been breathless, then sliding his thick arousal between her thighs until she came again. "I suppose I could have."

"I suppose."

He opened the car door for her. After she climbed in and he shut the door, she hoped that was the end of the conversation. She didn't want to talk about what they'd *done* last night. She wanted to *do* it.

After a silent drive back to Joy's, they entered the quiet house. A low burning fire crackled in the empty great room. "Joy and Walter must have gone to bed," she said and set the bag of goodies and the Bigfoot slippers on the dining room table. "I'm going to do the same after I get a little work done."

Without a word, they crept up the stairs. When they reached her room, he let out a sigh, furrowed his brows and scratched the back of his head.

"What's wrong?" she asked.

"Nothing really." He lifted a shoulder. "I've been trying to remember...what exactly were we doing last night that kept you from talking?"

Still facing him, she reached behind and opened the bedroom door. Grabbing him by the front of his coat, she dragged him into the room. "I think we were doing something like this." She rose on her tiptoes and brushed her lips across his.

"Is that all?" he asked as they began unzipping each other's coats.

"There might have been a little more to it." She shoved his sweater over his hard abs and chest, then let him pull it over his head. Her nipples hardened as she stared at his naked chest. Anxious to be skin to skin, she removed her sweater and bra, while he took care of her jeans and panties. Then he quickly stripped the rest of his clothes off, until they were both completely naked, their bodies mere inches apart.

He cupped her bottom with both hands, and lifted her. She wrapped her legs around his back and her arms around his neck, then pressed her breasts against his chest. Instead of heading for the bed, he moved her against the wall.

He dragged his mouth along her neck. "It's all starting to come back to me," he murmured against her ear, his hot breath sending a shiver of anticipation straight between her thighs. Holding her bottom with one hand, he reached between them, gripped his erection and nudged the tip against her sex. Meeting her gaze, he slowly slid inside of her. Once seated to the hilt, he gripped her rear with both hands.

"Now that your memory is back, should we stop?" she teased, knowing there was no way in hell she'd let him leave her room. Knowing deep down that if what they had together ended up being only a sexual affair and nothing more, she'd take whatever she could from him. A relationship based solely on sex wasn't her style, but she could compromise where Owen was concerned. She might end up with a broken heart later, but as he filled her, completed her, she didn't want to think about the consequences. He made her feel alive, wanted, desired. Right now was all that mattered. She'd learned a long time ago that the future could be unpredictable. Instead of worrying about a future that might not happen, she wanted to soak up every moment possible and enjoy being in his arms.

His breath puffed against her neck as he released a low chuckle. "There's no way I'm stopping now."

He pulled out, then thrust. She closed her eyes and pressed her head against the wall as a delicious tremor zipped through her body. "Not even if Bigfoot came crashing through the door?" she teasingly asked on a gasp.

Rocking his hips, he kissed her. When he tore his mouth away, he met her gaze. Her breath caught. The intense desire, the open intimacy in his eyes filled her with hope and love. "Not even if Ian crashed through the door." He moved them to the bed. When her head and back hit the mattress, he thrust inside of her. "It's no one's business what we do," he murmured against her ear. "I've wanted this for too long to stop."

With her heart soaring, she clutched his broad back. His muscles bunched with each pump of his hips. The soft hair lining his chest tickled her nipples. As her orgasm drew near, she pressed open-mouthed kisses wherever she could reach. Never in her life had she thought she could have this—a gorgeous, sexy *and* intelligent man making love to her. He might not love her the way she loved him, but he wanted her as much as she wanted him.

As pressure built low in her belly and spread between her thighs, her heart raced faster. She *loved* Owen. She'd been lying to herself to protect her heart. She wasn't half in love, or kind of in love with him. She full out, without a doubt, was crazy in love with the man. And it scared her. She gripped him tighter, raised her hips and spread her legs wider to meet every one of his thrusts. Loving him scared the hell out of her. If he walked away, if he looked at this as just a fling, the loss of him would leave a void in her heart and soul.

When he raised his body and braced his arms along either side of her, he dipped his head and kissed her. Refusing to think about anything but them, this moment, she met his kiss, and mimicked every powerful rock of his hips with her tongue. Every delicious slide of his hard arousal set her on fire. When he gripped her hip with one powerful hand and moved faster, harder, the slow burn growing in her core ignited.

Tearing her mouth from his, she dropped her head to the

mattress, closed her eyes and gasped. A kaleidoscope of beautiful colors burst behind her eyelids. Inner thighs quivering, pure pleasure burst from within and radiated out, shocking every single sensitive nerve ending. As her orgasm multiplied, her inner muscles clenched and drew him deeper.

His breathing grew more labored. His movements became shorter, faster. "Beautiful," he said, and stared down at her. "You're so damned beautiful."

His words, his amazing touch, his familiar, masculine scent collided together. She came in a rush, whispering his name over and over until he released a low, harsh groan.

Pulling out quickly, he released himself. Seconds later, he dropped his body on the bed and rolled onto his back. She turned her head and smiled when she caught him grinning at her. "You're amazing," he said, then dropped his gaze to her stomach. "And I need to buy condoms." Pushing himself upright, he then reached for his undershirt and used it to clean her stomach.

"If you don't, you're going to run out of shirts," she managed to say while trying to catch her breath.

Chuckling, he moved to the center of the bed, and took her with him. "No doubt, because I don't think I can keep my hands off you."

Snuggling against his chest, she curled next to him and ran her hand along his lean, hard abs. "That makes two of us."

He kissed the top of her head, then reached down and touched her chin. Too comfortable and sated, she didn't want to move. "Look at me," he coaxed.

With a groan, she rolled onto him. Chest to chest, he ran his hand down her back. "I meant what I said about Ian. What we do is none of his business. I...ah...I'm not saying I want to hide our...relationship. I just don't want it to affect our careers."

She let out a sigh of relief. They were so in sync and always on the same page. "I agree." She glanced at his chest and feathered her finger through his soft hair. "So...this isn't just a...ah...casual, let's have sex while we're out of town fling?"

He gripped her bottom and pushed her body up until they were nose to nose. Spearing his hands through her short hair, he held her head. "When it comes to you, there's never been anything casual. I told you I've waited a long time for this. I'm not planning on going anywhere."

As he gave her a long, lingering kiss, his heart beat hard and fast against her own. She'd tried to tell herself she was maybe half in love with Owen, but had realized the truth tonight. She loved him. Heart and soul, she loved him. He hadn't said he loved her, but what he had said had disintegrated the last barrier guarding her heart.

He wasn't planning on going anywhere.

After he reached for the lamp on the nightstand and turned it off, he pulled the sheet and comforter over them. Her body completely satisfied, her heart filled with hope and love, she laid her head against his chest and closed her eyes.

CHAPTER 18

FRIDAY

RACHEL STIRRED, HER active mind still caught between a fuzzy dream state and full consciousness. Clips of memories filtered through her head as she snuggled against the pillow and burrowed deeper under the covers. When Owen's sexy grin filled her hazy thoughts, she took herself back to yesterday. To the playful teasing in his car, to the festival, to last night. Releasing a sigh of satisfaction, she replayed the way they'd made love, how he'd used his hard, gorgeous body to coax orgasm after orgasm from her.

A throb built between her thighs and she knew the one person who could fix it. Her body still lazy, sleepy and languid, she forced her arm to reach next to her.

Empty.

Damn.

Wishing Owen was still in bed, she shoved her hand between her thighs and cupped herself. She couldn't help being greedy where he was concerned. She'd waited four years to touch him, hold him, live every fantasy she'd conjured about him. And now, it appeared they were a...couple.

Abandoning her need for sexual release, she rolled onto her

back and rested her hands under her head.

They were a couple.

Knowing the type of man Owen was, she believed that he'd meant everything he'd said last night.

This isn't a casual fling, and he doesn't plan on going anywhere.

Thoughts of a bright future, one filled with fun holidays, family gatherings, a houseful of children, and late night love sessions filled her mind. Owen came from a good family. She'd had the opportunity to meet his parents a couple of years ago and had instantly liked them. Down to earth, loving, they were good people and had raised a fine man. Growing up with her flaky mother, she and Sean never had much. Holidays were just another day and there were no family gatherings. To be able to have a future filled with love gave her courage and hope. Giving herself to Owen, her whole self, allowing him to see the emotions she'd kept guarded would require trust. She trusted him, but being with him made her realize she hadn't trusted herself. She needed to have the courage to be open with him, to not allow herself to close off the moment she didn't understand a new emotion. Still, she wasn't silly enough to believe Owen was in love with her like she was with him. She also knew that dreaming of the future when things between them were still new wasn't necessarily smart. But it was hard not to become caught up in a fantasy when her reality hadn't always been the greatest.

She stared at the rotating ceiling fan, reality now rearing its ugly head. They had an investigation to solve, a killer to stop and a missing boy in need of rescue. Although on the fence as to whether or not she wanted to pursue being a CORE field agent, she still had a job to do. She glanced at the clock on the nightstand. Just past six. She had time before she needed to shower and make their eight o'clock meeting with Jake and the Michigan State Police Inspector, Marty. Curling on her side, she let her eyes drift shut, then immediately popped them open. Tearing the sheet and comforter from her body, she quickly gathered her toiletries. Who was she kidding? Instead of lazing in bed, she had work to do.

As she showered and moved through her morning routine, she made mental notes of what needed to be done…things she should have done last night instead of going to the festival and messing around with Owen. Not that she had any regrets, but Josh's life was at stake, and because of their investigation, Bill had been murdered.

Now ready to attack the day, she headed for her bedroom. As she turned the knob, she glanced down the hall where Owen's bedroom door remained partially opened. Needing to gather her thoughts and do a little brainstorming, she entered her room, grabbed a notepad and pencil, then headed to Owen's room. She knocked on the door and popped her head inside.

"Morning," she said.

He closed his laptop, pushed the chair away from the desk and stood. "Morning." Eliminating the distance between them, he pulled her into his arms and gave her a kiss.

"Why didn't you wake me?" she asked and gave him a light swat on the arm.

He took her free hand. After leading her to the bed, he sat on the edge while she remained standing between his legs. "You looked all soft and peaceful. I felt kind of guilty for keeping you up late."

"You don't look like you're feeling guilty."

He grinned. "Okay, maybe I don't feel *that* guilty. I'm a guy and it's in our nature to be selfish." He grabbed her rear and pulled her closer. "When it comes to spending time with you, I'm very selfish."

She gave into temptation and kissed him. Her body immediately came alive. Before things spun out of control, she quickly stepped back. Wagging a finger, she shook her head. "If we're going to get anything done, I think we'll have to make sure a bed isn't in the room."

He leaned back on his elbows. "Who needs a bed?"

Her mind instantly conjured all the other places they could make love. Before she let her body rule her head, she moved across the room and took a seat in front of the small desk in the corner. "On that note," she said with a smile. "I want to talk about a few things."

He straightened and grew serious. "Us, you mean."

"I...ah...no. I wanted to talk about the case, where we are with it and what needs to be done." While she did want to talk about them and define their relationship, now wasn't the time. "Unless...did you want to talk about us?" she asked anyway. Based on his assumption, maybe *he* wanted to talk about their relationship.

Relief crossed his face. "I thought we covered things last night, but if I wasn't clear...I don't want what we have to stop anytime soon."

Okay, now he was opening up a can of worms. Now she questioned exactly what they had together. She had major feelings for him. Not like, but love. Maybe she'd read him wrong. Maybe this was just sex to him. "Good. I don't want that to happen, either."

"Thanks for the enthusiasm."

She cocked her chin and looked at him. "What's that supposed to mean? I'm totally enthused. You want sex between us to not stop anytime soon." *Damn it. Think before you speak.* "Sorry, what I meant—"

He held up a hand and sent her a wry smile. "You meant exactly what you said. And I'm an ass for not making myself clear." He shoved off the bed, then knelt in front of her. "When I told you this wasn't casual, I meant it. We're good together. In and out of bed." Taking both of her hands, he held them to his chest. "Do you realize that other than my family, you've been the only other constant person in my life? I look forward to my mornings because I know you'll be the first person I talk to. The nights...when I'm out of town, I can't stand it if I miss your call or don't have an excuse to put a call in to you."

Heart racing, she stared at their joined hands. "I...I've felt the same way for a long time."

He tilted her chin and snared her gaze. "You're important to me. And I'm not about to take what's happening between us lightly. I don't want casual, I want complex. I want to give what we have together a shot."

Throwing her arms around his neck, she kissed him. When she pulled away, she smiled. "I want to give us a shot, too."

Grinning, he looked over his shoulder at the bed, but she cupped his chin and forced his attention back on her. "Don't tempt me."

"I'm not," he said and had the nerve to look innocent. "I was just stretching my neck. Of course, if you want to, we could—"

"Nope." She chuckled. "Well, I do, but we have to work."

He rose and went back to his spot on the edge of the bed. "All work and no play...when was the last time you had a vacation?"

"Christmas."

"I'm not talking time off, I'm talking getting on a plane and flying off to someplace fun vacation."

"Never."

Shock crossed his face. "Never?"

"How could I? I had either Sean to take care of, or school, then there was the Army, now my job...there just never was a good time to up and leave. If I did, I'd feel...selfish and guilty."

"You put too much responsibility on yourself." He leaned back on his elbows again. "That's going to change."

"Really? Got a magic wand on you?"

He looked to his crotch. "Well...I don't know if I'd call it that."

Laughing, she acted as if she was going to throw the notepad at him.

"Be nice," he warned with a grin. "I'm taking you on vacation. I think some tropical island resort would work, don't you?"

She instantly pictured him shirtless and lying on a beach, the sun dipping as the waves lapped along the shore. "That'll definitely work. But for now, *we* have work to do. We're supposed to meet with Jake in an hour."

"Fair enough. Let's get at it."

"Okay." She looked at her notes. "We need to stop at the university's human resources department and hope they have that list of visiting professors for us. I didn't have a chance to dig into their database last night to see if I could find something dating back further than last year. Like you said, we really need to make sure none of the current faculty had been here at any point prior to their current position."

"Like Stronach?"

"Yeah, he's on my radar. And not because he's an ass."

"Mine too. He orchestrated the Bigfoot festival at a time of year when he knew Hell Week was a possibility."

"Plus he considers it nothing more than a legend. It's a stretch, and doesn't make him guilty of anything but being eccentric." She tapped the pencil against her lips. "Okay, Jake took care of speaking with former deputies…"

"I guess that means you didn't have a chance to look into GSI?" He rose from the bed. "What were we doing that kept you so busy?" he asked with a grin and moved to the opposite side of the room where he began rummaging through his suitcase.

"No, I didn't. And don't start with that again." Damn, she hadn't even jotted down the name of the company that had provided Wexman University with the malfunctioning security equipment. The dean's secretary had called just as she had entered her brother's hospital room. Distracted and focused on Sean, she'd forgotten about it. Last night, she'd intended to research the company after the festival, along with the visiting professors, but once Owen had her clothes off, she couldn't think about anything but him.

She glanced at Owen's laptop. Time to rectify her inexcusable absentmindedness. Every CORE member had the same computer system. Hers was a little more elaborate, but for what she was looking for, his would do. She opened his laptop, and froze.

Her throat closed as she stared at an email from Ian. His message had been a reply to an email Owen had sent yesterday afternoon. She scrolled down, and as she read through Owen's original email, each and every one of her fantasies fizzled and died, along with her hope for a future with Owen. Betrayed, shocked and hurt she looked across the room and glared at his back as he pulled a black sweater over his head.

"Rachel has proven that she, as we already know, is an excellent investigator," she read the first line out loud, then looked at him again.

He turned and smoothed out the front of his sweater. His eyes were unreadable, his face expressionless. "Ian wanted me to keep him updated on our progress."

"This isn't just about our progress," she countered, her voice rising. "It's about *me*."

"What I wrote wasn't bad."

"Really? Let me refresh your memory." She looked to the laptop screen. "That being said, I'm not sure Rachel is qualified to work in the field. While she has led an aggressive investigation into the Hell Week disappearances, emotionally, she does not yet possess the strength required when dealing with a murder victim. She even voiced her concerns to me and has admitted to having second thoughts about working in the field." Glancing at him, she shook her head. "Ringing any bells?"

Narrowing his eyes, he moved to the edge of the bed and sat. "I know exactly what I wrote. If you continue to read, you'll see that I gave you a lot of props, especially considering you're also dealing with what's happened to Sean."

"Aren't you a prince? Thanks so much for the *glowing* report." She slammed the laptop shut, then scooped up her notepad and pencil. "And for sharing something I admitted to you in private."

He shot off the bed and blocked the door. "Where are you going?"

"To my room." She needed time to think. Alone. Professionally, she'd trusted Owen. Personally, she'd been ready to dive head first into a full-blown relationship. But he'd betrayed both her professional and personal trust. That email would keep her chained to the desk and locked in CORE's evidence and evaluation room. If Ian didn't think she was capable of running an investigation and dealing with murder victims, there wasn't a chance in hell he'd give her a position in the field. Whether she wanted it or not.

"Rachel." He gripped her shoulders. "Answer me honestly. Do you really want to be a field agent?"

"That's not the point." She shook his hands off and threw her arms in the air. "You of all people knew how much I wanted this."

"And now that you're doing it, you're miserable." He sighed and shook his head. "Honey, I know this week has been hard. There are days you act like a fish out of water. That's one of the reasons why I bought all that stuff and turned Joy's dining room into a mock evidence and evaluation room."

She knew everything he said was true, but it still infuriated her that *he* would make himself part of a decision that didn't concern him. People had been making decisions for her since she could remember. Her mother had decided Rachel should play the role of mommy to Sean in order to continue with her carefree, screwed up lifestyle. The Army had decided she'd been more suited to a desk job, and so had Ian. And while there was a very strong chance she'd choose working behind the scenes at CORE versus in the field, it should be *her* choice to make.

"Look," he said, and reached for her, but she stepped away. He dropped his hands to his side. "You obviously saw Ian's response."

"Right. Keep an eye on her," she quoted.

"Exactly. So no harm done."

"No harm done? You've possibly jeopardized my career. And on top of that, it's obvious I'm not the lead on this investigation, after all. Ian humored me by making *you* my babysitter. And you went along with it. Come on, Owen. After everything you said, after we…I told you something in confidence. When I was down and vulnerable, I trusted you. I trusted that I could talk to you about how I felt about seeing…" She glanced away when Bill's lifeless, gruesome image emerged. "Your email, whether it's true or not, takes away my opportunity to decide what's best for me."

"Being in CORE's evidence and evaluation room is what's best for you. That's where you thrive. And I'll be honest, that's where I want you. Not out here where there's a chance you could get hurt or worse."

"Keep the little woman locked safe in a closet," she said with an eye roll. "Doc Brown, time to refuel the Delorean and leave 1955 behind. I *do* have combat training and can take care of myself."

"I know you do, but when was the last time you used it? Basic training?"

"I'm not doing this. Please move. I need to look into the security company."

"Not until we've finished discussing this."

"There's nothing more to discuss. You win, Ian wins…I don't want to work in the field. Okay?"

"No, it's not okay. I don't want this coming between us. And for whatever it's worth, although I don't think you're qualified to work in the field, I *do* know how important being here is to you and I want you to have the chance to finish what you started. Despite what you think, I'm not here to babysit you. I'm here to guide you."

She'd known for days she wasn't qualified to deal with certain parts of field work—like dead victims—but to hear Owen say it? That hurt. Bad. She'd tried hard to keep herself, her emotions in check. She'd failed miserably the day they'd found Bill's dead body. While she'd held up throughout the day, she'd unleashed those tremulous emotions later. Cried for Bill, for his family, all while an overwhelming amount of guilt had plagued her. Owen had witnessed her breakdown. He'd held her, then later loved her body. And while he hadn't put in his email to Ian anything about her emotional collapse, she'd read between the lines. She couldn't hack it, and the only thing she *could* hack was a computer.

She glanced at the clock on the nightstand. "We leave in

forty minutes. Let me go to my room and look into the security company before we go."

He kept the door blocked. "Are you going to let this come between us?"

She didn't want it to, but in her heart she knew it would. She'd trusted him and he'd betrayed that trust by not being upfront with her...by not supporting her. He'd made love to her, made it clear he'd wanted a relationship, but how could they have anything—professionally or personally—between them without trust and reinforcement?

He, of all people, should have supported her. Beyond the intimacy they'd shared, he understood her better than any of the other CORE agents. Her throat tightened with the strong urge to cry. Instead of telling Ian she was unqualified, he should have come to her first. Talked to her face to face. Told her Ian had wanted updated reports on her progress. Shown her how to move past the emotional side of investigating. In the four years they'd worked together, they'd made a great team. Team members should never forget their partnership or to support each other. Owen had forgotten that. He'd gone behind her back and what he'd written left her hollow.

"Well?" he asked and took a step forward.

She clutched the notepad to her chest. "At this point I'm wondering how much of an us there really was." The acknowledgement broke her heart.

He widened his eyes, then immediately narrowed them. When he reached for her, she took another step back. Dropping his hand, he shook his head. "I want there to be an us. I also want you to know that I've never said anything to Ian about how you dealt with finding Bill."

The betrayal thickened and her skin prickled with unease. "You've talked to Ian?" That was a news flash. She hadn't spoken to her boss once the entire week. Of course she'd reported in, but only via email and had assumed the same for Owen.

"Only a few times, but I told you I didn't bring up anything—"

"I don't care what you talked about. I care that you didn't bother to tell me." She smacked the notepad against her thigh. "I care that you didn't have the balls to say what you thought of me—as an investigator—to my face. But, I suppose that would've made for some pretty shitty pillow talk, huh?"

He'd wanted their relationship to become complex, now it had become beyond complicated and tainted with ugly betrayal. She loved him, but based on his actions, he made it clear he didn't feel the same or even remotely close. He might care, but not enough to be completely honest.

Insecurity squeezed her chest. Damn it...his opinion mattered. What he thought of her mattered. Not just as a woman, but as a fellow agent. She'd worked hard to prove her worth to CORE. Now she realized sex with Owen had been a huge mistake, and she questioned whether she could move past this.

His face reddened as he gripped her shoulders. "Our personal life has nothing to do with our professional one. If you haven't noticed, I've let you take the lead during this entire investigation."

She tried to shake his hands off, but he held her steady and drew her closer instead. His familiar scent, his nearness was a painful reminder of how close she'd been to finally fulfilling her fantasies. "You *let* me take the lead? What a joke." God, she felt like a fool. "And while you were *allowing* me to be the lead, did it ever occur to you to give me a few pointers? Did you ever stop and think that maybe giving me a little advice might have helped?"

"I...up until we found Bill, you were doing fine."

"And then?" she asked, even though a part of her didn't want to know. Insecure and unsure of herself, she wasn't sure her ego could handle another blow.

He gave her a slight shake. "When I found you in your room on the floor crying...I knew in my gut that you weren't cut out for this. Rachel, honey, I've been doing this for a long time. And I remember each and every victim I've seen. I don't want that for you. I don't want you struggling to find ways to erase the memories."

She shoved his chest and finally freed herself of his grasp. "Is that why you had sex with me? To help erase my memories?"

"Don't," he warned, his tone low, foreboding. "Don't you dare throw that bullshit in my face." He took a step back. "That was a shitty thing to say."

"Going behind my back was even shittier." She reached for the doorknob, then paused at the threshold. The tears that had been threatening to fall blurred her vision. "Jake's expecting us. I'll meet you in the dining room in thirty minutes."

"Rachel."

She paused, but not wanting him to see the tears streaking down her cheeks, she kept her back to him.

"I'm sorry," he said, his voice low, raspy. "For whatever it's worth, I care about you."

Her heart squeezed, while her throat tightened. She'd already shown him too much emotion this week and refused to let him see how close she was to breaking. Without a backward glance, she closed the door behind her, then rushed to her room. The moment she locked the door, she slid to the floor and let the tears fall. When she rested her head against the door, she drew in a deep breath and swiped at her face.

Screw him and get it together.

Even if she wasn't cut out to work in the field, she'd finish this investigation. Scratch that. She'd *solve* it.

With new determination, she pushed off the floor and went to her laptop. Her head hurt and her heart ached, but she needed to do a quick check on the security company. The sooner they found Josh and stopped the killer, the sooner she could return home and back to business as usual. And she would make damn sure things would go back to the way they were before she'd stupidly made love to Owen. Besides, she'd just spent the past year being a bitch to him. She could manage to maintain her well-balanced bitchiness for more years to come.

As she sat on the bed and opened the laptop, his scent,

lingering on the sheets and pillows, assaulted her senses and took her back in time. To only a short while ago when they'd made love, slept together and had decided to give their relationship a shot. Fresh tears sprang into her eyes.

She didn't want to be a bitch to him. She wanted to love him. But how could she love a man who had betrayed her trust?

Breathing hard, Owen surveyed the damage to his room. The moment Rachel had closed the door he'd launched his suitcase. It now lay haphazardly on the opposite side of the room, on its side, the contents scattered across the floor and bed.

Why did she have to be so damned stubborn? Why couldn't she realize he was right and only had her best interests in mind?

He knocked a pair of jeans off the bed. How could she even think he'd had sex with her as a way to help her deal with Bill's murder?

"Bullshit," he muttered and dropped onto the mattress.

He hadn't lied when he told her he cared about her. But he hadn't told her the whole truth. He was crazy about her. Lust might have had him interested in her soft curves and sassy mouth, but lust didn't fill his chest with a longing for something more. Like the opportunity, or the hope of sharing a life together.

Yeah, he was in that deep. Running a hand through his hair, he realized he had to act fast to make things right between them. He didn't want them heading back to Chicago with their argument weighing on their shoulders. Conjuring up worse case scenarios, he could easily picture Rachel going back to her sarcastic self. Back to calling him a douche bag and treating him as if...damn, as if they'd never made love.

Made love.

He shook his head and reached for some of the clothes on the bed. Sex. They'd had sex. Love had never entered the equation. He righted the suitcase. Then why in the hell did it feel like someone had just ripped his fucking heart out of his chest? Why couldn't he shake the tension from his shoulders or stop his gut from clenching every time he pictured the shock and hurt widening her green eyes?

He'd done what Ian had asked. Gave his boss updates and an honest assessment. While he stood by his evaluation, deep down, he'd wanted her to prove him wrong. He'd wanted her to step up her game and prove she could be a candidate for assignments away from the desk. But at the same time, he'd selfishly wanted to keep her locked in CORE's evidence and evaluation room where she would be safe and far away from atrocities she could witness. Make that, atrocities she *would* witness. Since he'd been with CORE he'd seen things that still made his skin crawl and his stomach nauseous. Crying over it didn't make those images go away. He'd learned a long time ago to mask his emotions, push past the vile things he'd seen and keep the end goal in mind—putting a criminal or killer behind bars.

Did it ever occur to you to give me a few pointers? Did you ever stop and think that maybe giving me a little advice might have helped?

He ran a hand through his hair, then hung his head. He'd been so concerned about making sure she took the lead and ran the investigation, despite Ian's orders, he hadn't wanted to interfere. Shit. He'd been so frickin' concerned about finding a way to crack her defenses, convince her that they deserved a shot at a relationship, it never occurred to him that he should talk about ways of handling emotions during an intense investigation.

"Fuck…she's right," he mumbled and tossed the clothes at the suitcase. He'd totally betrayed her trust and confidence. How could he have been so asinine? How could he not realize that going behind her back would eventually jeopardize their professional and personal relationship? Hell, if any of the other guys at CORE had gone behind his back and bitched about how he'd handled himself during an investigation, he'd seriously consider kicking their asses. There was a code among the members of CORE and he'd just broken it.

Now he didn't know how to make this right. He cared about her, more deeply than he'd realized. She made him want more out of life. She made him think about the future, and not just his future with CORE.

At thirty-seven, he'd considered himself a confirmed bachelor. Constantly on the road, there had never been time for a committed relationship. But being with her, watching the way she interacted with Joy and Walter, how devoted and nurturing she was to her brother, he realized that behind her sarcasm and dark humor, she had a sweet side.

This past week with Rachel made him also realize he was missing out on life. He'd spent years making sure he kept his career on track. After the shit he'd dealt with in the Secret Service, he'd made it his goal to solve every case that came his way, to prove time and again that what had happened in Italy was the last mistake he'd ever make. Not paying close attention to his surroundings while in Rome, dismissing a seventeen-year-old brat as nothing but a nuisance had been a mistake. But he'd made a bigger one with Rachel.

He hadn't paid attention to what she'd needed and hadn't considered that his actions might result in a reaction that could cost him something he probably didn't deserve. Rachel.

To have her, hold her, make love to her, then lose it all because he'd been too stupid to understand what she needed? He couldn't let that happen. He didn't want to go back to using business as an excuse to talk to her in the morning, then again at night before he went to bed. He wanted to wake up and fall asleep next to her. While he'd been trying to crack her defenses, she'd disintegrated all of his. Now he needed to be honest with her. Hell, he needed to be honest with himself.

He'd fallen hard for Rachel and now he could lose her.

His stomach rolled with anxiety and his temple throbbed with self-loathing. He glanced at the clock. Time to meet Rachel downstairs.

After grabbing his coat, he slid into his boots. When he opened the door, he caught Rachel closing hers. The slight puffiness around her eyes made his stomach roll again. He'd made her cry, and hated himself for his stupidity. But he'd hate himself even more if he didn't right his wrongs and do everything possible to prove to her that they deserved a shot.

"Ready?" she asked and zipped her coat.

"Yes...no." He took several quick strides to reach her. "Rachel, I'm—"

She held up a hand. "Me, first."

Relief settled his stomach. Maybe she'd given their argument some thought and was still willing to give them a chance.

"GSI stands for Guaranteed Systems Incorporated."

Damn. Back to business.

"The reason Jake or the security guards at Wexman probably didn't know the name of the company is because it's kind of super secret. Remember the university's head of security telling us the equipment was delivered from an unknown recipient and that all they knew was it had been donated?"

"Yeah."

"GSI builds custom security systems for the government and fortune five hundred companies. I'm talking major, high tech, cutting edge stuff that could possibly give the term Big Brother a whole new meaning. They don't have a website, or list any of their products or security solutions."

"How'd you find all this out then?" he asked then wished he could instantly retract such a ridiculous question. Rachel loved hacking into places considered off limits.

After confirming his stupidity with a "you're a dumbass" look, she pulled a notepad from her pocket. "Ever hear of Guarinot?"

"Yeah, it's a security company. My neighbor uses them."

"Guarinot is more than a residential security company. They're not only a government contractor, but they have a bunch of employees who have top-secret security clearance. You and I both know that kind of clearance is—"

"Yeah, that's big time."

"Well, GSI is linked to them. I literally found one small mention in a government document dating back thirty years and only recently made public. Linked that to Guarinot, then did a little snooping."

"Are you thinking this company and the killer are somehow linked?"

"Not sure about that. But what I did find is a GSI employee, with top secret security clearance, who is linked to Josh Conway."

"Who?" he asked, growing impatient. Rachel was known for her melodramatic build-ups. While he normally liked when she kept him hanging onto her every word as she dished the details, he wanted answers. Now. He wanted to find the missing kid, stop the killer, then use his energy to make things right with Rachel.

"Robert Conway. Josh's dad, who's also the senior engineer for GSI and, get this…a graduate from Wexman University."

"Josh's dad graduated from Wexman? When?"

"Twenty-two years ago."

"Which means he was here when the no hazing policy went into effect and might have some answers for us."

Her eyes brightened. "Yeah, like how is it that the security equipment he donated to the university happened to malfunction the day before his son was kidnapped?"

CHAPTER 19

DETECTIVE NICK MERRETTI looked up from the report he'd been working on and absently glanced at the small calendar sitting in the corner of his desk. He stared at the X's he crossed out daily and realized he hadn't put an X through today's date. After doing so, he leaned back in the squeaky office chair.

Five months and nineteen days until retirement.

He couldn't wait. No more tedious reports. No more victims. No more murderers. Just him and Gracie. He and his wife had big plans. Sell the bungalow, buy a condo in Fort Myers, Florida, and enjoy carefree days with nothing on the agenda but the beach and golf.

He glanced at his partner, Leon, who sat across from him, their desks pushed together. While his partner was on the phone, Nick opened his desk drawer and pulled out the brochure of the golf community where they planned to retire. The condos were nice, homey and nothing ritzy. With three bedrooms, his kids and grandchildren would be able to visit without having to stay at a hotel. Maybe he'd teach his grandson, Cody, how to golf. The boy—

Leon leaned across his desk and gave Nick's a smack. "Sure, I'll get Detective Merretti for you. Hold on one second." He pulled the phone away from his ear and covered the receiver. "Remember the John Doe we found at Parkside

Motel? You know the one who had his junk cut—"

"What about him?" Nick asked.

"I've got a deputy sheriff on the phone who says he might have a connection to our John Doe." He shook his head. "Nick, he thinks his wife has been living in Marietta, Ohio for the past eighteen months."

Nick shoved the brochure back in the drawer. The gruesome brutality of that particular case had haunted him. He and Leon had worked every angle without any results. Other than the man's DNA, which wasn't in the national DNA database, they had no way to ID the victim. The ME had been able to give their John Doe a rough age guestimate of thirty-five to forty-five, but that did them no good. They'd scoured missing persons reports for months, but without a photo ID and no idea where the man originated, they'd eventually had to call it quits. John Doe had become a cold case.

Until now.

"Patch him through to my phone," Nick told Leon and picked up a pen. When the phone rang, he quickly answered. "Detective Merretti."

"Morning, Detective, this is Deputy Sheriff Dave Keppler with the Washington County Sheriff's Office."

"Morning. My partner says you have some info pertaining to a John Doe case."

"I've got better than that," Keppler said. "I've got his wife."

Nick refused to let his excitement surface. They'd had leads in the past that had ended up being nothing but a wasted effort. "His wife? How can you be sure? And why is she coming forward eighteen months after her husband was murdered?"

"It's a long story. Can you come here and meet her?"

Nick covered the receiver. "Leon, see how long of a drive it is to Marietta, Ohio," he said, then returned to the call. "Why can't the wife come to Detroit? Is she incarcerated?"

"More than you could imagine," the deputy said, his tone filled with both sympathy and disgust. "Eighteen months ago, I answered a call from a farmer claiming he found a dead body in his field. When I arrived, I realized the woman wasn't dead, but she was pretty close. Someone stabbed her—at the minimum—twenty-one times, then bludgeoned her with a tire iron. She spent six months in a coma. When she woke, she couldn't speak or move."

Leon rapped his knuckles on the desk then held his hand up and mouthed, "Five hours."

"And now?" Nick asked and glanced at his watch. They could be in Marietta by one.

"She's a quadriplegic, but her speech therapist is using this gadget that's allowing her to speak."

"What's the woman's name?"

"Vivian Saunders. The husband's is Arthur Saunders."

He jotted down the names, then handed them to Leon.

"Does she know who attacked her and killed her husband?"

"Yes, Detective. Her daughter."

The fifteen minute drive to Jake's office had been hell. When Owen had wanted to apologize and right his wrong, Rachel refused to speak with him about anything but the investigation. In between the few comments she made, she'd gnawed on her damned pencil, something she hadn't done for days.

Now they sat, side by side, in Jake's stuffy, cramped office, waiting for Robert Conway, the missing kid's dad, and his wife to show. Marty O'Reilly, the inspector from the Michigan State Police Field Service Bureau, stood behind Jake's desk, where the sheriff remained seated. The inspector kept his arms folded across his chest as Rachel told Marty and Jake what she'd learned about Robert Conway and Guarinot Security.

"That's some decent info," Marty said when she finished, his tone complimentary and yet smug. "Is that all you've got?"

Rachel frowned. "Well, for now. And I think it's more than decent. The malfunctioning equipment is key. The fact that the missing boy's father was probably the one who donated it…I don't think that's something we should overlook."

"Could just be a coincidence," Marty countered. "Could be one has nothing to do with the other."

Owen had enough of this guy. For Marty to dismiss the evidence as coincidence had him wondering not only how up to speed the inspector was, but if he was ready to take over the investigation.

Jake's phone rang. He quickly answered, then said, "I'll be right there." He rose and wound his way through the tight office. "Robert Conway is here." He looked to Marty. "I'm grateful for your assistance, but unless he directs his questions to you, I want Owen and Rachel to take the lead with Conway. They've been here all week and Rachel knows his son. Agreed?"

Marty's face reddened, but also softened with relief. "Whatever," he said, and turned his back on them as if more interested in the county map hanging on the wall than them.

The uncomfortable silence in the office thankfully lasted for only a few minutes. Between Marty, who pouted like an angry kid, and Rachel, who refused to even look at him, claustrophobia might have squeezed him out of the room.

Jake introduced them to Robert Conway, a tall, well-dressed guy who looked to be in his forties and obviously took his gym membership seriously. After introductions were made, Conway ran a hand over his close-cropped, blonde hair.

"I just flew halfway around the world to get here." He fisted his hands, then dropped into the metal folding chair Jake had set up for him. "I had to walk away from a top secret job because you people can't do your fucking job. I want to know everything," he demanded, and directed an angry glare at Marty. "And I mean now."

The state police inspector pushed off the wall, and twisted his mouth into a mocking smile. "The sheriff and the private investigators he's hired have been handling the investigation. I just got here yesterday."

"Yesterday?" Conway shifted his anger toward Jake. "You waited until yesterday to call in the professionals? Sheriff, I'll have your badge for this. Understand? If something happens to my son, I'll make sure you won't even be able to work as a fucking meter maid. I'll—"

"Mr. Conway," Rachel interrupted. "I can assure you that we've been doing everything possible to find your son."

He slammed a fist on the desk. "Bullshit."

"If you continue with your threats and profanity, I'll escort you from my office," Jake said in a calm voice the belied the tension rolling off his shoulders. "This is a courtesy, nothing more. Trust me. We want your boy found just as much as you do."

"A courtesy?" Conway looked to Marty. "Do you have any idea who I know? I'm well acquainted with some of the most powerful—"

"Doesn't matter," Marty said. "The sheriff's right. The information we have pertaining to an ongoing investigation isn't public record."

"That being said," Rachel added. "We would like to share with you some of the details. We're also hoping you can answer a few questions for us."

Conway looked away for a moment. "Fine. Whatever." He waved his hand.

"Will your wife being joining us?" Rachel asked.

"No. She's at the hotel...thirty miles from here, by the way. I don't know what the hell is going on in this town, but I couldn't find a room. Which was a total pain in my ass." He crossed his ankles. "She's suffering from a migraine. This whole thing with Josh has her...she's not taking this well."

"Did you meet your wife while you were attending Wexman University?" Rachel asked.

"No. I met her a few years after I graduated."

"From Wexman, right?"

Conway released an exasperated sigh. "Yes. What does this have to do with anything?"

Rachel held up a finger. "When you were at Wexman, do you remember anything about the university initiating a no hazing policy?"

"Yeah." He looked to the ceiling and squinted. "I was a

junior, I think."

"Do you know what happened to cause this policy to go into effect?"

"How the hell should I know?" Conway leaned forward. "Mind telling me where this is going? Because I got a missing kid out there." He pointed to the door. "And if I don't get some answers, I'm calling the FBI. I don't need a bunch of backwater cops and a couple of private investigators, who don't know their heads from their asses, wasting my time." Focusing on him and Rachel, he sent them a look of disgust. "Don't you people have some cheating housewives to spy on?"

Keeping his temper in check, Owen forced a chuckle. "Mr. Conway, I can assure you that Rachel and I are quite competent to handle this investigation. But your cooperation is necessary. The insults…aren't."

"Fine. Waste my time." He folded his arms across his chest. "No. I don't remember anything about the no hazing policy. Anything else?"

Rachel sent him a smile. "Thank you. Now about the security equipment you donated to the university."

"What about it?"

"Why did you donate the equipment?" Rachel asked.

"I make sure things are secure for a living. Since my son was attending Wexman, I wanted to make sure there were extra security measures. The system I donated wasn't top of the line, but the model was only a few years old and used to be one of our best sellers. I got it for next to nothing and told the university president if it wasn't installed, they'd never see another dime from me. Trust me. President Lambert doesn't want that to happen. I've been very generous."

"Why is that?" Owen asked.

"Wexman's engineering program is excellent. Over the years, I've personally hired over a dozen graduates." He glanced around the room. "I'm trying to be patient with you people. Now I demand you tell me what this has to do with my son."

"Mr. Conway," Jake began, "your system malfunctioned the

night before Josh was kidnapped."

Conway looked around the room, then shook his head in disbelief. "Impossible. That system has an impenetrable firewall. The only way it could be disabled is if..." He moved to the edge of the metal chair and poised himself as if ready to run. "I need to speak to President Lambert. Now."

"Why is that?" Owen asked.

"Because he has the codes to disable the system."

Owen looked to Rachel, who met his gaze with a raised eyebrow. "And he's the only one with this code?" he asked, when he refocused on Conway. "Wouldn't the head of security have this code, too?"

Conway nodded. "Of course he would. But in order to keep it secure, I instructed Lambert to make sure that code wasn't public." His face growing red and mottled, he cracked his knuckles. "The reason I donated the system was to keep my son safe. I need to head to the university and find out what dumbass messed up my system. I also want the name of the guard on duty that night." He shook his head. "How in the hell could someone take a kid from a dorm room without being seen?"

"He wasn't taken from his room," Rachel answered. "He went missing after he left the residence hall."

Relief crossed Conway's face. "So Josh isn't missing because of me...thank God." He blew out a deep breath. "Anything else? Because while you people attempt to do your job, I'm going to the university to get my own answers."

"There's nothing more," Owen said and looked to Rachel, then Jake. Prior to meeting with Conway, they'd agreed not to show Conway the copy of the photo of Josh. Even Marty had been onboard. After meeting Conway, Owen couldn't be happier with that decision. The man would likely raise holy hell if he saw the picture, and they needed him to keep his cool and not interfere with the investigation. "As for President Lambert, he—"

"Have you ever heard of Wexman Hell Week?" Marty asked.

Shit. They'd also agreed not to discuss anything about the other missing kids. Adding to the father's worry when they didn't have solid evidence that there was a serial killer, even if they believed it to be true, hadn't been part of the plan.

"What? Are we back to the hazing crap again?" Conway stood. "This is bullshit. After I meet with Lambert, I'll be making a few calls. The four of you will be lucky to have jobs by the morning."

Marty took a step forward and pressed his knuckles against the desk. "Back to the hazing crap." He kept his attention on Conway. "Wexman Hell Week has—allegedly—been going on for the past twenty years."

"What are you talking about?" Conway asked. "It's been going on longer than that. Universities across the country have no hazing policies, but it doesn't mean fraternities aren't still doing a Hell Week. They just toned it down so pansy-ass kids don't get hurt and call their mommies."

Rachel cleared her throat. "Mr. Conway, for the past twenty years, nine boys pledging with different Wexman fraternities have gone missing. Actually, Josh makes number ten. And each abduction takes place during Hell Week."

Conway glared at the sheriff. "You knew about this? You knew and did nothing to stop it? You're done, Sheriff."

"The sheriff has nothing to do with this," Owen said. "The university refused to get rid of the fraternal organization because the alumni wouldn't hear of it."

"If anything happens to my son, I'll do more than shut down the fraternities. I'll bulldoze the place until it's nothing but a pile of rubble." Conway stood and moved to the door. "I'm done with this. The president and I need to have a long...talk."

"Lambert is in Wyoming," Rachel said. "He left a few days before Josh went missing. You'll have to speak with Xavier Preston, the dean who's acting on his behalf. I'd be happy to give you his phone number. Actually, Owen and I were planning to head to the university now. If you want to follow us, we can take you to his office."

"No." Conway held up a shaky hand, then ran it down his face. "No. I...I'd rather talk to Lambert." With a deep frown, he looked to the floor. "I need to check on my wife. Call me if you have anything."

After Conway left the room, Marty grabbed his coat. "Sheriff, got a private place I can use to make some calls?"

"I thought we agreed not to bring up Wexman Hell Week," Rachel said before Jake could respond.

"No. You three agreed. The only thing I agreed on was not showing Conway a picture of his abused son hanging from a wall. Besides, I find it hard to believe a guy with top secret access wouldn't know the school he sent his son to had an alleged serial killer stalking it."

"I can," Jake said. "The last sheriff never asked for any help and most of the locals and students acted like it was a legend, not a reality. Even your office blew me off after the hoax six years ago."

"I also doubt the university mentions a possible serial killer in their recruiting letters." Rachel tucked the pencil she'd been holding behind her ear. "Are those calls you plan to make going to be to your lab?"

"They are. While I'm taking care of that, I want you two—"

"We're good." Owen stood. "Like Rachel said, we're heading to the university."

Rachel also stood. "When we cross referenced our list of faculty and staff, we didn't consider visiting professors. Human resources is supposed to supply us with that list."

"Sounds like a long shot," Marty said. "I'll have Jake call you if I get any lab results."

When Marty left the room, Jake also rose. "I have a feeling Robert Conway is going to make some trouble. Don't be surprised if Marty throws all of us under the bus."

"After how the state police disregarded your last victim, I don't think Marty and his division will get off clean if that happens." Owen followed Rachel to the door. "We're doing everything we can. Conway's angry, and rightfully so."

"It's Friday," Rachel reminded them. "We're running short

on time. If we don't get a break, Conway's going to be more than angry. He's going to be grieving over his dead son."

"Good morning, Puke," he said to the pledge as he stepped off the ladder's final rung. "Today's the big day. Are you as excited as I am?"

He turned on the lantern, then swung it in the puke's direction. The boy winced and turned his head away. In the process, the pledge revealed the horrible purple bruises and raw abrasions coating his neck.

A small sliver of guilt pierced his chest. He'd gone a little too far yesterday. He'd strangled the puke with the twine until the boy had almost reached the edge of no return. More times than necessary, he'd choked him, then allowed him to live...only to die today.

"Those look painful. Nothing to worry about, though. By the end of the day, you won't feel a thing." He moved to the boy and pulled a piece of cold, burnt toast from his pocket. "Open wide and eat your breakfast. Because today is such a special day, I've decided to make something extraordinary for your dinner," he said as the boy slowly chewed. "Do you enjoy lamb?"

When the boy didn't answer, he pulled a water bottle from his pocket and offered him a drink. "Do you know that in Christian teachings "Lamb of God" refers to Jesus Christ because he sacrificed himself to God in order take away the sins of the world? There are some that argue that the significance of "lamb" is derived from the notion of a scapegoat." He gave the boy more water. "Someone who takes the blame for another person's actions."

He stepped away, then went to the corner of the room. After finding a rag, he doused it with the remaining contents of the water bottle. "You, my dear Puke, are my lamb. You are the sacrifice that will take away the sins of your father."

"It sounds like I'm the scapegoat," the boy said, his voice

low and raspy likely due to yesterday's game of choke the pledge.

As he wiped the boy's face and cleaned off the dried blood around his cracked lips, he smiled. "In a way I suppose you are. I didn't plan on discussing theology, but here's another way you can look at this situation. Do you remember what you told me about Hell Week?"

The pledge slowly nodded, then hung his head. "The guys from the fraternity said whoever was taken was a Hell Week sacrifice."

"Yes," he said, thrilled to share this new insight with the boy who would save him from twenty-five years of nightmares. "When you told me this, I considered that perhaps all of my pledges were somewhat of a sacrifice, but I realized I was wrong." He tilted the puke's chin until they were eye to eye. "God commanded Abraham to sacrifice his son, Isaac. Before Abraham killed his son, the angel of God stopped him, and told Abraham, 'Now I know you fear God.'" He cupped the boy's face. "You are my Isaac, my true sacrifice. The role of Abraham belongs to the devil who not only spawned you, but...tormented me." He held the boy's face tighter. "I'm playing God now. No, I won't have your father killing his own son, but his actions, the choices he made twenty-five years ago, are what put Hell Week in motion."

He rested his forehead against the puke's. "Unfortunately there will be no angel of God coming to your aid. I'm truly sorry for that." He quickly drew back and held the boy's shoulders. "But your father will know fear. He will comprehend at the most heinous level that for every action there is always a reaction."

"You're going to...kill me because of what my father did to you?" the boy asked, his eyes filling with hatred and tears.

"He's given me no choice."

"Sir," the puke whispered, then cleared his throat. "There's always a choice. You don't have to kill me for whatever he did. If it was that bad, go to the police."

He loved the boy's determination, and while he should have

gone to the police years ago, that choice had been taken from him. His selfish mother had not allowed her child justice. "You would want to see your father imprisoned?"

The puke looked away. "No."

"But you don't want to die for his sins."

"No," the boy repeated, louder, stronger.

"Well, you will. You see, your father cannot be tried for his sins. Michigan law has a statute of limitations for rape."

Shock rounded the puke's watery eyes. "R...rape?"

"Yes, Puke. Rape." As he went back to the corner of the room and tossed the towel on the bench, the memories of that night haunted him, drilled a black hole into the depths of his soul. "Everything I've done to you this week, your father did to me twenty-five years ago." He turned and faced the pledge. "He made me trust him. He made me think that if I suffered through his horrifying, painful, juvenile games, that I would be allowed into his circle." He shook his head in disgust. "I wanted to desperately be his brother, to feel welcomed, to know that I had a group of men I could always count on when needed. Then he betrayed my trust."

"Is that why you kept asking me if I trusted you? Because you wanted to betray me?"

"Yes," he hissed, proud of his intelligent puke. "That's exactly right."

"This...rape...who did my father do it to?"

He stood in front of the boy again. "I think you know the answer."

Tears streaked down the pledge's face as he nodded. "I'm so sorry."

Grief for what he would later do to the boy filled his heart and tightened his stomach with regret. He touched the boy's cheek. "I'm sorry, too. Tonight will not give me pleasure." Holding the back of the boy's head, careful of his wounded neck, he kept the grief and regret at bay. "Joshua," he whispered. "The savior, the deliverer...the meaning of your name is so fitting. Because I know in my heart your death will save me and at the same time, deliver your father into the bowels of hell."

He quickly turned away, shut off the lantern and gripped the ladder. "Because we've become so close, I won't lie to you. Tonight will not be quick, nor will it be painless. But it will be necessary."

"Sir," the boy called.

He stopped on the second rung, and looked over his shoulder. "Yes, Puke."

"Will Junior be here tonight?"

"Yes."

"Will you kill her, too?"

He chuckled. "Yes, Puke. I just haven't decided whether to kill her before or after I kill you." He continued up the ladder.

"Sir," the pledge called again.

He stopped. "Yes, Puke?"

"Please kill her first."

CHAPTER 20

RACHEL SHRUGGED OUT of her coat, then draped it on the bed. After Owen had parked the car, she'd quickly climbed out and headed inside Joy's. Too many times today he'd brought up this morning's argument and had tried to apologize. The betrayal too fresh, the wounds too raw, she wasn't ready to dissect their relationship—if there was even a chance of one—or accept his apology. She needed distance.

A sharp rap at the door made her stomach twist. *Damn it.* Why couldn't Owen give her space?

"Shorty, you in there?" Joy called and knocked again.

Relieved Owen wasn't on the other side of the door, she turned the knob. "Hey, Joy. How are you?"

"About ready to sneeze my frickin' face off. Did you see all the flowers downstairs?"

When Rachel had entered the house, a flowery aroma had assaulted her nose. Once in the dining room, she'd discovered the source. A dozen plus bouquets, baskets of flowers and plants littered the dining room and spilled into the great room. "Yes, they're beautiful."

Joy wiped her red nose. "At a distance. My allergies are killing me. Got anything I can take? Walt's heading into town for that frickin' festival, but won't be back for hours."

Sean also had bad allergies. Rachel had made it a habit to keep her purse stocked with allergy medicine should he need it.

"You're in luck." She rummaged through her purse. "One of these should help." She handed her the bottle of pills.

"I owe you, Shorty." She popped a pill and dry swallowed. "How'd it go today?"

"Not well." Defeatism wasn't normally her nature, but with one dead end after another, and her fight with Owen, she couldn't help allowing pessimism to creep to the surface and take hold of her. "The visiting professor route was a no go. Josh's dad was a jerk and no help at all. The inspector from the state police hasn't heard back from the lab yet..." She sighed and dropped onto the edge of the bed. "On the bright side, we stopped and saw Sean. He's doing great. Dr. Gregory is releasing him tomorrow morning. Do you mind if he stays here?"

"Of course not. We've got plenty of room." Joy swiped at her watery, bloodshot eyes. "Is he going to go back to school?"

"I'm not sure what he wants to do yet. He's really broken up about Josh...so am I for that matter." She crossed her legs and hugged herself. "I'm really worried, Joy. If we don't find Josh...until him, Sean's never had many close friends. I don't know how he's going to cope with this."

"Sometimes life's a bitch, which is why I tend to be one." She half-smiled. "We've all got a lot to cope with right now. You bring your baby brother to The House of Joy and we'll cope together."

Rachel swallowed around the lump in her throat. For all her gruffness, Joy was a kind woman. "Thank you."

"You know how you can thank me? Help me sort through those frickin' bouquets. I want to write down the names of everyone who sent flowers, but don't want to get near them."

"Sure." Even though she wanted to open her laptop and do more research, she could use a break. A tedious task was just what she needed to take her mind off her brother, Owen and the investigation. "I'll be down in a few minutes."

Seconds after Joy left, there was another knock at the door. She looked to the bed and scooped up the pills Joy had left behind, then went to the door. "I could have brought them down," she said as she turned the knob.

Owen filled the doorway.

"Oh, it's you."

"I saw Joy leave your room. She looked like she was crying."

"Allergies," she said and held up the pills. "What's up?"

"I'm going to head over to the festival with Walter. Do you want to come?"

Memories of their time there yesterday flooded her mind. Before the longing for what could have been took root, she shoved those memories aside. "No. After I help Joy with the flowers I want to recheck what we'd cross-referenced and look at what we have again. I keep feeling like we're missing something."

"I can stay and help."

"No," she said louder than she'd intended. "I'm...I'd rather do it alone."

He shoved his hands in his back pockets and looked to the floor. "Want me to bring you back anything? Yesterday, I saw you eyeing up the stand selling funnel cakes."

"Nope. I'm good," she said even though she *had* eyed up those funnel cakes last night. But she didn't want anything from him. Not after what he'd done to her, and potentially to her career with CORE. She also didn't want him to be sweet or sexy, but unfortunately, he was both. While her feelings for him hadn't changed and she still loved him, he'd not only crossed the line with his email to Ian, he'd broken the trust between them.

Finished with their conversation and needing to distance herself from him, she started to close the door.

He stopped her, then with lightning speed, gripped her shoulders. "I can't apologize enough for sending Ian that email. Hell, you won't even *let* me apologize."

"Apology accepted. You can go now."

Giving her a light shake, he drew her closer. "Stop. Please, just stop with the bullshit and listen to me. Let me make it right. I'll call Ian and tell him—"

"Don't. I don't need or want you calling Ian." She fought to ignore his nearness, his familiar scent. His words and touch both distressed and calmed her. If she let him contact Ian, he could smooth things over by explaining away his original report. But even if she did let him, it didn't change the fact he'd gone behind her back, or that he didn't think she was cut out to work in the field. "Once we're back in Chicago, I'm going to need time to decide what I'm going to do."

He tightened his grip. "You're not leaving CORE because of me."

She shrugged him off her shoulders. "Get over yourself. There's no way in hell I'm quitting my job." She crossed her arms over her chest. "What I meant is that I need to decide what's the best direction for me and Sean. I doubt he'll want to stay at Wexman, and if that's his choice we'll need to look at new schools. As for me…I need to reevaluate my career goals."

"And us?"

Although hurt and angry, she couldn't erase her feelings for him in a matter of a few hours. But she knew that with time, the love she felt for him would fade to nothing. For now, she'd have to maintain her distance and remain professional. Stay focused on the investigation and her brother's well-being. "I told you there can't be an us."

"You ready, Owen?" Walter called from downstairs.

Owen looked over his shoulder toward the staircase, then back to her. The regret and anguish in his eyes made her knees weak and her stomach knot with despair. She'd wanted him to hurt as badly as she did, but because she still loved him, she hated seeing him miserable.

"I can't apologize enough for my actions." He rubbed the back of his neck, and tightened his jaw. "I know what I did doesn't show it." He dropped his hand to his side and took a step closer. After placing a soft kiss to her cheek, he rested his forehead against hers. "I'm crazy about you, Rachel," he whispered, his voice raw, husky, then he quickly drew back and moved toward the staircase.

As she watched him go, a part of her wanted to run after him and tell him she loved him, and that they'd work through this. But how could they?

I'm crazy about you, Rachel.

She went back into her room, sat on the edge of the bed and fought the urge to cry and throw herself one hell of a pity party. The man she was in love with was crazy about her, yet she could no longer trust in him.

Rather than give in to a crying jag, she decided a distraction was definitely in order. She headed downstairs. When she reached the bottom step, she looked to her left and saw Owen at the open front door. He glanced over his shoulder and snared her gaze. The determined look in his eyes told her he wasn't finished. But he'd have to learn to deal with his mistakes, because she *was* finished. There would be no more hot, love making sessions. There would be no more playful, sexy exchanges. There would only be business and professionalism.

After he closed the door, she hugged herself.

"Cold?" Joy asked from behind her.

"No. I'm fine." She nodded to the flowers in the dining room. "Ready?"

Joy held up a pen and piece of paper. "Yep. The funeral director is sending his son by later to pick up all the bouquets. Thank God."

She picked up a gorgeous arrangement. "Why aren't they being sent to Hal's?"

"They *are*. Only my brother won't accept them and tells the delivery guy to haul ass to my house." Joy took a seat at the dining room table. "These flowers are nothing but a terrible reminder that his son's dead. I know it, because each time I walk past them, I think of Bill."

"What's Hal going to do after the funeral?"

"Meaning?"

"Just a few minutes ago you brought up coping. How's Hal going to cope with the loss of his son?"

"He's not going to hurt himself, if that's what you're asking.

Hell, when he came back from Vietnam, I was worried sick. He'd changed, you know? But he told me he didn't dodge bullets for two tours to come home and put one in his head. He's a strong man. Like with his wife, he'll never get over losing Bill, but he'll cope." Joy leaned back in the chair. "Besides, he has Bill's dog to take care of now."

When she pictured the sad Golden Retriever, a lump formed in her throat. To shake the image, she dug through a bouquet and found the card. After she told Joy the name of the sender, Joy had her move the bouquet to the foyer. When the funeral director's son arrived, Joy wanted the flowers and baskets immediately out of her house.

They continued in silence until Joy finally said, "Walt and Hal are best friends. Bill was like a son to him. Since Bill's…death, he's been quiet. He's been worried about me and my brother, but I know this is killing him just the same. He's also back smoking like a frickin' chimney." Joy shook her head. "The man doesn't think I know it. He's always trying to cover it up with cologne, but I got a nose for things."

"So, it bothers you that he smokes, yet you chew tobacco."

"Cigarettes are disgusting."

"And spitting in a cup isn't?" Rachel read off another card, then after putting the basket in the foyer, she dropped into a dining room chair. "Can I ask you something…personal?"

Joy lifted a shoulder. "Only if I'm allowed to do the same."

"Fair enough. Does everyone know you and Walter are a couple?"

"We're married, so yeah."

Rachel looked to Joy's hand where a ring *should* have been, and half-laughed. She hadn't seen that one coming. "How long have you been together?"

Joy folded her hands together and rested them on the piece of paper. "Walt moved to Bola about sixteen years ago. At the time, I'd been widowed for eight years. My last husband…he wasn't a good man. He liked to beat the shit out of me." She narrowed her eyes and set her mouth in a grim line. "The only good he ever did me was dying and leaving me financially secure. Anyway, back when Walter came to Bola, I was accepting boarders, and had one room available. When he moved in, it was supposed to be temporary."

"Was he here for work?"

She nodded. "He had a nice accounting job at the mill...just retired last year. But that's not the only reason he moved to Bola. See, Walter always had a thing for Bigfoot, and this area is known for sightings. When he was a kid, he and his dad went camping for the weekend in the woods outside of Munising, that's in the Upper Peninsula of Michigan. Anyway, he claims that late one night they heard what sounded like a bear lumbering through the woods. His dad told him they needed to abandon the tent. When they got inside the truck and his dad flipped on the headlights...there was Bigfoot staring right back at them." She grinned. "When I first met him, I was convinced he was nothing but a crazy son of a bitch."

"But?"

"Half of Bola claims they've seen Bigfoot. Hell, even my daddy said he did. Same with Hal. So I was used to crazy." She released a wistful sigh. "Walter...he's a good man, Shorty. When people meet me, most times they don't know what to do with me. Not him. He gets me. Gets that I'm not good with all that expressing myself bullshit. You know what I'm saying?"

She glanced at the cork and dry erase boards hanging on the dining room wall. Owen had bought those items for her because he'd understood that she'd been missing her evidence and evaluation room and knew she'd had a hard time transitioning from the desk to the field. She thought about how he'd held her the night she'd broken down over Bill's murder, about how she'd told him her career concerns and how his words of assurance had bolstered her confidence. Owen might *get* her, but she didn't get why he'd betrayed her with the ugly email he'd sent to Ian.

"A few months after Walt moved in here and got to know the area, he found a beautiful place along the river and thought about buying it. I was so pissed off about him leaving." She rested her chin in her hand. "I was a bitch to him for days. So he finally says to me, 'Joy, does treating me like shit mean you love me?'" She chuckled. "The man threw me for a loop. And I said, 'Yeah, you damn fool. What are you going to do about it?' Well, he said he loved me too, but didn't want to live with a bunch of boarders. I was sick of having a houseful anyway, the house was paid for and I didn't need the money. Plus Walter had a good income. So after the last tenant moved out, we got married. Our fourteenth anniversary is next month. Valentine's day."

Holy cow, Joy was a romantic. *Who knew?*

"My turn," Joy said. "What's going on with you and Owen?"

Her face heated. Had they been obvious? "Nothing."

Joy laughed. "That's not what it sounded like the night before…or the night before that. Sorry, Shorty, I couldn't resist." Her smile waned as she picked up the pen. "You're being as bitchy to him as I was to Walt when I thought he was moving out. So again, what's going on?"

"I…it's complicated."

"Do you love him?"

Yes. She stood and retrieved another bouquet. "I told you, it's complicated."

"Nothing complicated about being in love. You either are or you aren't. Appears to me and Walt that you both *are.*"

Rachel read the name off the card. After leaving the flowers in the foyer, she picked up a vase filled with blood red roses and angel's breath. "Aren't these roses beautiful?"

"Don't change the subject. Now talk."

She released a sigh, then set the flowers aside. "It's one sided."

"With the way that man looks at you, I don't get that impression at all."

"I…it can't work between us."

"Because?"

"Owen and I work together, so that's a problem."

"So."

"So, it's an issue. How can I face him day after day when he..." She grabbed the vase and took it to the foyer. When she returned to the dining room, Joy was leaning back in her chair with her arms folded across her chest.

"What'd he do to you?" she asked, her tone quiet, yet indignant. "If he hurt you, I'll string him up by his—"

Rachel held up a hand. "No need to go there." She sat again. "This is my first assignment in the field. Normally I work in the office."

"Right. You like your evidence and evaluation room so much Owen turned my dining room into one for you."

"True. I do love my place at CORE, but for the past couple of years I've been begging my boss to give me a chance to work in the field. After hearing stories from the other agents, I felt like I was missing out on something. I wanted some action and adventure, you know what I mean?"

Joy lifted a shoulder. "I'm a homebody. But I understand what you're saying. So what's the problem? From where I'm sitting, you haven't caught a killer or found that boy, but you've been working your ass off trying."

Rachel stared at Joy, wishing she could blurt out everything. She'd never had a close friend she could confide in, and while she could use a sounding board and Joy's advice, she also didn't want to look like a fool. She'd had sex with Owen knowing it could affect their work relationship, and done it anyway. She'd thought with her body and heart, rather than her brain.

"Come on, Shorty. Spit it out. Unless you're too chicken."

"Fine." She gave into Joy's taunt. "Owen went behind my back and told our boss I wasn't *emotionally* cut out to work in the field. Happy?"

Joy dropped her gaze to the table. "No. That doesn't make me happy at all," she said softly. "How'd it happen?"

Rachel hesitated at first, but when Joy finally looked at her, and she'd caught the anger and empathy in the other woman's eyes, she spilled every detail. When she finished, she stood and grabbed a lovely basket fill with hearty greens. "So? Am I wrong to be mad at him?"

"Hell, no. But..."

Great. This was the point where Joy would tell her she'd blown everything out of proportion. Rather than hear what Joy had to say, she read the name off the card, then took the basket to the foyer. As she reached for another bouquet, Joy cleared her throat.

"If you don't sit your butt in the chair and hear me out, I'll strap you in and make you listen."

"Joy, I don't know if I want to hear what you have to say. My mind is made up. Owen threw me under the bus. He took a private moment and...just forget I even brought it up. Let's finish with these flowers. I have work to do."

"No doubt he fucked up," Joy said, her voice rising. "But turn it around."

"I would have never done that to him," she countered. "If I had any concerns, I would have talked to him first, not gone behind his back."

"Maybe so, but let's say you've got a new agent working for your company. Let's say you realize that this new guy isn't completely qualified to work in the field. You're concerned he could maybe put the company or another agent at risk. What do you do?"

With her stomach knotting and her head hurting, Rachel slumped into the chair. "I'd tell my boss," she admitted and rubbed her temple.

"Because?" Joy prompted.

"Because that new agent, depending on the assignment, could get himself or one of our seasoned agents killed." Shit. Owen *had* done the right thing, just in the wrong way.

"Exactly. Because you're not new to the company, and you have a close relationship, Owen should have come to you first. But I think, in the end, you know what he did was the right thing." She rested her chin on the back of her hand. "Besides, you did say you didn't think you were cut out for working in the field, right?"

"Yes, but when I was ready, I wanted to be the one to tell

my boss. I wanted it to be *my* decision."

"Well, you're still here and still working. Finish what you started, then go to your boss. Who knows, by the time you leave Bola, you could be kicking ass and taking names. Your boss might be begging you to take on assignments."

Rachel smiled. At one time, she'd believed she could kick ass and take names. But fantasy and reality didn't always mesh well. Still, Joy had a point. About her job and Owen.

She needed to go back upstairs and work. Hell, she needed to give herself a moment to digest this entire conversation. "Thanks for listening, and for the advice."

"What are you going to do about Owen?"

"I don't know." She picked up the final bouquet, an interesting, yet unattractive blend of rhododendron and lavender. "I need to think about it. Right now, I want to remain focused on finding Josh and stopping a killer."

"Shit, that thing is frickin' ugly." Joy nodded to the bouquet. "I have a gorgeous rhododendron bush in the backyard that I love, I even have lavender, but putting them together that way just doesn't do them justice."

"Agreed. But, it's the thought that counts."

Pen in hand, Joy prepared to write. "Who was so thoughtful?"

Rachel gently moved the flowers aside and plucked out a card. "Kaylie Gallagher."

"Bill's girl? What's the card say?"

"I'm terribly sorry for your loss. Bill was a special man."

Joy's eyes filled with tears. "Sounds like that girl really liked Bill."

Rather than tell Joy the truth, that Bill and Kaylie had had a platonic relationship, she kept quiet and took the flowers to the foyer. When she returned to the dining room, Joy was wiping her eyes with a tissue.

"I should have her over for dinner," Joy said. "Bill would want us to look out for her. You know, Saturday he called me. I just got home with the groceries and didn't have time to bullshit." She drew in a shaky breath. "He was so excited, too.

And what'd I do? Blew him off." Regret filled Joy's eyes. "I felt bad and tried calling him on Sunday, but he was sick...drugged. Now I wish I would have let him talk longer."

"You can't beat yourself up for that." Rachel mustered a grin despite her heavy heart. "What was he excited about anyway?"

"Kaylie. I guess she'd just gotten to the residence hall and told Bill they should go for lunch the next day." She smiled. "That boy had it bad. You met her, is she pretty?"

As she brought Kaylie's image to mind, her thoughts drifted to what the girl had told her and Owen. That the last time she'd seen or spoken to Bill was the Friday the locks had malfunctioned. "Dark hair, blue eyes...she's kind of plain, but attractive," she said. "Do you remember what time Bill called you Saturday?"

"Actually, I do. It was around five and I was pissed off that running errands put me behind. I was going to make a roast, but didn't have the time. We ended up eating leftovers."

"Did Bill say anything else about Kaylie? Was she there visiting a resident or just stopping by to see him?"

"Don't know. Like I told you, I cut him short." Joy frowned. "Why all the questions?"

"Just curious," she said, and moved toward the staircase.

"Shorty," Joy said, her tone cautionary.

"Seriously, Joy. It's nothing."

"If you say so." Joy eyes held the touch of suspicion as she rose from the table. "Since the boys are at the festival, I'm just doing sandwiches for dinner, unless that's what you had for lunch."

Anxious to head to her room, Rachel climbed a couple of steps. "We skipped lunch."

"Well then, I made coffee cake this morning. Want me to bring you up a slice?"

She raced up the steps. "Thanks, I'm good," she called.

"It's only one-thirty. And you should eat something," Joy shouted as Rachel reached her room.

Her stomach flipped, then somersaulted as she closed the

bedroom door and rushed to her laptop. She couldn't eat anything right now, not with apprehension and unease curling through her belly. Kaylie Gallagher had lied to them. And she'd been at Stanley Residence Hall the evening Bill and the boys had been drugged. Had she left before Bill took sick and Josh and Sean had gone to the study session? If so, her cause for suspicion would lessen. The security camera in the foyer had been moved after Bill passed out, and after the boys had left. Meaning, the killer or accomplice had remained in the building.

Although tempted to call Owen, she decided to wait until she was armed with more information, and called Adam Lynch, Wexman's head of security, instead. Before she jumped to any conclusions, she needed to find out if Kaylie had been filmed leaving the building before the camera had been moved. If not, the little liar had just become her number one suspect.

Hell, at this point, she'd be their only suspect.

Detective Nick Merretti shook Sheriff Deputy Dave Keppler's hand. "Thanks again for calling us," he said and introduced his partner, Leon.

"Are you kidding me? For the past eighteen months, Jane...I mean, Vivian, has been a mystery we've all wanted to see solved." He rapped on the hospital room door. "When I first saw her in that field...it's a miracle she's alive."

Before Nick could ask the sheriff deputy about Vivian Saunders's attempted murder, the door opened. A pretty, young brunette greeted them. "I'm Elizabeth Cormack, Vivian's speech therapist."

"Call her Bunny," a synthesized voice said from across the room.

He looked over the speech therapist's shoulder to where a woman sat in a wheelchair. With gray sprinkled throughout her dark hair, and jagged scars running along her cheeks and forehead, Vivian Saunders vaguely resembled the driver's license photo Leon had pulled up before they'd left Detroit. Leon had also pulled up her husband's driver's license. Due to the acid that had melted Arthur Saunders's flesh, he'd been completely unrecognizable and in no way looked like the thick haired, heavy set, forty-eight year old smiling man in the photo.

"She's right, you can call me Bunny," the speech therapist said with a smile. As she led them toward Vivian, her smile waned. "Vivian's been nervous about your visit."

Nick looked at the computer equipment in front of Vivian's wheelchair. "Why's that?"

"Yesterday was the first time she's been able to tell her story." Bunny stood behind the wheelchair, stroked Vivian's long hair, then rested her hands on the woman's shoulders. "It's not a pretty one."

Movement on the computer screen caught his attention, just as the synthesized voice said, "Bad."

"Did she just do that?" Leon asked, and moved toward the computer equipment.

"Yes." Bunny beamed. "I was able to get the equipment on loan. This is a state run facility and while the equipment is decent, this sip and puff technology isn't in its budget."

Leon frowned. "Sip and what?"

Bunny repeated herself, then she went on to explain how the equipment worked. "Vivian started on it yesterday and is a natural. By lunch, she was talking up a storm." She stepped away from Vivian, then pushed a chair next to the wheelchair. "Please, Detective Merretti, have a seat. I'll call the nurse and see if she can have more chairs brought—"

"I'm good," Leon said, while Dave nodded in agreement.

"Okay, then. Vivian, are you ready?"

The woman grunted and blinked once.

"Good. Detective, she's all yours."

Nick sat, and pulled a notepad and pen from his suit coat pocket. During the five hour drive from Detroit to Marietta, Ohio, he and Leon had discussed how they'd handle the interview. With the first real break since finding the John Doe in the motel room eighteen months ago, his heart raced with anticipation.

Time to finally get some answers.

"Vivian, my partner and I pulled up your driver's license. You're last known address is Sterling Heights, Michigan, correct?"

He looked to the screen, but was met with a grunt instead.

"Did you live with your husband and daughter?"

Another grunt.

"According to Dave, you claim your daughter killed your husband and attacked you. What is your daughter's name and were you present when your husband was murdered?"

Vivian captured the straw-like device with her tongue. As words developed on the screen, the synthesized voice droned from the computer speakers. "Daughter Holly. Not there. Holly told me."

"Can you explain what happened? I'm sure it's difficult to work the equipment, but I'm hoping you can give me specific details. If your daughter is responsible for your husband's death and your injuries, we need to find her."

"Holly home from Michigan U. Art not home. She took me dinner I woke up in field."

Nick read the screen to make sure he heard her correctly. "Okay, so Holly is a student at Michigan University. She was home from school. Your husband wasn't there, so she took you to dinner, correct?"

Vivian grunted and blinked.

"Were you drinking alcohol or do you think she drugged you?"

"Drugged. Drank coffee. Woke in field."

Nick looked to Dave. "The day you found Vivian…do you know if a tox screen was done?"

"I have her records," Bunny said, and picked up a tablet similar to the one his kids bought him for Christmas. Only Bunny knew how to use hers. "Yes. A tox screen was done." She puckered her brow. "They found Rohypnol."

"Okay." He focused on Vivian. "Your daughter drugged you, drove you from Michigan to Ohio, then what?"

A tear curved over the uneven scar on her cheek. "Confused. Scared. Weak. Drag by hair to field. Stab gut."

"Did she talk? How did you know your husband was killed?"

"Told me."

"Did she say why she killed him or how?" Without DNA evidence, there was no way to confirm Vivian's story. But, if she knew details kept from the press, they might be able to use her statement as circumstantial evidence.

The tears stopped as Vivian narrowed her eyes and worked the straw. "Acid head hand feet. Cut penis. Stab him. Took teeth. My fault."

"*My* fault?" he quietly repeated.

"It's probably the auto correct," Bunny said.

Vivian grunted and typed. "MY fault!!!!!"

Nick sat at the edge of the chair. "How was his murder your fault, Vivian?"

"Rape Holly."

Disgust coiled through his stomach. "Holly's father was molesting her?"

Another grunt. This time stronger, louder.

"And Holly got even," Leon said, then pushed off the wall he'd been leaning against. "You knew he was molesting your daughter and did nothing about it."

Nick glared at Leon. While he'd come to the same conclusion, he hadn't planned to attack Vivian. He didn't want her shutting down before he had all the answers he needed. "Did you know, Vivian?" he asked, and kept his tone light and empathetic.

More tears trailed down her face. "No. Should have. Been doing to her since twelve. She twenty-two in May."

Bunny touched the woman's arm. "I told you, it's not your fault. Tell the detectives the rest."

Vivian released a sigh, then captured the straw again. "Art like to take Holly to Parkside motel. She went ready to kill. Found out truth. Had enough."

"Found out the truth about what?" Nick asked.

"Art not real dad. Holly mine Art adopted her."

Nick sat back in the chair. "Okay, so Holly finds out the man she thought was her real dad, the man who had been molesting her for nearly eight years, is her adoptive father and snaps. Correct?"

Vivian grunted.

"She violently kills him, then lures you by taking you to dinner, drugs you, then drives you five hours from home, where she tries to kill you, too."

Another grunt.

"Dave," he said to the sheriff deputy. "Can you run Holly Saunders's driver's license for us? Let's also get her social security number, any credit cards in her name, bank accounts…hopefully she's left an electronic trail."

"Sure thing. I'll call the Sheriff's Office."

When Dave stepped out of the room, Nick turned to Vivian. "What your daughter did was *not* your fault. You can't blame yourself for something you didn't know about. What you can do is try and think of where Holly might go. Friends, family? I know she's not at your house, a new family is living there."

During the drive, Leon contacted the owner of the three thousand square foot home. The landlord had said that the Saunders had been renting the house for two years, that they were excellent tenants until they stopped paying rent eighteen months ago. At that point, he'd gone to the house, tried contacting them, and after two months without hearing from them, sold their belongings and found new tenants.

"We new to area," the synthesized voice said. "Art had own business. We travel a lot. Didn't have many friends. No family. Holly quiet. Few friends."

Well, that explained why no one filed a missing person's report for either Vivian or Arthur. Nick released a sigh and hoped to God Holly wasn't smart enough to cover her trail. While what she'd done to her mother and Arthur had been premeditated, this was—plain and simple—a revenge killing. The question was…if someone else wronged her, would she kill again?

"What about Holly's real dad?" Leon asked. "Vivian, you said Holly found out the truth...that Art was her adoptive father." He shook his head. "Could be she blames him for what Art did to her, too."

Damn, his partner was good. "That makes complete sense," Nick said, loving the new direction they were taking. "Holly finds out her real dad gave her up, only to stick her with a pedophile. If she's making people pay for what Art did, I'd say her real dad might be next in line."

"But that was eighteen months ago," Bunny countered. "She could have already...killed him and moved on to who knows where."

True, damn it. "We won't know until we find him." He turned to Vivian. "One last thing and we'll let you rest. Who's Holly's real father?"

CHAPTER 21

RACHEL CHOMPED ON a pencil and glanced at the clock. Four-fifteen. She'd spoken with Wexman's head of security, Adam Lynch, two hours ago. How hard was it for the man to email the security footage from last Saturday?

Her patience at its limit, she picked up her cell phone to call Lynch. The phone rang before she had a chance to dial. Marty O'Reilly's number popped on the screen. Anxious to hear what the inspector had to say and hopeful they might finally have some solid evidence, she answered.

"Jake asked me to call you directly," Marty said.

Hello to you too. "Great. What'd you find out?"

"The photo was printed off a standard photo printer. The techs were able to tell what type of printer was used, as well as the brand of photo paper. Unfortunately, both are common and can be bought at just about any office supply store. Even if we find the printer, it doesn't mean the owner was the one who used it."

"Did they analyze the actual photo?"

"Yeah. They gave me a ninety-five percent confirmation that the male hanging from the wall is Josh Conway."

She'd met Josh several times and could give a one hundred percent confirmation, but kept her mouth shut. No need to be snarky to Marty, not when she wanted and needed his help.

"They couldn't tell the location," Marty continued, "but

based on the rock walls and floor, one of the techs suggested a root cellar, which are common in older homes in this area." He paused and shuffled papers. "Okay, the rope used on Bill Baker is standard and can be found in any hardware store. Baker's shirt had the same mineral powder on the shoulder and collar as your lab found on your brother's clothes. So we have an obvious link there."

A chill swept through her. Her brother had come close to being a victim of more than just a brutal beating.

"The rest of Baker's clothes had traces of dog hair, which matches the hair also found on your brother's clothes. Other than that, nothing."

Damn it. "And the note left on Baker?"

"This is interesting. Jake gave our lab every Hell Week note, dating back to the first disappearance, along with the ones left on your brother and Baker. The handwriting analyst said the writing on the Baker note was a good match to the others, but she concluded that a different person wrote it."

"The accomplice."

Marty released a sigh. "Yeah, I'm starting to buy into your theory. Only, I'm wondering why the accomplice wrote it. This killer has been doing this for a long time, without any slipups. Why let the accomplice write the note?"

"Maybe he didn't know she did."

"Or maybe Baker's death isn't related to Hell Week at all," Marty suggested. "If Baker's tox screen came back positive for Rohypnol—"

"But mineral powder—the same exact cosmetic mineral powder—was found on both Sean's and Bill's clothes," she argued. "That's not a coincidence."

He blew out another breath. "True. But without the drug connection, as it stands, Baker looks like he could have also been an accomplice and the killer wanted to get rid of him."

While she knew how Bill's death, and how the circumstances surrounding the boy's initial kidnapping looked on paper, she firmly believed Bill was an innocent victim. She didn't see the point in arguing with Marty, though. She was going with her gut instinct, and he was basing his assessment on forensic evidence.

A message showed up in her inbox. Finally, Lynch pulled through and sent her the security footage from last Saturday. After thanking Marty for the information, she hung up the phone and opened the file.

She quickly cued the footage to three o'clock. Joy had said that Bill called her around four and told her about Kaylie making plans for lunch the next day. Bill's shift had started at three, meaning Kaylie had entered Stanley Residence Hall at some point within the hour.

As she fast-forwarded the footage, her stomach twisted with anticipation, then suddenly dropped. She slowed the footage as Kaylie swung open the door and entered the foyer. Bill wore a big grin as Kaylie approached the desk. At this point, she wished the footage contained sound. She'd love to hear the exchange. Based on Bill's body language, the way he smiled and puffed his chest, it was obvious he liked Kaylie. Oddly, she was all smiles, too, as she leaned over the desk and talked. She touched him...a pat on the arm, then another on the hand. She said something else, and Bill's smile grew enormous.

"Must've just asked him to lunch," Rachel murmured.

Kaylie pushed away from the desk and turned. Bill looked up, his smile falling slightly. Melissa approached the desk and gave Kaylie a half hug. They exchanged a few words, then Melissa waved to Bill and she and Kaylie walked away. Before Kaylie was out of camera range, she glanced over her shoulder. Wearing, what Rachel considered, a shy smile, Kaylie said something, waved, then disappeared from the screen.

Rachel leaned back in the chair and watched as Bill picked up the phone a few minutes later. She looked at the time on the screen. Four o'clock. "So he calls Joy here," she said, then rewound the footage. After a few minutes, she realized Kaylie had never signed the guest roster. "Strike one, Kaylie. Let's see if there's any more against you."

She fast-forwarded, watched students passing in and out of

the foyer, then came to the familiar part when Sean and Josh's pizza was delivered. Checking the time stamp, she slowed the footage. Josh and Sean were now in the foyer, talking with Bill. As soon as they left, Bill covered his mouth and ran out of camera range. Even though she'd already watched all of this and knew what was coming, her skin prickled with dread and unease, just as the camera was slowly moved.

After rubbing her arms, she paused the video. "Kaylie never left." She quickly reached for her cell phone and called Owen. As his phone rang, she stood, then grabbed her boots. When the call rolled into his voice mail, she left a message, then ended the call. After lacing her boots, she tried Jake's phone, which also went into voice mail. She swore, grabbed her coat, then headed downstairs.

"I was just going to see if you wanted something to eat," Joy said as Rachel hit the bottom step.

"No time." Rachel zipped her coat, then rushed down the hall. When she reached the foyer, she paused. "What the...?"

"The funeral director's son picked up all those frickin' flowers. It's nice to be able to breathe again."

"It's not that. I just realized I don't have a car."

Joy's eyes grew large as alarm crossed her face. "Where are you racing off to?"

"I need to get to Owen and Jake. Neither one of them are answering their cell phones."

"What's the point of having one if you don't frickin' answer?" She shook her head. "What's going on?"

She quickly told Joy her suspicions.

Joy's cheeks grew red as she narrowed her eyes. "That little bitch. I'm coming with you."

"No. No way. I could be dead wrong and don't need you kicking Kaylie's ass. Please. Can I borrow your car?"

With a huff, Joy left the foyer. Seconds later she came back holding a set of keys. "It's in the garage." As she handed over the keys, she gripped Rachel's hand. "Don't do anything stupid. Find Owen or Jake. Hell, even Walter. If this girl is capable of kidnapping young men and killing Bill, who knows what she'll do to you?"

As Owen stood next to Jake and watched the crowd, he wished—for the millionth time—he were back at Joy's. Although he'd love to warm up next to an extremely naked Rachel, he knew that wasn't going to happen anytime soon, if at all. But he'd take Rachel's icy attitude over the frigid temperatures he was exposed to now.

"When Stronach proposed the Bigfoot festival, didn't anyone suggest he do it in the summer?" Owen asked, and pulled his knit cap over his ears.

"He insisted on doing it now," Jake said, then sipped from a thermos. "Dumbass said he wanted his students to experience the festivities."

"Dumbass is right." He nodded to the thermos. "What do you have in there?"

"Coffee, but I wish it was whiskey." Jake greeted an older couple as they walked past them. "I was really hoping the state police lab had more for us. Hell Week has been hanging over Bola for twenty years. It needs to stop."

Owen eyed the sheriff. "You said you were in the Marines."

"Yep."

"And from Pittsburgh."

Jake nodded and took another sip. With a sigh, he looked at Owen. "Something you want to know?"

"Just killing time."

"Ever serve in the military?" Jake asked. "Or are you a former cop turned PI?"

"U.S. Secret Service."

Jake whistled, then chuckled. "Didn't see that coming. How do you go from being a Secret Service agent to private investigating?"

"Long story."

"I thought we were killing time," Jake said with a grin. "Okay, I'll bite, 'cause now you've got me curious. I was with

Marine Division Recon—1st Reconnaissance Battalion."
Familiar with the different branches of the U.S. military,
Owen knew that meant Jake was part of the Marine Air
Ground Task Force of the U.S. Marine Corps Reconnaissance
Battalions. In other words, he was a badass.

"Got out in '06 right when we were in the middle of
Operation Iraqi Freedom." Jake's smile fell as he looked to the
crowd. "We were patrolling in a Humvee. It hit an IED, killed
the driver, and injured the rest of my team. One guy lost an
arm. The other sustained burns over sixty percent of his
body...I got lucky. Took shrapnel to my back and leg. Missed
my spine by that much." He held his fingers less than an inch a
part. "I only had to spend two months in the hospital, but by
that time, my tour was up and I chose not to reenlist. I saw
enough fighting to last me a million lifetimes."

After a moment, Jake released a sigh. "I had a fiancée,
Naomi, waiting for me. We were both from Pittsburgh, but
while I was overseas, she moved to Bola. She wanted out of
the city so bad, she plopped herself right in the middle of
nowhere." He smiled. "She worked as a nurse at Dixon
Medical Center. And when I moved here, Bola was looking for
a sheriff." He took another sip from the thermos. "I think the
only reason I got elected was because the other guy running
against me was a Townie—and not a popular one."

"Being a veteran probably helped."

"That and Naomi ran a hell of a campaign. She was popular
with the Townies. Hell, if she ran for sheriff, I'd bet anything
she would've been elected." Jake clenched his jaw as he
narrowed his eyes. "She left me about a year later when she
realized she couldn't do the small town thing, after all." He
sighed. "Okay, your turn."

Owen gave Jake a shortened version of what he'd told
Rachel about his time with the U.S. Secret Service. After he
explained how he'd ended up with CORE, Jake frowned.

"So, your boss waited until you were down, then recruited
you?"

"That's Ian's MO with every one of CORE's agents."

"Even Rachel?"

"No." Owen chuckled. "She's the exception. After she got out of the Army, she entered the Chicago Police Academy, but couldn't pass their psychology tests." He grinned. "Rachel doesn't know how to obey the rules and has issues with authority."

Jake half-laughed. "I can see that. I thought she was going to rip Marty's head off the day he told her he was taking lead on the investigation."

"No shit," he said, while thinking about the way she'd basically ripped his head off over the email to Ian. "Anyway, Rachel hears about CORE, and applies for a job. Ian doesn't even bother with an interview and sends her a 'thanks but no thanks' letter. Instead of taking the rejection, she hacks into CORE's computer system. After she disengaged every firewall, she sends Ian an email telling him his system blows ass—and those were her exact words—and if he wanted, she'd be willing to fix it."

"That's balls. He could have gone to the police. He *should* have gone to the police."

"Not Ian," Owen said with a grin. "He reviewed her resume again, saw what she did when she was with Army Intelligence, then must've realized it's better to have Rachel working for him than someone else. He went to her apartment and hired her on the spot. I'll never forget the day she walked...there's Walt." He changed the subject before he said too much. Jake didn't need to know how he'd been intrigued by Rachel's big green eyes, red hair, lush lips and curvy body the moment she'd walked through the door.

Jake laughed. "Smooth transition." He waved at Walt. "Maybe one of these days we'll grab a beer and you can tell me what's with you two."

Owen welcomed the warmth infusing his cheeks, but not the reasons for it. Instead of dwelling on Rachel and how he could make things right between them, he greeted Walter. "Cold enough?"

Walt tugged on his ugly earflap hat. "Nah. This ain't

nothing," he said even as a shiver wracked his body. "Jake, been looking for you. I wanted to talk to you about Bill's funeral."

Sensing Walter was going to discuss something personal, Owen edged away from the two men. "I'm going to walk around. I'll meet up with you later. Walt, I want to leave as soon as this thing shuts down. The cold might be nothing to you, but it sure as hell is to me."

After he left the two men, he weaved through the crowd. Fortunately, the polka band had only been scheduled for last night. Unfortunately, the country trio playing now wasn't any better. They sang like a pack of whining dogs, and either the cold had affected their ability to play an instrument, or they just couldn't play worth shit.

When he reached the edge of the crowd, he turned and watched the hundreds of people milling around the town square. Some morons had donned Bigfoot masks, making them look like distant cousins of Chewbacca. Then again, those morons were probably warmer than him. At least their faces weren't exposed to these ridiculously low temperatures.

Besides, who was he to call anyone a moron? Because he had to play by the rules, he'd screwed everything up with Rachel. Instead of obeying his boss, he should have gone to Rachel first. He should have told her that Ian wanted detailed updates as to how she'd conducted herself during the investigation. Even if he'd been upfront with her, there was no doubt in his mind that he would have given Ian an honest report. If she wasn't ready to work in the field, she could jeopardize herself, another agent, an assignment and even CORE. But he hadn't been upfront with her. Instead, he'd betrayed her trust. He'd not only taken something she'd said and used it against her, he'd allowed his need to keep her safely tucked away in CORE's evidence and evaluation room, and his love for her, to skew his judgment.

He froze. *Love?* Hell, yeah. What else could explain why his chest ached and his stomach knotted every single time he considered she might not have anything to do with him outside of work? He'd told her he was crazy about her, and that was the truth. But his actions, her reactions, had made him realize this was more than sexual infatuation. The thought of never having the chance to be with her, on every level possible, made him sick, especially because if that happened, the blame would lie solely on him. He could have controlled the situation. He could have told her the truth. He could have *showed* her how much he valued and loved her by giving her the honesty and respect she deserved.

Now he was fucked.

She'd made it clear she wanted nothing to do with him. While he couldn't blame her, he also couldn't walk away without a fight. He'd done just that when he'd left the U.S. Secret Service. Instead of fighting for his reputation after he'd been exonerated, it had been easier to walk away and start fresh. Granted, leaving the Secret Service and joining CORE had ended up being the best career choice for him, but the way he'd handled the situation had haunted him for years. Regret had made him a workaholic. He'd kept busy so that he couldn't stop and consider what his life might have been like had he fought for what he wanted.

As he stood at the fringes of the crowded square, watching the band, the people with the Bigfoot masks, it occurred to him that maybe he hadn't fought for his reputation because he hadn't cared enough. Maybe, deep down, he'd been ready to leave the Secret Service, but couldn't admit it to himself. While he'd loved what he'd been doing in Italy, there had been times when he'd longed to come back to the States, where he could be closer to his family. But it had been more than that. He'd grown...bored.

His breath hung on the frigid air as he released a deep sigh. Shit. Why did it have to take Rachel walking away from him to make him realize he'd wasted too many years hanging onto a regret that—in the big scheme of life—hadn't even mattered? As his stomach balled at the thought of losing her, he clenched his jaw. Screw that. Rachel would *not* walk away from him. This time he'd fight. Because this time, the fight was worth it.

Professionally, personally and physically, they were more than good together. More than that, he did love her. Now that he could wrap his brain around the emotion that had been nagging him for a long time, thinking the "L" word was becoming easier and easier. Telling Rachel how he felt? Well, telling and showing were two different things. And before he opened up, laid his heart on the line, he needed her to *see* his love in action.

Headlights pulled him out of his thoughts. He looked over his shoulder as a dark SUV slowed along the curb and stopped in front of a wooden barricade. When the passenger side window opened, he took a step forward.

"Owen?" a woman's familiar voice called.

He took another step, then caught Melissa, Jake's receptionist, leaning across the SUV's center console. "Hey. Is something wrong?"

"I don't know. Marty called the station and said he couldn't get in touch with you or Jake. I guess he and Rachel are looking for you two. He said everyone needs to get to Wexman immediately."

As anticipation thrummed through his veins, he looked over his shoulder and did a quick scan of the crowd. When he didn't spot Jake, he moved closer to the SUV. "Where's Jake now?"

"I already found him. He sent me after you."

Then why not call him? Owen dug into his coat pocket and retrieved his phone. Shit. He'd missed a call from Rachel. "Thanks for the heads up. I'll head to Jake's office—"

"Hop in, I'll give you a ride."

He'd parked in the lot outside of the Sheriff's Department. Rather than waste time and hoof it in the cold, he opened the passenger door and climbed in. "Appreciate it," he said and closed the window. He dropped his cell phone in his lap and held his gloved hands in front of the vents. "Any idea why they want to head to Wexman?"

As she did a quick U-turn, she shook her head. "Beats me. Apparently Marty didn't think I needed to know." She stopped at a stop sign, then turned the SUV down the road leading to the Sheriff's Department. "I'm just a girl sending a message."

"Too bad he didn't give you a message to send," he said, and picked up his phone. Rather walk into Jake's office unprepared, he hoped Rachel's voice mail could give him an indication of what had been discovered that had them rushing to the university.

"You misunderstand. *I'm* the one sending a message," she said, reached to her left, then swung.

A wooden baton connected against his forehead. The unexpected blow jarred his head, made him dizzy, and warped his vision. The phone fell from his ear as he raised his hand and reached for the steering wheel. Before he could veer them off the road, she cracked his hand with the baton, then elbowed him in the jaw. Blood instantly coated his tongue as his head jerked back. She jabbed him in the stomach, then nailed him in the groin. Dazed and writhing in pain he reached for the weapon, and caught it as she swung.

She let go, slammed on the breaks and threw the SUV into PARK. Breathing hard, she pulled a butcher's knife from inside her coat and stabbed him in the thigh. Not about to let the others fall into Melissa's trap, he swung the baton and connected with her shoulder. She let out a furious cry, then thrust the knife up, slicing through his coat and penetrating his forearm. As he tried to hit her again, he reached for her throat, made contact and squeezed.

An eerie smile tilted her lips as she grunted and dragged the knife. Excruciating pain radiated from his arm as she sliced. He fought to hold the baton, fought to choke her until she lost consciousness. But she twisted the knife, dug deeper into his flesh. Wave after wave of dizziness exploded in his head. His grip on the baton loosened. Terrified of losing consciousness, he dropped it, let go of her neck and went for the knife.

She punched him in the throat. Wheezing, his eyes watering, blood soaking his coat, he clutched his neck. She ripped the knife from his arm, grabbed the baton, then swung. Hard.

The instant the weapon slammed against the side of his head, he fell against the seat. Caught between fading into a black oblivion and consciousness, he struggled to keep his eyes open.

"Give it up," she said, her voice tinny and distant over the buzzing in his head. "You've been invited to Hell Week, and as you can tell...I won't take no for an answer."

As his eyes drifted shut, the engine revved and the SUV lurched forward. Then everything went black.

Rachel parked Joy's car outside of the Sheriff's Department, climbed out, then sprinted toward the town square. Pushing her way through the crowd, she didn't slow down until she spotted Jake. She rushed to his side, and gripped his arm.

He pulled her aside to where there were fewer people. "What the hell happened?" he asked, his voice and face filled with alarm.

"I tried calling you and Owen," she panted. "I couldn't get an answer." She inhaled and tried to catch her breath. "Owen...I need to find him."

"He's over there somewhere." Jake pointed over her shoulder, then pulled out his cell phone from his coat pocket. "Sorry. Looks like I missed your call. What's going on?"

"I think Kaylie Gallagher might be the woman we're looking for."

He looked up from his phone and frowned. "The grad student Bill liked? What makes you think—?"

"I watched the footage from the security camera again," she began, then told him what she'd seen, or rather what she hadn't. "Plus she lied about that last time she was with Bill."

He pulled off his knit cap, then scratched his head. "Look, I'm not saying we shouldn't question her again, but that's a pretty big leap."

"Yes, but—"

"So she lied to you, or maybe she got her days confused.

Either way, that doesn't make her an accomplice to kidnapping and murder."

Frustrated that his reasoning made sense, she looked away. Her already elevated heart rate took another jump. "Well, she's right over there. Why don't we ask her?"

Jake raised a brow, then replaced his knit cap. "Why don't we?"

Kaylie stood with a couple of girls Rachel recognized from the interviews they'd conducted at Stanley Hall. As Kaylie raised a Styrofoam cup to her mouth, her eyes widened when she saw them. "Sheriff, Ms. Davis, how are you?"

"Good," Jake said. "Mind if we talk to you for a sec?"

"You guys go ahead," Kaylie said to the girls. "I'll catch up with you in a minute."

As the girls walked off, Rachel searched the crowd for Owen. She didn't find him, but she did find Walter, and waved him over.

"What's going on, Sheriff?" Kaylie asked.

Refocusing, Rachel turned her attention on Kaylie. "Were you at Stanley Hall the night Josh Conway and my brother were kidnapped?"

The steam emanating from Kaylie's cup caught on the breeze. She nodded. "I was there, tutoring Melissa."

"When did you leave?" Rachel asked.

"Around eight. I needed to get back to my apartment before eight-thirty. It was my dad's birthday and my mom wanted me to Skype them. Everyone but me was going to be there, but at least I could help sing Happy Birthday and watch my dad blow out the candles." Her hands shook as she raised the cup to her lips. "He's sick and we're not sure how many more birthdays he has left. I wanted to be there, but Professor Stronach wouldn't give me the time off from my TA job."

"TA?" Jake asked.

Kaylie sent him a tired smile. "Teaching Assistant. I work about twenty hours a week as Stronach's TA. Between my scholarship and the TA job, next semester's tuition is covered. I only have one more year left, but I won't be applying to be a

TA again. It's too much work and takes away from my courses."

"As Stronach's TA," Rachel began, "shouldn't you have been at the library for his study session? You know, the one Josh and Sean were supposed to make?"

"I...ah...yeah." She nodded. "But I lied to him and told him I was sick. If I couldn't go home, I wasn't about to miss seeing my dad blow out the candles for a study session Stronach could run on his own. Look, he can't know that I lied or I could lose my job. That's...that's why I lied to you."

Kaylie could lose more than that if she'd helped with the kidnappings and had murdered Bill. Rachel shoved her gloved hands in her pocket and fingered the tip of a pencil. "Okay, I can see why you lied about being at Stanley Hall, but your timeline doesn't work."

"How so?" Kaylie tilted her chin and narrowed her eyes. "I got there at around a quarter to four, worked with Melissa until six, then another girl until eight. If you don't believe me, just ask her. Her name's Emma and she was one of the girls I was with a few minutes ago."

"We will," Rachel said. "Before we do that...I watched the security camera footage from last Saturday. You said you and Bill weren't in a relationship, but you looked...friendly. Plus, another source said you invited Bill to lunch on Sunday."

Kaylie pressed her lips together. Her chin trembled as she nodded. "I did. Bill is...was a sweet guy. I really liked him. Wexman has a strict policy about university employees dating students. I wouldn't get in much trouble considering I'm the student, but I didn't want Bill losing his job over me." She looked to the ground. "Being away from home, especially with what's going on with my dad...Bill lost his mom and he knew what I was going through. Being with him..." She shook her head. "If there's nothing else, I'll introduce you to Emma and she can verify the time I left Stanley Hall."

"I didn't realize how much you liked Bill," Rachel said with sympathy. Although still suspicious, she began to wonder if she'd pegged Kaylie wrong. If Kaylie *had* left the hall at eight, then she couldn't have helped kidnap Sean and Josh. "It was really thoughtful of you to send his family flowers."

Kaylie wrinkled her brow. "I...didn't send flowers. I wanted to, but I just don't have the extra money. But I *am* going to the funeral on Monday, whether Stronach likes it or not."

"Kaylie, I know you sent flowers. I personally pulled the card from the bouquet, which was an odd one, by the way. Rhododendrons must've been hard to get at this time of year. Expensive, too."

"I told you, I didn't send any flowers and I certainly couldn't afford to special order a bouquet even if I did. If you don't believe me, go ahead and check with the florist or check my bank account."

Rachel smiled, even though disappointment settled in the pit of her stomach. "We will," she said, although she knew in her gut they probably wouldn't find anything. Kaylie had tried to keep her relationship with Bill secret, and for good reason. But that didn't make her a murderer or kidnapper. Add on the fact she'd left the dorms *after* the boys had been taken...damn, they were back to zero suspects. "In the meantime, let's go meet Emma."

With a curt nod, Kaylie led them through the crowd. When she spotted the girls they saw her with earlier, she quickened her pace. "Emma," she called. "Can you come here?"

The young girl's eyes grew round as she came over to them. "What's up?"

"Did I tutor you last Saturday night?" Kaylie asked, her tone strong and angry.

"Yes."

"Can you please tell them what time we worked together?"

Emma nodded. "Kaylie came to my room when she was finished tutoring Melissa. It was around six."

"And when did I leave?"

"Around eight."

"Thanks. I'll be with you in a sec." After Emma went back to the other girls, Kaylie turned on them. "Happy? If not, I'll give you my bank information. I don't have any credit cards, but you can go ahead and waste your time checking to see if I'm lying about that, too." Tears filled her eyes. "You know, I really liked Bill. He was the one person in this crappy little town that I could talk to. And now he's gone." She wiped a tear with a gloved finger. "Can I go now?"

Although Rachel empathized with Kaylie, and no longer suspected her, she would check her bank account and whether or not she had any credit cards just to be certain. "One more minute, please." Kaylie might not be a suspect, but she might be able to answer a few lingering questions. "Did you see Bill before you left the dorms?"

"No, which surprised me. He knew I was going to leave at eight and always walked me to my car...even if he wasn't supposed to leave the building during his shift."

"On Monday, did he tell you that my partner and I asked him to go to the lab to get blood work?"

"I didn't talk to him on Monday." More tears streamed down her cheeks. "I was...hurt and mad when he didn't answer my calls on Sunday. Now I'll never know why he blew off our lunch."

Rachel knew, but wasn't going to disclose that information at this point in the investigation.

Kaylie pulled a tissue from her pocket, then wiped her nose. "Like I said, I'll give you whatever information you need to get you to believe me. But...no one except Melissa knows about Bill and me. Even though he's gone, I'd like to keep it that way. I don't want Bill to look bad and I don't want Stronach to know I lied."

"We'll be discreet," Jake said and touched Rachel's arm. "Right?"

Rachel fought to mask her frustration. "Right. Thanks for being cooperative," she said, then turned away. She took a few steps, then stopped.

"What?" Jake asked.

"Hang on," she said, then quickly caught up with Kaylie.

"What is it now?" Kaylie asked.

"Melissa...you tutored her until six so she could make the study session."

"That's right."

Rachel smiled, while her stomach jumped with excitement. "Thanks," she said, then rushed back to Jake.

"That went well," he said with disgust. "Poor kid is mourning the guy she liked and you drilled her as if—"

She waved her hand. "I'll apologize later. Right now, we need to find Melissa."

"Melissa?"

"Yeah, she needs to explain why she lied about going to the study session."

"You're reaching, Rachel. I *know* Melissa. She's been working for me for over a year."

"Okay, then if she went to the study session, why didn't I see her leaving the building before the camera was moved?"

He puckered his brow. "Maybe she left after."

"The session started at seven. The camera was moved at ten after." She shoved her hand in her pocket and accidentally pricked her finger with the tip of the pencil. "I can't believe I missed it."

"Missed what? I'm not a mind reader. What in the hell are you talking about?"

"Stronach gave us a list of the students who went to the study session. We questioned all the kids on that list. Melissa wasn't one of them." She pulled out her cell phone, just as Walter finally approached them. "Hey, Walt. I'm looking for Owen."

Walter looked from Jake to her, his eyes holding the hint of concern. "Jake, you look ticked. Everything okay?"

"I'm not sure." Jake dialed a number on his phone. "But I'm going to find out."

"Owen?" she reminded Walter.

"Oh, yeah. I saw him about fifteen or twenty minutes ago over there." Walter pointed to the vacant street flanking the town square. "He was talking to someone in a SUV."

The phone went slack in Jake's hand. "What color?"

"Hard to say…maybe dark blue or black."

"Melissa drives a dark green Chevy Blazer." Jake ended the call. "And she's not picking up." He shook his head and winced. "Shit, Rachel. She's the first person who found that photo of Josh. She'd told me the picture had been slipped under the door, but she could have easily—"

"Who gives a shit?" Rachel dialed Owen's number again and started moving. At this point, none of that mattered. Not now. If Melissa was the accomplice they'd been looking for, she was dangerous and…damn it. Why wasn't he answering his cell?

Jake grabbed her arm when she reached the street. "Where are you going?"

"He's not picking up." Panic crawled from her belly to her chest, and squeezed. "I've got to find him and—"

Jake's phone rang in his hand. He quickly glanced at the screen.

"Owen?" she asked.

Please let him be okay.

While he shook his head and answered, Walter touched her shoulder. "What do you need me to do, Shorty? I ran into a couple of the state policemen earlier. Want me to get them?"

"Hang tight." She dialed Marty's number. "Let me call their boss. He could get to them faster."

As she stepped away from the two men and waited for Marty to answer, her panic morphed into absolute dread and fear. The streetlamp Jake stood near created eerie shadows across his ashen face. When Marty answered she quickly told them about Melissa and then asked him to have his men do a quick search for Owen. After telling Marty to meet them at Jake's office in ten minutes, she pocketed the phone, just as Jake ended his call. "Who was it?" she asked.

"A detective from Detroit." He tapped against his smart phone. "Short version…he's looking for the daughter of two victims. One was the girl's adoptive father, the other, her mother. The dad's dead, the mom should have been." The light from his phone glowed as he gave the screen another tap.

"The daughter allegedly did it and this detective thinks she might head here if she already hasn't."

They didn't need this right now. If Melissa did something to Owen...she couldn't think about it. She had to keep her emotions intact and her focus on finding him and Melissa. "Deal with this detective's case later." She started toward the sidewalk leading to the Sheriff's Department. "We need to concentrate on finding Melissa." *And Owen.*

"I think we just did," Jake called.

She stopped and turned, then rushed back to Jake. When he handed her his phone, her stomach dropped. "Oh my God," she whispered and stared at the driver's license photo of Holly Saunders. "That's *her*." She looked up at Jake and caught the guilt in his eyes. "How could you know?"

"I'm a fucking sheriff, I *should* know who works for me." He started to move. "She's been playing me for a year. I trusted her."

She lengthened her steps and kept pace with him, leaving Walter behind. "Let it go for now. Why did this detective think she'd come here?"

They reached the Sheriff's Department, and Jake whipped open the door. "For her *real* father."

Rachel's throat tightened with fear. "Her real...who is he?"

"Xavier Preston."

CHAPTER 22

WHERE THE HELL is Junior?

He stopped pacing the living room and checked his watch. The little bitch was supposed to have been here twenty minutes ago. Of course she would choose tonight of all nights to be late.

"How many times have I told her?" He punched his palm as he moved back and forth in front of the bay window. "No more deviating. No more—" He moved the curtain aside when headlights suddenly glistened off the icy patches coating the driveway.

Finally. Now he could move on with the regularly scheduled program. He smiled at his reflection in the window. No. What he had planned for tonight wasn't exactly part of his normal Hell Week, but it would be superbly satisfying. And busy. He had to initiate the pledge. His smile fell as he envisioned the heinous, violating act he had no desire to perform on the boy. Unfortunately, it must be done to come full circle. Afterward, the pledge would die, and so would Junior. Yes. He had a busy night ahead of him. As to which order their deaths would come?

His pledge had asked him to kill Junior first. And he'd loved the idea, had loved the bloodlust in the boy's voice when he'd made the request. Junior had showed utter disrespect to Hell Week the night she'd smashed his pledge's toes. Considering what the boy would endure before being killed, he'd honor his final wish. He would...

"Son of a *bitch*." Uncontrollable rage tore through him as he quickly moved away from the bay window and whipped open the front door. "Fucking bitch," he muttered as he rushed to the SUV.

"Hi, Dad." Junior said with a smile as she opened the passenger door. "Look who I brought to the party?"

The interior light revealed one of the buffoons from Chicago. Now he had to kill *three* people tonight. He scrubbed a hand down his face, and masked his temper. He needed to keep her at ease and in his circle of trust. If he showed any indication that he hated her, that just looking at her disgusted him, she might grow wary and run. He had no time for that particular nonsensical stuff. Not if he wanted to keep an agenda. Not if he wanted her dead.

"Junior," he said as he approached the passenger side of the SUV. "What is the purpose of bringing *him* here tonight?"

She opened her coat and craned her neck. "Not sure if you can see it, but he choked the crap out of me when he was trying to..." Turning away, she drew in a ragged breath. "He tried to rape me."

He looked to the man. "Very well. But you do realize what this means, correct?"

Junior nodded and hugged herself. "I'm sorry, sir. I didn't want to bring him here, but I...I defended myself and after he passed out, I didn't know what else to do." Tears spilled down her cheeks as she started kicking snow. Kicking the tires. Manic, she pulled at her blond hair. "I was so worried if they found him, he'd lie. Tell them I...I don't know. All I knew was that I couldn't let them find out about us," she wailed. "I'm so sorry. I'm so, so sorry."

As a victim of rape, he should empathize. Because he hated Junior, and planned to kill her anyway, he felt nothing. While he didn't want to kill the investigator, and possibly place himself in a precarious situation, he abhorred rapists. No one knew about the old well on his property. The last person who had any recollection of its existence was dead. Her old bones mingled with those of his past pledges.

"Enough." He moved toward the motionless man and gave him a slap. When the investigator didn't respond, he turned to Junior. "What did you do to him?"

"I...I hit him with a baton the sheriff gave me to keep in my car. Thank God," she finished with a shiver.

"Let's get him inside." He reached for the man, Malcolm, if he recalled correctly, and hefted him from the seat. Malcolm roused a bit, but not enough. He gave him another slap. When the buffoon's eyes slid open, then rolled back, he hit him again. Nothing.

Irritation swam through his head, but he kept it in check. He shoved Malcolm from his seat and let him land face first in the small snow bank flanking the driveway. Malcolm raised his head and gasped.

Grinning, he hauled the man up, steadied him, then told Junior to help. Together, they dragged him into the house. When they reached the trapdoor, Malcolm began to regain consciousness. "Quickly," he told Junior. "Open the door."

"Wouldn't it be easier to kill him upstairs? He's heavy and I don't see how we're going to haul him back up the ladder."

"Now, Junior," he ordered.

She jumped, and did as he demanded. Idiot girl. Dragging dead bodies from the basement required minimal effort. His ancestors had ensured easy access to the root cellar after they'd blown a hole in the ground and erected the house. An exit stood in the far corner of the basement and led to the side of the yard. The door, while crude and in bad disrepair, had been kept hidden from sight by overgrown hedges for as long as he could remember.

By the time he hauled Malcolm down the basement ladder, he'd wished he had used the old, outer door to the cellar. The man's dead weight had been cumbersome, and had made navigating the rungs difficult. But he didn't want Junior aware of the exterior door. He wanted her trapped in the basement with the others. If she were to escape, he had no doubt she'd run. Maybe not to the authorities, but that was a risk he wasn't willing to take. After all, he had plans for a future outside of Bola.

Breathing hard, he dropped Malcolm to the floor, removed the man's gun, then placed it on the workbench. As he quickly retrieved rope, he noticed blood smeared across the sleeves and chest of the beige, wool sweater he'd put on before Junior arrived. A trickle of dread slipped down his spine. He would have to be careful. Junior had used more than a baton to thwart her attacker. Much more, based on the amount of blood.

"Sir," she cried. "Your sweater."

"Yes." He began tying the man's legs together. "Are you sure you only used a baton?"

"He had a knife. I...he must have cut himself when we were struggling."

"And where is this knife now?" he asked as he flipped Malcolm over and twined the rope around his wrists.

"I'm not sure exactly. I'll go check the car."

"Leave it. We'll take care of it when we're finished." With his breathing now under control, and his heart rate returning to normal, he stood and glanced at the pledge. "I can't allow this minor setback to interfere with tonight's initiation. My pledge has worked hard this week, and deserves to be honored."

He wiped his bloodied hands on a towel and approached the pledge. "This morning, we had a nice long talk, didn't we?"

Stony-faced, the pledge stared at him. "We did."

"So you know what's to come?"

While he kept his face expressionless, his Adam's apple bobbed. "I do."

"Well, I don't," Junior whined.

"Why don't you tell her, Puke? Tell Junior the last details of initiation."

The boy kept his eyes locked to his. "Your father plans to rape me, as my father had done to him."

As Junior gasped, he touched the puke's cheek. "It will be quick, but it will be painful. I'm sorry, Son. But, I have no other choice."

The boy's eyes filled with tears. "There's always a choice."

He smiled. "Not in this instance. But I did mull over your earlier request, and I'm very fond of granting a man's dying wish. Understand?" He leaned forward and pressed his mouth against the boy's ear. "She will die first. That is a promise I intend to keep."

He stepped back. "Junior, grab me the broom." While he waited for his idiot daughter, he bent and began unfastening the boy's ankle restraints. "If you believe in God, you might want to start praying for—"

"Look out," the pledge shouted.

He turned, just as Junior slammed the broomstick against his head. Dazed, he shook his head and tried to push off the rock floor. She hit him across the back. He rolled to his side, and she cracked him in the groin. Howling in pain, he tried desperately to move, his sole intent on murdering the bitch he'd spawned. She jabbed the stick into his kidney. As he bowed, the broomstick clattered the floor.

The boy grunted and pulled on his restraints. "Leave him alone, Melissa."

"Fuck off, " Junior said, as she quickly snapped handcuffs around his wrists. "Bet you didn't see that one coming, huh, *Dad*?"

Stunned, he lay on the floor. Memories from twenty-five years ago suddenly came at him in a rush. Being held down, restrained and helpless. Being...violated.

She bent down until they were face to face. "Hello?" She rapped his throbbing head with her knuckle. "Anyone home?"

Her taunt, the evil lurking in her eyes, gave him the strength to push on to his knees. She stood and let him. "Comfortable?" she asked. "I hope so, because I've got one hell of a story to tell you before I rape and kill your pledge." She looked over her shoulder to where Malcolm lay motionless on the floor. "Oh, and the private dick, too." Grinning, she pulled a butcher's knife from inside her coat pocket. "Don't worry. I'm not going to kill you, Daddy Dearest. Someone needs to be punished for these murders."

The pledge whimpered and drew flat against the wall as she approached the boy. "So your dad raped my dad?" She made an X over the boy's heart, but did not break the skin. "Kinda gross, don't ya think?"

"Melissa," the boy said. "You don't have to do this."

"My name is Holly, and that's not what I asked you." She sniffed. "God, you stink." As she turned away, she chuckled. "Actually, I *do* have to do this. Just like my daddy had to do all of these dumbass Hell Weeks. See, when I met him and he let me in on his secret, he kept telling me that Hell Week would bring him full circle. What Daddy didn't realize was that I was on the same mission."

His mind still thick and foggy, the rock bit into his knees as he swayed. "Junior," he warned. "You're making a big mistake."

She turned and pointed the knife at him. "No. *You* made the mistake. What's funny is that you kept thinking I was constantly making mistakes." She laughed, the eerie cackle bounced off the walls as she squatted in front of him. "Remember when I first came to you and told you my story?"

He nodded. How could he forget? When she'd first arrived on his doorstep, she'd been a scared, pitiful, timid little mouse of a woman. She'd been abused by her mother, accused of violent behavior toward children and animals, and had killed a man to save her virginity. Although he'd wanted nothing to do with his child, he'd hated that she'd suffered, hated that she'd been left powerless. Because he'd understood what she'd gone through, he'd wanted to give her the empowerment to take control of her destiny. Show her that she could be strong, and teach her that she didn't have to serve as another's doormat.

Now, he tasted fear. The woman squatting in front of him was nothing like the one he'd met eighteen months ago. He'd once considered her harmless, pathetic. The smug arrogance in her crazed eyes told him otherwise. Junior had played him for a fool, and the game wasn't over.

"I remember," he finally said.

"Me too." She grinned and flicked the knife against his sweater. "The way you ate up my story was priceless." She glanced over her shoulder and looked at the pledge. "This brilliant, pompous academic believed every piece of bullshit I gave him. But now I know why."

Facing him again, she nodded. "Yes. Now I know why. You'd been raped during *your* Hell Week all those years ago. How old were you? Eighteen? Nineteen? Either way, it explains why you're stuck in the past and why you've done these incredibly childish things to Josh." A small smile tilted her lips as she leaned forward. "I didn't know about Hell Week when I found you. Honestly, I planned to kill you the day we sat on your porch and drank your shitty iced tea. But you intrigued me that day. I knew you were hiding something dark and I wanted to know all about it. And once you finally told me your dirty secret, I knew killing you would be too easy."

He sat on his heels and considered what she'd just said. "Why did you want to kill me?"

Her eyes narrowed as she pursed her lips. She cocked her head and also sat back on her heels. "Josh's dad raped you, right?"

He nodded.

"Once? Twice? Were there others?"

"Once, which was more than enough."

She smiled. "So true. But imagine it happening on a weekly basis for...oh...let's say eight years." Her face contorted into a sarcastic wince. "Yeah, I think I've got you beat." She stood. "In more ways than one."

Junior moved to the corner of the room, and retrieved the metal bat. "I've pictured slamming this into your head more times than I can count."

"I don't know why," he said with honesty. He might have been, on occasion, a little rough with her, but he'd never struck her or touched her in a sexual way. But it sounded as if someone had molested her for years, and that violation to her body and mind had warped her. In a small way, she'd piqued his curiosity, yet the need for survival overrode his need to know what had caused her to seek vengeance against him. He thought about the hidden door in the back of the basement. While fear lingered on his tongue and tightened his chest and throat, survival had his stomach jumping with awareness. When the moment was right, he would take his chance and run.

"He doesn't know why," she said on a chuckle. "Hello? Because you gave your parental rights away when I was born, my stupid mother not only married a pedophile, but let him adopt me. My entire life I thought he was my real dad. During those eight years when he abused my body...it sickened me that a father would treat his own flesh and blood in such a vile and disgusting way."

After pocketing the knife, she raised the bat. "Then one day, I was in the attic. Hiding." She twirled the bat like a baton. "How pathetic...twenty years old and hiding in the attic because my molester was home and I was alone in the house. But something good happened that day. While I sat there for hours, waiting for him to leave or for my mom to come home, I started sifting through boxes. That's when I discovered *you*." She stopped twirling the bat, then pointed it at him. "That's when it all clicked." She cocked her head. "Or, maybe the better word is *snapped*."

The disturbingly sinister way she said "snapped" caused his skin to crawl with dread.

"Yeah. I admit, I definitely snapped. I thought...how could a man give his own child away to a monster?"

Guilt settled in his chest. "I didn't know. If I had, I would have—"

"What? Taken me in? Or put me in the system so I could go into foster care? Because I have a feeling that's *exactly* what you would have done. You didn't want me. Not then, not now. The only one who wanted me was that sick fuck, Artie."

"Who?" he asked, keeping his eye on the bat and preparing for a blow.

"You didn't even know who adopted me? And you thought *I* was pathetic." She pounded the tip of the bat against the floor. When she calmed, a serene smile crossed her face. "Remember the man I told you I killed? Well, I kinda lied about that. Not about killing him, trust me, Artie is dead. But I was no virgin. He took that from me when I was twelve. So you know what I took from him?"

His head swam and his stomach grew nauseous. He didn't want to hear anymore and hoped to God she'd shut the fuck up and move on with her business. Kill Malcolm or maybe the pledge, so he could run. He glanced away and caught sight of the investigator's gun on the workbench. Too far away. Too risky. The woods were his only safe bet. He knew them like the back of his hand. He would lose her in them, then when it was safe to return, rid his basement of any evidence of Hell Week, then leave this godforsaken town.

"I'll tell you what I took from him." She smacked the bat against her palm. "His teeth, his eyes, the skin on his face…his dick." Smiling, she gripped the bat. "Then I took care of my mother."

A fuzzy image of Vivian shifted through his mind. He hadn't seen her in twenty years, had never felt any emotion toward her then, but hated her now. She should have done what he'd asked her the moment she'd told him she would be expecting *their* baby. She should have aborted and saved them all from having to ever endure…Junior.

"That was another lie," Junior said. "Mom needed to pay. She'd brought that piece of shit into my life and she needed to pay for what he did to me. Now you do, too."

She spun, then swung the bat, hitting the pledge in his exposed stomach. As the boy grunted and cried, she leaned against the bat as if it were a crutch. "Wow, that felt good. I really want to do that to your head, but you did teach me one good thing. Patience. And my patience is paying off quite nicely."

He ignored his pledge and focused on Junior. At this point, her arrogance might be his only salvation. She thought she had him cornered, but didn't know about his escape route. She would slip up and he would be ready.

"Patience is a good virtue to possess," he said. "I've spent twenty years perfecting it."

"Funny, it only took me eighteen months."

"Yes, and your patience has paid off. You have me trapped and at your mercy. But, have you thought about how this will look once the authorities arrive? You claim that I'll be held responsible for these murders, but what about you? Aren't you worried I'll tell them about you?"

He'd expected a flicker of self-doubt, but had been wrong. Junior straightened her spine, then tossed the bat aside. "Those mistakes you accused me of weren't mistakes. I purposefully took Sean Davis because I knew who his sister worked for. Yeah, Sean bragged about the fancy private investigation firm she worked for and I wanted her involved. I wanted you worried and nervous, but you, in all your pompous arrogance, didn't blink an eye. So I had to up the ante. I drugged the security guard with the same stuff I used on the boys, then used his truck. I could have let him live, because I know I didn't leave any evidence behind, but that was just too easy. Did I mention that I left a note on Bill?"

Fury replaced his fear. "You stupid bitch."

She wagged a finger. "I'd say I'm far from stupid. Guess what else I did. I took a picture of Josh hanging against the wall, and *pretended* it was sent to the sheriff." She gave him a big grin. "Brilliant, huh?"

Although he seethed with hatred, he returned the smile. "No, Junior. You set yourself up as my accomplice. You said yourself that the state police were involved. Did you consider that they would analyze this note you left behind or the photograph? A handwriting analysis will prove—"

"Jack shit," she shouted. "It'll prove nothing. Yes, they'll be looking for an accomplice, but they won't be looking for me. I've already set someone else up to take the fall, and it's working out quite nicely."

"How nice for you."

379

"Thank you, I thought so." She pulled the knife from her coat pocket. "Now that you know all the gory details, let's get...gory. Who should I start with? Your precious pledge or the private dick?"

Owen played opossum, and fought the urge to move. Xavier Preston had bound his hands and wrists. Preston's daughter—Melissa/Holly—had taken him by surprise in the SUV and had cut and bludgeoned him. He'd lost blood. How much? He wasn't sure if the ache in his head and sheer grogginess was due to the baton she'd cracked against his skull or the wounds to his thigh and arm. Either way, it didn't matter. At this point, he needed to find a way to stop her before she killed him and the boy.

"Well," Melissa began, "I'm thinking I should go for your precious pledge. He's been pissing me off all week."

"He's done nothing to you," the dean said, his tone desperate but laced with anger.

"And you've done nothing to him," she countered. "You talked a big game, but instead all you did was hose him off and feed him gross food. Oooo, scary." She laughed. "What's even scarier is that I get the impression you actually like him. Hell, I think that even if I didn't fuck you over, you'd feel more for him than me. So, yeah. I think Josh needs to go first."

Metal scraped against rock. Owen couldn't see her from his position on the floor, but pictured her running the blade of the butcher's knife along the wall next to Josh.

"Wait," she said. "You never told me...how do you normally kill your pledges?" When the dean didn't answer, her footsteps echoed on the floor as she moved into his line of sight. She picked up the bat. "Do you need a little encouragement? Or are you going to answer me?"

"I strangled them," the dean shouted from behind him.

Owen slid his eyes closed when she walked past him. "Boring. Effective, but boring. Seeing as how this has ultimately become *my* Hell Week, I'm going to have to spice things up...one slice at a time."

"Junior—"

"Stop calling me that! I fucking hate it. I hate you." Drawing in labored breaths, she moved back to the corner of the room. Owen slid one eye open just as she picked up a crowbar. "I used a tire iron on my mom. My trusty dusty knife, too." She waved the blade. "Right now, I think I could do something rather interesting with both of these."

When she moved out of view, Owen inwardly cursed. He lay only a foot away from the ladder, but without being able to move his hands or feet, he couldn't risk making a move just yet. He'd have to wait until she went to work on Josh. While she was distracted, he would find a way to loosen the rope.

The boy's screams pierced his ears and resonated throughout the basement. Taking a risk, Owen curled onto his right side and brought his knees to his stomach. Excruciating pain shot through his right forearm and impaled his brain, making him dizzy and nauseous. Sucking in a deep breath, he used his injured arm and shoulder to shove himself to his knees. His left leg throbbed as fresh blood soaked his jeans. He quickly shifted his body and turned his back to the ladder, then held back a gasp.

Blood oozed from the slice Melissa had made along the center of Josh's chest. With her back still to him, he glanced at the dean, who stared directly at him, then nodded toward the corner. Owen looked, and spotted his gun on the workbench. He had no idea if anyone knew where he was, or who had taken him. As far as he was concerned, he was on his own. With retrieving the gun his sole focus, he kept his eyes on Melissa's back, widened one leg, shuffled the other one until both legs met, then moved his bound feet.

"I'm not sure how doctors perform chest surgery," Melissa said. "But I'm assuming they pull back the skin and crack the ribs, right?" She glanced over her shoulder to the dean. "I thought it would be fun if I pulled his beating heart from his chest. According to Professor Stronach, some cannibalistic cultures ate the organs of their enemies as a way of displaying their victory. Think about it. Wouldn't eating Josh's heart be an excellent way to truly come full circle? To truly show his father, your enemy, that in the end you're the victor?"

The dean pushed off his heels. "That's disgusting."

"So says the man who has killed nine innocent boys. Really, Daddy. Your morals are incredibly...warped."

When she met Owen's gaze, his hope deflated, but his determination grew stronger. Melissa was beyond sick. If he didn't stop her, they were all dead.

"What do you think you're doing?" she asked him, as she approached. Blood dripped from the knife and left a trail. "I guess I should have started with you, after all."

When she reached him, she kicked his chest. He fell back, but quickly pulled his legs and feet from under him.

"My idiot father was right about one thing," she said. "You and your partner are buffoons. You two are so fucking clueless, even after all the bits of evidence I left for you. If you'd done your job, you would have caught my dad, saved the boy and...well, honestly, you could've never saved the boy. He'd seen my face and knew me from the dorms." She tilted her head. "Yeah, he would've died anyway. Now you will—"

A door slammed on the main floor. Melissa craned her neck and looked up toward the ladder.

"You're screwed, Junior," the dean said with a chuckle. "There's no way out but up, and it sounds like the *buffoon's* friends are here."

"Actually, I'm not. The only one screwed is you." She smiled, then zipped her coat. "Yep, I know about your secret door, *Daddy*. God, you're an idiot. Have fun in prison. I have a feeling your fellow inmates will make your Hell Week look like playtime."

As she took off, Owen kicked the back of her knee. Her leg buckled. She fell forward, the hit jarring the knife from her hands. He quickly squirmed his body back and kicked the workbench and shouted for help. The gun fell just as she retrieved the knife.

"I would have enjoyed killing you, but you're not worth it," she said, then ran across the room until the darkness swallowed her.

****

Spurred by frustration and fear, Rachel gnawed on a pencil and trudged through the thick, wet snow. She couldn't stop thinking about Owen, or...the blood they'd found inside Melissa's SUV.

"Not too far, Ma'am," one of Marty's men called after her.

"Kiss my ass," she mumbled. As she edged around the corner of Dean Xavier Preston's century home, she wished she were carrying a gun. When they'd arrived, and discovered Melissa's dark green Chevy Blazer, Jake had insisted she stay outside and near the SUV until he and Marty cleared the house. Meanwhile, Marty had ordered one of his officers to head around the back of the house to secure the exit. Unfortunately, Jake's deputies and the remaining men on loan from the state police had been needed at the festival for crowd control. "Bullshit." She kicked the snow. Those men were needed here.

Damn it, I'm needed in there.

Her rational, logical mind understood Jake's position. While she was a licensed private investigator and also licensed to carry a concealed weapon, she didn't have the experience for a situation like this. Melissa, rather, Holly Saunders, was a dangerous, unpredictable killer. But the bitch had gone after Owen. Her stomach clenched.

Please, let him be okay.

She couldn't imagine never seeing him, touching him, loving him. While she'd said some awful things to him and had acted as if there wasn't a chance in hell they'd ever—

Sucking in a breath, she stopped dead. Icy fingers of dread crept along her spine as a figure emerged from the overgrown hedges running along the side of the house. The glow from the moon revealed long dark hair and Rachel knew, deep in the depths of her soul, that figure was the bitch herself.

Biting hard on the pencil, she crouched and hid behind a fat pine tree. Moving the branches slightly, she waited and watched. Melissa looked from left to right, then took off running. With the element of surprise on her side, and afraid of losing Melissa in the woods, Rachel shoved the pencil in her pocket and sprinted after her.

Once she entered the woods, she realized she'd reacted too quickly. She should have called out to the officer at the front of the house. Without a flashlight, without a weapon, she couldn't see or protect herself. She considered her phone, but instantly changed her mind. The glow from her cell could alert Melissa's attention.

Rachel stumbled over something, cracked her knee and scraped her hand. Screw it. She scrambled to her feet, reached into her pocket and pulled out her phone. Slowing to a jog, she kept her eyes wide as she hit the speed dial. When Jake answered, a small sense of relief filled her.

"She's in the woods," Rachel whispered. "West of the house. I'm on her—"

Melissa swung her leg through the air. Rachel dropped the phone and raised her hands. She knocked the bitch's booted foot away before it connected with her head. Taking advantage of Melissa's exposed torso, she double jabbed her stomach, then sent an uppercut straight to her jaw. As Melissa's head shot back, Rachel gave the woman a solid kick in the gut.

Melissa fell to her knees and clutched her midsection. With vengeance and fear for Owen driving her, Rachel kicked the other woman's head.

Melissa tucked and rolled, sprang up and raised her arm. A sliver of moonlight reflected off the blade of a knife.

Raw fury ripped through Rachel. She shot her hand out and gripped the other woman's arm. Melissa pressed forward. The tip of the knife snagged Rachel's coat. The bitch might have her by at least seven inches and thirty pounds, but Rachel knew how to fight dirty. When the knife met skin, she acted fast. She kneed Melissa in the belly, then the crotch. As the woman gasped and grunted, Rachel head butted her. Blood spurted from Melissa's nose. Ignoring her throbbing head, Rachel threw herself at Melissa, knocking the woman to the ground.

Melissa surprised her. Rolled them over and over until a large pile of rock stopped their momentum. At a disadvantage,

Melissa pinned her with her weight, and swung both her fist and the knife.

Rachel blocked the knife, but took a hit to the cheek. She ignored the taste of blood and punched Melissa in the throat. The woman gasped and clutched her neck with her free hand. She raised the knife with intent, but Rachel shoved her back. Crawled on top of her, then slammed Melissa's wrist against the rock. The knife fell from the bitch's hand. Rachel reached over the rock to grab it, but met nothing but air. Confused, but more worried the woman had another weapon, she went for one of the rocks.

Melissa punched her in the kidney, then the jaw. Rachel fell to her side and kicked, but Melissa dropped her knees on Rachel's back and gripped her head. She slammed Rachel's head against the ground and shoved her face into snow and icy mud. Her heart beating out of control, the need to breathe overwhelming, Rachel wished to God she had called for help from the start. She wished she hadn't been such a pansy ass and had forced herself to carry a gun. Owen and Sean's images rose in her foggy mind. Who would look after brother? And Owen...why couldn't she have just forgiven him and told him the truth? Told him she loved him.

"My daddy was right," Melissa panted close to Rachel's ear. "You and your partner are useless buffoons." She pressed on Rachel's head. "You should have seen the way I gutted your buddy. Cut him from the groin up to his—"

Stop this bitch.

Rachel squirmed her body and tried to buck Melissa. The woman pressed harder. "Fucking die," she whispered against Rachel's ear.

Not today.

With everything to lose, and in desperate need to breathe, Rachel twisted her arms, reached above and behind, and clawed Melissa's face. Melissa's grip loosened as she cried out. Rachel quickly pulled her head from the snow and mud, dragged in a deep breath, then elbowed Melissa in the gut. The woman grunted. Rachel rotated, reached into her coat pocket and latched onto the pencil. She pulled it free and stabbed Melissa in the cheek. Before the woman could grab it from her, Rachel plucked it from her face, and with her free hand, pinched Melissa's bloodied nose. As Melissa howled and swung her fists, Rachel focused on what the bitch had done to Owen. She cocked her arm back, and using all of her strength, slammed the business end of the pencil against Melissa's ear and shoved it hard.

Melissa froze. Moonlight chased shadows across her wide eyes and gaping mouth. Then her body violently shuddered. Rachel shoved her off, then quickly moved to her feet. As she stared at the convulsing woman, she used the back of her coat sleeve to wipe the mud and snow from her face.

She'd beaten the bitch, but there was no sense of triumph, only loss. If what Melissa had said was true, the killer had taken the man she loved.

Melissa's body stopped jerking, then stilled. Rachel gave her a swift kick to the side. Nothing. Good. She walked a few feet and scooped up her glowing phone. Before she could hit her speed dial, heavy footfall drew near.

"Rachel," Jake shouted.

She turned and caught the beams from flashlights dancing along the trees. "Over here," she rasped, then cleared her throat. "Over here!"

Jake and one of Marty's men rushed to her. While Jake pulled her close, the officer checked Melissa. He whistled, then shook his head. "Death by pencil. Never thought I'd ever see something like this."

Jake pulled away and gripped her shoulders. "I want to kick your ass for going after her yourself."

"Go ahead and try. I've got another pencil in my pocket."

He wiped a stray tear off her cheek. "Owen's freaking out. I almost kept him tied up to keep him from going after you."

Hope flared in her chest as she grabbed his hands. "He's okay?"

"He will be."

"Sheriff," the officer called.

They turned and stepped toward the rocks she'd slammed into during her fight with Melissa.

The officer aimed his flashlight down into a wide hole. "What do you make of this?"

Rachel peered into what she assumed was an old well and immediately saw a femur. She swallowed against the bile rising in her throat, took a step back, and then started to walk away. "I think we found the missing boys."

Jake caught up with her. "Let me help you back."

She shrugged him off and forced her legs to move faster, then faster until she took to a full sprint. When she reached the front of the house, she slowed, saw Owen sitting on the front porch step, then rushed to him.

He winced as he pushed off the step, then pulled her into his arms. "What the hell were you thinking?" He hugged her tight and made every blow she'd taken from Melissa come alive in the worst way. "She's dangerous...she could have killed you."

"She's not so dangerous anymore," she said with a mixture of remorse and relief.

He pulled back, and gently cupped her face. "I'm sorry."

"It was me or her." She touched his swollen jaw. "Owen, I...when I thought..."

He placed a soft kiss on her lips. "Later. I'm not going anywhere. Ever."

CHAPTER 23

RACHEL SAT IN the chair next to Owen's ER bed and took a sip of coffee. When she winced, he cracked a smile. "That bad?"

She set the cup on the stand next to his bed. "It's worse than the stuff you've brewed."

"So, I've got that going for me," he said, and propped his good arm under his head. "We'll be out of here soon. And I guarantee once we're back at Joy's, she'll—"

"She'll do what?" Joy edged around the corner and kept her teary eyes on Rachel. "Pamper the hell out of you?" She touched Rachel's face, examined the bruises on her cheeks, before folding Rachel into her arms. "You okay, Shorty?"

Rachel nodded. "Just some scrapes and bruises."

Joy drew back and held Rachel's hands. "Is that a self-diagnosis or did an actual doctor tell you that?"

Rachel released a tired chuckle. "Yes, an *actual* doctor examined me."

Joy looked over her shoulder and glanced at Owen. She let go of Rachel's hands then moved to the bed. "That's one hell of a goose egg." She nodded to his forehead, then sucked in a breath when she looked at his forearm.

"It looks worse than it is," he said, more concerned with

Rachel than himself. She'd killed a person. Yes, out of self-defense, but would the guilt over taking a life eat at her?

"Says the man who just took thirty stitches to his arm and another fifteen to his thigh." Rachel stood next to Joy. "Plus, he has a concussion."

"And the boy?" Joy asked. "How's he? Walter said he was cut up pretty bad."

Owen glanced across the ER. Less than ten feet away, the doctors and nurses tended to Josh behind a closed curtain, prepping him for a room. "Where is Walter?"

"Parking the car. Now about that boy."

"Physically, his doctor thinks he'll be okay," Rachel said. "He's dehydrated. His left foot and toes are broken, and he has a laceration along his chest. As far as they can tell, no muscle or organ damage, but they still need to run a CT scan and want to keep him for a few nights." She hugged herself and stared at him. "He was lucky."

Josh was more than lucky. What Xavier Preston had had in store for the boy was vile and perverse. But what Melissa had planned to do...Owen slid his eyes closed and tried to erase the image.

"Heads up," Jake said.

Owen opened his eyes and looked at the sheriff.

Jake thumbed behind him toward the ER's wide, glass doors. "Marty's been watching the parking lot. He called and said Bob Conway's on his way in."

"You're not going to arrest him in front of Josh, are you?" Rachel asked, her eyes wide and holding the hint of disbelief. "The kid's been through enough. I think you're better off waiting until his dad leaves the ER."

"What are you guys talking about?" Joy asked. "And don't give me none of that police business crap."

When no one answered, Owen cleared his throat. "We believe Bob Conway tortured Preston when he was a student at Wexman."

So your dad raped my dad? Melissa's haunting question rang through Owen's mind. He didn't *believe* Conway had tortured

Preston, he *knew* in his gut the man had taken a Hell Week hazing to a level so foul, it had corrupted Preston's mind.

"While the doc was taking care of Owen," Rachel began, keeping her voice low. "I borrowed Jake's laptop and looked into Wexman's database. It's the same one Owen and I went through earlier this week. Only we were looking at students who'd *graduated* from the university. Because Preston is the killer behind Hell Week, I looked to see if he'd gone to school there. Turns out, he was at Wexman the same time Conway was, too."

"Conway could have saved his son this morning," Jake said with loathing.

Rachel turned when the ER doors slid open. "And here he is now. What are you going to do, Jake?"

The sheriff looked away and hooked his thumbs on his belt. "I'll wait."

"Where is he?" Bob rushed to them and grabbed Jake's arm. "Where's my son?"

Rachel pointed. "Behind that curtain."

Without another word, Conway hurried over, then ripped the curtain back. "Josh. Oh my God." He stood at the end of Josh's hospital bed and fisted his hands. "Son...I...your mother and I have been so worried."

Josh licked his cracked lips, then twisted his mouth in a mocking smile. "Liar," he accused, his voice surprisingly strong considering everything he'd been through this past week.

Conway glanced over his shoulder at them, then quickly back to his son. "That's the medication talking. You've been through a lot. Let me talk to your doctor. I want to have you moved to a *real* hospital."

"I'm not going anywhere with you." The heart rate monitor hooked to Josh's chest began to ping in quick successions. "You make me sick."

"Josh, I'm not about to allow your mother to see you like this," Conway said, his tone forceful and warning. "You need to shut your mouth and get your rest." He turned toward the doctor who had been working on Josh. "How long before he can be moved from this shithole?"

"You're a rapist!" Josh's face twisted with agony as he tried to push off the bed. The nurse and doctor quickly pushed him down. "Because of you, nine people died," he shouted. "*I* almost died. And now...you're dead to me."

As if the boy had never spoken, Bob Conway shook his head. "I'm having him removed from here within the hour," he said to the doctor. "Have him ready."

"Sheriff," Josh called, his voice desperate, pleading. "Are you hearing this? This man is a rapist."

Jake looked to Rachel. "So much for waiting. Call Marty and tell him we're ready for him," he said, then went after Conway.

"This is preposterous," Conway ranted as Jake read him his rights. "What the hell are you arresting *me* for?"

"Obstruction of justice, Mr. Conway." Jake finished cuffing the man, and started to lead him away. "You knew this morning who had your son and didn't say a thing."

"Bullshit. I didn't know anything."

"He knew?" Josh cried. "What do you mean, he *knew*?"

"Look," Conway began. "I didn't know, but when I heard Preston was dean, I suspected."

"And you didn't say anything?" Josh's face contorted with hatred. "Let me guess. You called your lawyers and put them on damage control. You wanted to make sure my kidnapping, my *kidnapper*, wouldn't ruin your precious reputation."

"Just keep your mouth shut," Conway ordered. "You don't know what you're talking about."

Josh laughed, but without humor. "No. I do." He laid his head against the pillow. "You know what Preston told me?"

"Shut up, Josh. I'm warning you."

"He said that you were the one who put Hell Week into motion twenty-five years ago." Josh closed his eyes and tilted his mouth in a small, wry smile. "He said you'd know fear. That you'd comprehend at the most heinous level...because for every action, there is always a reaction." He opened his eyes. "He said I had to die for *your* sins. And you were going to let it happen to save your sorry ass."

"I wasn't going to let you die." Conway jerked away from Jake's grip. "I was trying to protect *us*."

"No. You were protecting *you*." Josh closed his eyes. "Just go away. I want no part of you."

Jake forced Conway to move. "I'll be free in a matter of hours," Conway shouted over his shoulder. "We'll talk this out. Everything will be fine. You and me, we'll be fine. We'll—"

The glass doors closed behind Conway and Jake, cutting off anything else the man had to say. Owen looked across the room. Josh met his gaze. "At least Preston showed some remorse," the boy said. "My father...I blame him for this."

Rachel went to Josh's side and held his hand. "What your dad did was wrong. But he didn't kill those other kids or kidnap you."

"No." Josh pressed his head deeper into the pillow. "He just created the monster who did."

Owen's chest tightened as Rachel smoothed the boy's hair from his face and kissed his forehead. Josh had a long road ahead of him. What his father had done, what Preston and his daughter had attempted to do, would likely require years of therapy.

Rachel stepped out of the way to allow the nurses and doctors to transfer Josh to a room. After they moved the boy out of the ER, she walked across the room and stood next to his bed. She looked exhausted, and he hated the scrapes and bruises marring her pretty face. He hated that she'd gone through what she had tonight, but would never doubt her *emotional* qualifications again. If anything, she'd proved to be one of the strongest people he'd ever known. She'd challenged herself, took risks and came out the victor. Hell, she'd challenged him and forced him to realize he could be a better man. That he needed to be if he were to prove to her they belonged together.

When she glanced at him, he reached for her hand. She leaned forward and took it, then closed her eyes and rested her forehead on their joined hands. He rolled slightly, and feathered his fingers through her short hair. When her warm tears fell along his skin, his throat constricted. She hurt. Not just on the outside. He wanted to take that hurt and swallow it whole. He wanted to tell her he loved her, and that she didn't have to heal alone.

"Rachel..."

She shook her head against their hands. "Not yet."

Back at Preston's, she'd been willing to admit something, but he'd stopped her. There'd been too many people around, and as much as he'd wanted to confess everything he'd been holding back, he'd wanted them to be alone where they could be open and honest with each other. Now *she* was the one holding back.

He rubbed the tension at the base of her neck. "Like I told you before, I'm not going anywhere. When you're ready, I'll be here for you."

Because...I love you.

Detective Nick Merretti entered my room. The somberness in his dark brown eyes filled my soul with fear and anxiety. "What happened?" I typed as quickly as my mouth would allow.

Bunny rushed to my side and held my hand. "Did they find her?" she asked him.

He nodded. "Yes."

"Xavier," my synthesized voice said. "He okay?"

Nick scratched the back of his head. "He's alive, but..." He sat next to me. "Vivian, Xavier Preston has been kidnapping and murdering college students for the last twenty years."

My chest tightened. I'd once been in love with the man. Together we'd created a child. My world tilted. My husband had been a child molester who preyed on my daughter. Blackness settled on my heart and soul. My daughter and former lover had been coldblooded killers. The people who had touched my life the most, the people whom I'd loved the most, had all ended up being monsters.

God, what is wrong with me?

"Thanks to you," Nick continued, "he's been stopped, and his last victim saved." He rubbed his temple. "Unfortunately, your daughter was killed. I'm sorry, Vivian."

Tears filled my eyes. Not for the young woman Holly had become, but for the adorable and sweet child she'd once been. Images of Holly filtered through my mind. Tiny fingers and toes. Chubby cheeks and ice cream kisses. I loved Holly more than life itself. A part of me would always love my little girl. If only I'd caught the signs. If only I'd been able to protect Holly from Art, take her away, sought help.

Since waking from the coma, I'd thought long and hard about what Art had done to my daughter. I tried to remember if I'd seen something inappropriate and wondered if I'd absently tossed it off as teenage angst. But there was never a moment I could recall that would have given me a warning or a red flag that something wasn't right in my home. Yet, I still blamed myself. Because I'd been blind to what went on under my own roof, my daughter was dead.

"My fault," I typed.

"No!" Nick smacked his leg. "*You* didn't do anything wrong. Your daughter killed an innocent man when she was in Bola. She helped Xavier Preston keep a nineteen-year-old boy prisoner in a basement for almost a week. She tried to murder you, and what she did to your husband..." He shook his head. "Vivian, I've been working homicide for nearly thirty years. Just because a kid is raised by a good parent doesn't mean they'll turn out to be a good person. Trust me, I've worked plenty of murder cases to know a mother's love could never erase the hatred your daughter carried with her."

I worked the straws and typed, "I surrounded myself with killers and a child molester. I am to blame."

Bunny squeezed my hand. "Don't you do this to yourself. I won't allow it. I won't allow you to feel sorry for yourself, or blame yourself for everything that's happened."

Fury clawed its way into my belly. My fingers and toes tingled with it. My head and heart pounded with it. "How dare you." I puffed into the straw and released a frustrated grunt. "Holly dead. Art dead. My ex-boyfriend a serial killer. I have right to feel sorry for myself."

"You've been feeling sorry for yourself for the past year," Bunny countered. "It's time to get mad and take your life back."

"Go back to fancy hospital you came from," my synthesized voice echoed through the room. "Don't need you. Don't have a life to take back. Sitting in chair no life. Everyone I love dead. I want to be dead."

"Well, that's no fun," my best friend, Lois, said as she entered the room. "I can't kick your ass in chess if you're dead." Disappointment lined her weary face as she stood behind Nick and crossed her arms. "I'm living on borrowed time. You, on the other hand, are wasting time. I've heard what your therapists have said. With intense therapy, there's no reason you can't regain control of your body. The problem is you don't have the will to do it. I listened at the door, and I get where you're coming from, but what I don't get is *why* you're going to let this defeat you."

"If I walk and talk, what would I do? I have nothing. No family. No money. Nothing."

"You have me," Lois said as she moved around Nick and took my other hand.

Bunny squeezed my hand tight. "And me. That fancy hospital I was working at fired my ass, so there's no going back." I slid my gaze to her and caught her smile. "And Lois is right. You can walk out of here if you work hard enough. I'm not saying you'll be running a marathon or doing backflips, but what you can do is share your story. By sharing, you can help others in similar situations."

"Yes," Lois hissed and bobbed her head. "I love that idea. But you can't help anyone if you give up on yourself." Tears filled Lois's eyes. "I love you, Vivian. You're my best friend and I need you to be strong. Before I leave this world, I need to see you walking. If I don't, I'll haunt your butt for an eternity."

My mouth twitched, but on the inside, I was smiling. "Love you," I typed.

"I certainly wouldn't want Lois haunting me," Bunny said. "So, does that mean you'll work your butt off and get on your feet?"

My vision blurred as I typed, "Yes."

Nick stood. "How is it possible for Vivian to walk?"

Bunny rose, too. "She sustained injuries to the lower part of her spinal cord, but with therapy, she could function normally. Like I said, though. No backflips or marathons. Unfortunately, when she was first admitted, there was a lot of swelling to her spinal cord, which caused the paralysis. The swelling has abated, but not fully. Medication is helping, though." She touched my shoulder. "I also believe mental health and will power has played a big part in keeping her mobility limited."

Was Bunny right? Was I keeping myself locked in my own personal prison? I used to be a strong person. I glanced at Lois, whose strength I've admired. She'd been fighting the cancer for a long time, and would eventually lose. I need to fight, so that I can be strong for her. I want to be able to wrap my arms around her when she needs me.

"Amazing," Nick said with a shake of his head. "It's late. I'm going to head to the hotel now and let you all get some rest. Vivian, thank you again for your help." When Nick reached the door, he paused and looked at Bunny. "One question. Why do they call you Bunny?"

While Bunny laughed, I typed. "Show him ears."

Bunny pulled her long, dark hair back in ponytail and revealed her peculiarly, elongated ears. "What's up, Doc?"

The following Tuesday, Rachel entered Ian's office and took a seat next to Owen. The past three days had been hectic. They'd spent Saturday and Sunday dealing with Preston and Conway, along with the crime scene at Preston's house. Monday was Bill's funeral, then the trip to Marietta. Through it all, she had dealt with moving Sean's things from the dorms and into Joy's house. Once Joy met Sean, she'd insisted he stay with her and Walter for the remainder of the semester. While she couldn't be happier with the arrangement, a part of her had wanted Sean to come home where she could keep a better eye on him. But she knew she couldn't keep him in a bubble forever, and Joy and Walter would make sure Sean was safe and well cared for.

Now that the investigation was over and her brother was in good hands, she needed to make some serious decisions. About her career. About Owen.

Considering she sat across from her boss, she had no choice but to deal with her career first. She handed Ian a hard copy of her final report. "I've also emailed you a copy," she said, as her nervous stomach did a little flip.

After Bob Conway had been taken away and Owen released, they'd gone back to Joy's. It had been nearly two in the morning by the time either one of them had made it to their rooms. Emotionally and physically exhausted, needing comfort, needing to know Owen was safe, she'd been tempted to sneak into his room that night, but had refrained. She'd also needed time to decompress and process everything that had happened.

She'd killed a killer. She'd taken a life and there were no do overs. Her nervous stomach grew nauseous. Dead was dead, and she was the reason Holly Saunders died. While she knew in her heart she'd been given no choice, and that if she hadn't fought, she might be the one lying six feet under, regret still ate at her. She didn't want to ever be put in a situation where her life might depend on another person's death.

Ian opened the file folder Rachel had handed him, flipped through a few pages, then closed it. "Give me the short version."

Rachel blinked and looked at Owen. "You're the lead," he said.

She'd hoped to simply hand over the report, then go back to business as usual. Bury herself in work, then go home and do…

Anything and everything to avoid Owen.

Although she'd accepted his apology, she'd never told him the truth. That she loved him. That she couldn't stand being without him. She'd almost told him Friday night, when they'd stood, bloodied and beaten, outside Xavier Preston's house. Coming off an adrenaline rush, she'd been ready to confess her feelings, but thankfully he'd stopped her. She'd needed to process her love for Owen, too. How her feelings could affect them professionally, and whether or not she was willing to take a risk and pour her heart and soul into a personal relationship with him.

When Ian cleared his throat, she glanced to her boss. "Sorry. Okay, short version…Xavier Preston was born and raised in Bola, Michigan. Twenty-five years ago, he attended Wexman University. It was during that time he pledged the Eta Tau Zeta fraternity."

"The same fraternity your brother and the missing boy pledged?" Ian asked.

"Yes. And during Preston's Hell Week, Robert Conway, who is the father of the kidnapped boy, Josh, tortured Preston."

"We spoke with Preston before the Michigan State Police took him," Owen said. "Turns out Conway took Hell Week hazing to a new level."

Rachel crossed her legs. "Conway abused Preston throughout the week, made him think the abuse was more about trust, then he betrayed him. On the final day, he used a broomstick to rape Preston, then told him he wasn't fit to join the Zetas."

Ian's dark brows rose. "I take it this was the incident that put the no hazing policy in effect."

She nodded. "Only because Preston sent an anonymous letter to the president of the university. According to Preston, his father didn't know about the incident, but his mother did and she refused to allow him to go to the authorities."

"I got the impression he was afraid of his mother, didn't

you?" Owen asked.

"Yeah, I did. Anyway, Preston leaves Bola, transfers to Michigan University, where he not only finishes his degree, but meets Vivian Williams. He gets Vivian pregnant, tells her he wants nothing to do with the baby, and signs away his rights. Vivian goes on to meet Arthur Saunders. They marry, and he adopts Vivian's daughter, Holly. Meanwhile, Preston returns to Bola after he finishes getting a PhD, and begins working at Wexman University."

Ian frowned. "The timeline doesn't work. The disappearances started happening twenty years ago."

"Right. Preston's mother died the year before the first student was taken. His father had passed the year before that. According to Preston, he had a hard time dealing with what happened to him. Every anniversary of Hell Week, he became more anxious and prone to violence. As he put it, he needed...*proper* therapy."

Ian leaned into the chair and sighed. "So begins the Wexman Hell Week."

"Exactly," Rachel said. "When the urge struck, if he wasn't living in Bola, he'd sneak back into town for a week of *therapy*. And once he was living there, he insinuated himself into Wexman's academic community, took a job as a professor, then later as a dean."

"Are all the missing students now accounted for?" Ian asked.

"We discovered an old well on Preston's property. It hasn't been used in over sixty years, except to dump bodies. The Michigan State Police have their labs working on what they've recovered from the well. They'll have to run DNA testing, but Preston confessed to not only using the well to hide the missing boys' bodies, but also Ethel Rodeck, his elderly neighbor. Preston said he didn't want to kill her, but she'd seen him put a boy in the well and he had no choice."

"There's always a choice," Ian said with a shake of his head. "Where does Holly Saunders fit in this?"

She glanced to Owen, who had heard, first hand, Holly

confess to killing her parents. "You're up."

"According to Holly," Owen began, "her adoptive father, Arthur Saunders, had been molesting her since she was twelve. When she discovered he wasn't her real dad, she said she snapped. She killed the dad, then went after the mother, who she blamed for the rapes. After that, she decided to go after Preston. She also blamed him for the years of molestation. When she had us all in that cellar, she told Preston she was originally going to kill him on the spot, but then she found out about his Hell Week secret and decided death wasn't as harsh a punishment as prison."

Ian folded his hands and rested them on the folder. "But Holly's mother survived."

She drew in a deep breath as she remembered yesterday's conversation with Detroit Detective Nick Merretti and Holly's mother, Vivian Saunders. "Yes. After Owen and I attended the funeral for Bill Baker, the murdered security guard, we flew to Marietta, Ohio and met with Holly's mother, Vivian." Her throat tightened. "Holly had bludgeoned and stabbed Vivian the night she'd killed Arthur Saunders, and assumed she'd killed her mom. Vivian spent six months in a coma and is now a quadriplegic. If it wasn't for her...I don't think." She paused to gain control of her emotions. If it wasn't for Vivian, Holly would have killed Owen and Josh, and would likely be running free right now. "I don't think we would have found Josh in time," she finished.

"How is it that Holly was able to not only get into the university under a false name, but work for a county sheriff?" Ian asked.

Jake had beaten himself up over being duped by Holly, but he hadn't been at fault. "The sheriff, Jake Tyler, ran a background check on her and also fingerprinted her before hiring her on as a part-time receptionist. Because Holly had never been fingerprinted, there wasn't a match. As for the name she was using...Michigan State Police are looking into it. They...we suspect Holly might have taken simple identity theft to murder. They're currently searching for the real Melissa

Channing."

Ian looked to Owen. "Anything else?"

"No, sir."

"Please give Rachel and me a moment."

Owen's eyes were unreadable as he stood, then left the room. After the door clicked shut, Ian rose from his chair. "Do you have anything else to add?" he asked and sat down next to her.

She suspected Ian wanted to discuss the email Owen had sent him regarding her emotional incapability to work a murder investigation. But rather than open herself up to that line of questioning, she played dumb. "No. That about covers it."

He smiled and turned the chair to face her. "I'll never forget the day you hacked into my system." His smile grew. "I was both furious and curious. And when I met you..." He shook his head. "Remember what you were wearing when I came to your apartment?"

Her cheeks heated. "Yeah, my pink polka dot pajamas. Can you believe I still have them?"

"I obviously don't pay you enough if you can't afford to buy new pajamas."

She half-laughed. "You're more than generous. They just happen to be my favorites."

"Well, when you opened the door, wearing those pajamas, you shocked me. And that's not easy to do. I don't know who I was expecting to meet on the other side of the door, but it wasn't a pint-sized, fiery redhead with a cocky attitude."

She straightened. "I know people shorter than me."

"They're called toddlers," he said with a chuckle, then sobered. "Rachel, I know you. I know you've wanted to work in the field for the past couple of years. I gave you that chance because you were going to go with or without the backing of CORE."

"I know about the email Owen sent you," she blurted, wanting to bring this discussion to a close. "And I'm okay with it. I'm okay with not working field assignments."

Ian's brows rose. "After two years of nagging me, you're

going to give up after one investigation?"

"I'm obviously not qualified. You know it. Owen knows it." She swallowed. "I know it."

"Because you showed emotion? Because you grieved for a victim?" He cocked his head and studied her. "I'd have been more worried if you *didn't* show any emotion." He stood and moved toward the window, then stared at the Chicago skyline. "And how are you handling killing the woman?"

"Fine."

With a half-smile, he turned slightly. "You shoved a pencil hard enough into her ear that it penetrated her brain. You're fine with that?"

Her stomach churned. "No. I would have rather she'd been arrested and sent to prison. But what's done is done."

"Yes. What's done is done," he echoed. "As you know, if any one of our agents kills in the line of duty, they're required to see a counselor. That goes for you, too."

Little did Ian know she'd already made the appointment. She needed to cope with killing another person before it drove her insane with guilt. "Of course."

"Once the counselor gives the okay, I'll assign you another case. At the start, I'll expect you to work with one of the other agents. Not Owen, though. I don't care if you two are together, but I can't have your personal relationship affecting your judgment in the field."

Her cheeks grew warm again. How Ian knew about her and Owen she couldn't be sure. At this point, it didn't matter. Ian was giving her what she'd *thought* she wanted. A chance to be away from the desk and out in the field. "You don't have to worry about me and Owen," she said.

He faced her. "I'm sorry. I thought you two—"

"We are...were...we need to sort some things out." She rubbed her temple. "Ian, I don't want to work in the field," she admitted. And as the words hung in the air an enormous weight lifted from her shoulders. "While I was in Bola, I missed my evidence and evaluation room. I missed *that* side of investigating process." She stood. "I don't want to carry a gun.

Right now, I'm not even carrying a pencil. I don't want to see a dead body up close and personal, and I certainly don't want to be put in a situation where it's my life or someone else's. Thank you for the opportunity, but if it's okay with you, I'd like to stick with my current position."

"That's your decision?"

Damn straight it's my *decision.* "Yes."

"Thank God," he said and relaxed his posture. "It's been hell not having you here. Honestly, I knew you did a lot, I just wasn't aware how much." He smiled. "Expect a pay raise."

Her heart rate jumped. "Thank you. If there's nothing else, I'll go see what needs to be cleaned up around here."

"Go home and rest. It can wait until tomorrow."

She thanked him again, and headed for the door.

"Rachel," he called as she turned the doorknob. "You did good."

Keeping her back to him, she smiled, then left the office. Owen grabbed her arm and steered her down the hall. When they reached the evidence and evaluation room, she tried to shake free. "What are you doing?"

He crowded her and pulled her close. "What happened with Ian?"

"Nothing."

"You were in there long enough, so I know it's not nothing."

"Okay, so it wasn't *nothing*. He offered me a position as a field agent, but I turned him down."

Concern clouded his eyes as he moved closer. His familiar scent tickled her senses and made her want to lean into him. But they had yet to discuss their relationship, and she still needed to figure out if they could even *have* a relationship.

"Are you sure that's what you want to do? I don't want that email I sent to Ian weighing in on your decision." He touched her chin. "I don't want what I wrote or how I treated you to be the reason, either."

She gripped a fistful of his shirt. "You have nothing to do with my decision. It's on me and it's what I want." She tightened her hold. "I've spent my whole life looking for adventure. I've envied you and the other guys who work here. You've all been to so many places, seen so many things. And all I do is sit in front of a computer." Loosening her grip, she smiled. "But you know what? I love what I do. It took this case to make me realize that there's nothing wrong with sitting in front of computer, that what I do is a huge asset to CORE. I'm not saying I wouldn't want a little adventure in my life, just not the kind that involves...murder."

His face relaxed. "So you're not quitting?"

She shook her head. "I told you before, I'm not quitting my job. I love my evidence and evaluation room too much to leave."

He cupped her cheeks, then swept the pad of his thumb along one of her fading bruises. "You know what I love?"

Her heart rate kicked up a dozen notches. "Bigfoot festivals?" she whispered. She loved him so much she didn't want to raise her hopes, only to have them plummet if he said something else.

"Not quite." His eyes sparkled as he grinned. "I love you, Rachel. And if you'll let me, I want to love you for the rest of my life."

Tears welled in her eyes. "I love you, too." She gave him a long, lingering kiss. When she pulled back, she wrapped her arms around his neck. "You do know I'm a total pain in the ass, right?"

"I happen to like your ass." He reached down and squeezed her rear. "So, by forewarning me that you're a total pain...is that your way of saying yes?"

She frowned. "I don't remember you asking me anything."

"Then I guess I wasn't clear." He took her hands in his. "I want to spend my life with you. Make a bunch of babies, get a couple of dogs, a house...Rachel, I love you. Will you marry me?"

She hugged him hard and quick. "Yes," she said, blinking back the tears. "Only...you want to make a bunch of babies. How much is a bunch?"

He pulled her closer. "Four, maybe five."

"Four or five?" She was in love with a mad man. "I love you, but you're crazy."

He kissed her forehead. "You said you wanted some adventure."

"I did, didn't I? And the only one I'd love to share those adventures with is you." She took his hand. "Let's get out of here. I haven't seen you naked in days and all this adventure talk is making me feel...adventurous."

"I know how to solve that." He looked around the evidence and evaluation room. "Do you know how many times I've fantasized about bending you over one of these tables and—"

"Stop." She grinned. "Don't tell me. *Show* me when we get back to my place."

He took her hand and kissed it. As they walked out of CORE she knew in her heart, life would never be boring. Not with Owen in it.

EPILOGUE

Six months later...

IAN SCOTT TOOK a seat in the last pew at the back of the quaint church. As the pianist played a beautiful melody, the wedding guests whispered amongst themselves, while the groom stood at the alter rocking on his heels. Owen Malcolm, normally cool and collected, looked as if he'd recently eaten bad Chinese food. His face was a shade too pale, and Ian hoped to God the man didn't lose his lunch while he exchanged vows with Rachel.

The doors behind him opened. His agents, Dante Russo and Lloyd Nelson entered. They both nodded to him as they took a seat in the pew in front of his. Moments later, Lloyd's partner, and his daughter Celeste's younger brother, Will, entered. The popular artist shook Ian's hand before sitting next to Lloyd.

Ian leaned forward. "Where are your sisters?" he asked Will.

"I just saw Celeste and John pull into the parking lot. Hudson and Eden are with them."

Ian checked his watch. The four of them had better hurry. The wedding would begin in the next five minutes. When he leaned back into the pew, he looked across the aisle and caught Joy Baker staring at him. He'd met Joy and her husband, Walter, last night at the rehearsal dinner. He wanted to dislike the brash and crass woman, but couldn't. She'd become a surrogate mother to both Rachel and her brother, Sean. And Walter had become the father figure Rachel had never had. They were a bit strange and eccentric, but good, solid people.

The door opened again. Expecting Celeste and the others, Ian turned. Jake Tyler, the Dixon County Sheriff who had brought CORE into the Wexman Hell Week case, entered and immediately took a seat next to Joy and Walter. Ian might have met Jake for the first time last night, but at this point, he knew the sheriff well. After the way Jake had handled the Hell Week case, and the glowing report Rachel had written about him, Ian decided it might be in his best interest to poke around Jake's background. He was always on the look out for unique individuals, with military and/or law enforcement experience, to come work for him at CORE. Ian had discovered some interesting and intriguing information about Jake, and knew in his gut the man would make an excellent investigator. Unfortunately Jake had to serve another year as sheriff, and based on what he'd learned about Jake, the man was too loyal to quit his post. With more cases than his current CORE agents could handle, he might have to make it so Jake had no choice but to resign and come work for CORE.

He glanced around the small church. One of these days, God was going to strike him down for his actions. He supposed while he was in the church he should offer up a prayer or two rather than consider how he planned to manipulate another man's life.

"Hi, Dad," Celeste whispered and touched his shoulder.

He let Jake go for the moment, stood and gave his daughter a hug. "Cutting it a little close, don't you think?"

"That's my fault," Eden said quietly, and gave him a peck on the cheek. "I was up late."

Hudson came up from behind and shook his hand. "Instead of morning sickness, Eden has *three* in the morning sickness. Hopefully it'll pass soon." He took his wife's hand, then kissed her knuckles. "She needs her rest before the baby is born so she can handle all those late night feedings."

"*We* need our rest," she corrected Hudson.

"But I don't have the right equipment."

Celeste gave her brother-in-law a nudge with her elbow. "I predict plenty of late night feedings and diaper changes in your future. Now, scoot in and leave room for John. I want to sit next to my dad."

Hudson shook his head. "Was that a psychic prediction?"

Celeste smiled. "Nope. I just happen to know my sister very well."

Eden grinned at Celeste, then greeted her brother, Lloyd and Dante before taking a seat next to Hudson. Eden looked great, Ian thought as he made room for Celeste. According to Celeste, thanks to therapy for her eating disorder, Eden had put on fifteen pounds before she'd become pregnant. Being with Hudson, and taking her time writing her true crime novel rather than climbing Network's corporate ladder, had softened her. She'd become more family oriented, more approachable. More likeable.

"John dropped us off and is trying to find a parking spot," Celeste said.

"He better hurry."

"He'll make it." She smiled. "So, three weddings in six months. You could start advertising that CORE is turning into a successful dating service."

He looked to the church ceiling. "God, help me. Next I'll have to provide child care."

"That's a brilliant idea. I know we'll be needing it in about...oh, seven and a half months."

He gripped her hand. "Are you and John...am I going to be...?"

She grinned. "Yes, Grandpa."

His heart swelled. *He* was going to be a grandfather. A year ago, he could only fantasize about meeting his daughter, and now she was a huge part of his life. She'd married one of his best agents, had a successful bakery just down the street from CORE, and now she was giving him a grandchild. Life couldn't be any better.

"Any room for me?" John Kain asked.

He wanted to thank John for bringing Celeste to Chicago, for marrying his daughter and creating a child. With his throat tight from too many unfamiliar emotions, he stood and gave the man a firm handshake, instead.

John took a seat next to Celeste. "You told him?"

"Sorry, I couldn't help myself. I think he's speechless."

Ian cleared his throat. "I'm not speechless, I'm considering how all these babies are going to affect business." He glanced across the aisle to where Jake Tyler sat with Joy. "I might have to definitely bring in some new recruits." He looked back to John. "Congratulations, by the way."

John grinned, then held his wife's hand. Seconds later, the music changed.

Celeste bumped him with her shoulder. "Time to stand."

Ian stood and turned toward the door. When Rachel appeared, with her brother on her arm, he sucked in a breath. She was absolutely beautiful. Her green eyes were bright, her pretty smile, huge. Ian quickly glanced toward the altar, and grinned. Owen looked the happiest he'd ever seen him. Hell, *he* was happy.

For Rachel and Owen, for Celeste and John, and for Eden and Hudson. All three of them had found something good in a world filled with so much bad.

At that moment, he took advantage of his location and sent a prayer of thanks.

For second chances, for his future grandchild, and for...CORE.

THE END

OTHER CORE TITLES AVAILABLE BY KRISTINE MASON

ULTIMATE KILL
BOOK ONE OF THE
ULTIMATE CORE TRILOGY

When the past collides with the present, the only way to ensure the future lies in the ultimate kill...

Naomi McCall is a woman of many secrets. Her family has been murdered and she's been forced into hiding. No one knows her past or her real name, not even the man she loves.

Jake Tyler, former Marine and the newest recruit to the private criminal investigation agency, CORE, has been in love with a woman who never existed. When he learns about the lies Naomi has weaved, he's ready to leave her—until an obsessed madman begins sending her explosive messages every hour on the hour.

Innocent people are dying. With their deaths, Naomi's secrets are revealed and the truth is thrust into the open. All but one. Naomi's not sure if Jake can handle a truth that will change their lives. But she is certain of one thing—the only way to stop the killer before he takes more lives is to make herself his next victim.

Enjoy an excerpt of Ultimate Kill...

ULTIMATE KILL
BY
KRISTINE MASON

PROLOGUE

How many narcissists does it take to change a light bulb?
One.
He holds the bulb while the world revolves around him.

"DID YOU FIND her?" He glared at the man he'd overpaid to find the one thing that belonged to him. Rage simmered in the depths of what most men might consider a soul. Not him. Essence, the nonphysical aspect of a person, that which survived after death and all of the other metaphysical, intangible drivel of poets and priests...that kind of shit was for pussies. He had one life to live and he'd live it to the fullest.

With her.

Carl Blackborne, the former CIA agent and the investigator he'd forced into his employment, shifted his gaze to the desk. "I'm sorry, sir, but...no. That's not to say that I didn't discover any new leads," he quickly added.

He followed Blackborne's gaze and looked at the handcrafted replica of the first ship ever built by his great-great-grandfather. Made of gold, and worth over three hundred grand, the piece had been in the family for five generations. "It's lovely, no?" he asked the investigator and touched the ship's golden mast.

Blackborne blinked. "Yes. Truly one of a kind, sir."

"If you break down what's in your savings and life insurance, it's worth more than you are."

"I...I don't know how to respond to that."

He ran a manicured finger along the golden stern and wondered if the ship would become damaged if he slammed it against Blackborne's over-sized head. "Of course you don't."

"Sir, if I may, I've exhausted—"

"Do you know how old my great-great-grandfather was when he built his first ship?" he asked and touched the life-like sailor standing at the helm of the golden ship. From what he'd been told, his forefather had been a ruthless son of a bitch. He didn't emulate the man, nor did he worship him. He didn't have to. Not when he was better than him. More powerful. More coldblooded. More merciless.

"No, sir, I—"

"He was twenty. Twenty," he repeated, sliding his gaze to Blackborne. "By the time he was twenty-five he was worth over one million dollars. That was in the mid-1800s. By today's standards, he would have been worth over twenty-five million. Amazing, no?" He waved a hand, and leaned into his chamois-soft leather office chair. "Over the past one hundred and fifty years, his company has endured many ups and downs. Right now, under my rule, it's up. I've had the foresight to take this company to new places. Literally. My planes, ships and trucks are worldwide. I've made this company a household name. Now that's amazing shit."

Blackborne rubbed the back of his neck. "Truly amazing, sir. But if you'll let me explain my new leads."

He folded his hands and rested them on the luxurious, handcrafted desk. Made of six different kinds of exotic woods, like ebony and Carpathian elm, it too was worth more than Blackborne. "By all means. It's not like I don't have anything better to do with my time. Right, Ric?"

Ricco Salvatici, his aide-de-camp and most loyal confidant sat stone faced, his focus on the investigator. "All the time in the world. I see no reason why Blackborne shouldn't waste yours."

Clearing his throat, Blackborne nodded. "Understood. Sorry, sir. I'll make this quick. When I was investigating her past, I came across family lineage that might be of interest. I thought that maybe—"

"How is this a new lead?" Blackborne wasn't the first investigator he'd hired, and based on the others, he could rattle off the woman's family tree by heart. Hell, he'd stripped that tree of its leaves and snapped the branches until she no longer had a family.

"Well, it's not exactly a lead, just a new avenue."

"My trucks travel down avenues all the time," he said, finished with Blackborne and their conversation. He'd had high hopes for the investigator. During his previous employment with the CIA, Blackborne had been known to successfully track terrorists and international criminals. Diabolically brilliant men who had the means to hide and, if they'd wanted, never be found. And yet Blackborne couldn't find a simple woman? Fucking useless idiot.

"I'm not interested in hearing about avenues—at all," he said. "I paid you a lot of money to bring me—"

"I told you I wasn't sure if I could find her," Blackborne countered, his voice rising.

His rage went from simmering to boiling.

No one interrupted him.

No one dared to shout at him.

He slid his gaze to the two men flanking the office's double doors. Santiago Ramirez, the Columbian he'd taken under his wing over fifteen years ago glared at Blackborne's back. So did Santiago's counterpart, former Russian heavyweight boxer, Vlad Aristov. He looked to Ric, whose mouth tilted in the subtlest of smiles. Knowing the chance of this conversation ending well was slim to none, the masochist would enjoy Blackborne's faux pas.

"She's obviously changed her name," Blackborne continued without apology. "Covered up paper trails, she has no immediate family, her friends and associates have no idea where she moved to...I've bribed several IRS officials and even they couldn't help me. That's why I thought if I could—"

"Pull up her family tree?" he asked with an easy smile that in no way matched the raw fury constricting his chest. "It's a brilliant plan. I wish my other investigators had the foresight to come up with such a unique idea."

"Thank you, sir." Blackborne relaxed and grinned, obviously not understanding sarcasm. "I appreciate the compliment."

He looked to Ric and caught the laughter in his eyes. "What would you need for this brilliant plan of yours?" he asked, transferring his attention to the investigator.

"More money and, of course, more time."

His last four investigators had given him the same request. They'd eventually come to him empty handed and wound up dead.

"I suggest we expand the scope and not just focus on her family," Blackborne said, his tone enthusiastic. "The friends and associates I checked with…these were people who knew her, or rather knew of her, when she was in her early twenties. As you know, she went off the grid around the time she turned twenty. I think if I go back further, say into her childhood, and find people she was close to then maybe—"

He raised a hand. "No."

Blackborne's face contorted with confusion. "Sir, we might be able to find a link from her childhood that could lead us to her current whereabouts."

"Might…could." He rested an elbow against the leather armrest and cradled his chin between his index finger and thumb. "If a broke redneck plays the lotto enough times, he might eventually win. If you give a seasoned whore the money to go to college and educate herself, she could go on to run a Fortune 500 company. Mr. Blackborne, what are the chances of a broke redneck winning the lotto and a seasoned whore going on to run a Fortune 500 company?"

Blackborne looked to the desk again. "Let me rephrase then, digging into her past may…I mean, it's probable…" He scratched his head. "Sir, I can't guarantee anything, I can only try this route."

He straightened and opened the desk drawer. "Not interested." His fingers stroked the AAC Evolution-45 silencer, a weapon ironically used by U.S. Military Anti-Terrorist units. He grasped the handle of the gun. "I know everything about her past. Her preschool teachers, her fourth grade Girl Scout troop leader, who she lost her virginity to during her senior year of high school." His stomach tightened with anticipation as he pulled the lightweight gun from the drawer and aimed it at Blackborne's head. "I know everything about her except where she is now."

Blackborne staggered back, holding his hands in front of his body. "Please, sir. This investigation—"

"Is over." He tensed for the slight recoil and pulled the trigger. As if the man had sneezed, a puffy mist of blood burst from Blackborne's face before he crumpled to the ground. He slipped the weapon back into the drawer, then pulled out a file from the hidden center console. "Well, that was a disappointment." He glanced to Ric who, in turn, looked to Santiago and Vlad.

"Get him out of here, then kill his wife and kids," Ric told the men.

Without a word, Santiago and Vlad picked up Blackborne and took him from the office. When the door closed behind them, Ric rose from his chair. "And the woman?" he asked. "Should I find another investigator?"

"No." He opened the file and stared at the eight by ten glossy of her. Although not beautiful in the classical sense, she'd caught his attention the moment he'd seen her. While she'd been bustling through the club where she used to work, taking drink orders, he'd pictured her naked, curvy body on his bed. Her long, straight brown hair fanning out along his silk sheets as she spread her legs and welcomed him. He had eventually made what he'd imagined into a reality. And after having her once, he'd wanted her again.

Only she hadn't.

That was her first mistake.

When she ran from him...that was her second.

After he'd found her, he'd tried to be reasonable. He'd tried to give her everything she would ever need, and she'd rejected him.

That was her last mistake.

He always got what he wanted. Always. Growing up with enough money to run a small country, the world and its contents were his for the taking.

She was his to take.

Ric pressed his hands against the desk and leaned forward. "You've spent eight years looking for her. Are you giving up?"

He looked up from the photograph and met Ric's eyes. Eight years. A lot had happened during that time, and over the years he'd assumed he would eventually grow tired of searching for her. But he hadn't. She was the one object his money couldn't buy. The only woman who had walked away from him without a second glance. He never understood why. Quite frankly, he didn't care whether she wanted him or not. She was a lost possession he wanted found. "Have you ever known me to quit anything?"

"Never." Ric smiled. "Now what?"

He closed the file, then returned it to the drawer. "Now we do things my way." He rose from the chair and walked to the windows. As he looked around the spacious backyard, he found his wife and two children sitting on the lawn having a picnic lunch. "Hiring another investigator isn't going to cut it. We've been down that road one too many times," he said and watched grape jelly drop onto his four-year-old son's pristine white shirt as the boy waved to him.

"And your plan is...?"

"Simple." He gave his boy a two-finger salute. "If I can't find her, I'll make it so she has no choice but to come to me. When I'm finished, she'll beg me to take her back."

"Interesting," Ric said, his voice laced with amusement. "And why would she come to you?"

He smiled as his wife frowned and worked on their son's jelly stain. "Because if she doesn't, I'm going to kill a lot of people."

SHADOW OF DANGER
BOOK ONE OF THE
CORE SHADOW TRILOGY

Four women have been found dead in the outskirts of a small Wisconsin town. The only witness, clairvoyant Celeste Risinski, observes these brutal murders through violent nightmares and hellish visions. The local sheriff, who believes in Celeste's abilities and wants to rid their peaceful community of a killer, enlists the help of an old friend, Ian Scott, owner of a private criminal investigation agency, CORE. Because of Ian's dark history with Celeste's family, a history she knows nothing about, he sends his top criminalist, former FBI agent John Kain to investigate.

John doesn't believe in Celeste's mystic hocus-pocus, or in her visions of the murders. But just when he's certain they've solved the crimes, with the use of science and evidence, more dead bodies are discovered. Could this somehow be the work of the same killer or were they dealing with a copycat? To catch a vicious murderer, the skeptical criminalist reluctantly turns to the sensual psychic for help. Yet with each step closer to finding the killer, John finds himself one step closer to losing his heart.

KRISTINE MASON

SHADOW OF PERCEPTION
BOOK TWO OF THE
CORE SHADOW TRILOGY

What happens when negligent plastic surgeons receive a taste of their own medicine...?

Chicago investigative reporter, Eden Risk, receives an unmarked envelope containing a postcard ordering her to watch the enclosed DVD...or someone else dies. No Police. After Eden watches the DVD, a gruesome, horrifying surgery, she turns to the private criminal investigation agency, CORE, for help. Only she hadn't expected that help to come with a catch. Her former lover, Hudson Patterson, has been assigned to the case.

Hudson would rather have another CORE agent handle the investigation. Two years ago, he'd screwed things up with Eden...bad. And as more DVDs arrive, Eden and Hudson find themselves not only knee-deep in a twisted investigation, but forced to deal with their past, and the love they'd tried to deny.

CONTEMPORARY ROMANCES BY KRISTINE MASON

KISS ME

When is a kiss...

After a series of bad relationships, Jenna Cooper wants a sex buddy—no-strings, no emotional involvement, and absolutely no expectations of commitment. She sets her sights on Luke Sinclair. A player and commitment-phobe, he'd make the perfect boy toy. Only Luke's tired of playing the scene and wants a serious relationship with Jenna, not a series of one-night stands.

...More than a kiss?

When Luke makes Jenna an offer she can't refuse, the sexual tension between them combusts and their emotional chemistry becomes too hard for Jenna to ignore. They both end up with more than either bargained for, especially when Jenna's wild past is exposed and threatens to tear their relationship apart. Now Luke will do anything to make things right between them, but knows it's going to take more than a kiss...

PICK ME
BOOK ONE OF THE
REALITY TV ROMANCE SERIES

For the chance of a lifetime...

To help save the TV reality show, *Pick Me,* from cancellation, Valentina Bonasera swaps her position as the show's Production Assistant, to play the role of Bachelorette, only to discover Bachelor Number One, rancher and sports agent, Colt Walker, happens to be her one and only one-night stand she'd snuck away from six months ago.

...Pick me.

Colt had never forgotten the hot, sensual night he'd shared with Valentina, or how she'd left him without so much as a note or her contact information. He'd spent months searching for the woman who'd given him a night he couldn't forget and thought he'd never see again. Now that she's in Dallas, he's determined to make her his...

LOVE ME OR LEAVE ME
BOOK TWO OF THE
REALITY TV ROMANCE SERIES

Love me...

Carter James, real estate agent for the hit reality show, *Renovate or Relocate*, has been crazy about the show's designer, Brynn Dawson, for years. He's been aching to take their friendship to a new level and when he gets his chance to spend a hot, sensual night with her and fulfill his wildest fantasies, he falls hard for Brynn. When the director of the show reveals that Brynn could possibly be fired, Carter knows he has to act fast before she's booted from the show. He'll not only jeopardize his reputation, but he'll go behind her back to help her keep her job. Knowing Brynn's pride is also at stake, he hopes his deception doesn't come back to haunt him in the end. He can't imagine life without the woman he loves.

...or leave me.

Brynn has been aware of Carter for years. How good he smells, his sexy smile, his lean, muscular body, his big, rough hands and what she'd like him to do with them. When she takes a chance by going from friends to lovers, she risks both her heart and their friendship, but discovers it's the best decision she could have ever made. Despite having her job on the line, she also knows that as long as she has Carter by her side, she can get through anything. Until she finds out what Carter's been up to. Hurt and betrayed, her emotions raw and her love for him tested, she'll have to decide whether she can move past the deceit and love him or if his lack of faith in her will force her to leave him.

ABOUT KRISTINE MASON

I didn't pick up my first romance novel until I was in my late twenties. Immediately hooked, I read a bazillion books before deciding to write one of my own. After the birth of my first son I needed something to keep my mind from turning to mush, and Sesame Street wasn't cutting it. While that first book will never see the light of day, something good came from writing it. I realized my passion and found a career I love.

When I'm not writing contemporary romances and dark, romantic suspense novels (or reading them!) I'm chasing after my four kids and two neurotic dogs.

You can email me at authorkristinemason@gmail.com, visit my website at www.kristinemason.net or find me on Facebook https://www.facebook.com/kristinemasonauthor and https://twitter.com/KristineMason7 to connect with me on Twitter!

Made in the USA
Columbia, SC
08 June 2020